Ethan moment **Holly's presence.**

Her swept-back locks exposed her long, elegant neck and straight, slightly upturned nose. But it was her vulnerability that got to him.

Despite her attempts to keep it all together, he sensed just below the surface she suffered and struggled with her son, the shop, everyday life.

He should step away. Instead, when she turned her head toward him, he found himself staring into her deep green eyes that had seen so much pain. A pain he could identify with. He'd lost his father at a young age, and several of his friends in Afghanistan. But even that couldn't compare to losing one's partner, one's soul mate.

He had no experience with that sort of loss, yet he felt the need to comfort. Protect. He wanted to draw Holly into his arms and absorb her pain and blend it with his own.

At twelve years old, **Kim Watters** fell in love with romance. An avid reader, she was soon hooked on happily-ever-after endings. For years she dreamed of writing her own romance novel but never had the time until moving to sunny Arizona, where the beauty of her surroundings inspired her to put her stories on paper.

Winner of the HOLT Medallion for Southern Themed Fiction, and the *Houston Chronicle*'s Best Christian Fiction Author of 1999, **Annie Jones** grew up in a family that loved to laugh, eat and talk—often all at the same time. They instilled in her the gift of sharing through words and humor, and the confidence to go after her heart's desire (and to act fast if she wanted the last chicken leg). A former social worker, she feels called to be a "voice for the voiceless" and has carried that calling into her writing. Having moved thirteen times during her marriage, she is currently living in rural Kentucky.

A Season of Love

Kim Watters

&

Somebody's Santa

Annie Jones

LOVE INSPIRED
INSPIRATIONAL ROMANCE

LOVE INSPIRED®

INSPIRATIONAL ROMANCE

ISBN-13: 978-1-335-28496-9

Recycling programs
for this product may
not exist in your area.

A Season of Love & Somebody's Santa

Copyright © 2020 by Harlequin Books S.A.

A Season of Love
First published in 2013. This edition published in 2020.
Copyright © 2013 by Kim Watters

Somebody's Santa
First published in 2008. This edition published in 2020.
Copyright © 2008 by Luanne Jones

This edition published by arrangement with Harlequin Books S.A.

For questions and comments about the quality of this book,
please contact us at CustomerService@Harlequin.com.

Love Inspired
22 Adelaide St. West, 40th Floor
Toronto, Ontario M5H 4E3, Canada
www.Harlequin.com

Printed in U.S.A.

CONTENTS

A SEASON OF LOVE

Kim Watters

For my children, Shane and Emily, who have provided wonderful anecdotes through the years and the inspiration to keep writing.

Though you have made me see troubles, many and bitter, you will restore my life again; from the depths of the earth you will again bring me up.
—*Psalms* 71:20

Chapter One

Another Christmas carol drifted through the airwaves and settled on Holly Stanwyck's shoulders as she sat in her deserted shop. Normally the music would soothe her, but not today. She needed some customers to walk through the front door of 'Tis Always the Season and buy enough merchandise to pay for the day's overhead expenses. Without being able to put out new offerings in the past few weeks, though, the odds of that happening were nil.

Taking a break from the computer, she opened her mail and stared at another past-due notice before she placed it in the manila folder with the others. The real meaning of Christmas and the reason for the store had died two years ago, along with her dreams of a happily ever after.

"Bah, humbug." Holly never thought she'd utter those words. Fisting her palms, she rested her chin against them and stared out at the tree behind the wrought-iron fence, its bare limbs scarcely darker than the clouds spitting snowflakes. Even the cold marble pillars and structure of the courthouse in the center of the square seemed to shrink under the weight of the early November storm. She blew her wispy bangs from her eyes.

She missed her husband. The store had been his idea; a way to keep Christmas in their hearts all year round and a way to sell the hand-carved wooden crosses, ornaments, figurines and crèches he made in the workshop behind their bungalow, along with other Christmas merchandise. Only one of his masterpieces remained, and with Jared dead, no new ones would grace the shelves.

In a few moments, she regained her composure and breathed in the scent of cinnamon wafting from the candle on the shelf behind her head. It reminded her of her grandmother's house in the suburbs of Chicago, and she envisioned Nana Marie's soft arms cocooning her in comfort. *There is nothing in life that you can't handle, child. Just put your trust in the Lord, and everything will be all right.*

Easier said than done. She didn't believe anymore and only went through the motions for her twelve-year-old son, Cameron. Still, Holly Stanwyck was no quitter. She would not lose everything she and Jared had worked so hard for. The new business venture she'd thought of last night would work. Refocusing on the words on the computer screen, she felt hope blaze through her. She'd get caught up on her bills and give Cam the Christmas he longed for.

Where was Cameron anyway? She glanced at her

watch and her heart sank. School had ended an hour ago. If he didn't show up in the next few minutes, she'd have to close up the shop and go searching for him again.

The bell above the door jingled. Quickly stuffing the folder under the counter, she stood and plastered on a smile, hoping her customer wouldn't see the desperation lingering in her eyes. "Welcome to 'Tis Always…" Her words died in her throat as the door shut.

A tall, dark-haired stranger stood behind her son, and the scowl on the man's face didn't bode well. Cam had obviously forgotten their numerous talks about stranger danger, even in the small town. But then again, from first impressions, she guessed Cam didn't have much of a choice. Knots formed in her stomach. This wasn't a social visit. What had her son done now?

The man's drab olive military-style coat did little to hide his muscular frame and only accentuated his height. Snowflakes clung to his cropped dark hair and dusted his jacket, but a few hugged his long eyelashes, outlining incredible but unsettling sapphire-blue eyes. His lips had yet to break into a fraction of a smile. She straightened her shoulders, refusing to be intimidated by him as she concentrated on her son.

"Cameron." She glanced at her watch again. "Where have you been?" Trying to keep the censure from her voice and keep her tone light, she failed miserably. "Thank you for bringing him back, Mr.…."

"You're welcome. It's Pellegrino. Ethan Pellegrino." He spoke as if she should recognize his name. His lips formed a straight line and fatigue bracketed his eyes.

He took his left hand off her son's shoulder and put it in his pocket, but not before fisting and then flexing his fingers.

Holly racked her brain but came up empty. She would remember meeting him, although his name did sound vaguely familiar now, as if she'd seen it written down somewhere in the recent past.

"Holly Stanwyck." Holly had enough manners to jut her hand out. The man didn't reciprocate. He stared at her outstretched hand and shifted his weight. How rude. Holly let her hand drop back to the counter.

After a few uncomfortable seconds, she picked up a pen and twirled it in her fingers. Glancing past his broad shoulders, she noticed the steady stream of snowflakes increasing outside the front window. More anxiety tightened the knots inside her. If the snow continued, she'd have to drag out the shovel by nightfall and, worse, drive in it. But that was probably going to be the least of her worries. What had Cameron done now that this Ethan Pellegrino had to bring him to the shop?

"Pleased to meet you, Mr. Pellegrino." *I think.* She glanced at the frown hugging her son's lips. "What's going on?" Her words added another layer to the growing tension. Uneasy, she walked to the other side of the counter, put her arm around her son and pulled him to her. At the man's immobile expression, her nerves threatened to dislodge the glass of water she'd drunk earlier.

"Your son should tell you."

"Cameron?" Her son pulled away, hung his head and

then kicked at an imaginary spot on the floor. "What have you been up to?" She clipped her words and tried to remain unemotional, but failed. Cameron had been getting into trouble a lot lately.

Who was this stranger residing in her son's body? He looked the same with his unruly dark blond hair and blue eyes, but his attitude had gone south. She needed to get a handle on it because in the next year or so, he'd be taller than she'd be. And more opinionated and more uncontrollable. The pen in her hand bent under the pressure.

"I took the long way here."

She ground her teeth as a scowl twisted Cam's lips. "With Patrick?"

"Why do you care who I walk with?"

Her son's new friend was bad news, but the more Holly brought that fact up, the more Cameron hung out with him instead of his other friends. Her grip tightened. She'd lost Jared two years earlier, and she was going to lose the store in a few months if things didn't improve. She couldn't lose Cameron, as well. "I care because I love you."

Her son's scowl deepened and he moved away when she tried to push his bangs from his eyes. "I don't see why you won't let me take the bus *home* after school. Everyone else does."

Holly sighed, refraining from the age-old saying of asking if everyone jumped off a bridge, would he follow? "Because I'm not there, I'm here, and you didn't want to go to the YMCA. And now there's apparently a good reason you're to come here, that's why."

"The YMCA is for babies. Why did Dad have to die?" Cam threw his backpack down and crossed his arms over his chest. "If he were alive, you'd be at home like Matt's or Tyler's mom."

At least she understood where the anger came from now. Communicating with her son lately had been harder than talking to the accounts-receivable people trying to collect on her past-due invoices. "Cam—I…"

Ethan Pellegrino shifted his weight, reminding Holly they weren't alone. Her shoulders sagged. Now was not the time to have a heart-to-heart talk with her son about the fact that even if his father were alive, she'd still work outside the home as she'd always done. She had no choice now, and once she faced the reality that the store would be going out of business soon, she'd have to find another job to pay her bills. She'd been a book-keeper before and could do it again, but she'd deal with that later. "What were you doing that Mr. Pellegrino felt compelled to bring you here?"

"Patrick and I were having some fun."

"Fun?" Holly sank against the counter and rubbed her forehead. Her shoulder muscles tightened, creating an instant headache. "You know I don't want you hanging around him. Thanks for bringing him to me, Mr. Pellegrino. I can take it from here."

The man crossed his arms, pursed his lips and glowered at her son. "Not until I hear him utter the truth about where he was and what he was doing."

"Excuse me?" Holly shoved her hands onto her hips and bit back her anger as she glared at Ethan Pellegrino.

Somehow she'd lost control of the situation. "You don't trust that I can deal with whatever *my* son has done?"

"It's not you. It's him. I doubt he'll tell you the truth. I'm familiar with teenagers."

"It's not like we did much damage," Cameron shot back.

"Cameron. Show some respect." Holly corrected her son. "You will not speak to an adult that way no matter what the situation is. Understood?"

Cam nodded and stared at the floor.

"Now, what did Cameron and Patrick do?"

"They spray painted my garage door." The man scraped his hand through his short hair as his gaze penetrated hers.

Cam had picked the wrong person to mess with.

Bile caught in her throat. Cameron had gone too far this time. The chat with the principal this morning had confirmed her son was heading down the wrong path. Holly felt powerless and overwhelmed by his attitude and change in personality. Inhaling sharply, she fought for control.

She was out of ideas on how to break through the wall Cameron had built around himself lately. Where communication had been easy when he was young, the moment he turned twelve and hormones kicked in, he'd turned inward and quit talking to her other than a few grunts here and there or to ask for money. "You spray painted Mr. Pellegrino's garage? Why?"

"Because I wanted to." Underneath all of Cameron's bravado, Holly sensed him ready to implode. His eyes flashed with anger, hurt and panic, emotions she identified with on a daily basis.

Tagging was a minor offense in Dynamite Creek, Arizona, and usually had some kind of monetary fine—something she couldn't afford right now. "That's not a good enough answer. I believe both Mr. Pellegrino and I deserve to know the truth."

Out of the corner of her eye, she watched the man shift his weight and continue to flex his hand as if testing out its strength while he glanced around the store.

"Because I heard that *he's* going to evict us. This is Dad's place. He can't do that."

"What? Where did you hear that?" The gnawing sensation took hold in her stomach and refused to let go as the realization hit. Mr. Pellegrino owned the building. She'd never met her landlord because he was supposed to be in Afghanistan. Jared had set everything up, and the past two years she'd signed the contracts with someone named Nan Emrey on the owner's behalf.

She knew she'd have to deal with her rent issues sooner rather than later, but she'd thought it would be with Nan, not the six-foot male taking up more space in her shop than she was comfortable with. And now, thanks to Cameron, that time had probably come; not that her son was responsible for her failure to pay the rent. The place Jared envisioned all through college and during their early married lives was about to disappear. More sadness consumed her. 'Tis Always the Season was one of the few remaining ties they had to Jared.

She stared into Mr. Pellegrino's immobile expression and shivered before she broke contact and refocused on her son.

"I heard it from Delany Wilson." Anger choked his voice and emotion hovered in his eyes. "She told the whole class. She said we were going to lose everything—the business, the house, our car—and end up living out of a grocery cart in the park across the street."

"That's not true, Cam." They weren't in danger of losing the house yet, because Holly had paid her mortgage and her maxed-out home-equity loan before her rent. "Mr. Pellegrino is not going to evict us from our house. Only the bank can do that. I promise you, though, no matter what happens we will not be living out of a grocery cart."

Holly had no idea what the future held in store for them. She did know that even if they had to eventually walk away from the house, they would not be homeless; both she and Jared had family in Tucson. She'd refused to let Cam know about all the money problems because she wanted to let him remain a child for a bit longer. Maybe she was doing him a disservice.

Cam wiped his nose on his jacket sleeve. Holly didn't correct his actions, hoping he didn't realize that she hadn't mentioned anything about the store. A quick glance at her landlord confirmed he'd caught on to her son's words, and their gazes met and held a few seconds before he glanced away. She knew this conversation was far from over, but she hoped Ethan wouldn't bring up the issue in front of her son. She had enough to deal with.

"Promise?"

"Promise. Why didn't you come to me, Cam?"

"Because I can't talk to you. You're always distracted. Or worried. Or busy." Cameron pursed his lips and flailed his arms.

Holly wanted to deny it, but she couldn't. Truth became claws of pain that ripped apart what remained of her heart. In spending so much time worrying about the house and the shop, she'd lost focus of her son.

Pulling Cam to her again, she put her arms around him and held him gently, cradling him. "I'm so sorry, honey. I—I don't— I'm sorry." Holly just stood and held her son. A tear slid from beneath her closed eyes. Cam squeezed her back, his thin body reminding her that he was just a child who needed help in understanding what happened around him.

Ethan cleared his throat. Holly still had to deal with the situation that had brought him here in the first place. No matter what Cameron was going through, she couldn't condone his behavior and needed to get a handle on it quickly before it spun further out of control.

Releasing her son, she lifted his chin and stared into his unhappy eyes. "I'm still upset by your actions at Mr. Pellegrino's house. You know what you did was wrong."

"Yes," Cam agreed halfheartedly.

"Good. And you know there's going to be a consequence."

"But—"

"No buts." After wiping her hands on her jeans, she glanced at her landlord, surprised to see such compassion before his expression closed. "We're going to Mr.

Pellegrino's house this weekend to remove the graffiti. Patrick, too, as soon as I talk to his parents."

"That won't be necessary."

Holly took a step back and openly stared at the man. With his arms now folded across his chest and his legs spread shoulder-width apart, she deemed him another force to be reckoned with. The tick in his jawline and the immobile line of his lips didn't help, either.

"It is necessary." She placed her hands on Cam's shoulders and spun him around to face the man. "My son needs to be held responsible for his actions. Why else would you have brought him here if you didn't want some sort of resolution, Mr. Pellegrino?"

"Please, call me Ethan. Point taken. I'll stop by tomorrow to set up the details." He rubbed the stubble on his chin and stared at her baldly. But it was the words he didn't say that concerned Holly. Her gut told her that when Mr. Pellegrino—no, Ethan—came by tomorrow, he'd have her eviction notice ready to add to the pile of past-due invoices underneath her counter.

"Welcome to 'Tis Always the Season." Holly glanced up from her computer the next day. When she saw who stood at the threshold of her shop, her heart began to beat rapidly inside her chest.

"Afternoon." Ethan Pellegrino took up more space than he should. A small gust of wind carried in the snowflakes and made her shiver, but that wasn't what stole her breath away and froze her spine into a straight line. Crossing her arms, she leaned against the counter.

His expression matched the snow-laden clouds in

the sky behind him. Not surprising, since she knew the nature of his visit today. She'd been expecting him, but that still didn't make today's conversation any easier.

Ethan rubbed his left hand over his five-o'clock shadow and broke eye contact for a moment. Hesitation danced over his features as he let out a sigh. "I won't sugarcoat the situation. I was going to come by at the end of the week. Yesterday's incident made it that much sooner. You know I'm here to collect the past-due rent as well as talk about the garage."

Holly stared at a bare spot on the counter. Heat stung her cheeks, and humiliation draped across her until the butterflies in her stomach begged for release. Four months behind in rent and more than one hundred and twenty days past due on most of her invoices, it had only been a matter of time. She'd just hoped she could get through Christmas and figure out another game plan before she had to close. "I know. Thanks for not bringing it up in front of Cam yesterday."

"I'd like to think I have more tact than that."

Her newly designed flyers on the counter caught her attention. Her idea was a good one, and people would hire her. People who came into the shop told her she had a flair for decorating, and she'd learned quite a bit from all the classes she'd taken at the local community college when they'd talked about opening the store. In about an hour, Cameron would come sullenly through the doors after school, and she'd had hopes they could fold, stuff and stamp the envelopes after he'd finished his homework. Unless Ethan gave her a reprieve, they'd have to scrounge boxes from the local market instead.

"I'm sorry. I don't have the rent. But I'm working on it. I just need a bit more time." Her voice squeaked and her fingers gripped the counter until her knuckles gleamed white. Jared had died with a life-insurance policy in place, but that had been eaten up by both their medical bills from the car accident, and things had been tough these past two years despite the social-security benefits. The rent due to Ethan had gone toward her mortgage payments, and the payments to her vendors had gone to her utility bills.

His expression remained detached. Unless he held her stuff as collateral, she could still sell the merchandise online and coordinate her decorating services from her home. It wouldn't be easy, but it was the only fair thing to do. He needed a renter who could pay the rent, and it would be easier for her to not have to worry about it anymore. But to give up Jared's dream… It would give her more time to focus on her son. She knew what she had to do even though the words were hard to form. "I'll vacate immediately."

A kaleidoscope of emotions flickered across his features but didn't match his words. "How much time do you need?"

Closing her eyes for a brief second, and knowing this was for the best, Holly shuddered at the thought of boxing everything up. Jared's hopes and dreams packed into a dark world and crowded together, lifeless, with no one to enjoy them. She fingered the carved baby Jesus ornament by the old-fashioned cash register that Jared had given her the day they'd opened the store, determination filling her every movement.

She would find everything in the store a new home and maybe bring in enough money to pay her mortgage and provide her son with a Christmas present this year. Straightening her shoulders, she flipped her hair back and met his gaze. "Well, if I can run a going-out-of-business sale for a few weeks, that should help. The rest I'll auction off online, along with the trees and fixtures. Today's November 3. Can I have until the end of the month?"

"Isn't this supposed to be your busy season?" When Ethan used both hands to pick up the Santa snow globe from the counter and shake it, Holly noticed the scars covering his entire right hand and disappearing under his sleeve. When she saw the nubs where his fingers should have been, she bit her bottom lip. Now she understood his hesitation yesterday about shaking her hand. More heat claimed her cheeks, because she'd assumed he was being rude. What had happened? And did she really want to know?

Yes… No. Holly warred with her answer as compassion filled her. The scars looked fresh, but she didn't have the time or the energy to open another place in her heart right now. Cameron and her money issues took up just about everything she had. She looked away, and from inside the globe, the jovial old man, the commercial epitome of the season, mocked her with his sack of presents. "It should be, but nothing's been *busy* since the economy went south."

Staring at the bits of white swirling around in the liquid inside the glass, Holly was reminded of her life right now. Drifting along but spiraling downward, resting at the bottom until someone came along and shook things up.

Like Ethan.

Not that she could blame him. Business was business.

When Ethan shook the globe again, she caught him looking at her over the top of the smooth glass. Lines were etched into the skin framing his deep blue eyes, but she sensed he had nothing to laugh about these days, either.

Her breath stalled, leaving her struggling to push away the strange, forgotten emotion gripping her heart. Moments passed before she managed to blink and break the effect he had on her. The snowflakes he'd carried in with him had melted, creating drops of water that glistened in his short, dark, wavy hair and on his jacket. Her instincts were to dust off the moisture so he wouldn't catch a cold, but she refrained from leaning across the counter and touching him with anything but her gaze. A day's growth of beard hugged the contours of his strong jaw, the intensity of his expression broken by his slight frown.

"What are these flyers for?" Ethan set the snow globe back on the counter, picked one up, then stared at the words.

Releasing her breath, Holly refocused on what should be the most important thing to her right now—making an income to pay her bills. "It's an advertisement for a holiday home-decorating service for people who are too busy to do it themselves this time of year."

"That's an interesting concept." Ethan looked around

the store pensively. An awkward moment passed between them as another Christmas carol filled the air. "Will it bring in enough money for you to get caught up?"

Holly found herself staring back into Ethan's blue eyes and felt a current threatening to pull her under. She floundered, trying to free herself from its grasp. Ethan Pellegrino confused her. She shrugged to relieve the tension building in her shoulders and arms. "Honestly? I have no idea, but I have to try."

The wind kicked up beyond the glass door, which protected them from the cold, even though the temperature seemed to drop inside. She shivered and pulled her black sweater tighter. Snow started to accumulate on the lawn across the street. Maybe she'd close up shop early and try to make it home once Cameron arrived from school. It wasn't as if she'd have much business this afternoon anyway, and they could take care of the flyers anywhere.

Ethan scraped his good hand through his hair and contemplated his next move. What was another month in the scheme of things? The thirty-six-hundred dollars was just a drop in the bucket of what he needed to operate his dog sanctuary, bring rescued dogs over from Afghanistan and introduce them to, or in some cases reunite them with, their new owners. "You can stay until the end of the year."

How could he kick her out before Christmas? Not only would he have a hard time reconciling that with God, Ethan also had his mom to contend with. She wouldn't take too kindly to him evicting the woman during the holidays.

"Thank you."

Ethan looked away from Holly's open expression and soft, feminine features to stare at the scars on his hand where his fingers used to be. He'd been one of the lucky ones. Along with the chaplain he was assigned to protect, two of his other comrades in the convoy in Afghanistan had been killed; one of them had been a father and the other a newlywed.

Why the Lord chose those three to die mystified Ethan. If anyone should have been called home, it should have been him. Nobody depended on him or needed him. If anything, he needed someone else since returning home from rehab. Buttoning a shirt and learning to write with his left hand continued to challenge him. Determination forced its way past the dissatisfaction as he shifted and flexed his injured hand. God had a plan for him, and it revolved around the new canine shelter.

"It's not a problem." Ethan would find the money owed from the rent elsewhere, especially since in his gut, he knew Holly wouldn't ever get caught up. Someone said charity began at home. Well, right now this was as close to home as he was going to get. He could still advertise for a renter, but with the three other storefronts available along the main square, it might take a while. As long as Holly made her utilities, what difference was it going to make? Peace settled inside him as he feigned interest again in the snow globe.

Dark blond hair fell to her shoulders and framed her

pale face, accentuating the dark circles under her green eyes. The black sweater she clutched around her only made her appear more fragile, as did the fact she barely came up to his shoulder. A light dusting of freckles endeared her to him more than he was comfortable with.

The woman looked as if she needed a break right now. The urge to shelter and protect her almost brought him to his knees. While his stint as an army chaplain's assistant had come to an end, he couldn't help who he was. He needed to think of something else.

"So your last name is Stanwyck. I knew a Jared Stanwyck. Any relation?"

When Holly nodded, his hope chose a quick exit.

"My late husband."

His mom had told him about Jared's car accident a few years back, but she'd failed to mention he'd left behind a wife and son. Another reason he couldn't evict her any sooner than the end of the year. "I'm sorry for your loss."

"Thanks. How did you know him?"

At her lost expression, his heartbeat accelerated. He picked up the carved wooden ornament sitting by the cash register. It was better than the similar one Jared had done in high school during shop class, but he'd recognize the talent anywhere. "We grew up a few blocks from each other and played ball together in school, but pretty much lost touch after graduation. I went into the military. He went to Northern Arizona University." He stared at her and then his injured hand. "If anyone… Never mind. I see Jared's work got better."

"It did. I used to have a lot of his stuff here, but it's

all sold, except for one of his earlier pieces. I'm sorry for your loss, as well."

"Thanks." Ethan put the figurine back down and his attention strayed to the empty fireplace along the wall, where she'd hung a few stockings, with more placed in the nook built beside it. The store had a pleasant feel and smell to it. As soon as he finished with the dog areas, he could use some advice on how to decorate the reception area he had in mind for Beyond the Borders Dog Sanctuary so it would look nice when he welcomed owners either dropping off or picking up their dogs.

He sniffed in the scent of cinnamon and listened to the sound of another Christmas carol coming over the speakers behind the counter. Lights twinkled on various-size fake trees, each pine with its own different theme. Larger ornaments interspersed with snowflakes hung from the ceiling, and wreaths of all sizes hung on the walls. Shelves lined the back walls, but even from here, Ethan could see they lacked merchandise.

He sensed Holly was in more financial distress than just behind in her rent and wondered if she was even going to make it through the holidays. The closer he inspected the store, the more gaps he found on the trees, shelves and walls. Would her last-ditch effort to set up decorations for other people work?

He hoped so. Even though he needed the rent money for his shelter, it wouldn't be coming from here. He'd already made up his mind and couldn't immediately evict his friend's widow. What a mess. He refocused on the snow globe with the Santa figure. Picking it up, he shook it again, creating a flurry of activity inside. The turbulence suited his mood.

"How much is this?"

"Twenty-four ninety-nine. I have others if you'd like to see them. They're right this way."

Holly had no idea why she prolonged Ethan's visit. She should be shooing him out the door so she could free herself from his closeness and plan her going-out-of-business strategy before Cameron showed up. Somehow she knew Ethan wasn't quite ready to leave yet, and all of a sudden she wanted his company to chase away the loneliness inside the shop.

Staring at the shelf along the back wall that contained what was left of her snow-globe merchandise, she wondered why the pretty glass orbs were her favorites. Was it because of the intricate work inside? The bright colors in some, the muted colors in others? The idea that each time she shook up the make-believe snow, she created a new scene?

She picked up one with a happy family opening presents on Christmas morning inside. Turning the key on the bottom, she wound the music box, shook the globe and set it back on the shelf, the strains of "We Wish You a Merry Christmas" keeping time with the swirling snow.

Ethan stirred next to her. He obviously wasn't comfortable with her choice, either.

He picked up one containing the manger scene. Ethan fumbled for a moment as he tried to turn the crank on the bottom to listen to the music inside, but without his fingers, the task was impossible until he flipped it into his injured hand and used the good one to start the music.

"What happened to your hand?"

Disgust, sadness and resignation flickered through his eyes as he looked at her, but his expression remained immobile. Holly forgot to breathe. In that quick instant his pain was her own—the death of a dream, a shattered life struggling to mend, a man trying to continue on as if nothing had happened, and yet in a flash everything had changed.

She knew it well. "I'm sorry. Forget that I asked."

"It's okay, Holly. You're not the first to ask and you won't be the last." Setting the snow globe back down on the shelf, Ethan pulled up the sleeve of his dress shirt, exposing more scarring that went to his elbow. "It looks a lot better than it did a few months ago. I served as an army chaplain's assistant in Afghanistan."

"What's that?" Holly never took her eyes off the man's arm. She wasn't repulsed, but she wasn't comfortable, either. Some people wore their scars on the outside, others on the inside and others in both ways.

"I was a bodyguard to whatever chaplain I was assigned to. This time it was a pastor, but I've protected rabbis and priests. We were heading out from our base camp when our convoy encountered a roadside IED. I was one of the lucky ones. The chaplain and two soldiers were killed along with two innocent civilians."

"What's an IED?"

"Improvised explosive device. It's technical words for a bomb."

"I'm so sorry. That must have been horrible for you."

Holly knew there was more to the story than just the spoken words, yet she dared not ask. Having closed off her emotions after Jared's death, Holly refused to let them open up again.

"I saw a lot of horrible things over there." Ethan looked as if he wanted to say more about that subject, but his expression closed again and she could almost see his thoughts shift. She braced herself for the next topic of why he was in the store. "Now, about the garage. I'll expect Cameron at eight."

"That works for me, but Cameron will be a bit testy that early in the morning."

"He's almost a teenager. I wouldn't expect anything less. It will be good for him." Ethan cracked a smile and studied the manger inside the snow globe again. "I'll take this one."

"But you don't have to buy anything."

"I don't have to—I want to." Back at the counter, he handed her his credit card, giving Holly her fourth transaction of the day. It wouldn't meet her overhead, but it would help cover something. When she went to wrap it up, he put his good hand on her arm, causing her heart to flutter. "It's a gift for you. We all have troubles, Holly. Sometimes it helps to know that we don't have to carry them alone."

Chapter Two

What had Ethan been thinking? Holly needed money, not a manger scene inside a snow globe. The irony that they were both in the same position but for different reasons would have struck him as funny if things weren't so complicated. Somehow, though, the action seemed right. For a moment, he saw behind her mask of exhaustion and fear and glimpsed the beautiful, caring, compassionate and vulnerable woman underneath.

The kind of woman Jared would fall for. He could, too, if that was what he wanted.

But wanting to protect her when he had to be part of her problem? Sure, he hadn't been the cause of her financial woes, but deep down he knew that being behind in her bills bothered her and he felt like a cad. His mom would have never gone over there and asked for the back rent. As soon as he met Holly Stanwyck, he knew he wasn't going to get it from her. Even if she did somehow come up with it, he wasn't sure he would take it and hoped her idea for the holiday decorating service panned out because she needed money.

The woman also needed some divine intervention right now. He'd add her to his prayers tonight and ask his mother to do the same. Knowing Nan, though, Holly was already on the list.

He slammed his car door shut. As a career soldier forced out because of his injuries, he'd never make it in the civilian world if he didn't toughen up. Right. He was just a big softy, regardless of which side he was on. He'd always had pieces of candy in his pocket for the Afghan children and biscuits for the stray dogs. Now he was opening a sanctuary for dogs to stay while their owners served on foreign soil and to help transport stray dogs adopted by servicemen overseas and reunite them stateside.

Head down to keep the lingering snowflakes from his eyes, and hands bunched inside his coat pockets, he headed toward home and the kennels in the enclosed porch of his house in town that he used as the temporary sanctuary. The permanent one was going to be at his family's farmhouse outside of town, but it needed to be refurbished before he could take the dogs out there. He needed money to do that; some of it he'd hoped to get from Holly. Now he'd have to look elsewhere, since his disability checks barely covered anything.

The lemon scent of cleaner and varied barks greeted him when he walked through the double French doors off the back porch.

"How'd it go?" Meredith, his cousin and fellow

board member of Beyond the Borders Dog Sanctuary, greeted him.

"As well as I suspected. There won't be any funds coming from the store anytime soon."

"I'm sorry to hear that. Holly's such a nice woman. She's just had a lot to deal with lately."

Ethan didn't bother to mention the incident with the garage door, seeing as he suspected Meredith was the one who had leaked the eviction information to the wrong person. He loved his cousin, but after being away so long, he'd forgotten her fondness for spreading gossip.

"Anything new with the little girl?" Ethan changed the subject. He didn't want to think about Holly anymore, or the tangible energy that had made the short hairs on the back of his neck stand at attention when his hand grazed hers as he gave her the snow globe. Meredith sat inside the kennel, stroking the little black-and-white mutt's head, and he saw the bandages covering both front legs where the dog had licked away all her fur.

"Pudding Cup will be fine. It's just nerves. She misses her mom."

"How about the big guy I brought in to Tim?" He'd found the injured stray mix huddled on the side of the road yesterday, and it reminded him of one of the dogs their patrol had rescued from the cruelty of an Afghan family. He couldn't ignore the mutt and had thoughts about keeping him, despite the fact Ethan needed to stick to his mission statement. There were other shelters in the area that took in homeless and abandoned dogs.

"He's going to be just fine. Tim thinks he's found a home for him already, so he said not to worry about the bill." Meredith was engaged to the local veterinarian, who also sat on the board and was willing to take care of any of their animals for cost.

"I'll have to stop by and thank him." And make sure the animal was going to a good home. Okay, so he was a sucker for dogs and kids and apparently widows behind on their rent.

Ethan rubbed his hand across his stubbly chin. "Anything else?"

"Yep." Meredith rose to her feet, causing Pudding Cup to whimper and follow her to the gate. "Another stray is being shipped over from Afghanistan, courtesy of your buddy Phil, along with the other one. Duggan and Jasper arrive Saturday, as do two more dogs on Wednesday. Their owners ship out next Friday."

"Great." Ethan wiped the snowflake residue from his face. His six temporary accommodations were more than full. With four more dogs coming in, he would be over capacity at seven, even though the two from Afghanistan would only be temporary until he could reunite them with their owners, who'd arrived home from their tour of duty last month. He could spill out into his living room, but he'd be over the limit and need a kennel license that much sooner. "Where am I going to put them?"

"Whose brilliant idea was it to provide a home for displaced animals when their owners left?"

"Mine, and you know it's a good one. It's one less thing for our local service men and women to think about while they're doing their tour. Most are fortunate to have family to take care of them, but not all." Ethan had started his studies to be a lay minister and had often counseled some of the enlisted men when the need arose. Leaving their pets behind ranked pretty high up there behind family, especially when they had to dump their companion in a shelter.

Being distracted could get a person killed. He knew that firsthand.

He stared at the nubs on his hand and tried to feel the forgiveness. The emotion refused to come. Five people died that day, and he wrestled with the guilt. Despite the fact he was assigned to protect the chaplain, he felt a responsibility to everyone he traveled with. He should have seen the IED. He knew the signs to look for. A strange vehicle on the side of the road, the wink of light reflecting off the camera lens set up to film the incident, the uneasy feeling harbored inside his gut because of the delay in getting the convoy started.

But he'd been distracted.

None of that mattered now.

What mattered as he stared at his scars and searched for forgiveness was that God had a plan for him. And it revolved around the sanctuary and taking care of man's best friend.

"You're just a bleeding-heart softy. That's what I love about you." Meredith gave him a hug. "I'll take Pudding Cup with me. I like the little girl, and Tim says it's no problem for me to drop her off at his office during the day. I think she'll recover quicker from her abandonment issues, so that frees up one kennel and then you'll have enough."

"Thanks. I appreciate that." For what seemed the first time that day, he smiled. Meredith was more like a sister than a cousin, and with a job in sales and marketing, she was an invaluable part of the team he'd selected for the board. He'd also asked her fiancé, Tim, and his mom because she owned the property that would house the permanent sanctuary. He should find one other person, to make the numbers odd in case they needed a tiebreaker, and he had yet to find someone with accounting experience so he could concentrate on the dogs and managing the sanctuary.

Things had happened so quickly. He'd probably gone about this the wrong way by accepting animals before he was ready, but the alternative would have been for his first resident, Sadie, to end up in the pound. It would work out. God's plan had been revealed to him during those long hours in the hospital and continued to be revealed daily.

Pudding Cup treated him to a good licking when he bent and scratched her behind her ears. Bear, the black Lab who had alerted him to yesterday's graffiti artists, whined and pawed at the metal fencing of his kennel, begging for attention. "I'll be right there, boy." His gaze scoured the cramped area again. "I need money to expand and move everything out to the farm."

"Keep praying. It'll happen. We'll get the grant money and more private funding. You'll see." Meredith picked up Pudding Cup and squeezed her gently. "Oh, there's one other thing." By the hesitant smile registered on her lips, Ethan knew he wasn't going to like the next words out of his cousin's mouth. "We're also getting a ferret. Seems like one of the dogs arriving Saturday thinks it's her baby. I told Private Smith it would be okay."

"But we agreed this would be strictly dogs. It's called Beyond the Borders Dog Sanctuary."

Meredith crossed her arms over her chest and stared at him darkly. "Then change it to Beyond the Borders Animal Sanctuary. As a member of the board, I have the right to speak up, as well. How can you break up a family? What kind of peace of mind would our soldier get if he didn't know both his pets were safe while he was away? I suspect we'll be getting calls for cats soon, too."

Ethan shoved his hand through his hair. "No. Absolutely not. No cats."

"We'll see about that." She gave him a dark look. "Just because you have a personal issue with the cute, cuddly creatures doesn't mean they shouldn't have the same consideration as dogs. They are all God's creatures."

"I'm well aware of that. I'm okay with cats. I just don't understand them. They need to go elsewhere. I'm having enough trouble raising the money and supplies for dogs." His cousin's scowl grew. Half Irish with red hair to match, Meredith was a force to be reckoned with when she was angry. "I'm not going to win this argument, am I?"

She shook her head. "They make medicine for that, you know. I'll make a cat lover out of you yet. I've gotta run, but I'll be back after dinner to help you walk them and transition Bear and Sadie for the night. You really need to get some volunteers in here, though, when the other dogs arrive."

"I'll work on it." Another item to add to his list of things to do for the shelter that grew longer, not shorter, with each passing day. And now to complicate things, he had a whole separate issue to think about.

Holly Stanwyck refused to budge from his mind.

Shadows from the early-morning sun stretched across the road in front of them as Holly drove to the other side of town Saturday morning. The digital clock in her car read 7:57 a.m. and she still had ten minutes to go according to Ethan's directions. Holly disliked being late. The scheduled 7:45 departure time shouldn't have been an issue, since she was an early riser. Too bad her son had other ideas. Holly had let him sleep as long as possible, but he still looked wiped out from the week, disgruntled and a bit dejected. He'd given her a hard time about getting up.

Instead of going to the early church service tomorrow, they'd catch the later one. Not that she really wanted to go, but she had to, for Cam's sake. It hadn't worked these past few months, but maybe being in the Lord's house would straighten him out since she hadn't been able to get through to him. She glanced sideways at her son and caught the scowl underneath the perfected look of boredom. Nothing seemed to have remained from his childhood, and her heart ached at the thought of how things used to be before Jared died.

So much had changed since the accident. Especially the past year.

Holly tried to lighten the mood inside her old Honda. "Mindy's manning the shop today." The high-school student worked for her part-time because Holly couldn't work seven days a week, keep sane and keep Cameron out of trouble, which apparently wasn't working very well. She couldn't really afford the student, but Holly hated asking her friends to continually pitch in. "I need to stop in and check on a few things, but any ideas on what you'd like to do after we finish at Mr. Pellegrino's house?"

"I wanna ride the quad again." He folded his arms across his chest and glared at her.

"You know we don't have them anymore." To help pay their medical bills, she'd sold both ATVs after Jared died.

"That's what I want to do. Patrick tells me they have two. You can let me go home with him after we're finished."

"You know that's not going to happen. Besides, we don't even know if they're coming today to help. They never responded to my phone call." Her fingers gripped the steering wheel a little harder as she turned the corner and merged with the rest of the local and tourist vehicles heading through the downtown area. She couldn't imagine not communicating with another parent had the roles been reversed. But then again, she had no idea what was going on inside Patrick's home, and she had never met his parents.

Silence accompanied them the last five minutes to

Ethan's house, where he waited for them outside by the garage with a can of paint and painting supplies. Arms crossed, he paced the small cement area in front of the 1960s-style single-story brick ranch house.

"Good morning." Holly spoke as soon as she exited the car. Too bad her inability to get her bearings had nothing to do with the sudden movement and everything to do with the man in the old T-shirt underneath his worn camouflage jacket and faded jeans. He still wore the same compassionate look he'd had inside her shop the other day, but underneath she sensed his uncertainty and awkwardness that probably stemmed from his injury in Afghanistan.

"Good morning." His gaze swept over her fleece-lined jacket and then back to her face, making her feel a bit self-conscious. A half smile broke the tension. "I'm glad you're here."

Heat consumed her cheeks. "Sorry we're late. I should have called. I would never back out on a promise or commitment. We just had a hard time getting out of the house this morning." She glanced around the driveway, not surprised to see her car the sole vehicle. "I take it Patrick isn't here?"

"Not yet."

"Then he probably won't show. I was only able to leave a message for his parents, and they never called back." Sorrow and a touch of anger burrowed into her heart. From what she'd gleaned from Cam's conversation the night of the incident, the idea had been Patrick's and so had the spray paint, but her son was just as guilty for going along with the plan.

"That's not your problem. I should have contacted them myself. Ready? After Cameron removes the graffiti, it shouldn't take that long to paint, but we may have to do two coats. We should be finished by eleven. If you need to leave earlier, I can drop Cameron off at the store."

"We? I thought this was Cameron's job."

"It is." Ethan rubbed his chin with the back of his hand, drawing her gaze along with it. "But I somehow feel responsible. If my cousin hadn't mentioned my hastily spoken words—about evicting the tenant because of the back rent—to her best friend, the busybody of Dynamite Creek, your son wouldn't have heard it from his classmate."

She looked at the black spray paint on the light brown wooden door. Holly nodded. "I see. Look, I understand your position. You need someone in there who can pay the rent, and being behind usually results in eviction. I get that. Now, as for the door, you're right, it would go much quicker if we all helped, especially because you haven't seen Cam paint yet." She glanced back at her car. Her son still sat hunched in the front seat. "Today, Cameron. The sooner you get started, the sooner you get finished."

Cam sulked as he stepped from the passenger seat and shuffled toward them. The preteen residing in his body screamed attitude. Holly needed to get a handle on him before he towered above her with his next growth spurt.

Ethan gave Cameron a pair of black work gloves. "Here, put these on."

"For painting?"

"You're going to remove the spray paint first. I doubt the paint for the garage door will cover the black markings very well." After kneeling down, Ethan wedged the yellow bottle with red lettering into the crook of his arm and used his good hand to open the top.

"What's that?" Cameron yanked on the gloves.

"It's supposed to remove the graffiti." Ethan poured some liquid onto a rag, set the bottle down, stood and then handed the cloth to Cam. "Just start rubbing the painted areas. It should come off."

"Me?"

"Of course." He winked at Holly, making her heart flutter until she tamped down on the emotion. Despite the two years that had passed since his death, her heart belonged to Jared.

"You're the one who did it. I'm here to supervise, not do the job for you. Your mom, either. Just be careful you don't get it on your skin or clothes." Folding his arms over his chest, Ethan stepped back.

What? she mouthed, raising her eyebrows and tilting her head to the side. Ethan put a finger to his lips and motioned for her to take a few steps back.

Once they were out of hearing distance, he leaned close to her ear, the warmth of his breath creating havoc with her breathing. "We'll help with the painting. This part is a lesson the boy needs to learn for himself."

"Sounds like you have experience," Holly replied softly as she inched away, needing to distance herself.

"I do. I wasn't exactly a choirboy in my youth." A fraction of a smile tugged at his lips, and his gaze slipped back to her son begrudgingly rubbing the saturated cloth over the paint.

"Really. What did you do?"

"Pretty much the same thing. I tagged a neighbor's garage door because he was old and crotchety. Back then, I didn't get to use any sort of remover. I had to sand the area first, apply a primer and then four coats of paint. Took nearly the whole weekend."

"Did you learn your lesson?"

"That was just one of many."

And yet it looked as if Ethan had managed to turn his life around, go into the service and almost die for his country. Her gaze flickered to his injured hand again and wondered if it still hurt and how he managed to do the day-to-day stuff that required two sets of fingers, but she was too polite to ask. Besides, that would mean opening up her heart again to the possibilities of establishing some sort of friendship or relationship with him, and that wasn't going to happen anytime soon.

"This stuff smells like your nail-polish remover, Mom, but it really works. Look. The paint is almost all gone." Cam broke into her thoughts, dragging them back to the garage door. A slight stain still clung to the beige paint, but it was much less noticeable now. She breathed a sigh of relief, realizing they wouldn't be there all day as she'd anticipated.

"Pretty much. Now you need to rinse the residue off. Then while it's drying I'll show you around."

"Show us around?" Cam dropped the cloth on the

newspaper protecting the driveway and yanked off the gloves.

"I'm opening a sanctuary for dogs while their owners are overseas."

"Dogs? Really? I wish we had a dog, not a stupid, silly cat."

Holly heard the criticism and hurt spew from Cam's lips. Her mouth opened and shut quickly as the blood now drained from her cheeks. Any words she could even think to say caught in her throat as she stared at her son and gulped for air. The person standing next to Ethan bore little resemblance to the sweet, innocent boy she remembered.

"Your dad brought Figaro home." That was all Holly managed to say. Pain ate through her heart again, and tears hovered behind her eyelids. How could she explain to her son that the cat was more than just a cat? Figaro was another link to the past she'd shared with Jared, just as Cam was.

Ethan broke the uneasy silence. "Cats are wonderful creatures and just one of God's many creations, Cameron. Pets come in all shapes, sizes and colors. The same as people. God made us all unique. He loves us all the same, despite our differences."

Holly squirmed at Ethan's mention of God. Of course, she should expect no less from a chaplain's assistant, but it made her uncomfortable, especially since she went through the motions for Cam's sake but didn't really believe or love the way she was supposed to.

"I want a dog that can play fetch."

Ethan caught the defiant look the boy threw at his

mother, and a subtle change hovered in the air between them. Clouds drifted in front of the sun, blocking out its temporary warmth, and the wind kicked up a notch, intensifying the clang of the wind chime on the front porch of his neighbor's house. Holly's soft gasp met his ears as her light floral fragrance drifted under his nose. Her stricken expression told him more than any words she could speak. The tagging incident aside, the boy was headed for trouble if there wasn't some kind of intervention.

He liked kids, had a special rapport with them. He'd started training as a lay minister after he joined the military, where he had high hopes of saving the world. He hadn't. Instead, five people had paid the ultimate price. But this wasn't about him, the pastor or the two soldiers and civilians with God now. Saving the entire world was His job. Opening the dog sanctuary and maybe helping a troubled boy find the right path in life was something Ethan could handle. Maybe. It was the least he could do for Jared. For Holly.

A thought struck him as he turned on the spigot, yanked the hose to the garage door and then passed it off to Cameron. Ethan knew he should check with Holly first, but he had only so much time to get through to the boy. "I have a solution."

"What?" Both she and Cameron spoke at the same time.

"I need a volunteer or two to work at the dog sanctuary. Cameron can come after school. He'll stay out of trouble, I'll get some much-needed help and the dogs will have someone to play with. He could ride the bus here after school. What do you think?"

"Really?"

"Really. Why play with one dog when you can play with several?" Encouraged by the hope blazing in the boy's eyes, Ethan shot a look at Holly and saw her cross her arms and draw her lips tight.

"Can I, Mom?"

"What about his homework?"

Ethan understood this was about more than just homework. She'd already lost her husband; this was about her son's safety. Despite his being her landlord, she didn't know him from any other stranger in town. He'd reassure her while Cameron rinsed off the door.

A strand of hair had fallen free from her ponytail and accentuated the curve of her jawline. Her soft lips graced him with a tentative smile, and her green eyes made him think of his childhood and rolling in cool, thick grass on a hot summer day. Ethan almost forgot why he stood in front of his garage. Almost. He pulled his gaze from her and refocused back on the boy and safer territory. Something about Holly brought out his protective side that, despite what had happened in Afghanistan, was a part of him that refused to go away. And that extended to her son, too.

"I'll make sure he gets his homework done."

"And how will he get home afterward?"

"I'll drive him there."

"I don't know…" Holly felt the weight of two pairs of eyes staring at her. This twist threw another item she had to deal with into her already-crowded mind. Pressure simmered underneath the surface.

"Please, Mom?" Cam begged her.

"Rinse off the door and give me a moment."

Holly should have realized her son wanted a dog. She did know that she couldn't handle the added expense or the time commitment, although the idea of helping out at the shelter was brilliant. Had her monetary worries removed her that far from her son's life? Had she been so focused on getting through each day that she had lost touch with what was the most important to her?

Yes.

Holly didn't like the answer that popped into her head. She didn't understand her son anymore. Jared would have told her to take her troubles to the Lord. Easier said than done. Holly blamed Him for taking her husband away from her.

Cameron quickly squirted the water onto the door and washed away the paint residue and chemicals. Then he handed the hose back to Ethan. "I'll get my homework done. I won't get into any trouble and I won't ask for a dog again. Please?"

Put like that, how could she say no? Easily. Her alternatives, though, were wondering how to keep Cameron away from Patrick or dealing with her son's sulking expression in the store after school. It would make him happy, settle the issue of Patrick and help Ethan out at the same time. In a way, she owed it to her landlord for letting her stay in the shop until after Christmas.

She still had to deal with the fact that she didn't even know Ethan that well. But he had to be good. He was a

Christian, retired from the military and had once been Jared's friend. Plus he was Nan Emrey's son, and she'd never had any issues or concerns with the older woman. Her gut told her it would be okay, but it wouldn't hurt to ask around about him tomorrow just in case. She could always change her mind if necessary.

"Fine. We'll try it out for a week. I'll pick him up, though, after I close the shop. Now shake on the deal and…" Holly turned to face Ethan, the last of her words garbled in her throat. Blood pooled in her cheeks.

This time Ethan had no problem putting out his hand as if almost daring Cameron to touch it.

"What happened to you, Mr. Pellegrino?" Cameron's eyes widened as he stared at Ethan's hand. His own hovered in the space around his head.

A muffled silence filled the space until Holly's strangled voice cut into it. "Cameron. Where are your manners?" Yet she'd asked the same question days earlier.

"Does it hurt?"

"Cameron Jared Stanwyck. Enough." Holly clenched her fists.

Ethan ignored her outburst and leaned toward her son. "Not so much anymore, but when the cold seeps in, it does bother me somewhat."

Flexing his thumb, the only remaining digit on his hand, Ethan stretched it toward Cameron. "Go ahead. You can touch it." He gave her a no-nonsense expression. "I've found talking about it instead of ignoring it helps."

When his gaze caught hers, Holly had a hard time remembering her name. His startling blue eyes had turned into deep, mysterious pools of uncharted waters, challenging her. She fought to gain control over her emotions. What was happening to her?

"Feels weird. How do you write and stuff like that?"

Holly's gaze remained averted, but she sensed Ethan's attention shift to her son. "I'm relearning that, or I do it with my left hand. It hasn't been easy, but I've discovered you can teach an old dog a new trick. Speaking of which, come on. I bet Bear is just waiting to learn something new today."

"Bear?"

"A black Lab that's going to be here for at least a year. He loves to play fetch with an old tennis ball. The temporary sanctuary's in the house until I can move it to the family farm outside of town."

When Cam ran ahead of them, Ethan faced Holly again and held out his injured hand. "Here. Your turn. We may as well get this out of the way, since I'm guessing I'll be seeing a lot of you when you pick Cameron up."

Seeing each other? Holly had no plans on that. She would make sure that Cameron waited for her outside.

"Holly?"

Blinking, she forced her thoughts back to the present. She inhaled sharply. She'd tried to keep from staring earlier, but her gaze had kept returning to his injured hand. She was curious. But to touch it?

Swallowing, Holly reached out. She stopped short. It seemed too intimate a gesture for someone she hardly knew, despite the fact Ethan and Jared had gone to school together. "I'm really not comfortable with this."

"And I'm not going to be comfortable with the idea of seeing the questions in your eyes all the time."

"But—"

"It looks worse than it really is, but I understand." Ethan shrugged and stared at his hand as he withdrew. "It does take getting used to."

"I'm sorry, Ethan."

Holly felt his pain again behind his mask of indifference, confirming there was more going on inside him than he let on. The bomb had taken more than just his fingers and five lives. It left behind a shell of a man, struggling to deal with everyday life. He suffered the survivor's guilt that ate away at the soul like a moth devoured clothing.

Holly wore it every day like a piece of her wardrobe.

She should have never insisted that she and Jared attend the Chamber of Commerce function when the weather forecaster had predicted the cold snap that would turn the melted snow into ice. But how was she to know in that brief moment she took her eyes from the road that the argument would be their last?

Chapter Three

Disappointment pooled around Ethan's shoulders as silence accompanied them to where Cameron stood impatiently by the back door. Holly's son had taken Ethan's injured hand in stride with the curiosity he'd expect from a child. Holly's reaction bothered him, even though it shouldn't. He didn't see the revulsion in her eyes like he had with others, but even now he noticed that her feet angled away from him and she stepped in close proximity to Cameron.

Why had he insisted she touch his hand? Why had he openly challenged her? What difference would it make in the scheme of things? She was his tenant for now, and in less than two months that would change. Then, of course, there was Cameron. But who knew whether that arrangement would last more than a week? More discontent filled him as he stared at the nubs. He didn't understand his actions himself, but he couldn't go back and change things.

If he could, the injury and loss of life would have never happened.

Let go, let God. The voice of the pastor who'd visited him daily in the hospital echoed in his brain. Four simple words; three if you didn't count the repeated one. Was it really that easy? He'd studied God's word, yet he found himself struggling to follow His commands. *Let go, let God.*

Ethan had no choice. In order to embrace the future, the past had to be forgiven and forgotten. Starting today.

"Come on in." He opened the back door and ushered them inside. Warmth spilled around them, along with the scent of lemon, antiseptic and dog. He heard a happy whine as he flipped the light switch, evicting the dimness from the west-facing room.

Nudging the door shut with his shoulder, he glanced around the small white kitchen, realizing the only color came from Holly's red sweatshirt. Nothing adorned the walls but a small black-and-white clock. Even the white curtains on the window over the sink blended into the background, as did the few appliances on the equally white Formica counter.

He'd packed up all his stuff and rented out the house while he was overseas, and hadn't made the time to unpack the boxes he'd pulled from storage and left in the garage. His house was just a house and not the home he'd left behind. But then again a lot of things had changed. He'd changed. Used to the constant company of people around him for the past several years, the quietness of his surroundings now, other than the two dogs, grated on his nerves.

He'd find the time today to breathe life back into his house.

Another whine sounded from the other room, louder this time since Bear had heard their voices. This time Sadie joined in along with the noise of the chain-link fence rattling as the dogs tried to escape their enclosures.

"Are they this way?" Excitement buried the indifference in Cameron's voice. Good. The boy hadn't gone too far down the wrong path yet. He could work with the spray-paint incident and the few other problems that simmered under the surface.

Maybe this was part of the Lord's plan for Ethan, as well. He'd had an old neighbor's intervention in his teens that helped steer him in the right direction. Now it was time for him to pay it back, not only with Cameron but with other boys, as well—Patrick being one of them if he ever showed up.

"Right through that doorway. Hang on, though. Let me get you some treats for them." Ethan grabbed a box from the pantry, pulled out two bone shaped dog snacks and then handed them to Cameron. Anticipation created a tangible energy inside the small kitchen, and he knew he'd made the right decision to have the boy help him with the dogs. Holly's signature light floral fragrance mingled with the other scents lingering in the air. He wouldn't turn down her assistance, either, if she decided she wanted to help in some capacity.

"Thanks, Mr. Pellegrino."

It felt right to have Holly and her son inside his home. They added warmth and companionship that were missing between the four walls. Possessions didn't make a home. People did. But allowing others into his life again besides his immediate family meant protecting them. Bile burned his throat and he flexed his throbbing hand, feeling the impression of fingers where none remained. Protecting people was something he wasn't good at anymore. So why the offer to have Cameron help him out?

Because right now, the need to think about the boy's well-being overruled everything else.

"You're welcome. This way. They're in the Arizona room." Ethan slipped past his guests and into the area to his left that used to be the back porch before the previous owner enclosed it. Six kennels filled the space, all lined up like soldiers during inspection.

But this was only temporary. As soon as he found more funding, he'd be moving to the permanent sanctuary outside of town. The vision of twenty-four more inside the old barn on the farm property filled his mind's eye as well as the big dog run in the pasture.

Focus on the future.

Cameron shook off his mother's grasp and ran to the first kennel. A smile broke out as he put his hand out for the black Lab to smell. Good. The kid knew how to approach a dog. And he showed an interest in them and an apparent love for them as he reached through the bars and scratched the dog behind his ears. That would make their time together go a bit smoother.

He glanced at Holly and momentarily lost himself

in her presence. With her hair pulled back in a ponytail and no makeup to cover her smooth, delicate skin,
she looked to be in her mid-twenties even though he
figured her to be closer to his thirty-five years. The
swept-back locks exposed her long, elegant neck and,
from this angle, a straight, slightly upturned nose. But
it was her vulnerability that got to him.

Despite her attempts to keep it all together, he sensed
just below the surface she suffered and struggled with
her son, the shop, everyday life. Ethan also knew he
hadn't made it any easier on her, but he had his own
dreams and issues. His gaze fell on his hand. Sometimes sugarcoating things didn't help; it only made mat-
ters worse. He'd given her to the end of the year, and his
offer to help her son would still be available to both of
them as long as the arrangement continued to work out.

He should step away and draw himself inward. Instead, when she turned her head toward him, he found
himself staring into her deep green eyes that had seen
so much pain. A pain he could identify with. He'd lost
his father at a young age, and several of his friends in
Afghanistan. He could identify with the hollowness,
the gaping hole, the huge cavity filled with darkness
that even these days God's light had a hard time driving
away. But even that couldn't compare to losing one's
partner, one's soul mate.

He had no experience with that sort of loss, yet he
felt the need to comfort. Protect. He wanted to draw
Holly into his arms, absorb her pain and blend it with
his own.

"What's his name?"

Ethan blinked at Cameron's words, stepped backward and concentrated on the dog as Holly knelt down by her son. He folded his arms across his chest and leaned against the door frame. "That's Bear. He'll be with me for at least a year. He likes to play ball. I've already taken him out for a walk, but in between the coats of paint, maybe you can let him run around the yard a bit and throw him a couple of balls."

"Hi, Bear." Laughter spilled from the boy's lips as the dog tried to lick his face through the metal fencing. In that instant, Ethan realized another thing that had been missing from his life. Not that he'd had anything to laugh about. That would change going forward. He flexed what remained of his right hand again, determined not to let anything stop him from his goals.

And maybe find love in the process.

A strange emotion gripped Ethan as he squatted down beside Holly outside the kennel of the cocker spaniel/heeler mix next to Bear. The tan-and-white spotted dog with the droopy ears stared up at them with big brown eyes. Love? Something as complicated as that was meant for guys like her late husband, not someone who would probably have nightmares of what happened in Afghanistan for the rest of his life, or carry the guilt of five deaths around his neck like a yoke.

"This one here is Sadie. She'll be here for almost two years." God willing he'd still be open then. More delays in funding meant he would have to pull more money out of his savings account to continue the renovations, because with more dogs coming in, he had to have more room.

"She's adorable," Holly whispered. He noticed her gaze dart toward Cameron, who had wedged his hand between the metal bars of the cage door and continued to scratch Bear behind his ears. "Maybe I should consider getting Cam a dog. In the future." Her sigh washed over him, filling him with that need to protect her from her thoughts. Ironically, he was part of the problem, not the solution, since her reprieve lasted until just after the holidays.

"Where are the rest of the dogs?" Cameron asked.

"Two dogs are showing up this afternoon and the other two arrive next week."

"What happens if you get another dog? There won't be any room." Holly turned to face him.

"I'm well aware of that. I'll have plenty of room once I move to the permanent place."

"But in order to move there, you need money. Like the rent from the storefront." Holly dipped her head and clenched her fists. But when she made eye contact with him again, resolve and resignation slid into her eyes. "What you're doing is a noble thing, Ethan. I'll vacate immediately so you can get another renter in there."

"It's going to take a lot more than those kinds of funds. The past-due rent isn't going to make that much of a difference. My original offer still stands. You have until December 31."

For a moment Ethan stared at the empty kennels and again envisioned himself in his new place with twenty-four kennels occupied and his sanctuary fully operational. Somehow he sensed the woman who barely grazed his shoulder and the boy kneeling in front of the other kennel would play an intricate role in this if he managed to pull it off.

The Lord worked in mysterious ways.

"Come on, the door should be dry by now. Let's put the primer on and then we'll come back and take the dogs outside for a bit."

"Aw, just a few more minutes?" Cameron whined.

"We'll come back." Ethan held his ground. The integral part of the intervention was taking a firm hand and making sure the preteen knew who was boss.

Fifteen minutes later, they all stepped back and looked at their handiwork. Holly grinned and scratched the back of her neck. "Now I know why I leave the painting to the professionals. Your area looks much better than mine."

"And mine." Cameron plopped his brush back into the paint tray.

"It's primer. It won't matter, anyway. Not once the topcoat goes on. I'll show you a quick, easy way to do it when we get to that step."

"It's a good thing you placed cardboard along the bottom. It saved the concrete driveway from the wayward drops."

"Yeah, it's a lesson learned the hard way." Ethan grabbed the brushes and rollers to rinse off with the hose. "If you study the driveway enough, you'll see the drops of paint from the first time I painted it six years ago when I bought the house. No matter how careful you are, you always make mistakes."

Funny. He could forgive himself for certain mistakes, but not others. But then again, a little paint on the concrete couldn't even compare to five people losing their lives because he was distracted. Careless.

If only he could wash away his guilt as quickly as he did the primer. The stream of water cleared. After shutting off the tap, he stood and shook everything out. "Good job, Cameron. We'll make a painter out of you yet. There'll be lots of painting needed in the new offices of the sanctuary. What do you say? Wanna come on board?"

"Sounds like too much work. Can I go back and play with Bear now?"

Ethan couldn't help but smile. At least the kid was honest. Cameron would probably rather go to the dentist than do any more painting, but at least he had energy for the dogs. Exercising the dogs took a lot of time, time Ethan could use for paperwork, or raising money, or cleaning up the kennels, if he didn't make that part of Cameron's responsibilities. "Just make sure you put him on the leash hanging on the wall before you take him outside."

"Sure thing. Thanks, Mr. Pellegrino." Cameron spun around and sprinted away, leaving Holly and Ethan to follow at a more leisurely pace.

"It's sunny today, so it should dry quickly. Then we can do a coat of paint. If that doesn't cover it, I'll do another one tomorrow."

"Tomorrow? But I thought we'd get it all done today."

He watched Holly swipe her fingers across her old sweatshirt, leaving gray streaks of primer in the process. That and the tiny splotches sprinkling her hair only added to her charm. It was all he could do not to try to remove some of the bigger blotches, but after his earlier thoughts about her surfaced, he knew that it wasn't a good idea. Instead, he focused on Cameron.

"That had been my plan, but keeping you here all day wasn't part of it, either. I forgot about factoring in the time frame of letting the coats dry in between applications. Cameron will have fulfilled his obligation after the first coat of paint."

"But—"

"If I do another coat, that is my own choice, okay? You have enough going on. Let's just keep it at that."

Holly reflected on his words. He understood, and that scared her more than the thought of losing the shop. Because if she ever decided to let go of what she had with Jared and started dating again, Ethan would be the kind of man she'd choose to go out with. But she wouldn't. Involvement with another man would only open herself up to more heartache and pain, especially if something happened to him. Besides, she needed to concentrate on her son and his needs. Once he was grown, she could focus on her own.

"I haven't seen Cameron this excited in a long time." *Since before Jared's death.* "Thanks for giving him the chance. I'm sure he'll do a great job with the dogs. And I doubt he'll give you any trouble with his homework if he's got something to look forward to afterward."

"He doesn't like doing his homework?"

"Not lately. Or pick up after himself, or do any of his chores." Her sigh filled the space between them.

"There's a lot of things he used to like to do but not anymore. His attitude these past few months has been… for lack of a better word…challenging."

Holly had to get a grip on it, or the spray-paint incident at Ethan's was only the beginning. Some days she didn't know where to turn. Jared would have told her to look upward and let everything rest in God's hands. Yet He hadn't answered her prayers to keep her husband alive. What made her think He'd listen to her now?

"I've worked with kids before. I'll see if I can get through to him."

He put his hand into his pocket but pulled it out empty. A pained expression flickered across his face, quickly restrained and replaced by one of resignation.

"Is something wrong? Did you hurt yourself?" She placed her hand on his forearm and compassion infused her. Only a bit lower and she could touch his hand. His injured hand. Did she want to go there? Only confusion answered her.

"No. I'm okay. I used to always have candy for the Afghan children. Sometimes I forget where I am. I don't carry it anymore."

"I'm sorry."

Ethan moved her hand from his arm and squeezed it gently before he let it drop. "What's there to be sorry for? For some reason God spared me but left me a reminder that He's in charge. Despite my teachings in order to be a lay minister and everything I've witnessed, I forget."

Unsure of what to say next, Holly trudged along beside him the rest of the way to the back of the house in silence. What could she say that wouldn't sound phony or unbelievable?

Holly paused in the parking lot of the shingled one-story redbrick building. Despite her almost weekly attendance, she still felt uncomfortable since her husband's death. This had been Jared's church, his parents' church and his grandparents' church before him in the old building that now housed the youth center and other Sunday school classes. It was as if they knew she didn't have the same beliefs, that she'd shut down her connection with God the same time He'd taken Jared away. Some days she felt the eyes of the congregation staring at her, drilling her as she sat in one of the back rows, as if they blamed her for her husband's death.

That wasn't too far from the truth.

Beside her, Cam shifted in his seat and refused to take off his seat belt. "Do we really have to go?"

"Yes, we really have to go. I let you sleep in, so you're stuck with the traditional service today. Come on, we'll go grab brunch after we're done." Not that she could afford it, but both of them needed some sort of treat. The Sunrise Diner wasn't too far from the store, and it catered to the folks who didn't have a lot of money to spend, unlike the more touristy places on the square.

Afterward, she'd drop her son off at his friend Tyler's house while she opened the store for a few hours since Mindy wasn't feeling well today. If the sunny weather held, the afternoon should be somewhat busy and she could reduce her inventory by making a bunch of sales. That would be less for her and Cameron to pack after Christmas.

If they even had a Christmas. So far she'd had no response to her seasonal decorating flyer, but it was still early in the season. She'd thought her idea had been a good one. Apparently, it wasn't.

The butterflies in her stomach increased with each step. She joined the streams of other worshippers entering the church, yet Holly still felt the isolation despite the beige welcome mat by the door. It was probably more of her own doing than anyone milling around her, though.

She and Cam wandered inside, stopping only to pick up a bulletin on their way through the door and into the interior. Grabbing one of the last open pews on the left side of the aisle, Holly sank down and stared at the tall white candles that graced the two candleholders on each side of the pulpit. Christine Preston, one of the store owners on her side of the street, made them, along with some of the other candles in other areas of the church.

Mrs. O'Leary, in her usual bright, tropical attire, sat behind the organ to her right, the pull of the music impossible to ignore. On each side of the building, three large, narrow windows allowed sunlight to stream in, casting a kaleidoscope of color on the stairs leading up to the altar.

Too bad her mood didn't match the tranquil setting. Especially when Ethan stepped through the double doors and sat down on the pew next to Cam. "Good morning."

"Morning." Of the few open seats left in the sanctuary, why did he choose to sit with them? As a local, he had to know a lot of people inside. But when he tilted his head and spoke into her son's ear, her heart fluttered at the sight of her son's grin. Whatever Ethan told him had adjusted his attitude. For the time being, anyway.

And here Holly thought the man would only help during the hours Cam was at the dog sanctuary. Apparently, she'd been wrong. She flashed him a smile, but sitting with him, despite her widow status, would have the tongues of the town gossips wagging. The last thing she needed was another rumor getting back to Cam, even if there was no truth to this one. Her son had taken her closing the shop after the holidays well, but he had yet to think about the alternative of how she was going to earn money. Or if he had, he hadn't mentioned a word to her.

But Holly thought about it constantly, even when she should be concentrating on the service. Moisture gathered on her palms as she dug into her purse to retrieve her paltry offering. Despite her problems right now, there were people worse off than her. She still had a roof over her and her son's heads and could still put some food on the table.

"So who's ready for Thanksgiving?" Pastor Matt rubbed his stomach and glanced at the front row, where his wife and two teenage boys sat.

The congregation laughed. Everyone knew the pastor appreciated food. They were barely into the start of November, but Holly had been more focused on Christmas than anything else. Like last year, she'd bring a pumpkin pie and loaf of homemade bread to her friend Kristen's house for the big meal.

"So in that spirit of Thanksgiving, along with the offering you've just given, I'd like to take some time to reflect on the meaning of a stuffed turkey, gravy and mashed potatoes by reading you the passage Thessalonians 5:16–18. 'Be joyful always; pray continually; give thanks in all circumstances, for this is God's will for you in Christ Jesus.' Notice it says 'in all.' And we know that God is there with us to help us through it all. And for that we have to be thankful."

Holly suddenly realized she was thankful for more than she thought. She had her house, her son and her friends. Her gaze drifted over Cam's head to where Ethan sat. Could she include him in her circle? Her cheeks warmed at the thought, especially when his lips turned up at the corners as he glanced her way.

"Now, during this time of thanksgiving, we start to think about our wants and needs." Pastor Matt continued, and Holly faced forward, determined to listen to every word the pastor spoke, instead of dwelling on the man who might be able to help her with her son. "Not that there is anything wrong with that, but sometimes we don't go to the right place to get those needs met. Do you turn to friends? Family? Significant others? Shouldn't you be turning to the Lord first?"

Maybe that was Holly's problem.

Instead of blaming the Lord for taking Jared from her because there was nothing that could be done about it now, she should be turning to Him to help her sort things out. Let Him help her with her needs instead of

trying to figure everything out. Maybe that was why
Ethan had been brought into her life. Still, letting go
of the past and moving forward challenged her way of
thinking and wasn't going to happen overnight, despite
Pastor Matt's comforting words.

"Great sermon today, Pastor Matt." Ethan stepped
into the refreshment line behind the man with the re-
ceding hairline that had started to gray at the temples.

"Did it help you?" Matt looked at him compassion-
ately. "So often I think I'm not getting through to the
congregation."

"It did." Ethan clutched his hands. He'd prayed along
with everyone else that by letting God attend to his
needs he'd be able to better deal with everyone else
with more compassion, mercifulness and forgiveness,
Holly and Cameron included.

"Good." Matt patted him on the back before he
grabbed a plate. "Now I can enjoy my snack knowing
I've done my job with at least one of my flock. Was
there something else you wanted to discuss? Like how
you can better participate in your church family?"

Ethan knew this was coming. Every week since his
return, the pastor had brought up the subject. This time,
though, he was prepared. "In a way. I have a new raffle
item for the Charity Ball next weekend."

"Good. We're always on the lookout for more stuff.
What is it?"

"Holly Stanwyck is starting a seasonal decorating
business. She'd like to raffle off her services." Ethan
glanced over his shoulder, looking for his tenant. He

hadn't exactly told her earlier that this was the idea that he had for increasing her new business, but if she left a stack of cards out with the raffle item, it was another way for her to get her name out there. Of course, he probably should have checked with her first. Now he had to tell her just what he'd volunteered her for.

Since it was his idea, he'd go along and help with the project as best he could. He had no decorating sense, but he could follow directions. If all worked well, maybe some of her skills would rub off on him when it came to accessorizing the office and waiting area for his new sanctuary.

"That's great. Get me her donation information so I can put it out with the other items before this weekend."

When Holly came into view with Cameron in tow, Ethan excused himself. "I'll get one of her flyers and deliver it tomorrow."

"One more thing before you go. Have you thought about helping out with the Youth Ministry?"

Ethan rubbed his good hand along the back of his neck. His gaze darted to Cameron before he made eye contact with Pastor Matt again. "I have. But I think I need to do it on a smaller scale than what you have envisioned, and not just within this church. There's several misguided youth here in town that could use some intervention. I plan on utilizing them at the sanctuary and teaching them God's word, as well."

Pastor Matt clapped him on the back again. "That's a great idea. And I think I have an excellent candidate for you if you haven't discovered him yet."

"Cameron Stanwyck?" Ethan set his plate down on

the counter and placed a few pieces of fruit and half a poppy-seed muffin on it.

"That's the one."

Cameron had a reputation. Not good. It looked as if his intervention had come just in time. Ethan's hand shook a bit as he picked up his food. After everything that had happened, was he ready for this? Yes. He'd make sure he had no distractions this time when he supervised Holly's son and any other boy he had out at the farm. He spied her in the thinning crowd. "I thought so. I'll get you that information about Holly's service this week."

Weaving his way through the room, Ethan planted himself next to Holly. "I have something I need to discuss with you. How about some breakfast? These snacks just aren't cutting it."

Cameron grunted his approval.

Too bad Holly couldn't muster up the same enthusiasm.

What could Ethan want to discuss with her? They'd painted the garage yesterday, and Ethan had said not to worry about the second coat, that he'd do it this afternoon on his own.

Maybe he'd changed his mind about letting Cam help him after school? Or could he have found a renter and needed her to vacate immediately?

She fingered the gold cross suspended from her neck when she returned his gaze. Lines furrowed his forehead and his lips zipped into a straight line. Her heart stalled. Whatever he needed to discuss didn't look good as she floundered in the depths of his gaze. It took a few moments for her voice to work properly. "Sure. We were going to the Sunrise Diner for brunch. Would you care to join us?"

Holly twirled her hair around her finger and stared out at the grayness pushing against the glass. The streetlight out front burned through a cone-shaped area of gloom, accentuating the empty sidewalk. Sunday should have been a good day for sales. With just a handful of customers wandering through her front doors, discouragement settled around her shoulders as she cradled the phone to her ear. "I don't know, Kristen, even running a twenty-percent-off sale isn't enough to entice people inside. Maybe I should just blow out all the merchandise and close up as quickly as possible."

"I'm so sorry. I'll keep praying that something changes. I know you've worked so hard to keep Jared's dream alive. Maybe that idea of Ethan's will work? I think it's brilliant that he thought to raffle off your services at the church raffle."

"That would be nice."

"And what's even better is that hc's going to help you with it. And he's helping you with Cam. Wouldn't it be great if something else came out of it, too?"

Kristen, the hopeless romantic. Holly wasn't interested in replacing Jared.

"It's starting to snow outside and it's bound to get worse. I've gotta run, Kristen." Holly said goodbye to her best friend, hung up and began shutting off the lights so she could go pick up Cameron.

She hated driving in the snow, especially now. The

weather had been worse that night the accident claimed not only Jared but also the life fluttering inside her womb. She still had nightmares about it. If anything happened to Cam, her only link to her late husband, she'd never forgive herself. She still hadn't with Jared and baby Olivia.

Chapter Four

"Hi, Cameron." Ethan met Holly's son at the end of his driveway Monday afternoon. Relief mingled with a bit of trepidation filled him. The boy had shown up, which meant he didn't have to go search for him or make that phone call to Holly, but it was also a big commitment. Sure, he was good with kids, liked them, wanted one or two of his own someday, yet his dealings with those Afghan children had been on a superficial level. This was different in so many ways. Somehow he knew, though, that God meant for him to intervene here. "School go okay today?"

The boy grunted a response, his gaze darting around him as if searching for something. "Where's Bear?"

"Inside with Sadie and the other two that arrived Saturday afternoon. Come on."

"They came. Yes!" Delight lit the boy's expression, and he quivered with excitement.

Ethan had had no doubts that this arrangement would work. Still, the boy's reaction made him happy.

A willing student always made things easier, but he was glad he hadn't brought Bear out to meet him, because he didn't want the distraction. "And two more are arriving this week. I'll introduce you to them, but no work until your homework is done."

"Homework?"

"Homework first. That's the agreement I made with your mom."

"That rots."

"Not really. Education is important." Ethan scratched the back of his neck. He'd gone into the military right after high school instead of college like Cameron's father, figuring life training was better than a formal education. He didn't regret his decision, but he'd changed his mind while serving by taking lay ministry courses online when he could and had just enrolled in a few night courses at the local community college to improve his business skills.

A few stray leaves crunched under their feet, and a crow cawed from the towering pine tree on the other side of the driveway as they made their way to the back of Ethan's house. A cool, crisp breeze laden with a hint of the encroaching winter made him snuggle deeper into his warm jacket. Some snow remained from last night's brief storm, and the temperatures had dropped.

Despite his love for his hometown and the numerous family members that remained, he disliked the cold. The winter weather wrapped around his body and seeped into his limbs. He dug his hands farther into his pockets to keep them warm. Opening the sanctuary in Phoenix hadn't been an option because of the extreme heat in the summer. That and the simple fact his mother had leased him the fifty acres of land outside Dynamite Creek that held the old family farmhouse and a barn at a rock-bottom price so he could operate Beyond the Borders Dog Sanctuary. Although right now he missed the warmth of the Valley and the Middle East.

Five minutes later, after the introductions to the newest occupants, Ethan poured a glass of milk and set out some apple slices, peanut butter and crackers. The boy would probably prefer the chocolate-chip cookies, but Ethan didn't want to feed him any unnecessary sugar before he had a chance to discuss what type of diet Holly followed.

"Here's a snack."

Discomfort lodged between his shoulder blades. Was he usurping Holly's role? Maybe a little, but he was also helping her, and that had to outweigh everything. The boy needed this; he needed the help, and the dogs needed the attention.

"So what do you have for homework?"

"Just math."

Ethan didn't buy that. He may not have kids of his own, but he'd already lived through middle school and he probably still knew some of the teachers at Dynamite Creek Middle School. Kids always had homework. Even over school breaks.

"Let's see your agenda."

"You don't trust me?"

"Should I?" He stared Cameron down. The boy held his gaze for a few seconds before he looked away. Ethan recognized that look of being busted; Holly's son had worn it the day he caught him and his friend spray painting the garage.

"No. I have social studies and science, too." Cameron pulled out the binder that held his notebooks and agenda from his backpack.

"No English?"

"It's called language arts now."

"Okay. No language arts homework?"

"No. I did it in class."

This time Ethan sensed the boy was telling the truth. "Good. So who's your language arts teacher this year?"

"Mrs. Metcalf."

He blinked and wrinkled his forehead. "She's still there? She's got to be near retirement now. She was one of my teachers when I went there."

"Really?"

Ethan almost laughed at the raised eyebrows and O-shaped lips. "Yeah, really. Don't look so surprised. I'm about the same age as your mom. If I remember correctly, your dad had Mrs. Metcalf, too."

"You knew my dad?"

"We used to be friends." Ethan squeezed his eyes shut and rubbed his face. An image of a high-school-aged Jared imprinted itself on the inside of his eyelids. He could see his father's influence in Cameron's features, though his blond coloring came from Holly's side. "I'm sorry he passed away, Cameron. I know it's got to be hard on you, eating you alive on the inside while you try to hide it from everyone else."

A scowl replaced the boy's earlier surprise and Ethan felt him pull away. "How would you know?"

The camaraderie they'd shared a few moments ago disappeared, but Ethan knew he had to reach out to the boy or he'd lose him. That wasn't an option. God had brought Cameron into his life for a reason, just as He'd given him the idea about the dog sanctuary. Maybe they were meant to help each other out; the dogs, too.

"I know because my dad passed away when I was just a year older than you were. It hurts. It leaves a hole in your heart and makes you feel like you're floundering in a sea of monsters. You don't know where to turn or who to reach out to. So you beat yourself up, lash out at the world, feel the injustice and want to hurt things, spray-paint things, maybe hurt yourself, too. But nothing changes the fact that he's gone, and you blame yourself."

White pinched the skin around Cameron's mouth, and anger flashed from eyes that looked so much like Holly's that Ethan was taken aback for a moment. Like mother, like son. Holly hadn't recovered from Jared's death, either. When the boy slouched at the table and buried his face in his hands, Ethan recognized the pain. He'd worn it so many times as a youth until it became a second skin. With the help of his old neighbor, though, he'd finally managed to shed it in high school.

"Come on. Get your homework done so you can play with the dogs." Ethan changed the subject and picked up the envelope that had slipped out of Cameron's agenda. Since it had Holly's name on it, he didn't open it, but he doubted it was a report card. "What's this?"

The boy flopped back into his chair, glanced at the envelope and then back down at his notebook.

"I asked you a question, Cameron. I expect and deserve an answer. If you can't have the respect to do that, then I'm not sure how well we'll work together with the dogs."

A stricken look flashed across his features. This time he had no trouble finding words to say. "You mean I can't work here after all?"

"That's a choice you have to make. I want an open form of communication and need to feel that I can trust you. We made a great start. Let's keep it that way."

"It's a letter from my math teacher. I'm not doing good. I mean, I just don't get the stuff we're covering. It all gets so jumbled up in my head."

"Does your mom know?"

Cameron shook his head. "She doesn't get it, either. I mean, she's good with numbers, but all this algebra stuff…"

"What is it?"

"She's just so busy all the time. And worried." Cameron played with his pencil in one hand and twirled his hair through his fingers with the other. "I can't talk to her anymore. Things used to be so different."

Ethan pulled out a chair and sat down. He'd made a promise to Cameron earlier, and he wouldn't go back on his word. The phone calls and paperwork could wait a few more minutes. "Want to talk about it?"

"Yeah. We used to have so much fun."

"It's hard trying to take care of everything by yourself. Life, just like math, can get pretty overwhelming at times. I'm sure your mom is doing the best she can. How many of these communications have you gotten?"

"First one." Cameron refused to look him in the eye.

"Try again."

"This is my fourth."

"And who signed off on them? Your mom?"

Silence filled the kitchen.

"You signed your mom's name, didn't you?"

Guilt flashed across the boy's features before he hung his head in shame.

Ethan dug his hands through his hair. Holly had more to worry about than she realized. His gaze rose, taking in the stark whiteness of the kitchen ceiling, but he wasn't really paying attention. *Thank you, Lord, for bringing me into Cameron's life.* That the boy needed more guidance was an understatement. He couldn't fault Holly. She'd done a great job so far, but he knew from firsthand experience now that he was opening the sanctuary how much time it took to run a business. She had a son and household to run by herself, as well.

"We're going to have a talk with your mom when she picks you up. Now, I have a few phone calls to make and some paperwork to do. Finish up your other homework and I'll come help you with the math. That actually was one of my best subjects, behind lunch."

"Lunch?"

Ethan tried to lighten the mood swirling around the kitchen. "Yeah. If they gave out grades for that, I would have gotten an A."

Cameron smiled. "You're okay, Mr. Pellegrino."

"Call me Mr. P. if that's easier, or Ethan if your mom approves."

An hour later, Cameron closed his math book and stretched. Ethan did the same. They did things differently now in school with the new programs the administration and government had put in place, but at least the fundamentals were the same. Cameron was a smart kid; he just needed to be shown by example and given an explanation how to do the problems.

Ethan pushed his chair back and stood. "Good work. Now, what else do you know about dogs?"

"They like to be played with?"

"And?"

"They need to be fed and have lots of water?"

"And?" Ethan sensed the boy was toying with him.

"They like to be scratched and petted?"

"All of the above, but you're forgetting one basic thing. They need to be cleaned up after."

"But I thought I was here to play with them."

"That's one reason, but you're also here to help. And that would include making sure that the environment is safe and healthy for them."

"What do I need to do first?"

Ethan threw Cameron his jacket and led him to the back porch, where he handed him a small rake and scooper. "I think you know what to do with these. And after that, their food and water dishes need to be washed out. Then, after you brush them, it'll be time to play."

Knowing that her son was in good hands, Holly had stayed open a bit later than usual to accommodate another decent sale. Her cat wouldn't be too happy with the delayed dinner, but Mrs. Hendricks had come in to buy several ornaments for her book-club ladies along with the remaining snow globes so she could start a family tradition with her new grandbabies. Business had also been good for a Monday and Holly had actually made a profit. If she could sustain it, she'd have a lot less to box up and sell on eBay and actually make more than a minimum payment on her credit cards for once.

Since she knew she'd get home too late to scrounge something together, she stopped at the grocery store to pick up dinner. Holly hadn't asked if Ethan had made any plans, but she'd picked up enough fried chicken and side dishes to feed them all if he didn't mind sharing his kitchen with them for the meal.

Recyclable cloth bags in hand, she stepped quietly from her car, not wanting to disrupt the scene playing out in front of her. Both Ethan and Cameron stood in the backyard, throwing tennis balls to Bear and Sadie. When Ethan placed a hand on her son's shoulder and pointed at something off to their left, the scene brought tears to her eyes. Cameron needed a male influence in his life.

The action made her miss Jared again.

"Hello?" Her voice wobbled. She had to get a grip on herself. Not only for Cam's sake but her own, as well.

"Hi, yourself." Ethan waved, a tentative smile on his lips, his gaze never leaving her face as she approached.

"Mom." Cam ran toward her and flung his arms around her waist. "You're here. Wait till you see what Oreo can do."

"Oreo?" Holly dragged in a breath of cold air and focused on her son. Her attention should be on him, not the man who sent conflicting emotions through her at a mere glance.

"One of the new dogs. She can catch a disc in her mouth and then bring it back. She's in her kennel now, but we can go get her."

"I can't wait to see it. I brought some dinner." Holly held up the bags. "I figured you guys would be hungry after a full day at work and school. You don't mind, do you, Ethan?"

"'Course not. Eating was his favorite subject," Cam broke in. "Here, let me help you and then you can watch me with Oreo."

The turnaround in her son caught Holly by surprise. She'd hoped Ethan would be a good influence on her son, but over time, not just in a few short hours. Holly took in Ethan's crooked smile and the way the light wind ruffled his wavy dark brown hair. She'd never noticed the slight dimples before, which added another dimension to his character. In her core, she felt a tiny ripple, somehow knowing she could depend on Ethan no matter what.

"Things went okay today?"

"Better than can be expected. There is a small issue with his math he needs to show you, but I think we've got a handle on it now. Other than that, Cameron's a great kid. He's just hitting that tough age to be a boy. Do you have anything else that needs to come inside?"

Holly shook her head and walked beside Ethan as they made their way to his back porch. Math. Ugh. She was glad Ethan had been able to help Cameron because what her son was studying wasn't her strong point. Accounting, yes; algebra, no.

In the kitchen, Holly pulled out the food while Ethan scrambled for plates and utensils. In the background, she could hear Cam talking to the dogs as he put dry food into their bowls. The scene held more promise of a future than Holly was accustomed to. Night had descended beyond the windowpanes, adding a cozier feel to the small kitchen than she was comfortable with. It almost felt like it had before with Jared. Their last meal. Except that time, she had the flutter of life inside her. Dinner hadn't been a good idea, but with everything Ethan was doing for her son, she felt compelled to return some sort of favor. Cam reentered the room, washed his hands and went to sit down.

"Wait a minute." Ethan stopped Cam from sitting at the table. "A gentleman always pulls out the chair for a lady." Ethan moved the chair back and motioned for Holly to sit. The action brought more than a flutter to her pulse. It brought back a simpler time, when the little things mattered.

Ethan took his seat, bowed his head and clasped his hands together. "Dear Lord, thanks for providing us with the food we are about to receive that comes from all Your good graces. In Jesus's name we say amen."

"Amen." Holly spoke the word, but it held little meaning for her. Would she ever be able to believe again like her late husband had, or the man sitting across from her? She'd tried on numerous occasions and continued to go to church, but she didn't feel it. She'd believed once, but in her sorrow and anger, she'd turned off her belief and tuned Him out. Despite what the Bible said, would God and Jesus welcome her back if she decided to do more than go through the motions? Would They hear her if she really prayed? And did she want to go there?

Each question brought more anxiety, and despite her lack of an appetite, her dinner disappeared in less than ten minutes. Holly's fingers trembled as she wiped her mouth and put her paper napkin on her plate to cover the chicken bones. She had a more immediate concern. "I got a phone call about my decorating business today. My first."

"Congratulations. And don't forget, the holiday raffle at the church is Sunday. You're sure to get more calls after that."

"There's just one problem." Holly almost couldn't get the words out of her mouth. "It's Saturday morning, and I'll probably be gone most of the day. The mayor wants his house decorated for his annual gala that night. Neither he nor his wife is up to it, and their handyman is down with the flu." Or that was what Mayor Moss claimed, but no matter what the excuse or charitable contribution, she couldn't turn it down. Her gaze froze on Cam.

"But, Mom, that's the day of the Fall Harvest Festival at the Community Center. You promised." Disappointment and anger chased away Ethan's progress.

"I know, Cam. We'll go. It might just be later than we expected." Guilt tore at her insides and the tension in the room threatened to suffocate her. They hadn't been to the festival since Jared died, but the decorating job was a big one, and realistically she wondered if she could handle it by herself.

She had to.

The job paid way more than she needed to put out for Mindy to work the shop Saturday as long as she was feeling better. It would help pay down some of her personal bills and put away some money for Christmas. Her gaze froze on Ethan. Would he expect her to pay some of her back rent with it? Everyone in town knew Mayor Moss came from old money.

Ethan must have read her mind, because he shook his head slightly. "Drop Cameron off here and he can help me with the dogs, especially the new ones arriving Wednesday. Then after we're done here, we'll come help you decorate. I haven't been to a Fall Harvest Festival since I graduated high school. It'll be fun."

"No, Mom. You promised we would go for the entire day. Just you and me." Cameron jumped up and toppled his chair back. White surrounded his tight lips and he visibly shook. "We haven't done anything fun since Dad died. All you do is work, and worry and cry when you don't think I'm looking."

Holly also stood, at a loss on how to deal with her son. She wanted to reach out and hold him, but her hands remained clenched at her sides. She didn't know what to say to him anymore, especially when he spoke the truth. Heat flushed her cheeks at the airing of their family problems. "Cameron. Please. We'll talk about this later."

"That's what you always say and it never happens."

Ethan's chair scraped across the tile floor. The tension in the room set him on edge, bringing his own issues to the forefront. "Stop it, both of you. I have an idea. Come with me."

He motioned for them to follow him into one of the rooms he'd converted into a gym. Beyond the treadmill and just past the weight machine, a punching bag hung from the far ceiling. The psychologist had told him that releasing his anger from what he called "the incident" would help with his emotional recovery. Maybe the same would apply to Cameron. Holly would benefit from it, too.

"You have a workout room?" Anger still rolled off Cameron. "We used to have a membership to the YMCA. I used some of the things in the teen center until my mom didn't renew." He glared at Holly and slapped his hand down on the weight machine.

"You know why I had to do that."

"When are we ever going to have enough money? And now that you're closing the shop, we'll have even less."

"But I'll have the decorating business."

"And even less time for me." The boy's shoulders sagged, his voice now barely a whisper.

Holly welcomed her son into her embrace. She closed her eyes and placed her cheek on top of his head. "Oh, Cam. I'm so sorry."

Ethan knew he'd made the right decision to bring them in here. They both needed to exorcise their anger and memories. He gave them a few moments before he broke the shattered breathing in the room. "This way."

He pointed toward the back corner of the room by the window.

"You have a punching bag?" Cameron broke away from his mother.

"Helps relieve tension and anger. I want you to walk over there and punch it. You, too, Holly."

First Cameron tapped the bag with his fist, then Holly. She shook her hand but then tapped it again. The bag barely moved. He'd expected the boy to do it, but not his mother. His plan might work better than he'd thought.

"That's the best you guys can do?" Ethan stepped in between them and egged them on, trying to re-create the energy in the kitchen. The therapy didn't work unless both Cameron and Holly could release their anger. He'd work on Cameron first.

"No!" Cameron struck the bag again with more force, but not enough to make it sway very far.

"Your dad is dead. How do you feel about that?" Ethan punched the bag himself, feeling the spurt of adrenaline through his veins. He needed his own dose of therapy right now, too.

Cameron punched the bag again, and this time, Ethan knew he'd hit it as hard as he could by his grunt. "It rots."

"You know what else rots?" Ethan didn't wait for the boy to respond as he punched the bag again. "What rots is that I don't have any fingers anymore on my right hand. What are you angry at, Holly?"

For a few heartbeats, Holly just stood there and stared at the bag. Anger, hurt and denial all took up residence on her face and in her stance. For a moment, Ethan didn't think she'd go along with his plan until he saw the resignation disappear behind determination. "I don't have my best friend and husband anymore." She focused on the bag and punched repeatedly. "He left me to deal with everything and it's tough. Tougher than it should be."

"And I don't have a dad anymore." Cameron punched the bag harder using both hands, each strike a little harder than before. "I have no one to play ball with or go fishing with or talk to."

"That's it. Let it out." Along with Cameron and Holly, Ethan continued to strike the bag in a staccato rhythm. Moisture gathered on his forehead and under his arms with the action. Soon, the white walls began to collapse in on him, suffocating him in the memories of that day in Afghanistan and the recurrent dreams every night. "And each time I look at my hand I know that I failed at my job. I let five people die because I wasn't paying attention."

"Why did you have to die on me? Why? I need you." Cameron yelled at the top of his lungs as he continually punched the bag and released some of the pent-up emotions he'd hidden away since his father's death. "Why did you have to die?"

Ethan caught Holly's stricken look as tears crested in her eyes before she fled the room. Somehow Ethan knew there had to be more than just survivor's guilt going on.

Chapter Five

Holly wiped her hands across her jeans and stared at her handiwork in the parlor Saturday afternoon. Somehow in just over seven hours, she'd transformed the mayor's three main living areas in his home into a Christmas wonderland. Of course, it helped having Ethan and Cam there to assist her with the last two. Her gaze wandered to where they stood by the tree, hanging the last of the blue and silver ornaments.

The changes she'd seen in her son in the week since he'd been going to Ethan's to help out every day after school were amazing. Her helpful, courteous and thoughtful son had returned, and Holly hadn't received one phone call from the principal. Cameron could continue to help out after school indefinitely, as long as that was what Ethan wanted.

Gathering her hair back into a ponytail again, she secured it with a hair tie as the scent of the newly cut tree filled her nose. Holly loved the crisp, outdoorsy aroma of pine trees. Sure, they were a mess and a fake one was more convenient, but other than the scent of gingerbread cookies baking in the oven, nothing conveyed the holiday season more.

A sense of accomplishment filled her as did a moment of melancholy.

The Christmas season had always had a special meaning for her. A renewal of sorts with the celebration of the birth of Jesus. Jared had felt the same way, which was one of the reasons he'd opened the store. Keeping the meaning of the season in their hearts had been important to him, and something she'd lost.

Her son, too.

The laughter had disappeared, lost on an icy road on a dark, wintry night. Pain tried to form inside her, but she pushed it away. She wouldn't allow the feeling to take over and ruin what promised to be a fun evening. Holly deserved it. Cam especially deserved it, and so did Ethan, since he would be joining them.

Somehow they'd all managed to survive, yet each of them carried around a guilt that clung to them like cling wrap. Sometimes the harder she worked at trying to straighten out her emotions, the more involved she became in them. Patience was the key, and she struggled with it on a daily basis. Especially lately. She closed her eyes, breathed deeply and sent up a silent prayer, something she'd been doing a lot more of this week, and it felt good. The first time had been hard, but it grew easier each time she tried. Comfort washed over her.

She glanced in Ethan's direction and saw an ornament slip out of his injured hand and hit the ground, breaking into two pieces. A look of disgust passed over his features as he stared at his hand. Holly knew he struggled with his own survivor's guilt and wondered why God had chosen this path for Ethan. One step forward in renewing her faith, two steps backward.

"No worries. We have plenty." Before Ethan could bend down, Holly walked over and scooped up the broken pieces and tucked them into her jeans pocket. Her heart went out to him again. Despite their workouts with the punching bag, neither one of them had been able to completely shed the pain from their pasts.

She smiled and picked up another ornament from the box. Energy coursed through her when their hands touched, and she pulled back. Ethan both confused and scared her. She wasn't looking for anyone else. Holly had already lost the love of her life. She couldn't handle another emotional involvement anytime soon.

"We could—"

"Always pull a few from the back of the tree if necessary." Ethan finished the sentence and Holly squirmed.

"That's what I thought, but they have so many, I think we should leave some of them in the box so we can actually see the tree."

Ethan's expression stilled as he descended from the first rung of the stepladder and moved in front of her. His gaze searched hers, as if trying to see past her layers of protection she'd wrapped around her heart. Conflicting emotions warred inside her, none of which she was willing to identify.

"I agree. Why bother with a real tree if you can't see it through the decorations?" He turned away from her and put the small, empty ornament containers back into their plastic storage boxes then glanced around the room. "Nice job, Holly. Once people see this, you're going to be getting a bunch of phone calls."

"Thanks." She attributed her breathlessness to all the work she'd done today and nothing more. It didn't matter that they'd worked well together, anticipating each other's needs, or that their conversations delved more into a familiarity that she'd only experienced once before with a man.

None of that mattered.

"You're welcome." His gaze focused on hers again, shutting out the music, the lights and everything else around them. Ethan opened and shut his mouth, clenched his fists and then turned away. "Come on, Cameron, time to put on the finishing touch."

Holly took her cue from Ethan. Concentrating on the here and now, and nothing else, she surveyed the rest of the room. Pride filled her. She had done a great job. Pine garlands covered with large white flowers and bows, clear lights, and blue and silver glass balls draped over the curtains and complimented the arrangement dominating the fireplace mantel.

White ceramic swans filled with more of the same white flowers and silver spray-painted twigs graced the tabletops. Tonight the white and silver candles would be lit, adding more charm and ambience to the room, along with the clear lights on the tree, where Ethan and Cameron were putting the finishing touches on the sixteen-foot-tall pine. Decorated with the same color scheme, it tied everything together.

She had transformed the room into a Christmas wonderland.

Holly's heart skipped a beat, though, as Cameron clambered up the ladder with the tree topper. "Cam—"

She bit down on her lip to keep the rest of her words inside when her son turned around and stared at her. He'd been a real trouper with all the decorating and had even come up with a few ideas himself of where things should be placed. He'd inherited both her and Jared's artistic talents. Cam wasn't a little boy anymore, and she had to remember that there was a teenager inside struggling to get out. She had to let him find his way even though she wanted to remind him to be careful. "You're doing great. Thanks for all your help today."

"We're still going to the festival today, right?"

Typical response. Cam was only helping her so they could go to the festival, but it still gladdened her heart that he wanted to spend time with her. Although she detected a bit of hero worship when he looked at Ethan. "Of course. I can't wait."

"Hang on a second, Cameron. Let me hold the ladder for you. I'm sure a trip to the E.R. is not what your mom has in mind for tonight if you fall." As if sensing her distress, Ethan walked over and held on to Cameron's legs to steady him as her son placed the ornate silver star at the top.

The fact that they had similar thoughts scared Holly. Because if she ever contemplated dating again or getting involved with another man, some of Ethan Pellegrino's characteristics would top the list of things she would look for.

"Done. Let's go." Oblivious to the emotions of the people around him, Cam scrambled down the ladder.

"Oh, Holly, it looks stunning." Edith Moss joined her. "I especially like the silver twigs. I would have never thought that bringing more of the outdoors inside would create such a charming setting. I'll make sure everyone knows that you did my decorating this year. I'm sure you'll get several clients, especially since this is so early in the season. But you know how crazy things get after Thanksgiving. This was the only time that worked for us."

"Thanks, Mrs. Moss. I appreciate the opportunity."

"No. Thank you. I can't tell you how relieved I am that it's finished. Now I can concentrate on the other things."

"Like the food." Mayor Moss rubbed his round belly as he joined his wife. Around them, caterers and staff busied themselves with the food setup.

Holly smiled at the portly mayor, whose adoring attention was on his wife. Married thirty-some years, and he still looked at her the same way he probably had the day they exchanged their vows. Something Holly wouldn't experience, because she and Jared had only made the ten-year mark. Yet she didn't begrudge them their happiness, and maybe someday, she'd experience love again, if she could let go of the past. If she wanted to go there.

Looking away, Holly clutched the envelope Mayor Moss had given her and tucked it into her purse. "All right, boys, let's put all the boxes back into storage and go. The Fall Harvest Festival is waiting."

* * *

The community center building teemed with life as they entered through the double doors twenty minutes later. Music from one of the local bands filled the air with the beat of a current hit, as did the scent of freshly popped popcorn.

Games lined the far side of the room and bounce houses for the smaller kids dominated the gymnasium to their right. Food vendors had set up along the back wall with the band and dance area stationed to their left.

"I see a friend of mine. Can I have some money?" Cam looked at her, hope, expectation and a tiny bit of trepidation in his eyes.

"Which one?"

"Tyler." Cam's gaze darted past her shoulder.

Holly's mouth went dry at the thought of the sixty dollars in her wallet because she hadn't gotten to the bank to deposit her check from the mayor. Forty of those dollars had been earmarked for groceries and the rest for the festival. Somehow she thought they'd spend it together, but her son seemed to have other ideas despite what he'd told her at Ethan's house Monday. Holly had known the day was coming when Cam would rather spend the time with his friends instead of her, but it still hurt.

"Okay." She opened her wallet and pulled out a ten-dollar bill. Cam had helped out quite a bit this afternoon, and Holly hadn't given him his allowance yet for the few chores he'd done this week. He deserved to have some fun with his friend. "Check back in an hour."

"How about two?" Cam slipped past her.

When Holly turned around, though, she saw her son walking toward a group of boys from school that didn't include his friend Tyler Adamson. Her shoulders sagged when she recognized the ringleader of the group. She should have guessed that Cam had an ulterior motive for coming here today. The low-slung pants on the four other boys, the ripped T-shirts and the baseball caps positioned to the side made her stomach churn. The furtive glances in her direction didn't help her nerves, either.

Ethan's gaze followed hers, and he placed his hand on her arm, creating that familiar tingling sensation in her stomach. "Do you want me to stop him?"

"No. I don't think causing a scene would be a good thing right now."

"Agreed. Let's see what kind of choices he decides to make tonight. One of them is Patrick, isn't it?"

"The one in charge. Two boys I can't identify, but underneath the long, uncombed hair, I recognize Tyler Smith, one of Cam's friends from grade school. I guess I should have asked which Tyler he was referring to. I don't understand how Cam fell in with that crowd."

"Sometimes it depends on where they are in their life at any particular moment." Ethan spoke as if he had personal experience, and Holly knew it to be true from their conversation while painting his garage door.

She waited for Ethan to elaborate and sighed as she watched Cam and his friends nod and knuckle-bang each other before they disappeared into the crowd. Holly wanted to follow, yet something in Ethan's gaze held her back. Cameron had already made a poor choice with Patrick and had paid the consequence. She could only hope that he'd learned from his mistake.

"So, I guess that leaves the two of us." Ethan gave her a half smile as his gaze lingered on the spot where Cam had just stood. Concern and hesitation clouded his expression.

"It does. For now. I don't trust those boys." Holly could feel they were on the same wavelength. The thought gladdened her and scared her. It felt good to share her concerns with Ethan, but opening up an area in her heart again could only lead to more pain. And yet with Cameron getting older and wanting to spend less time with her, the idea that she didn't want to spend the rest of her life alone erupted in her mind. The earlier image of Mayor and Mrs. Moss and how happy they were didn't help, either. Tonight she was going to forget about everything else and have fun.

"Me, neither. What would you like to do?"

"Let's walk around and take a look at all the activities first. Since Mrs. Sanderson took over, there's bound to be a few surprises." Holly moved into the stream of traffic, needing to surround herself with other people besides Ethan and the strange emotions he had awakened inside her.

Coming to the festival had been a good idea in theory, but it had been her and Cam when she'd imagined it, not her son running off with a group of so-called friends and leaving her with Ethan. From the looks and the number of people who stopped to talk to them, though, the town gossips were going to have a lot to talk about tomorrow. She threw caution to the wind.

It had been a long time since she'd really had fun, and she was glad Ethan was here with her.

"Looks like the bouncy castles are a big hit." Piles of shoes thrown haphazardly outside the Princess Castle and Dinosaur House along with the squeals of young children confirmed that.

"Cameron used to love those." They walked by a crowded craft table containing the materials to make sand art in a plastic bottle. Holly recognized a few of the younger kids from church and smiled at their parents. "He also loved making things. I still have one of his sand creations in my china cabinet. Now all he seems to make is trouble. Well, up until last week, that is. His turnaround is remarkable. Thank you."

"You're welcome. He's a pleasure to be around. I think he's going to be just fine."

"I hope so." Holly wasn't sure how much more stress she could handle, even though things seemed to have gotten better in the past week, thanks to Ethan's intervention. And maybe, just maybe, God was listening to her prayers and they were starting to work.

"He will." He grabbed her hand and squeezed it gently. "Let's try the cake walk." Ethan pulled her to the booth that contained a table laden with various cakes and pies. "We can still get in on this round."

He handed two tickets from the ten he'd bought earlier to the woman standing next to the boom box and motioned for Holly to step on a numbered circle behind his. The music started and both Holly and Ethan moved from one circle to the next. Holly laughed as she jumped into his circle. He turned, his hands grazing her waist to keep her from falling over. "No fair. This is my circle."

His touch exhilarated and frightened her and she hadn't felt this carefree in a long time. Playfully, she pushed him from the circle. "Keep moving. You can't hog it all to yourself."

"If that's the way you want to play."

But before Ethan could make his move, Holly jumped away and ahead of him to the next circle, the music keeping time with the tempo of her heart. More laughter filled the air as she moved from circle to circle, only once glancing back to catch a smiling Ethan looking at her. She turned away but not until after she returned his grin.

Just a few more hops and she'd be back to her favorite number. The music stopped just as she reached nine. The woman running the booth pulled out a number from her paper bag. "Number nine is the winner."

"Holly, that's you." Ethan stepped over and high-fived her.

"Yes. Cam will be so excited." Holly put her name on the chocolate-mousse cake to collect before they left, an extravagant dessert she would never allow herself to buy because of the cost. "And because you bought the ticket, we can all share this tonight after the festival closes."

"Sounds like a plan. So how do you feel about bobbing for apples?" Ethan pointed to the next booth over, where adults behaved like kids as they dunked their heads into the big horse trough filled with water.

"Go for it."

"Only if you do it with me. It looks like they're giving away some pretty good prizes." He pointed to the sign behind the trough. "I wonder if anyone's won the $100 gift card yet."

Holly didn't want to get her face wet and chance her mascara giving her raccoon eyes, but the idea that she could win a generic gift card that could be used at any number of stores caught her eye. She could use it to help buy the present that Cameron longed for this year.

"You're on." She looked around the crowded room again in an attempt to locate her son but only managed to catch the attention of her neighbors. She smiled and waved but this time managed to hand the booth attendant two of the tickets she'd bought before Ethan could.

"Okay, no use of hands or feet or any other body part is allowed," the volunteered droned. "No getting help from your neighbor, either."

Ethan winked at her. "There goes that idea."

Holly blushed under his scrutiny. "Why, Ethan, you didn't strike me as someone who broke the rules."

"Let's just say I like to think outside the box. Which one do you think I should try for?"

"How about the green one in front of you. It doesn't look too battered."

"The green one it is, then."

A few moments later, Holly wiped the water from her face after having come up empty in her attempt. The apples were hard to get a grip on, and the harder she tried, the more the apples seemed to mock her attempt. Ethan, on the other hand, was still trying to snag the green one. She watched in fascination as he managed to grab the stem of the apple and pull it from the water. Holly wasn't exactly sure if that was the correct way to play, but she clapped and cheered along with the rest of the crowd.

"Let's see what you won." She took the apple from him and compared the colored thumbtack pushed in the bottom to the chart on the sign. "Well, it's not the $100 card, but it looks like you're the proud owner of a $15 certificate to Marc's Hobby World."

"Terrific. You can use it as a stocking stuffer for Cameron."

Holly handed Ethan the towel she'd just used to wipe her face. His words made her breath catch in her throat. The selfless action sent a jolt into her bloodstream that refused to still, but she needed to refuse. He was already doing enough for her by letting her stay in the shop and assisting with Cameron, whom she hadn't seen since the evening began.

"Better yet, why don't *you* give it to Cameron for all the help he's doing for you. Here, you missed a spot." Using the corner of the towel, she reached up and dabbed the droplet of water clinging to his sideburn. The action, so innocent on her part, seemed to change something between them as they stared at each other, the noise and the people fading into the background. "Finish drying off. I'll go collect your prize."

Ethan stared after Holly as she slipped away.

"Ethan Pellegrino. I'd heard you were back. Good to see you again."

Glad for the distraction, Ethan turned toward the voice and recognized his former classmate immediately. Whatever had just happened between him and Holly needed to be stopped. He had other things to think about, like his dog shelter, learning to work with his right hand again, learning to trust his instincts so he didn't make another fatal mistake. "Jeremy Foster. How's it going?"

"Not too bad. Yourself?"

Ethan took in Jeremy's police uniform. Somehow his old high-school friend's career choice surprised him. Jeremy had had a bit of a wild streak in him as well, and they'd both had their share of scrapes with adults in the past. But then again, who better to understand the youth in this town?

"Glad to be home for good. What's with the uniform? I thought you were more interested in politics."

"Still am, but from a different perspective now. Who knows, though. Maybe I'll run for police chief once Phillips retires."

"He's still around?" The police chief had been old before Ethan left for the service. The man should be well past retirement age and planted on one of the community benches lining Main Street along with all the other retirees.

"Yeah, he plans on dropping dead in his office with his uniform on."

"That doesn't surprise me."

Holly returned and handed him his gift certificate, but before she could slip away again, Ethan put his hand on her arm. "Have you met Holly Stanwyck?"

"Can't say that I have. Pleased to meet you. Jeremy Foster."

"You, too." Holly shook his hand and smiled tentatively.

Ethan didn't appreciate the length of time it took Jeremy to release Holly's hand even though Ethan had no claim to her heart. "Anything interesting going on in town?"

With one more casual glance at Holly, Jeremy focused back on Ethan, his professionalism returning. "Just the usual, although there seems to be a lot more vandalism and mischief happening. Word has it it's a bunch of kids. If you see or hear anything, let me know."

"Will do." Ethan glanced over and saw that the blood had drained from Holly's face. She'd obviously connected the incident with his garage door. Could the issues be related?

"I'd better run. I'm on the clock. Again, it was nice to meet you, Holly. Call me if Pellegrino gets out of line." With that, Jeremy strode away into the waning crowd.

"I wonder where Cam wandered off to." Holly broke the silence between them.

Ethan's gaze searched the room. Cameron and the other boys were nowhere to be seen. During the hour they'd been there, he'd kept his eye out for Holly's son. He hadn't seen him in a while, and his gut told him they were not in the building. "Let's go check outside."

"Outside?"

"I doubt they're inside one of the bouncy castles."

After stepping into the cool, crisp night, Ethan took her arm and guided her along the sidewalk that led to the parking lot. But instead of heading toward the lighted area where all the cars were parked, he strode in the other direction, away from the lights and people.

The smell of cigarette smoke assaulted his nostrils once they reached the back of the building. In the darkness, an orange glow hovered in the air, as if passed around from hand to hand. In the shadows, he made out a group of six figures, one of them most likely Holly's son.

Holly gasped. "Cameron wouldn't, would he?"

"We're about to find out. Cameron Stanwyck, show yourself."

"Run." A boy's hushed tone broke the stillness. Shadows melted into the night and footsteps pounded against the blacktop.

Ethan managed to filter out which was Holly's son and step in front of him to keep him from running.

"Cam, what were you doing out here?" Holly's strangled voice thrust a knife through Ethan's heart. Her vulnerability when it came to her son affected him on a more personal level than he cared to admit. He wasn't the boy's father, but Ethan felt a responsibility to Holly, Jared and the community to keep Cameron from making the same mistakes he had.

"I wasn't doing anything."

"No? Then what's this?" Ethan kicked at a cigarette butt.

"The other boys were doing it. I was just standing here."

Ethan sniffed. At least it was only cigarette smoke he smelled, but given what he'd seen of the other boys, something stronger was probably going to follow sooner rather than later. It didn't matter the size of the town—drugs and alcohol abuse were everywhere. He stepped closer. Ethan's intervention with Cameron had come just in time. "Try again."

"Ethan, stop. Please." Holly placed her hand on his arm. "This is my problem."

He knew he was treading on Holly's parenting skills, but even in the dim light, he could see that all the blood had leeched from her face again. Moisture pooled in her eyes and the skin between her brows furrowed.

"Not anymore."

"Yes, it is." She fisted her hands and planted them on her waist. "Cameron, we will discuss this on the way home. Now, go to the car."

"Look, Holly, it's not just cigarettes. They've been drinking." He pointed to the ground by Cameron's feet. "Before you get in the car, pick up the empty bottles and go throw them in the trash."

Cameron didn't say a word confirming or denying the truth as he collected the bottles and slunk toward the trash can nearby.

"Are you undermining my authority, Ethan? I'm Cameron's parent, not you." Anger simmered beneath her breath.

"I'm well aware of that, but there's nothing wrong with getting some help. What do you think would have happened if Officer Foster had found the boys? Especially since alcohol was involved."

"I believe my son when he tells me that he was just standing there."

Ethan scraped his hand through his hair. "Do you know anything about guilt by association?"

Holly sighed. "No." Her shoulders slumped again. "I feel like such a failure."

"You are not a failure, Holly. Far from it." He tucked a loose strand of hair behind Holly's ear, the gesture sending a wave of compassion and the need to protect her through him. He leaned in a fraction, his gaze lingering on her lips. What was he thinking? Neither he nor Holly needed that complication right now. He valued their tentative friendship that he hoped could survive the eviction after next month. "You've done a great job with him. But he's at that tough age where he's testing his limits and your patience. You have enough to worry about. Please let me help."

Holly stared at him and finally nodded as a silent Cameron returned and kicked at a small rock on the blacktop.

Ethan crossed his arms and faced him. "You have a decision to make, son. Your fair-weather friends, who have obviously already turned on you since they're no longer here, or the dogs. Think long and hard about what each of them means to you and let me know. You can't have both."

Chapter Six

Soft light filtered through the front window of the shop as Holly sat behind the counter midafternoon Monday. Outside, city workers strung holiday lights on the trees across the street in the town square and on the trees lining the sidewalks. Colorful red and green banners hung from the streetlights, adding an even more festive feel along with the large Christmas tree filled with ornaments of different shapes and colors. Each of the businesses, Holly's included, had hung exterior Christmas lights around their windows, adding to the quaint feel of the small town.

Too bad the mood outside didn't reflect the one inside her shop, despite the dwindling merchandise. Yesterday's sales had emptied more shelf space, but it wasn't enough. She was too far in debt to remain open and keep Jared's dream alive. The bare Christmas tree in the corner sported a new for-sale sign, and in between customers she'd spent the past hour rearranging all the figurines, wooden nutcrackers and candlehold-ers into more visible positions.

Despite the lights, the music and the scent of the holidays, the Christmas spirit had passed over her this year.

Holly pulled up Cameron's grades online, rubbed her eyes and stared at the computer screen. She had more immediate things to worry about. How had Cam's grades dropped even further? When she'd checked just over a week ago, they'd been Bs and Cs. Now they were Cs and Ds. Cameron had always been a good student.

She'd failed her son. In fact, she didn't even know him anymore. How had he gotten involved with Patrick and his cigarette-smoking, beer-drinking buddies? Despite her talk with Cam after church yesterday, Holly didn't know if he'd been serious when he'd chosen the dogs over his so-called friends.

Another Christmas carol drifted around her in the stillness of the shop, and even the scent of pine brought her no comfort today. For the first time since they'd opened the shop, Holly turned around and slammed the radio off. She couldn't handle it any more than she could stand to see the twinkling lights making the remaining leaves shimmer across the street. With Thanksgiving only a week away and more and more phone calls about her decorating business coming in, her days and nights were stretched thin, and tonight she was supposed to go see the winner of the church auction. She now had less time for her son, especially since she didn't see him right after school anymore. Was that why his grades suffered?

Clicking into each individual teacher's highlighted name, she stared at the number of missing or incomplete assignments. More caged butterflies begged to be released from her stomach. "But he's done them. I know he has. Why hasn't he turned them in?"

Holly dropped her head into the palms of her hands. *Where did I go wrong, Lord?*

Sometimes she felt so alone.

It wasn't supposed to be this way. Her clenched hands banged down on the spot on the counter where the stain had worn away over the years and rattled the pens. God was supposed to be there for her. So where was He? She'd been reaching out again, but even He abandoned her. Why did she even bother? She knew the answer. Cameron. And maybe, just maybe, despite it all, a small piece of her still believed.

If God wouldn't talk to her, she knew someone who would. Holly picked up the phone and dialed Kristen. While she waited for her friend to answer, Holly cradled the receiver and picked up the pen holder her son had made for her in first grade. She ran her fingers along the ripples of the old soup can where he'd glued a hand-drawn stick figure of Santa along with colorful wrapping paper to cover the tin. Another speck of paint chipped off the bottom, reminding her that nothing lasted forever. Nothing. With stiff fingers, she brushed it to the floor and set the pen holder back by the register.

"What's up, girlfriend?" a breathless Kristen answered. In the background, Holly heard her friend's three-year-old banging on what sounded like a pot. She winced at the noise, remembering those days well. Her friend sounded flustered.

"Nothing. Sounds like you're busy."

"I'm never too busy for you. Wait a second till I plant the kids in front of the TV for a few minutes. I'll be right back."

"Okay." Holly twisted the phone cord until the room grew silent, her gaze wandering outside the large store-front window, and caught sight of a dead leaf clinging to a branch, yet fluttering helplessly in the breeze. Holly knew how the leaf felt, if it had that ability. *Hold on, little fella. You can do it.* But seconds later, a gust tore the leaf from its mooring and carried it away.

Holly refused to suffer the same fate. Unlike the leaf, her destiny wasn't so short-lived, and despite closing the shop at the end of the year, she'd make things work out. She'd also figure out how to deal with her son and get his grades back up.

"I'm back. So what's wrong?" Kristen asked.

Holly's confidence faded, though, as she stared at the computer screen again and pushed the print icon.

"Cam's about ready to fail this semester."

"Uh-oh. What do you mean?"

"I just checked his grades. They've gone down since last week. He's not turning in his homework. There's only four weeks left, and I don't know if he can bring them back up to A's and B's or if he even wants to. His attitude really stinks right now."

"But I thought that Ethan was making sure his home-work was done before Cam worked with the dogs."

"He is, and I check Cam's agenda and work almost

every night." Holly twirled a section of hair around her finger. At this rate, she'd have a bald spot by Christmas. "I've been so worried about the store and keeping a roof over Cam's head that I've failed him. I don't know my son anymore, and that hurts worst of all."

"You haven't failed him, Holly. This is just one of those stages. He's about to hit his teen years. Something else is going on. Go talk to Ethan. You need to get this taken care of right away. Just give me a few minutes to pack the kids in the car and I'll be right over to watch the shop."

"I can't let you do that."

"Yes, you can. Tony's at work and dinner's in the Crock-Pot. The kids love 'Tis Always the Season. It'll give them a change of scenery. I'm not taking no for an answer."

Twenty minutes later, Holly pulled up slowly to Ethan's house and saw both the man and the dog Bear walking up the middle of the driveway. Catching him unawares gave her a few moments to study him. Ethan was taller than Jared but had the same slim build. His hair was a bit darker, and now that it was growing out from the military cut, she noticed the curls. But that wasn't what made her pull her bottom lip between her teeth.

His slumped shoulders and slow gait as he glanced through the mail that he'd retrieved from his mailbox spoke of a man with his own set of problems and worries. She knew the feeling well and found herself wanting to put her hand in his and squeeze gently to let him know he wasn't alone, but that would place her in an emotional position she didn't want to be in. She had enough to deal with already, and putting herself back out there would only lead to more pain.

She pulled up next to him, rolled down her window and then breathed in the cool, crisp air, laden with another hint of winter. "Hi, Ethan."

"Holly?" A surprised Ethan glanced up from the stack of mail. "What are you doing here?" Creases formed between his eyes, and his lips curved downward, accentuating his five-o'clock shadow as he leaned through the window. "Cameron's not coming?"

"He said he was, but I'm not sure anymore." Holly swallowed and managed to keep the emotion from her voice. Breaking down in front of Ethan was not an option. Not when she knew he'd put her first. They were friendly to each other because of Cameron and the store, nothing more, despite the fact her heartbeat accelerated a bit, like it was doing right now. With all her other distractions, she hadn't really noticed how handsome he was. Well, maybe she had just a little.

Her gaze drifted to his right hand. Even that didn't bother her quite as much as before, yet as he stared down where she'd looked moments earlier, she knew he hadn't forgotten her reaction to his injury.

"What's going on?" The frown still tugged at his lips.

"I'd like to show you something. Hang on." She placed the car in Park, unbuckled the seat belt and turned off the ignition. After Ethan moved away from the door, she grabbed her purse and stepped out, glad her friend had convinced her to see him. Kristen was right. Since Ethan monitored Cam's homework before her son could work with the dogs, he had a vested interest in his grades. If they didn't improve, Holly would stop the arrangement.

He held up his mail. "Let's go inside. My hands are a bit full." Once Ethan dumped the stack on the kitchen table, he turned to Holly. "What did you want to show me?"

"Cam's grades. I pulled them off the grade portal." She gave him the paper and set her fists on her hips. Inhaling sharply, she caught the scent of freshly baked chocolate-chip cookies and dog. "I don't understand what's going on."

Ethan's brow furrowed even more as he rubbed the back of his neck. His eyes widened and his lips pursed. "I don't, either." His gaze captured hers, pulling more oxygen from her lungs. The sincere tone of his voice told her more than his words. "He has done his homework."

"I know he has. I check almost nightly." Holly sank into the kitchen chair and rested her forehead against her palm. The confusion in her stomach went north and created havoc in her brain. Something had changed between them Saturday, and despite what her brain wanted, her feelings and emotions wanted something else. Or to at least explore the possibilities. Her blood chilled as she stared up at the man who'd suddenly made her want things again.

"Something else must be going on."

"But what?"

Ethan glanced at his watch as he strode around the cramped room. "If Cameron is coming here, we'll know in about five minutes. If he doesn't show up, then it may take a bit longer, because we'll have to go find him."

Holly appreciated his words. Maybe that was why she'd come here in the first place. She could have dealt with the situation with her son at home and over the phone with Ethan. And yet, she'd wanted to see him, talk to him, just be near him.

"Would you like a chocolate-chip cookie? Fresh out of the oven." Ethan changed the subject and held out a blue plastic plate.

Her stomach growled at the tantalizing smell, reminding her she hadn't eaten anything since breakfast, her lunch still in the mini refrigerator at the store. "You baked them?"

"I'm crushed that you think I'm helpless in the kitchen. I can bake. Sort of." He gave her a slight grin. "Okay, so I used a package from the refrigerated section, but it's the thought that counts, right?"

"Of course. I'd love one. All I need now is a glass of milk." Add her grandmother's lilac scent and she'd be transported back to the simpler days of her childhood.

"That can be arranged." Ethan set the plate down in front of her and pulled three glasses from the cabinet. Then he retrieved the milk and poured some into two of the glasses. "I'll pour Cameron's when he gets here."

Holly bit into the warm cookie and let the chocolate burst across her tongue. How long had it been since she'd had the time to do something as simple as baking cookies? Too long. Since before Jared's death. She hadn't even cheated by using a frozen or refrigerated package from the store like Ethan did. These days she relied on packaged cookies from the store shelves for Cam's lunches.

She stared as Ethan dunked his in the milk first and then took a bite. "What? This is the only way to eat them."

"You know, I like milk and chocolate-chip cookies, just not together like that. I don't even like root-beer floats, but I do like root beer and vanilla ice cream separately."

"You don't know what you're missing." He popped the rest of it into his mouth. "Sometimes we even put in cream soda or, my personal favorite, orange soda. It tasted just like those things we used to buy from the ice-cream man who drove around the neighborhood every weekend."

"The ice-cream man. Wow. I haven't thought of him for years. They used to have someone who drove around during the summer, but I haven't seen him lately." Holly savored another bite. "These are pretty good for not making your own dough. I remember making chocolate-chip cookies from scratch with my grandmother. She was a traditionalist. We even sifted the flour before we put it in."

"Yeah, my grandmother was like that, too. There's something to be said about the time before cell phones, three hundred television channels and handheld computer games."

The sound of footsteps clomping up the back steps caught her attention right before the back door opened and Cameron careened inside. "Mom? What are you doing here? Who's watching the store?"

Ethan took a step back and busied himself with pouring a glass of milk.

"Kristen is at the shop right now. There's something I need to discuss with you, and it couldn't wait until after dinner. I pulled a copy of your current grades off-line this afternoon. Is there something we need to talk about?"

Cam refused to make eye contact and kicked the floor with the toe of his shoe. "No."

"Then how do you explain your grades?"

"Can I go see the dogs, Mr. P.?"

"No." Ethan glanced at Holly as he set the milk and the cookies on the table. If he had to choose an adjective or two, he'd describe her as *vulnerable* and *lost*. Not a good combination, because it brought out that need to protect her again. "You need to answer your mother. I won't tolerate any disrespect, remember?"

Cameron glanced at him before he exploded on his mother. "Fine. I hate school. I hate homework. And sometimes I even hate you. I wish you had died instead of Dad."

"What?" Holly gasped and sank back in her seat. All color fled her cheeks, and shock pulled her jaw open. Tears gathered in her eyes, causing Ethan's instincts to overload. He had to get a handle on this situation before it spiraled further out of control.

"Sit down." Ethan yanked out a chair. The boy needed some heavier intervention and fast. He seethed. Where had Cameron learned this type of behavior? No one should ever be on the receiving end of those words. "You will never speak to your mother like that. Do you understand me?"

Out of the corner of his eye he saw Holly clench her fingers and stand. "I can handle this, Ethan. Cameron, put your backpack on. We're going home."

"But I don't wanna go home." Cameron flew into his mother's arms. "I'm sorry, Mom. I didn't mean it. I love you. It's just so hard—"

Holly cradled him back. "I know, sweetie. I know. I'm sorry that I haven't been there for you like I should have been. Like I should be. Why don't you come back to the shop and do your homework there, like the old days? Just me and you and some hot chocolate."

"Because I like it here. I like the dogs. I like Mr. P. I want to come here after school."

"Then what's going on with your grades, Cam? They're all C's and D's."

The boy remained silent.

"When I opened up each subject, most of your homework was missing. You did it all. I know because I checked it. What did you do with it?"

The only sound in the room was their breathing and the whining of the kenneled dogs.

"I think I know what's happening." Ethan paced the small area. Someone was bullying Cameron. The accusation would be a strong one, but he wasn't about to let Holly and Jared's son flunk seventh grade. "Patrick's been taking your work and turning it in as his own, hasn't he?"

The boy held his mother tighter. Ethan captured Holly's tortured gaze, her pale skin and large eyes. Knots twisted his gut as he wrestled with what decision to make. He'd been wrong before, couldn't trust his own judgment half the time, yet somehow he knew he wasn't wrong about this.

"I bet he also told you that if you told anyone, he'd beat you up. What's Patrick's last name?" A sinking feeling developed in the pit of his stomach. There'd been a similar incident between some boys when he'd been in middle school.

"Dennison."

"And I bet his dad's name is William." His feelings were justified. "Did it happen again today?"

Cameron shook his head. "There was no homework last weekend. I tried to stay away from him today after what happened Saturday night, but he followed me around. He wouldn't leave me alone and kept calling me names."

"I'll go talk to your principal tomorrow, Cam. I won't allow this to continue." Holly kissed the top of his head.

A look of relief flitted across her son's face. "Will you go, too, Mr. P.? Principal Buchanan is mean and old. He might scare my mom."

"Cameron. Mr. Buchanan and I get along fine."

"Please? I want him to go, Mom. He is the one helping me with my homework."

"Is that what you want?" Pain laced her voice and deepened the green of her eyes.

When Cameron nodded, Ethan caught the adulation on Cameron's face as he glanced at him. By her sharp intake of air, he realized Holly caught it, too. When Ethan had come up with the idea of Cameron helping out with the dogs, he'd never intended for the boy to bond with him. Holly's son needed to find a different father figure, one who could keep him safe. "This is something your mom needs to take care of, Cameron."

"Please?"

Great. Being manipulated by a twelve-year-old was a bit unnerving. "Only if she wants me to."

"Please, Mom?"

"If that's what you want and if Mr. Pellegrino is free, then he can come with me."

Ethan was glad to see that he wasn't the only one feeling cornered. "Let's see what you've got for homework today. After you're done, I've decided that instead of working around here, I'll take you out to the real sanctuary and show you around. Holly, you're welcome to join us unless you need to go back to the shop."

"I'd like that. Let me ask Kristen if she can close up."

"But what about everything we have to do?"

"You do your homework, Cam, and I'll do your chores so we can leave as soon as possible. I think after a day like today, we all need to have a little break." Holly glanced over Cameron's head at him, her expression closed just a fraction.

In that moment, he realized that Holly had interpreted her son's wants correctly and she wanted to keep them from spending too much time together alone. It was as if they were a family, not too different from the one he'd established with his patrol back in the Middle East. The kitchen shrank under the weight of the responsibility he wasn't sure he wanted. Because then he had to protect them. But could he when he didn't even trust that he could protect himself?

"This is it. The final home for Beyond the Borders Dog Sanctuary." Ethan turned off the county highway and into the long, winding driveway defined by tall ash, sycamore and pine trees. Swatches of fall color still clung to the remaining leaves, and a hint of smoke from a neighbor's fireplace drifted through the air. Last week's snow had melted but had left muddy patches in the ruts where the gravel had disappeared over the years.

"Wow. It's beautiful," Holly marveled. "It's hard to believe we're only fifteen minutes from town."

"Do you get a lot of deer out here?"

"Deer, elk and an occasional cougar or bear." At Holly's soft gasp, Ethan leaned over and patted her hand. Mistake. He found himself wanting to hold it, which would be impossible. Her hand moved under his, bringing back the memory of her revulsion of his injuries. He pulled away. "Don't worry. It's been a while since we've seen any other wildlife besides rabbits and coyotes."

At the last bend in the driveway, the old two-story farmhouse came into view. A fresh coat of white paint covered the wood siding, and the dark red shutters on either side of the four windows complemented the front door. Two benches and a rocking chair graced the porch running the entire front of the house, and an empty birdbath added a homier feel to the home Ethan's great-grandfather had built.

Brown dotted patches of the front lawn, but next spring and summer, he envisioned replacing the shrubbery in the front and adding some flowers, as well. He'd have to ask Holly for her opinion. Repainting had been the easy part; he'd just followed what had already been done.

"It's gorgeous."

"Are you going to live out here, Mr. P.?" Cameron piped up from the backseat.

"Eventually." Ethan looked at Holly's son in the rearview mirror. "I'll want to be near the dogs once we make the move."

"What about your house in town?"

"I'll rent that out and use the money to pay the mortgage and my bills."

"That makes sense." Holly crossed her arms.

Ethan eased his car to a stop, his hands gripping the steering wheel a bit tighter than normal. The sensation felt odd because of his missing fingers, but that would just be something else he had to get used to. The temperature inside the car had dropped noticeably with his insensitive words. If Holly wasn't paying the rent on the store, she probably had trouble making her mortgage payments, as well. He hoped that wasn't the case, because the thought of Holly and Cameron without a home didn't sit well, especially when he was lucky to have two. Well, the bank still owned part of one, and technically his mother owned this one, but by Holly's pale face and tight expression, the damage had already been done.

"This place is cool." Unknowingly, Cameron

changed the subject when he jumped out of the car and ran toward the dormant grass between the house and the barn.

"Cam, wait." Holly struggled with the broken lock.

"Doesn't work." Ethan opened the door and helped her from the car. "Cameron will be fine. There's nothing out here that can hurt him." Setting his hand against the small of her back, he escorted her over the uneven ground where her son had run moments earlier. The action spoke of the possibility that there could be something between them if either one was looking for that. He knew Holly wasn't. He wasn't, either, but dropping his arm to his side left him feeling incomplete in a way that had nothing to do with his missing fingers.

He shook his head to clear his mind and focus on what should be the most important thing right now. "I'll show you the barn and runs first and then the inside of the house. Cameron, over here."

The traditional-looking two-story wood barn had also been treated to a new coat of red paint that matched the house. As Ethan pulled the barn door open, it creaked. A musky scent of old hay filled his nose, and darkness interrupted his vision until he flipped the switch to his right. A lone lightbulb suspended from the ceiling chased away most of the shadows. "This place needs to be rewired and a lot more lights added."

"Lights would be good. So would a bit of heat. I think it's colder in here than outside." Holly pulled her jacket closer.

"It probably is. Last night was pretty cold. Until I can afford to put in a central-heating and air-conditioning unit, I'll be using portable heaters and lots of old blankets in the kennels." Ethan walked to the center of the barn and surveyed the large, open space.

"Manny and his son have already demolished the horse stalls so I'll have room for twenty-four kennels, twelve along each side. The back will be for storage and up front, when I install some plumbing, will be the bathing area."

"Manny?"

"My handyman. His wife is sick so he took the day off to take her to the doctor."

"What are you going to use the upstairs for?" Cameron ran over to the rickety ladder leading to the loft.

"Be careful, Cam."

"Don't climb on that. It's not safe," Ethan ordered as the boy put his foot on the first rung. "I haven't decided yet. They used to store the hay up there, but maybe the cats will go up there."

"Cats?"

"My cousin has accepted a ferret, so cats aren't too far behind."

"Do you have a problem with cats?" Not appreciating his tone of voice, Holly crossed her arms and glared up at him.

Ethan scraped his hand through his hair, remembering that Holly had a cat. A cat Jared had brought home for her. He was scoring points left and right with her today. "Not at all, even though I can't say I understand them. They're just not my favorite of all God's creatures, and I'm not sure where to put them."

Holly relaxed. "Cats certainly keep you on your toes,

that's for sure. Maybe you can convert one of the up-stairs rooms of the house into a cattery. I don't think kenneling them here would work very well."

Holly's idea rattled around inside his brain. The old farmhouse had four bedrooms upstairs, and he only needed one. He could use one for the cats, another for any other type of creature—like the ferret or a reptile or bird—that showed up and still have one for a work-out room. Plus he had the attic.

"That would probably work. Being as curious and agile as cats are, I'd have to enclose the loft, and if one of them got out, it could get interesting with all the dogs. Separate accommodations would be a good idea." And that was where Holly's expertise would come in, if she and Cameron stayed around. He had no idea how long the arrangement would last, but he hoped it would be awhile. The thought of not seeing her and her son almost every day left an empty hole in his heart. "Come on, let me show you what I've got planned for the outside."

He ushered them outside and took in what remained of autumn outlining the large backyard where the run would go. What little remained of fall contrasted with the pine trees interspersed among the deciduous ones and amazed him. He'd missed the change of seasons overseas, but God had really outdone himself this year. And continued to do so. From the snowfall they'd al-ready experienced, it looked to be a winter with a lot of accumulation, especially in the higher elevations as he took in the white-capped mountains to his left.

Turning away from the beauty, he locked the freshly

painted barn door and realized he was going to need a security system on the house and the barn, too. More money he didn't have, but he had a lead on another grant.

Had he made a mistake in trying to take on such a big endeavor? There was still so much to do and more calls coming in about his sanctuary every week. Three more dogs were scheduled to arrive mid-January. He had to be ready. The alternative for the dogs wasn't an option.

Let go, let God.

No. He hadn't made a mistake. He felt it in his bones. All those hours in the hospital bed had given him plenty of time to think and reflect on his life and pray about what to do next. God had opened a new door for him. *New doors,* he thought as he watched Cameron run through the grassy area destined to become the play area for the dogs.

Mentoring boys on the edge of becoming delinquents had to be another part of that plan and would give him the extra volunteers that he needed to run a successful sanctuary.

"It's really beautiful out here. I'm sure the dogs will love it. This will be the dog run?"

"Yes. Manny and I have already started to dig the holes that will hold the posts for the chain-link fencing. Once that's in, I can move the dogs out here. Of course, there's still a lot of work, but it will get done." Eventually. He could only afford to pay the handyman for so long until more funds came in. Rubbing the back of his neck did little to relieve the instant tension. He needed at least six more hours a day to accomplish what he needed to do, and most of them had to be daylight hours. But God only provided them with a finite set of time, broken down by day, hour or minute, and he had to make it work within that time frame.

"Is there anything I can do to help?"

"As a matter of fact, there is." Ethan glanced down at Holly. He wanted to reach out and grab her hand, hold it and share this with her. Make her a more permanent part of his life and sanctuary. Whoa. He'd never had those thoughts before. Must be the idea that he'd just slipped another year closer to his mid-thirties. Besides, Holly was still in love with Jared, and any thoughts of getting involved with the single mom outside of helping with Cameron had to be stopped. He had to ignore the fact that his heart lightened when she was around and he enjoyed talking with her.

"I've seen what you've done with your shop and the mayor's Christmas decorations. I need some advice on how to decorate the foyer and office area downstairs as that will be what people see when they stop by."

"I can do that."

And yet, Ethan saw the hesitation in her eyes. He knew she was thinking about her store, her decorating business and spending time with Cameron. He also knew she felt she had a responsibility to him in order to make up for the rent she couldn't pay.

He didn't see it that way, but he'd already tripped over his words twice today and hurt her feelings. Trying to vocalize something when he couldn't formulate a valid sentence in his head wasn't worth it, either. The day he walked into her shop with Cameron in tow, he'd made the decision to let her remain through her busy season and try to rent it out after the new year.

Despite his financial needs, he still stood by that decision, even though it might cost him more in the long run, and he wasn't just thinking about money.

Chapter Seven

"Hi, Holly."

"Ethan." Holly's heart pounded when Ethan walked through the front door of 'Tis Always the Season. She didn't know if it was him or the pretty, petite blonde accompanying him that left her lungs out of oxygen and her stomach behaving as if there were a million butterflies trapped inside. Especially when the woman stood a tad bit closer to Ethan than Holly thought appropriate.

She knew a lot of people in town. The bottle blonde with the notepad and a more than casual interest in the shop remained a mystery. Holly stood behind the counter and gripped it tightly to keep from charging around the other side. "Is there something I can help you with?"

"Oh, no. I'm just here to look around and take some notes." She grabbed the pen clipped to the top of her notebook before flipping open the cover.

The woman's dismissal surprised her. So did the way Ethan placed his hand on the blonde's arm and gave her a guarded smile. More butterflies took flight. Funny, he never looked at Holly that way. Not that she wanted him to or anything like that, but what she interpreted as a protective gesture only reinforced the loneliness that crept up on her at the most inopportune times. Like now, for example. Forcing her mouth shut, Holly started to rearrange the Christmas-themed pens in the display canister. Santa needed to go next to Rudolph, not the snowman.

"Then let's get started. But first, I'd like to introduce you two. Beth, this is Holly. Holly, Beth."

"Pleased to meet you." Dropping the pen with the red package attached to the top next to the Christmas tree, Holly held her hand out to the woman, hoping her dislike didn't show. Ethan aside, she couldn't explain the sudden discomfort in Beth's presence. Maybe it was the freshly styled hair, the makeup or the perfect manicure. Or all three.

"Likewise." The woman's quick, limp grasp barely qualified as a handshake, her interest more in the man next to her. Beth's close-set eyes held a predatory gleam as she leaned closer to Ethan. The chill in the room did not come from the light breeze playing with the remaining leaves on the trees outside her front window.

Holly dropped her hand back on the counter and inhaled sharply, the woman's words finally registering in her brain. "Taking notes?"

"Yes." Her gaze flickered around the store, distaste etched in her perfectly made-up face. "I'm here to see about renting it once your lease is done at the end of the year. Now, Ethan, I don't have as much time as I'd like because of prior commitments, but please show me around."

A possible renter? Holly's spine fused into a straight rod. In all her preoccupation with Cam, closing shop and her new business, she hadn't even considered that Ethan would be showing the place while it was still occupied. But business was business, and she suspected he needed the money just like she did, especially after her visit to the permanent sanctuary outside of town yesterday and seeing how much Ethan had left to do.

She should be glad he had the opportunity to rent the place out with all the other spaces available in town, but her emotional side still resisted the idea that the shop had to close and she would give up on Jared's dream.

A dull pain spiderwebbed out from the base of her neck that even today's cranberry-scented candle couldn't alleviate. She refused to follow Ethan and Beth or hover anywhere near the couple. She didn't need to; she could hear almost every word the woman spoke, her loud cackle drowning out the Christmas music playing in the background.

"A Christmas shop? No wonder the place is going out of business."

Ethan's reply remained a mystery, but the woman's quick writing in her notebook worsened the pounding in Holly's skull. Not that she'd expect Ethan to defend her as a business owner, but she did as a friend, unless she'd totally misjudged him. After reaching in the top drawer for her bottle of pain relievers, Holly shoved two in her mouth and chased them down with this morning's warm water.

"And these colors and murals are awful. I presume I can paint the walls?"

Each word struck a dagger into Holly's heart, and she sank down into her chair. She and Jared had worked so hard painting the walls and deciding which murals they should do in the spirit of Christmas. Holly's favorite was the one of Santa standing next to the real fireplace on the opposite wall. Her gaze wandered to the small, framed picture she kept of her late husband by the cash register as she picked up the wooden ornament he'd carved for her.

The action brought her no comfort today. The shop was going away soon, and she'd be left with nothing but memories and heartache.

"Within reasonable guidelines. Of course, the cost will be yours. The lease only covers major issues, not cosmetic ones." The tone in Ethan's voice changed, and out of the corner of her eye, Holly watched him take a step to his right.

"And what about plumbing? I need at least three sinks." Beth placed her hand on Ethan's arm and squeezed gently, screaming high maintenance and territorial.

"You're welcome to change the interior to what you need, again at your own cost. However, the exterior and any signage have to be approved by the city historical society since this is listed as historical property." Holly detected another subtle change in Ethan's tone.

"Perfect. I don't suppose you know any plumbers, do you?"

Holly almost gagged at the woman's purr. If that was

what men wanted these days, she was glad not to be out there dating. Her occasional loneliness didn't matter; she had friends. When she wanted to share a funny story or some other news, she had friends. If she needed to escape the confines of her home or store when Cameron was out, she had friends. And now Ethan had joined that rank, despite the occasional closeness she felt around him or the weird sensations inside her heart.

But date? She had no reason to date even if that was what she wanted, which she didn't. She had her hands full with her son, even though things seemed to be turning around. Well, that was until she saw his grades. The butterflies returned to her stomach. Their appointment with the principal was in an hour.

"Plumbers? Not offhand, but I can ask around for you." Ethan smiled at Beth again, but it died quickly when he made eye contact with Holly. Did she catch that look of desperation in his eyes, or had she simply imagined it? Now he looked quite content to be standing next to the woman who wanted to be his future tenant.

Holly looked away first, rearranging the pens again back to their original order, and wished another customer would walk through the doors and take her mind off Ethan and Beth.

No such luck. And there was only so much she could do behind the counter.

"That would be perfect." Out of the corner of her eye, Holly saw Beth move in a tad bit closer to Ethan as she pulled a tape measure from her purse. "Can you help me take some measurements? I want to make sure that everything will work out to my specifications."

"Of course." But he didn't sound very happy about doing it.

After ten agonizing minutes of rearranging her sparse shelves and tree ornaments, Holly sighed in relief as the woman finally made a move to leave and take her cloying scent of expensive perfume, her notebook and her condescending attitude with her.

"Ethan, let's run over to the Sunrise Diner, grab a bite to eat and discuss all the details."

Ethan glanced at his watch and then back at Holly. His intense gaze pulled the air from her lungs. "I only have time for a cup of coffee. Holly and I have an appointment at one o'clock that we can't break."

"Thanks for your time, Mr. Buchanan." Ethan stood up and tugged at his collar, impatient to leave because he'd spent way too much times here in this very office. The man behind the desk had changed. He liked the slightly younger, more in-touch principal more than the old, strict one from his youth, but being in here brought back times he wasn't too proud of. Fortunately his neighbor, old man Witherspoon, had helped straighten him out, just like God had made sure Ethan was now there to set Cameron on the right path.

"Yes, thank you." Holly stood up, as well.

"You're welcome." Mr. Buchanan stood and offered his hand to Holly and then to Ethan. "I'll be making an appointment to see Patrick's parents this afternoon and have a talk with all the teachers affected by the homework issue. If you have any other questions or concerns, you know where to find me."

"I do have one request." A smile tugged at Ethan's lips. Despite it all, he'd had some good times inside these walls.

"Sure. What is it?"

"I need to use a restroom."

"No problem. It's right across the hall. Just sign in at the front and get a visitor sticker." Mr. Buchanan leaned back in his chair and hid a grin behind his stern face. "But that's all. I can't allow you to roam the halls during school hours. It's against district policies. And behave, Mr. Pellegrino. Stories about the frogs in the cafeteria still circulate in these halls. It wouldn't be good to have to reprimand a Purple Heart recipient for misconduct, now, would it?"

"No, sir. Holly?" Heat crept to Ethan's cheeks as he helped Holly to her feet. He didn't realize that prank all those years ago would still echo in the conservatively painted brick walls.

"Frogs?" They left the principal's office. "Frogs? I don't think they have frog legs on the lunch menu."

"They don't. My friends and I let a bunch of frogs loose in the cafeteria the last day of school in eighth grade. We really didn't like the head lunch lady."

"And I'm letting you help with Cameron?" Holly's laughter belied her words.

Despite everything going on, her attitude had lightened over the past hour, and for a brief moment he wondered what it would be like if they were to go out and do something that wasn't related to Holly's business or the sanctuary or Cameron. Maybe they could attend another event like the Fall Harvest Festival or go to the movies.

Wrong. Because that would be a real date, something they agreed to do together, independent of what anyone else wanted or needed. He wasn't going to go there.

"Let's just say I had an intervention that summer." He signed them both in at the register on the front counter and handed her a visitor sticker. "I only had a few more problems after that."

"Which would be?"

Ethan held open the door leading into the hallway. Memories hit as soon as they stepped through. This time, though, the visit to the principal's office had gone much better than previous ones. "One of my old neighbors left his garage door open one day, so my friends and I took his motorized wheelchair out for a spin." Shame and remorse filled him. "It was fun, but we rode around so long, we ran the thing out of juice several blocks from the house and had to push it back."

"Sounds like you learned your lesson."

"More than that. When my mom found out, she marched me across the street to apologize and sign me up for free labor. I had to mow his yard that summer, rake his leaves in the fall and shovel his driveway in the winter." More memories filled him. "We actually bonded because of that incident, and Mr. Witherspoon ended up paying me a few bucks each time I helped him out, once he felt I paid for my crime. He was like another grandfather, one I could see on a daily basis." Ethan glanced up, wondering if Mr. Witherspoon could see him now. Because of his influence, he'd changed his life. Now Ethan had been given the chance to pay it back with Cameron and other boys in his position.

"He never had any children, so when he died, he left me a small inheritance. Enough to put the down payment on my house in town. I was also a pall bearer at his funeral."

Holly reached down and squeezed his right hand. "He sounds like a special person. I'm glad you had him in your life. And despite the frogs and the wheelchair and whatever else you did, I'm glad that you're in Cameron's life. These past few weeks have made me realize that he needs a man's influence."

Ethan tried to pull away, but Holly's grip remained strong. She held up his hand and smiled as she enclosed her other hand over his. Then she gently ran her fingers over the nubs.

His heartbeat quickened and moisture broke out on his forehead and under his arms. Unsure of what to say and needing an escape, Ethan spied the restroom sign. He needed to get away for a second. "Excuse me."

He opened the door, went inside and crossed the white tile floor to the sink. The cold water splashing against his face relieved some of his tension. He'd wanted Holly's acceptance, but now that he had it, he wasn't so sure it was a good thing. Or was it? *Okay, Lord, I'm trusting You on this one.*

Glancing up, an errant chuckle escaped his lips as he stared at the wads of dried toilet paper clinging to the ceiling. Things hadn't changed in here, but they were changing at an amazing speed in other areas. God was good.

Forty-five minutes later, Ethan let out a whoop at the mailbox. Maybe things at the school hadn't changed over the years, but like the oncoming winter, he sensed a change in direction with the sanctuary and maybe, just maybe, with Holly. The sun seemed to shine brighter, and in his mind's eye, he could see the renovated barn clearly along with the brand-new fencing of the dog run. He inhaled the crisp scent of fall underlined with a hint of burning wood. "Thank you, Lord."

He pulled out the check for twenty thousand dollars from one of the prominent state representatives from Phoenix with a promise of yearly contributions. Meredith's letter campaign had worked. The retired military officer believed in the sanctuary. Believed in him.

Adrenaline surged through his veins, and he couldn't wait to get started. Things could only get better.

"Dear Lord, thank You for the food and drinks before us." Ethan's strong, unwavering voice drowned out the almost-muted professional football game playing on the television in the family room at Kristen's house Thanksgiving Day. "This table is full of Your abundant blessing. May all of us know that all good gifts come from You, and may each and every one of us serve Your heavenly will on a daily basis. Thank You also for bringing family and friends together to share this day of Thanksgiving in Your loving presence. And bless those who are still overseas fighting for truth and freedom and especially for those and their families who have paid the ultimate sacrifice for their country. Amen."

Belief and hope in his voice mingled with a touch of sorrow as he squeezed Holly's hand. She did the same before she released his, knowing he thought about the men who had died beside him. "Amen."

"My turn," Kristen's daughter piped up from the children's table, a rectangular folding table placed next to the elegant dining table that sat the fourteen adults. "Rub-a-dub-dub, thanks for the grub. Yeah, God!"

Everyone laughed at Kira's words and began to pass the platters and bowls of food around.

Abundant blessings was right. Kristen had outdone herself again. Not only was the main table full of food and guests, there was also the children's table of eight, and the five teenagers and Cameron sat at the counter. Most of the people in attendance were family, but her friend always invited people with nowhere else to spend the holiday. With both Holly's parents gone now and then Jared, and the rest of her small family in Tucson, Holly now fell into that category. But what was Ethan's story? He had family here. Even though he'd told her his mother went to Phoenix to be with her sister and he'd stayed behind because of the dogs, she knew there had to be others. So what story had Kristen concocted to get Ethan to sit by her side?

She grabbed the bowl of cranberry sauce and plopped some on her plate. When would her friend realize Holly wasn't interested in replacing Jared?

Or was she just fooling herself? Glancing out of the corner of her eye, she watched Ethan pour gravy on

Kristen's grandmother's turkey and potatoes. The gentle way he treated the ninety-year-old woman endeared him to her and reminded her that there was more to him than he let on. He carried his scars on the inside, too. No doubt he had nightmares about the day that changed his life. They had that in common.

Two kindred souls, trying to make sense of the useless deaths while struggling to achieve a normalcy that always seemed beyond their grasp.

"Gravy?"

Holly's heart beat a bit faster as she caught his gaze. This time she saw him as a man, not a landlord or as someone helping her to keep Cameron in line. A man with hopes and dreams and feelings like she had. Catching her lip between her teeth, she nodded. "Yes, thank you."

"So tell us, Ethan, how does it feel to be back in Dynamite Creek after being on tour so long?" Kristen's husband, Tony, spoke from the head of the table.

Before Holly looked at Tony, she spied the tightness around Ethan's lips and sensed him stiffen. She knew firsthand he had a hard time talking about his time over there. In fact, outside the accident that took his fingers, he hadn't talked about Afghanistan at all. From the few articles she'd read online recently, most people didn't understand the returning vets or what it took to assimilate back into the general population, especially injured ones.

"It's good to be back. A little cold, but I'll get used to it again." The way he flexed his right hand made Holly wonder if it bothered him. If there weren't so many people around, she might have grabbed it and tried to massage some warmth back into it.

What was she thinking? Feeling the heat explode on her cheeks, she shoved some turkey into her mouth and chewed.

"It has been an unusually cold fall so far, and I can't believe how much snow we've gotten so early in the season. I can only hope that doesn't mean it's going to be a horrible winter. Now, who needs more cranberry sauce?" As if sensing his discomfort, Kristen held up a small white serving bowl.

"I imagine it gets pretty hot over in Afghanistan. Kind of like Yuma or Lake Havasu on a bad July day. And wearing all that gear and being away from family, that's gotta be tough." Tony kept talking, even after Holly saw Kristen poke him in the stomach.

"You know, I just don't understand this war or why our men and women are over there. Now, World War II, that made sense." Kristen's grandmother spoke up. "Why are we there again? The deaths, the violence, it seems so senseless. I can't watch the news about it anymore."

"I know what you mean, Nana," Kristen's cousin said from the other end of the table.

Ethan tensed even more, and Holly saw him struggle to not jump from his seat and storm out the door. Before the conversation spiraled out of control, Holly placed her hand on his arm, squeezed gently and stared into the old woman's faded blue eyes before she made eye contact with everyone at the table. "We're there to defend freedom. Something this country was founded on. Something we shouldn't forget."

"You're right. Nana, we should all be thankful for our military and all that Ethan and his fellow soldiers have done and sacrificed for our freedom," Tony said.

When everyone at the table voiced their agreement, Ethan's muscles relaxed, yet the tranquil mood of the day had changed.

"Did you know Ethan's building a dog sanctuary outside of town for our service men and women who don't have anywhere for their pets to go while they're away?" Holly pursued a neutral topic.

"And I'm helping out," Cameron announced from the counter. Holly saw him puff up with pride, and it gladdened her to see him so interested in something. Her heart stalled for a moment. Or was it the attention he received from Ethan? Attention that he hadn't been getting from her because of her preoccupation with the shop? "I get to feed and play with the dogs, and when the sanctuary is fully operational, I'm going to be on the staff. Isn't that right, Mr. P.?"

Those weren't the exact words Ethan had said to Cameron, but the boy had been a big help to him, and he liked having him around. He liked having Holly around, too. She helped drive away his loneliness and made his nightmares recede. She brought him hope.

Ethan caught her gaze. He hadn't had a chance to mention his more permanent solution to her yet because of timing issues, but that had to change. Holly's stunned expression told him she wasn't particularly happy about it, and he couldn't blame her. Again he'd overstepped his boundaries with Cameron. "With your mother's permission, of course."

"Mom?"

"We'll discuss this later, okay?" Holly hid behind a wall of hair as she stabbed at her pile of mashed potatoes. Gravy slid out of the gash she'd put in the side and spilled into her green beans, but she didn't seem to notice.

"Okay." Holly's son wasn't pleased with the answer.

"Dogs?" Kristen's grandmother spoke up next to him. "I like dogs. Always have. Too bad my Fred was allergic to them. Maybe I should get one."

"Nana, I bet Ethan would be happy to bring a few into the nursing home for a visit." Kristen broke in, saving Ethan from a reply.

"That's a great idea. I've heard stories of how animals, dogs in particular, are good for the emotions of the elderly and shut-ins," the woman he identified as Kristen's sister Kate piped in. "I bet the dogs are lonely without their owners. No offense, Ethan, I'm sure you take really good care of them, but it could be beneficial for all of them."

"None taken." He acknowledged the blonde before his attention returned to Holly. Having Cameron and even Holly at times helping with the dogs had been helpful for all of them, too. He liked their company, and if he wasn't mistaken, they liked his, as well. Their gazes caught as she looked up from her plate and gave him a half smile, but it was the compassion written in her eyes that made his pulse accelerate.

"Dogs are good for everyone." Her hand covered his

and she squeezed gently. For a moment, he forgot about the others gathered in the room, the food, the football game in the background and the nightmares from Afghanistan. The warmth of her touch before she pulled away put hope in his heart.

"I'll speak with the manager when we drop Nana off tonight." Tony's words broke the connection.

"So is that all you're doing, then? I'd heard Pastor Matt was trying to recruit you as the youth pastor for our church," Kristen's father said from the other end of the table.

Ethan shook his head to clear away the lingering effects of Holly's gaze. He had to focus on the here and now, not on the woman who carried around the same amount of emotional baggage as he did. "He's trying, but I've got another idea in mind." He eyed Holly's son but remained silent. If these people didn't know of Cameron's troubles, he wasn't about to be the one to tell them. "I'm also working with another organization to rescue abused dogs, get them out of Afghanistan and reunite them with the men who'd adopted them but then got shipped home."

"Interesting. You hear so much about the poor people over there, but you never really hear about much else. I guess they would have dogs just like the rest of us." Kate scooped out more mashed potatoes onto her plate and held up the bowl. "Anyone else?"

"I'm good, thank you. Yes, they do have dogs and cats but unfortunately, they don't think about them in the same way we do." Ethan wiped his mouth and stared at his empty plate, thinking about Scooter, the yellow mutt that had strayed into camp one night, bloodied and battered from abuse. His appetite disappeared. The dog had ended up losing his mangled leg and one eye, and as far as he knew, Scooter was still in that base camp. Ethan expected a phone call any day requesting his services to help bring Scooter stateside.

The redhead he recognized as Stephanie with the twin girls spoke up from the far end of the table. "Finding the funding and supplies must be a challenge." She turned to her daughters. "Girls, quit fidgeting. You may be excused, but take your plates to the kitchen first."

"It has been. But I've been praying a lot and sending out a lot of letters. I'm finally finding support." Like a moth drawn to light, his gaze sought out Holly's. He wanted to reach for her hand and feel the connection, feel complete, but her attention was focused on her son.

"Praise be to God. It's important for our men and women to know their pets are safe while they're away." Kristen's mother, Hannah, broke in and began to pile the empty dinner plates. "Keep doing what the good Lord is telling you to do. Everything will fall into place. You'll see."

Kate's husband, Cory, snapped his fingers and pointed at Ethan. "I know the general manager of that pet-food chain store. Sometimes he gets in broken or damaged bags of food and doesn't know what to do with them. I'll make sure he has your name." He pushed back his chair and patted his belly. "Another wonderful meal, Kristen. Thanks for putting up with us again this year."

"No problem. I love having you. All of you." At her

direct stare, Ethan shifted in his seat. "Does anyone need anything else?"

"No, dear. Boys?" She motioned for the teenagers to step forward. "Start clearing the table, please. Ethan, we sometimes get donations that aren't quite resalable at the church thrift shop. I'll make sure to save all the towels and blankets for you," Hannah announced, daring anyone to refute her.

Despite the noise and activity, Ethan sat there stunned. God continued to answer his prayers each and every day with the generosity being bestowed upon him. *Let go, let God.*

He had, or at least was trying to, and things were starting to fall into place. This time he caught and held Holly's gaze. But would He answer Ethan's other prayer? The one with the mixed-up feelings about the woman beside him that he had a hard time putting words to?

"Ethan likes you." Kristen handed her a rinsed plate.

Denial sprung to Holly's lips, but she couldn't force the words out. Something had changed between her and Ethan over the past few weeks, even today, and it frightened her. Entertaining any type of romantic ideas with her soon-to-be former landlord was out of the question. Holly's hand shook as she set the plate in the dishwasher in front of the last one she'd put in. "We're almost out of room here. We'll have to do the rest by hand."

"Quit changing the subject. He likes you. You know it and you're running scared."

"He's just being friendly and helping out with Cameron," she retorted a bit defensively. There, she'd said it. The truth. So why did it hurt? Could Holly be a tad bit jealous of her son because of the attention Ethan was giving him? Nonsense. She only had platonic feelings for the man.

Ethan and Tony brought in another stack of dishes from the other room and set them on the counter. How many more dishes were there? And they hadn't even started on the pots and pans yet. Holly let out a groan, but she wouldn't trade Thanksgiving at Kristen's for anything. Now she knew how the turkey felt, though, before her friend had put it in the oven. Full didn't even compute in her brain.

"Almost done in there?" Ethan grinned at her before he turned away and headed back out the door.

Why had the air just disappeared from her lungs?

"Really?" Kristen rinsed off another plate. "I see the way he looks at you. And I see the way you look at him."

"We're just friends," Holly protested. Maybe a bit too much by the looks of things. Kristen's eyebrows almost touched her bangs.

"Right." A smile split Kristen's face. "You've got it all wrong and you're lying to yourself. I can see you're interested. He's a good man. I think you should give him a chance."

Holly's fingers tightened around the plate until her knuckles turned white. Anger, denial, fractured by her confused feelings about Ethan, punctured her thoughts.

"I'm not interested in replacing Jared, Kristen, and you know that. He was the love of my life."

Kristen sighed and grabbed the dish towel from the counter to dry her hands. Then she placed them on Holly's shoulders and squeezed gently. A frown furrowed her brows and concern laced her voice. "Holly, I know this is hard, especially around the holidays, but Jared is dead. He's not coming back and you know it. You've got to move on."

"Is it time for dessert yet?" Kristen's niece, Molly, stuck her head through the kitchen door.

Without missing a beat, Kristen grabbed a pitcher and handed it to the ten-year-old. "Not yet, but if you help us out, we may get done that much sooner and then it will be time. Why don't you empty all the water glasses and then water my plants on the back porch? And when that's done, we'll be that much closer."

Holly's reprieve ended when the girl sped from the room, full pitcher in hand. Despite having eaten too much of Kristen's good food, butterflies still managed to find room inside. She had to straighten out her friend once and for all. "Look. I know you mean well, but when I'm ready, you'll be the first to know, okay?"

"You're never going to be ready. I know you. Hiding away and sitting home alone, focusing on Cameron or work, isn't the answer."

"But I promised Jared that I would love him forever."

As Kristen scrubbed at the large turkey pan, water sloshed out of the sink. "And you will. He was your husband and Cameron's father. Did anything Pastor Matt say last Sunday sink in? Our physical hearts may not be that big, but God gave our emotional hearts enough room to love many times over. I love my children. I love Tony. I love my parents even though they drive me crazy most of the time. I love you like a sister, which is why I'm being so hard on you. God has given you the ability to love a lot. He's given you room. It's up to you to decide what to do with it. Live again, Holly. It's what Jared would have wanted. If the roles had been reversed and you had died, wouldn't you have wanted Jared to find happiness again?"

"But—"

Kristen held up a soapy hand. "Don't answer. Just think about it."

Holly fell silent. What could she say? Kristen didn't understand. None of her friends did. They still had their spouses, their happily-ever-afters. They didn't know the pain of waking up in an empty bed and reaching out to feel the warmth but only finding cold sheets. They hadn't experienced the loneliness of not being able to share news of their day, the loss of security or the hardship of raising a child by themselves.

Looking out the window over the sink, Holly watched Ethan play football with a few of the other men and the teenage boys. Cameron's face lit up with the attention. She swallowed and held back her tears. Her son deserved so much more than she could give him.

"Ethan's a good man. Look at the way he interacts with Cameron and the other kids. Don't you think God might be taking an active role in this by bringing two lonely people together? Things don't happen by coincidence. There's always a bigger plan. We might not understand it at the time, but eventually we will. On His time and terms."

Finished with scrubbing the turkey pan, Kristen rinsed it and handed it to Holly to dry. "Hello? Anyone home? I know you're here because I see you, but I don't think you're really *here*. You always seem to withdraw at the mention of God lately. He hasn't forsaken you."

"Some days it feels like He has."

"He hasn't." Kristen pulled her hands from the soapy water and wiped them on her apron before she put her arms around Holly's shoulders and squeezed. "As a parent you know you have to let your child or children live their own lives and learn from their mistakes as well as their triumphs. As our Heavenly Father, God allows us to do the same, but He is always there when we need Him. Now, back to Ethan. Take a good look at him and open your heart to the possibilities."

Through misty eyes, Holly continued to stare out the window. Maybe Kristen was right. Maybe it was time to let go of her past and live again. And possibly love. In only a few years, Cameron would be grown and off to college and Holly would be by herself. Lonely and alone. Is that what she wanted? Yes no—maybe not, but could she allow herself to open her heart again?

Chapter Eight

Ethan's first Thanksgiving back on American soil was turning out to be a good one—aside from the mention of Afghanistan over dinner. Great food, great company, and his favorite football team had won by scoring a field goal in overtime. Kristen's family had come up with solutions to some of his needs at the sanctuary, and something had shifted between him and Holly. God was on his team.

Winded from the physical activity of playing football with the guys, he leaned over, placed his hands on his knees and tried to catch his breath. He smiled at Holly as she looked at him through the kitchen window. Her serious expression put him on edge. He broke the contact and glanced in Cameron's direction and saw her son approaching with a basketball. Everything was good there. A quick surveillance of the rest of the yard reassured him that nothing seemed out of the ordinary. Something was wrong, but he had no clue as to its origins. Sometimes he just couldn't figure women out.

"Can I ask you something, Mr. P.?" Cameron motioned him away from the other people in the backyard.

"Sure." He glanced at the window again, but Holly had disappeared. Ethan righted himself and they headed toward the shed, where Tony had hung a basketball hoop.

Cameron took a shot, but the ball hit the backboard and dropped to the ground. Ethan retrieved the ball and bounced it between his two hands before he lobbed it into the air. The sensation felt strange at first, but he realized he didn't need all his fingers to shoot a basket. The ball rimmed the hoop and dropped in.

Cameron retrieved the ball, took another shot and missed.

Ethan knew what he was going to do with the open spot next to the barn where the cement had already been laid. "Next time you're at the farm, I'll teach you how to shoot. I don't think we have time today."

Cameron missed another basket.

Ethan retrieved the ball again and lobbed it back to Cameron. "You're not concentrating. What's bugging you?"

"I don't know." He dribbled the ball with more force than necessary. "School. Everything. My mom."

At the mention of Holly, the Thanksgiving meal became lead in his stomach. She had been rather distracted lately, and even today her attention had wandered during the meal. Her serious expression a few minutes ago bothered him more than it should. Was there something else wrong? "What's up with your mom?"

"I know she's lonely. She doesn't laugh anymore,

and all she does is work. I wish she'd be happy again. Like she used to be."

"What do you mean?" Ethan lunged for the ball before it slipped past him. Cameron's aim needed work. This time, instead of giving the ball back to Holly's son, he dribbled it himself, the steady beat keeping rhythm with his heart.

"She was always singing and laughing, and she told the most amazing jokes. She was always smiling and cooking and there for me—it's just different now. I want my old mom back."

"It can be tough. Losing someone you love can be very difficult, and everyone has a different grieving period. It takes longer for some than others." The ball smacked against his palm until Ethan trapped it. He wasn't in the mood to play basketball anymore and sensed the moment had passed for Cameron, too.

"But it's been so long." Cameron fisted his hands. "Sometimes I don't feel like I exist anymore. That she doesn't care."

Ethan digested his words. "She loves you very much, Cameron. That's why she works all the time. To make sure you have what you need. But I think there's something else that's bothering you. What is it? Maybe I can help."

The boy kicked at some gravel littering the court. "I want another dad. Someone like you." The color drained from the boy's face. "I mean, I loved my real dad. Is it wrong that I want another one?"

Ethan's heart contracted. If God had given him a son, he would have wanted him to be just like Cameron. While Ethan didn't know what was in store for his future, he knew that somehow Cameron was involved. So were other boys at risk. He'd tucked away the idea of Pastor Matt's Sunday sermon on hearts and loving for future reference but hadn't thought he'd need it so soon. "I think God made our hearts so big so we could love lots of people that come in and out of our lives. Your dad will always have a special place there that no one can compete with, but there's a lot more room."

"Do you think my mom's heart is big enough?"

Was it? Ethan had to choose his words carefully. He couldn't speak for Holly. "I think your mom needs more time. When you love someone and have them taken away from you, there's a healing process that needs to happen. She might not be ready yet." Despite the late-afternoon sunshine, his day dimmed. Holly affected him more than he liked to admit.

"Will she ever be?"

"That's up to her."

Kristen rang the bell hanging from the back porch. "Dessert time. Last one in gets nothing but crust."

"I'll race you." Cameron sprinted away before Ethan could react.

He let Holly's son win, not because the boy was younger, but because Ethan was digesting the words he'd spoken to Cameron. He couldn't deny any longer that he had feelings for Holly. He just hoped his advice worked not only on Cameron, but for himself, as well.

"Can you help me make something for my mom for Christmas?" Cameron turned away from Bear's kennel after he finished feeding the dog the day after Thanksgiving.

"What did you have in mind?" The idea that Cameron had come to him for help lightened Ethan's mood, yet concerned him because of the boy's growing attachment. Despite the positive interest from Kristen's family members and friends yesterday, another rejection for funds for the sanctuary had turned the promising day into one filled with more questions than answers. Sure, the check he'd already received was enough to complete the renovations on the barn and get the dog run ready, but he still needed food and supplies. The community was willing to chip in, but even their resources wouldn't be enough in the long run.

Was he doing the right thing? He'd made a mistake in judgment before and it had cost five people their lives. He'd misjudged some of Cameron's actions, like at the Fall Festival when he'd caught the boys smoking. Yet the boy had turned around, and something in Cameron's eyes today made Ethan think that all was not lost. He had to let go of the past and remember that God was in charge and that things came about on His time, not Ethan's. Things happened for a reason. Just the idea that he was brought into Cameron's life when he seemed to need Ethan the most was something he couldn't ignore.

"My dad had a shop in the shed behind our house. I used to go in there and watch him work sometimes. I want to use his tools to make something for her, but he always told me never to use any of them by myself. Obviously, I can't ask my mom."

Right. Jared had always talked about having his own woodworking shop one day, and he was glad that Cameron's dad had made that dream come true before his untimely death. Jared would be happy to know that his son showed an interest in learning how to use his tools, and Holly shouldn't mind because she hadn't disposed of them, so she was probably saving them for Cameron when he got older. "Sure thing. How about if we do it on Saturday while your mom's at the store?"

Holly heard the sound of power tools and voices coming from the large shed in her backyard when she stepped from her car. Not just any voices, but Ethan's and Cameron's. Normally she didn't come home for lunch, but today she'd forgotten to bring the small gift for the baby shower that she was attending this afternoon, which left her no choice.

Awareness of where Ethan and her son were punched her in the stomach and left her nerves raw and exposed. Jared's woodworking shop was inside. She hadn't been in there since her husband's death. She couldn't face it. Her fingers clenched her purse strap and all moisture fled her mouth as she slowly crossed the yard. The open door beckoned, and drawn to it, she couldn't refuse where her feet took her.

Guilt over the accident and the memories of Jared inside the shop were more than she could handle. Pain tore through her, ripping apart any thread of composure she had left.

Today of all days was the anniversary of Jared's and Olivia's deaths.

Tears poured down her face as her fingers gripped the threshold, the scent of cut wood filling her nose as she peeked inside. Nausea hit her hard. The aroma that she used to love made her tears flow faster. Through the haze, she spotted Cameron and Ethan bent over the workbench working on a cut piece of wood. She still couldn't face it. "No."

She barely heard her whisper or the guttural moan as she pushed herself away and stumbled backward. Her purse dropped to the ground right before her knees sank into the dead grass. Wrapping her arms around her middle, she curled up into a quivering mass of emotion. Her fingers squeezed her sides as if trying to release the blackness consuming her from the inside.

"Mom?" She heard Cam's voice as if coming through a fog.

"Holly? What's wrong?" Within seconds, Ethan was at her side.

"What are you doing in there?" Holly glanced up just in time to catch the stricken look on her son's face. She tried to reach out but her arm dropped to her waist.

"We— Nothing." Cameron shrank before her eyes. Her inability to control her fragile emotions had hurt her son. Moisture burned the back of her eyes again. The person she loved and who meant the whole world to her now had retreated back into the shed.

"Cam, wait." Holly swatted at her tears, stood and stumbled after him. Once inside, she rubbed her eyes, trying to regain her composure. Her chin trembled as she inhaled a shaky breath and looked at her son standing behind the workbench where Jared used to make his masterpieces. How tall and proud he stood and seemingly so grown-up. She bit her bottom lip and tapped her hands against her mouth, fresh tears lingering in her eyes. Her pain refused to subside. Sawdust littered her son's hair and stuck to his cheeks and chin. With a watery smile, she dusted them off as she used to do with Jared. The memory blazed another trail of tears down her cheeks. "I'm sorry. I— It's—just—this was your father's place. I—I'm having a hard time, that's all."

Through a haze, her gaze swept across the small interior, and she remembered the love that Jared had put into making that space his refuge. Shelves lined the walls, the cubbies and holders filled with every tool imaginable. He'd even built his own movable bases so that his saws and other necessary items could be positioned where he needed them. Countertops hid more drawers until every space in the area had been utilized to its fullest capacity.

"I used to love sitting in here with your father, watching him make his creations."

"Mr. P. is helping me make something, but I can't show you just yet."

Jared had been the same way when he was making a gift for her. Like father, like son. Her lip trembled and her legs lost the ability to hold her weight. She collapsed onto the stool in the corner and buried her head in her hands. She knew she should have disposed of everything, yet she couldn't. Not then, not now, even though the money she could sell it for would pay for quite a few things.

It would be like giving Jared up again.

Kristen was wrong. Pastor Matt was wrong. She couldn't do it. She couldn't give up her dead husband like that and make room for someone else. Her heart wasn't that big. She wouldn't replace him despite her loneliness or any other emotion that snuck up on her.

She heard Ethan shift in the doorway. He'd only been trying to help her son, but he'd unknowingly entered a place that he didn't belong. She couldn't bear it. Not today. Not any day. She still felt Jared here as strongly as she did days before the accident. This spot was off-limits. It had to remain Jared's. She glanced from her son to Ethan and then back. "I don't want you in here, Cam. You, either, Ethan."

"But, Mom." Hurt and anger laced his expression. "You ruin everything." Cam fled from the shed.

Holly stumbled from the stool and heard it clatter behind her. She tried to squeeze past Ethan, but he held her in place. "Holly, please. I'll take the blame. I won't come back in here, but don't do this to Cameron. This was his father's stuff. He should be using it. It's what Jared would have wanted. Jared is dead. Despite how much you want it, or how much I want those five people in Afghanistan to come back, it's not going to happen."

He lifted his hand as if to touch her face but let it drop loosely to his side. More words hovered on his lips, but no sound came out. In his expression, she saw her own horrors and found herself in his arms.

She did know that, but it still didn't make it right. All she knew was that she needed to allow herself to grieve and work through Jared's death, but she couldn't. Not with the knowledge she held inside her. Clinging to Ethan's shirt, her fingers clawed at the flannel fabric. His warm embrace cocooned her, made her feel almost complete again, which confused her even more. Tears spilled down her cheeks and saturated the redchecked cloth as she tried to purge herself and let go. "I still don't understand. Why did he have to die on me?"

"I don't have an answer for that. Only God does." Ethan's fingers rubbed the small of her back, trying to massage away her pain. It felt right holding her in his arms, right to lean his cheek against the crown of her head, right to whisper words of encouragement and forgiveness in the still air around them.

She raised her head, her eyes full of tears and a remorse that sucker-punched him in the gut. There was no denying it now. Somewhere, somehow, he'd fallen for Jared's widow.

"I was driving that night. I killed him."

He stiffened at her words and understood the responsibility weighing on her. They both had been put in positions that had resulted in horrible outcomes. The nightmares of what happened in Afghanistan hadn't decreased, and each night the images of his friends and colleagues, their faces frozen in motion at the time of the blast, lingered in the deep recesses of his brain. What images of that night tortured Holly? Could he make them go away?

"It wasn't anyone's fault. Quit beating yourself up over what can't be changed." He should listen to his own advice.

He stared down at Holly's tearstained face, sensed her vulnerability and her despair. It matched his own.

Two lonely people, struggling with the knowledge that their actions had caused other people to lose their lives. It was a heavy guilt to bear. After wiping the tears from her cheeks, his hands cupped the sides of her face.

In a trance, he leaned down and gently kissed her lips, as if he could wipe away the pain of her loss and maybe lose some of it himself. He had to let her know she wasn't alone anymore, unable to share her burden. He deepened the kiss, trying to purge not only her memories but his own, as well. His heart pounded, crashing against his rib cage, unused to his reaction to Holly. She made him feel alive again. Whole. Ready to let go of his past and embrace whatever the future held in store for him.

Holly trembled and returned his touch, her soft gasps encouraging him to deepen the embrace. Her fingers laced through his hair, pulling him closer. It all felt so right, holding her, kissing her, creating a new bond between them that had nothing to do with Cameron. His heart lightened.

A few moments later, she stiffened and pulled away, her fingers covering her lips. Her flush disappeared, the white a contrast to the dark wood-stained shelves lining the walls. More tears filled her eyes, twisting his gut so that it resembled the mass of wood shavings piled on the floor. "No, I can't do this. Just go. Go away and leave me alone."

"I'm sorry. I didn't mean for that to happen." But was he really sorry? He'd be lying if he said that the kiss had no effect on him, because it was more than just a physical reaction. Confusion coiled inside him like a snake ready to strike. What he'd just done was wrong, and Holly was paying the price.

"I am sorry, Holly. I'll go now." Ethan scraped his fingers through his hair, his voice scratchy with emotion and remorse. The last thing he'd wanted to do was hurt her. He'd overstepped his bounds. In the shadows clinging to the back corners of the shop, voiceless faces stared back at him: Jared, the pastor, his men, and the woman and child he should have protected. Until both he and Holly could come to terms with their loss, neither one was free to move on.

After Ethan left the shed, Holly sank to the floor, a sob managing to escape from her throat. What had just happened? Ethan had kissed her, and she'd kissed him back. She'd done nothing to stop him, instead encouraging him to deepen the embrace. She'd kissed another man. Kristen would be happy. Holly was miserable.

And it wasn't because she didn't enjoy it. It was because she did.

She'd ignored her promise to Jared.

She fingered the wooden whistle attached to her key chain that Jared had carved for her their first Christmas together. The anniversary of his death, the death of their dream and their second child, hung heavily in the air.

Would she ever find peace or forgiveness?

Lord, I'm so confused. I don't understand what You want from me. What is Your will? What do I need to do?

Only silence surrounded her in the warm, almost suffocating air. *Answer me. Please.*

No response, but what had she really expected? God hadn't answered her in her darkest hours after Jared's death or her miscarriage. He didn't answer her now, which made her struggle. If God existed, why did He allow such pain and suffering? Why did He call some people home and leave others behind? Yet how could she account for the miracle of birth or the beauty surrounding her? Or how sometimes in the stillness of the morning and again at night she could almost feel a comforting presence wrapping around her? But why didn't He answer now when she needed Him?

More pain sliced through her midsection, making her relive the agony of that night in the hospital. She'd known her husband was dead, that she'd killed him, and that she'd also killed their unborn child, Olivia.

More alone than ever, Holly pulled herself up off the floor, stumbled to the door and across the brown grass to the back porch. From her vantage point, she could see that only her car was parked in the driveway. A momentary relief filled her. Ethan had left, but had he taken Cam with him?

Cameron. He'd never seen that emotional side to her before because she'd always managed to hide it behind closed doors. Her nails dug into her palms and her teeth worried her bottom lip. A different anxiety emerged. The back door banged open when she pushed on it. The loud thump resounded in the dim kitchen. "Cameron?"

No answer.

She sped through the house searching for her son, even going as far as to look under his bed. Only Figaro's golden eyes stared back at her. Sitting back on her heels, she grabbed her cell phone and dialed Ethan, tapping her foot impatiently until he picked up on the third ring. "Is Cameron with you?"

"He is. I figured you needed some time."

Holly clutched the phone. "Thanks."

"Would you like to talk to him? Here."

Holly heard Ethan transfer the phone. Soon her son's breathing filled her ear, but no words accompanied it. Her stomach clenched and pain stabbed her behind her eyes. She'd messed up big-time and her son had paid the price. More emotion covered her like an unwelcome blanket. "I'm so sorry, Cam. I overreacted. We'll talk about it later, okay? I love you."

It took him a few heartbeats to respond. "I love you more."

"I love you most. I'll see you at five, okay?"

"Bye, Mom." He disconnected the phone.

"Bye, Cam. I'm so sorry." Her words shattered the stillness inside the room. Cameron had been terrified by her reaction. All he'd wanted to do was make something with his father's tools. He had every right to. She grabbed a T-shirt lying outside the hamper and pressed it against her face.

Ethan was right. It was what Jared would have wanted. But maybe it wasn't that her son was using the tools, but Ethan himself.

He'd made himself a part of their lives, first by helping out with Cameron and then by kissing Holly. Her fear grew. Ethan was taking over Jared's place. She tried to picture her late husband in her mind's eye, but

Ethan's face surfaced. Wiping away her tears blurred the image like a Picasso, but the pieces remained even after she opened her eyes and dropped Cameron's shirt into the hamper.

She'd get through this. She had to.

More shadows crept into Cameron's room. Holly walked to the window and gazed outside. The dark clouds emerging from the west matched her mood. There'd been no snow predicted today. Sweat slicked her clenched fists. Maybe she should cancel attending the baby shower and reschedule her appointment with Abby to talk about setting up the Christmas decorations at the bed-and-breakfast. Ethan could bring Cam home and then she could hibernate and take care of some things around the house. No. Her head battled with her emotions. She needed the company of her girlfriends right now and the money that another decorating job would bring in.

Fear would not win.

"Hi, Holly. It's so good to see you again. Come on in." Abby Preston ushered her into the renovated foyer inside the old Victorian bed-and-breakfast she owned and gave her a hug.

Holly returned the embrace. "You, too, Abby."

"Thanks for coming on such short notice. It'll be nice to catch up, though." Abby directed her into the empty parlor, their shoes clicking against the tile and then the wood floor. A hint of spiced apple drifted through the air from the candle burning on the fireplace mantel.

"Definitely. I wish we had more time to chat at those chamber mixers, but there are always so many distractions." Holly settled herself on the frosted blue fleur-de-lis, Queen Ann–style chair. Despite her anxiety of going to the monthly gatherings, Holly knew that she needed to make an appearance every so often to keep up on what happened around Dynamite Creek.

"I know. When I first moved here, I knew no one. Now I don't seem to have a moment's peace." Yet from the smile on the blonde's face as she took a seat on the matching sofa, Holly guessed it didn't bother her a bit.

Holly's fingers ran along the ornately carved chair arms as her gaze flitted around the cozy room spruced in a blue-and-gold theme, mixed with antiques and time-period replicas. She imagined the small Christmas tree in the corner filled with cherubs and bows and garland draped over the heavy, full-length curtains and fireplace.

"That's Dynamite Creek for you." Sometimes the town wasn't very welcoming to outsiders. Holly had grown up in Flagstaff, but the town had welcomed her with open arms because of Jared.

Despite her California background, Abby had no trouble fitting in, and it wasn't just because she was related to one of the original founding families. Her husband, Cole, a local, had had a harder time because of some bad business dealings, but he had managed to work things out. Now he and his partner, Robert, had a booming business in renovating the older houses in town, which was probably why Holly was here to talk about Abby's Christmas decorating for the Bancroft Bed & Breakfast.

"I know." Her laughter filled the area. "Would you like some coffee and a slice of banana bread? Mrs. Wendt brought it by earlier."

"I'm fine, thanks. Maybe I'll take a slice to go."

"You'd think by osmosis I'd learn how to bake, living with Cole and wedged between the two prize-winning bakers in town, but that's just not the case. It still bothers me that Cole is a better cook than I am, but then again I don't have to spend much time in the kitchen and can mingle with our guests."

"Which you're good at. And trust me, having a man who knows his way around the kitchen is a good thing. Especially toward the end." Beside her, Abby shifted, her belly starting to protrude with her first child. The woman had blossomed the past few months in more ways than one.

"Yeah, I've heard I'm in for a fun time. Pretty soon I won't be able to see my feet and Cole will have to paint my toenails for me."

"But it's all worth it. You forget about everything, even the pain, when the doctor places your baby in your arms for the first time." The joy, the happiness, the intense emotion of love and protectiveness. The bond created by sharing the experience. Her fingers curled into fists. *Stop it. Stop going there.* This was Abby's moment. The woman, like most of the town, knew nothing of Holly's miscarriage after the accident, and now was not the time to mention it. "Have you had any cravings yet?"

"Bacon and soup of all things. Are you okay?" Concern laced Abby's brow.

"I'm fine. Really. Just a bit tired, that's all."

"And why wouldn't you be? Running two businesses all by yourself and raising your son. I know I couldn't do it alone. I'm so blessed to have Cole." Abby's hands flew to her cheeks, but Holly could still see the redness underneath. "Oh, Holly. I'm so sorry."

"It's okay, Abby. That's life." Holly had found her true love, but he'd been taken away from her. Would she find happiness again if she wanted to? Ethan's face intruded into her thoughts again and she remembered the feel of his lips on hers along with all the emotions behind the caress. It was all Holly could do not to cover her mouth. She pushed all the memories away.

Despite Holly's recent thoughts of how she missed being in a relationship, Jared had been the love of her life and she had no plans to replace him. She couldn't go through the pain if she allowed herself to fall in love again and something happened to him, too.

"Now, let's see what you want me to do and I'll give you a quote."

A look of relief crossed Abby's features at the change in conversation. She stood and headed back toward the double doors. "Your flyer came at just the right time, you know. I wasn't sure how I'd get this place decorated for the holidays. We're just so busy these days, and I don't quite have the energy I used to, if you know what I mean. This is one of the rooms on the list, of course the living room is where the main focus would be."

"I do, and that's why I'm here." This was Holly's second potential big Christmas decorating job, and she'd do better to focus on that instead of Ethan. She stared at the large living room and fell in love with the architecture in here, too. "You've done an amazing job of renovating the interior and bringing it back to its former glory. I can see a twelve-foot Christmas tree in the corner, decorated with Victorian-style bows and ornaments. Garland strung across the windows and doorways and a wreath over the fireplace. What colors do you want to use?"

"I don't know. Surprise me. You'll have to wrap garland around the staircase banisters and deck out the dining room, as well."

"Of course, and I envision red and white poinsettias in the dining room. What about the guest rooms?"

Abby put her hands on her back and stretched. "If you have the time and we don't go over budget, I'd like to see something on a much smaller scale done in there, too. At least some kind of centerpiece for the dressers and maybe some garlands—oh, and wreaths in every front window."

Holly remembered the days of an achy back and equally sore feet. Which reminded her again that it was a small price to pay for the miracle of birth and holding an infant in your arms for the first time. This time when tears threatened, Holly managed to keep them at bay. She would not break down again. "What type of decorations do you have?"

"Not much but the exterior lighting, which Cole and Robert have promised to put up tomorrow. Most of what my grandparents left behind was old and didn't fit the theme I have in mind."

"May I see them? I might be able to save you some money by incorporating what you already have with other things and create something new. If anything, they can be used in the guest rooms if the colors don't match."

"That would be awesome. They're in the old garage out back. We can load them in your car and you can take them with you. If they don't work for me, maybe they will for someone else. Or you can donate them to charity."

Twenty minutes and a trunkful later, Holly accepted a slice of banana bread. "Okay, then, let me get to work on it. I'll get back to you tonight if possible with the proposal."

Abby put her hand on Holly's arm and squeezed gently. "Holly, you're hired. I have three thousand dollars to work with. I have faith that you'll be able to make this place a showcase and get more customers in the process. I need it up by next weekend, though. Is that going to be a problem?"

"Not at all." She thought of her schedule and currently pending commitments. Who needed sleep? Of course, with her schedule filling up so fast, she was going to have to rely on Kristen to help out with Cameron on the nights she couldn't be home. There was only so much she could do while she worked at the shop. Maybe she should just close down and be done with it. Turmoil reduced her to tears and she walked quickly to her car. She wanted to hold on to her late husband's dream as long as she could, because once it was over, she'd have to finally say goodbye to Jared.

Chapter Nine

"Pastor Matt, can I talk to you for a minute?" Holly stopped the man at the entrance to the community room after the service. Now probably wasn't the best time to connect with him, but given her schedule, her choices were limited. And if she gave herself more time, she'd probably chicken out.

His gaze softened as he reached out, placed his hand on her shoulder and squeezed gently. "Of course. Did you want to talk here or in my office?"

She glanced back and forth across the crowded room. With the official kickoff of the holiday season now, energy filled the crowded space, yet seemed to miss her. She swallowed. Would she ever feel it again? Could she allow herself to? "Maybe outside in the foyer? I need to keep a look out for Cam."

"Of course. Right this way." He ushered her back into the foyer and over to a quiet corner. "What seems to be troubling you?"

Holly stared at the small pile of toys placed under

the Christmas tree between the double doors leading into the sanctuary. Collecting presents for the less fortunate was a mission the church did every year. She and Jared used to donate, but that had stopped the year after he died. A lot of things did while she tried to deal and cope with her grief. She was still trying. But it was important to share what little she had with others who were less fortunate. And so was keeping a routine. And helping others.

"I—I'm— I don't know. I feel so lost and alone."

Pastor Matt rubbed his chin. "And this time of year doesn't help, does it?"

Holly shook her head.

"Survivor's guilt is a hard cross to bear. But you don't need to bear it. Jesus did it for us. He died so we might live. I know it's easier said than done, but search your heart. Challenge those irrational thoughts. You are not to blame, Holly. Grieve for Jared, but do not accept that responsibility. You did everything possible that night to keep yourselves safe."

"But I don't feel that I did. I took my eyes off the road. We were having an argument. I should have been paying better attention." The numbness that she associated with her thoughts of the accident surfaced again. Her fingernails dug into her palms and she bit down on her bottom lip.

"Who hasn't taken their eyes off the road at least once? Do you change your radio station? Or talk on your cell phone? Or look over at Cameron when you're talking?"

Holly nodded.

"Of course you do. I don't know of one person who can say that they pay attention one hundred percent of the time. Don't focus on the burden of guilt, Holly. God gave you a gift. You survived for Cameron. Each day He gives us is a gift. Use it wisely."

Holly closed her eyes for a moment and let his words sink in. Was there anything else she could have done that night? No. She hadn't been driving too fast, and she'd turned her steering wheel in the direction of the skid. But being on a hill with a sharp curve at the bottom along with the stand of trees…deep down, Holly knew that there was nothing she could have done.

Pastor Matt picked up her hand again and held it between his. "There are a few support groups in Flagstaff that gather weekly for people to help each other through their grief." Something caught his attention and he glanced over her shoulder, a pensive look coming into his eyes. "You're not the only one who needs to go."

Holly turned and met Ethan's gaze.

"Thanks, Pastor Matt."

He squeezed her hand gently before he released it. "Anytime, Holly. My door is always open."

Holly slipped back into the community room and found her son and Ethan, each with a plateful of food.

"Mom, what are we doing later?"

Her son straightened his shoulders and lifted his chin. The top of his head almost reached her eye level. When had Cam sprouted up? And when had he lost his little-boy softness? And outgrown his clothes? His long sleeves barely came down to his wrists and his pants neared the flood stage. She had to siphon money from the grocery budget and take him shopping this week.

Holly knew Cameron wanted to go out to the sanctuary, and she thought about her schedule. She needed to talk to Ethan, though, before she made any commitments, in case he had other plans. "You have a rehearsal this afternoon."

"Do I have to do it?" Cam kicked the floor with his sneaker, a scowl on his face.

"Yes. Some things are not negotiable. The Christmas pageant was short of shepherds this year, and Mrs. Stocker needed more boys."

"They still do the Dynamite Creek Christmas pageant?"

"Yes. Next weekend at the old Jensen place outside of town. Not too far from the sanctuary, if I remember correctly. Pastor Matt does a wonderful job with the narration, but this year it could be interesting if it keeps snowing. Cam played baby Jesus when he was an infant." Holly's memories flew back to that night and the reaction of the crowd when they realized it was a real baby instead of a doll. Her heart swelled and a smile curved her lips. "Of course, he doesn't remember. Not that I'd expect him to, but it was still special just the same."

"I don't want to do it." Cam continued to scowl and kick the floor.

"Why not? It's an honor to be asked. Even I did it as a kid. Call it a rite of passage for the kids of Dynamite

Creek." Ethan crossed his arms and raised an eyebrow, as if daring Cameron to challenge him.

"Really?" Cam's attitude spun a one-eighty.

"Really. I played a shepherd, too. I got to chase around Mr. McDermott's pesky goat all night and try to keep him from eating all the props. Do they still use live animals?"

"Yes, but not as many as they did years ago. The year before Cam's birth, the three wise men came in on camels, but now they use horses. And I think there might be a goat or a few sheep."

Cameron looked at Ethan with the hero worship Holly had uncomfortably grown accustomed to before her son high-fived him. "Fine. I'll do it, but only because you did. There's Tyson. I'll be right back."

While Cameron ran off to talk to his friend, Holly used the opportunity to speak her thoughts. She'd had all night to think about it, and this morning's sermon on opening your heart to receive all that God had to offer could have been written for her. She truly was blessed to have what she did even though there were days when it was easy to forget. Pastor Matt's stories of those who had lost everything in last month's hurricane moved her deeply and made her more aware that even when things looked the darkest, there was always a light to show you the way. You just had to be open to it.

And her talk with Pastor Matt a few minutes ago gave her more clarity on her role in the accident. She started to accept the idea that she wasn't really responsible at all.

"Look. I've been thinking about the wood shop.

I—I— It's okay for you and Cameron to use it. I'm sorry I got so upset yesterday. It was just such a surprise to find you in there."

Cam was the one she really needed to tell, but her son had withdrawn again, making it difficult for her to speak to him in the small amount of time they could actually spend together.

"I'm sorry we didn't ask permission." Ethan's gaze darted around the crowded room before he reached over and pulled her out of the way of a group of rambunctious teenagers.

His fingers remained on her arm, creating a crazy sensation again that she was afraid to put an emotion to. The unspoken kiss lingered in the air between them, yet Holly wasn't ready to bring it up. She swallowed the lump in her throat, stepped from his grasp and then wiped her hands against her black slacks.

"Apology accepted." Holly hated to have to say her next words but what choice did she have, especially when Kristen wasn't available? Sure, Cameron was old enough to be left alone for a few hours, but recent history, excluding the time he spent with Ethan, told her another story. She stared at the checkered pattern on the beige carpet before she met his gaze again. Money was finally coming in, but at what cost? She had less time than before, when she actually needed more time to spend with Cameron, but what bothered her more was her son didn't seem to care. After Christmas things would change. "I have to run and do a bid for a potential decorating job in an hour and then stop by to check on Mindy at the store before we leave for the rehearsal.

If you don't mind taking Cam with you, you can use the shed. That way he can finish up whatever he was working on."

Later that afternoon, Ethan watched Cameron nail the last board into place. Fixing Holly's porch after they'd finished up in the woodworking shop reminded him of all the things that still needed to be done at the sanctuary and his house, for that matter. But teaching Holly's son the basics in carpentry and other useful skills could only be beneficial in the long run when he wouldn't be around. Not that Ethan had any plans of leaving Dynamite Creek, but everything eventually came to an end. As much as he'd love to keep Cameron around to help with the sanctuary and see that he followed the right path into adulthood, in another year or two, Cameron's thoughts would be elsewhere and Ethan would need the spot open to help another at-risk kid.

Using the back of his hand, he wiped the sweat from his forehead despite the cold, late-fall air around them. Stepping out the back door with a tray wedged against her hip, Holly looked so young in her faded Northern Arizona University sweatshirt. Too young to be a widow. But then again so was Stephanie Dodd, a young mother and the wife of one of the men killed under his watch. A senseless death. A needless one. If only he'd been doing his job right. Instead of looking for the ambush, he'd been distracted by the stray dog running around on the road. He'd been worried that the convoy would hit it.

No one should have died. He should have realized

the dog had been a decoy. A movie reel of images tumbled around in his mind, the signals from his brain tossing around the contents of his stomach. He'd held Mike Dodd in his arms, his own blood mingling with Mike's as he tried to staunch the flow from his wounds. *I don't want to die. Say a prayer for me. Tell Steph that I love her, little Jacob, too.* His breaths came in gasps as he tried to talk while his life spilled out of him in a stream of red. Blood, dust and chemical smells surrounded them as did the sounds of moans and yelling and gunfire. Light had faded to black and the next thing Ethan knew, he was in a hospital in Germany.

"Are you okay?" Holly handed both Ethan and Cameron a glass of water.

"Fine." Ethan blinked and stared at the scenery around him, so different from the dusty brown of Afghanistan. He drank the entire contents in one try, but nothing could erase the memories that bombarded him now in the daylight hours, too.

Holly's eyebrows rose a fraction before she drew them in close, her breathing changing to a quicker tempo. "Thanks for fixing that for me, guys. Now I don't have to worry about anyone hurting themselves."

"Not a problem." Cameron straightened his shoulders again and looked at Ethan with trust and adulation written in his expression.

The boy misplaced his trust in him. Holly, too, because he was the wrong person. He'd be better off cutting any ties to them while he still had his heart intact. Or most of it, anyway. The kiss in the shed had affected him more than he cared to think about. He still needed to learn from his past mistakes before he could move forward.

And if she was looking for protection, she'd be better off with someone else.

At the store Thursday afternoon, Holly dug through the boxes she'd taken from Abby's place. The musty odor permeated the candy-cane-scented air and dust settled in her nose. She sneezed. Abby had been right. There wasn't much use for the stuff as it was, but she could turn some of it into other things. Maybe. If she could find the inspiration between all her worries.

"What do you think?" She held up some hand-painted wooden ornaments.

"Pretty ghastly. So is this." Kristen pulled out a bag of cheap plastic holly leaves and berries. "Although Figaro might like to play with it. So how's Ethan?"

Holly's heart fluttered at the mention of his name. She didn't dare tell Kristen about the kiss. Or her reaction to it. Her friend would only encourage the romance, if there was one, to continue. Confusion clouded her judgment. It had been so long since she'd been on the starting end of a relationship, she had no idea what the signs were anymore. "Okay, I guess."

"Only just okay? Don't you see each other every day?"

"Not always." At least not anymore, but she kept that information to herself. "Cam is usually waiting for me in the driveway when I pick him up."

He used to walk with Cameron to her car and say hi. What had changed over the past few days? She didn't have to rack her brain for too long. Heat seared her cheeks and her fingers instinctively found her mouth. The kiss must have affected him, too, and he realized as she did that any type of relationship between them was out of the question. Too bad her heart didn't seem to be following her head's lead.

"Regardless of what you think or want, there is nothing between us now, or will be in the future. I'm sure Ethan feels the same. Now, let's think of a way we can use all this stuff."

Holly wished she could wipe the knowing look flittering through Kristen's eyes. "I got it. No more talk about Ethan." She glanced down at the ornament in her hand. "It's interesting to think this stuff is older than we are."

"And hopefully we've aged better."

"Well, some of us have." Laughing, Kristen picked up a box of round, plastic ornaments of various colors.

"Look who's talking." Holly continued to pull things from the box. "I was hoping there would be something in here I could use."

"Yeah, someone was going for the cheesy, retro seventies look. You know, next year when Cam's looking for a costume, you can glue some old garland to a green sweatshirt and attach these and he can go as a vintage Christmas tree."

Holly sank back onto her heels and snapped her fingers. "That gives me an idea. My neighbor threw away some old picture frames and broken footstools. I can glue these onto them and create a unique montage to hang on the wall or place by the fireplace. Individually, these are awful, but put them together…" Holly laid a bunch of the ornaments on the floor and interspersed them with a few sprigs of the plastic holly leaves she'd torn from the stems. "And you've got something stunning."

"And instead of glass and a picture, you could put a mirror inside the frame or figure out how to make a candleholder out of it. Or use it as a door hanging instead of a traditional wreath. You could sell them in the shop to spruce up the remaining merchandise and put them up online. And why stop with Christmas?" Kristen's excitement filled the air.

"You're right. Old costume jewelry, buttons, broken antique dishes. Even old hardware." Holly fingered the silver ball she'd taken from the box before she held it up. Giddiness took hold, probably from lack of sleep. "Look. A tiny disco ball." She stood and pointed her finger in the air before jutting it down across the front of her body, and wiggled her hips. "I think I've just discovered another source of income."

Kristen joined her and jutted her hip out along with her arms. "And I bet you can pick up more real cheap at the thrift stores in Flagstaff as well as some vases. These cheap plastic balls would probably look pretty good wedged inside. And then you could glue some poinsettias or other holiday flowers around the bottom and even to the top."

"Or I can glue the ornaments and stuff to the vases and create one-of-a-kind centerpieces, too." Holly giggled and continued her little jig with the silver ornament dangling above her head.

"Mind if we join you?" Ethan stepped through the door after another man, carrying a notepad and tape measure.

Both Holly's and Kristen's laughter died. Holly shivered from the blast of cold air and dropped her hand with the ornament to her side, her moment of joy escaping like the warm air inside the shop. Ethan had brought another potential tenant inside.

Reality hit. What good would it do to make more stuff to sell when she would have no place to sell it?

A cold wind seeped through Holly's jacket as she sat on the blanket she'd brought to watch the pageant Saturday night at the old Jensen place. She was glad she'd told Cam to wear his long johns underneath his shepherd's outfit and wished she'd done the same. The cold from the ground had a way of penetrating the layers of cloth. She shivered, glad the production was only thirty minutes long. Her fingers curled around what remained of the cup of hot chocolate provided by Kiwanis Club.

Around her, the gathering crowd settled into their lawn chairs or blankets in the dim glow cast by the temporary lighting brought in for the event. To her right, the choir paged through their music; the only other words that would be spoken tonight would be Pastor Matt's. His voice broke the quiet murmur of the crowd, announcing the show would start in five minutes.

She glanced around, only too familiar with the setting. A stable had been set up directly in front of her, its thatched roof of palm fronds stirring in the light breeze. Two false, old, stucco housefronts faced her, creating the intimate feeling of a small town among the dead grass and dormant trees.

The old Jensen place was the perfect spot. Out in the country and away from the town's lights, she could get a real sense of what it was like to live before electricity. Sure, they had temporary lights set up so people wouldn't trip and fall, but the muted lights only cast the glow down. The inky black sky dotted with millions of stars and planets winked back at her in the frosty air.

"Mind if I join you?" Ethan held up another blanket and smiled down at her tentatively.

"You're here?"

"I wouldn't miss Cameron's acting debut for anything. I even told him a few things about keeping the goats in line."

"Good things, I hope," Holly teased lightly.

Ethan feigned innocence and put his hand to his chest. "Of course."

That he would come and watch Cam's performance filled her with gladness. It would mean so much to her son. It meant a lot to her, even though she tried to deny that her heartbeat had accelerated and that she had someone to share the moment with. Glancing around, she realized there wasn't any other room near the front. She moved to the corner of her blanket, well aware that it would be a snug fit for both of them. Since there was no room for his blanket on the ground, Holly had a different use for it in mind as another small gust of wind rattled the remaining leaves on the trees surrounding the natural amphitheater. She patted the spot next to her. "Um, sure. Have a seat."

"In a second." After he dropped the blanket down and strode away, Holly pulled the wool over her lap before Ethan returned a few moments later with two cups pinched between his fingers. "I haven't had hot chocolate in years. Here's another one for you." He settled down next to her, still a little too close for her comfort.

"Thanks. I'm sure Cam will be glad you made it."

"How about you?" When he gazed into her eyes, all thought fled her mind and all the breath from her lungs. It had been a week since the kiss in the shed, yet only hours since she'd last thought of him. His name was constantly in Cam's vocabulary, his image not too buried in her memory, and his kiss still lingered on her lips.

"No comment. It got colder than I thought it would tonight." Her voice came out a whisper and she drank some hot chocolate to occupy herself. The warm liquid coated her tongue and warmed her from the inside as Ethan's gaze did from the outside.

Ethan shifted a bit closer to her as if trying to block out the slight breeze. "What time did you get here?"

"Five o'clock."

"Two hours ago? You didn't just drop Cameron off?"

"It seemed silly to drive home just to turn around and come back. I did get some reading done while I sat in my car until people started showing up."

"You're freezing. Here." He pulled the blanket from her lap, draped it over her shoulders and wrapped her up.

"Thanks." She snuggled into the blue wool, which felt like a warm embrace and smelled like him. For someone who wasn't interested in starting a new relationship, she sure had a funny perspective on things. Maybe? Her gaze swept across his maimed hand. He'd been injured and could have been killed during his tour of duty. It didn't matter, though, that his time of service was done now. She knew only too well how a life could change with a simple drive to a Chamber of Commerce function on a cold, snowy night.

A few moments of silence ensued, as if he was testing out a new topic before he spoke. "Looked like you were having fun the other day."

Embarrassment flushed her skin as she thought about her impromptu dance with Kristen. "I was a bit excited about some possibilities we discovered in that box of old Christmas stuff from the Bancroft Bed & Breakfast. If all goes well, I've just found another stream of revenue."

"So did I."

Those three simple words and his serious expression told her more than if he shouted it from the hill behind the makeshift stable.

"You found a new tenant for the store." She knew she should be happy for him, but she couldn't muster anything up. Breathing became a chore and her vision clouded.

"Yes. I'm sorry."

"You have nothing to be sorry for. That's business." Yet she couldn't keep the emotion from tainting her voice.

The electronic bong sounded, signaling the start of the pageant, but some of the sparkle was gone. All along she knew that she'd have to close the store, but knowing without a doubt it was a reality gripped her in a viselike hold. The death of a dream. Jared's dream. But having an end date also filled her with relief.

She could quit pretending, but she'd also have to put Jared's memory to rest, too.

Disloyalty stabbed at her and made her shiver again as the actors playing the townspeople took their places, some hanging laundry, a few tending to the fire, while others gathered around in conversation.

"You forgot gloves, didn't you?" Ethan whispered in her ear.

"It was enough just getting here on time. Cam wasn't exactly excited about coming."

"Yeah, well, to be honest, I wasn't too happy about doing it myself. It kind of ruins the reputation in school."

"Thanks for not sharing *that* part with Cam."

"You're welcome. Like I told him, it's a rite of passage." He picked up her free hand and held it between his as if trying to warm it but he never let go. It felt wrong and right to be sitting there holding his hand. Wrong because it might give people and Cameron the wrong impression if someone saw them, but just this moment right, because she felt as if she had someone she could lean on, depend on and help her through each day.

Mary, riding a donkey led by Joseph, strolled onto the scene. "Mary's my second cousin Deena's daughter, Lilly," Ethan said.

"So you had another reason for coming tonight. Why aren't you sitting with your family?" Holly whispered harshly so as not to disturb the performance for those around her. She knew he'd had to have had more family here than just his mother.

"Because there are too many of them and I prefer the view from over here much better." The warmth of his breath in her ear created havoc with her insides. Her friend was right. Ethan did like her. The kiss confirmed it, too. For both of them. It would only take a small movement of her head to connect with his lips and allow herself to feel again and bask under the attention.

No! Her back straightened and she focused on the scene playing out in front of her. Mary and Joseph had been turned away at the inn and the owner was showing them the stable.

The spotlight dimmed, and a soft tenor voice filled the air. Holly allowed the music to swirl around her. She needed to focus on the play and not the man beside her.

"Look. There's Cam. The one in the blue with the off-white headpiece." Holly motioned her head toward the three boys walking up the trail with a sheep and two goats. After arriving at the predetermined spot, her son stretched his fingers toward the fire one of the older boys had started in the fire pit. Beside him a goat that kept trying to eat the rope was tied to his arm.

The audience twittered at the antics of Cameron trying to keep the goat from eating his costume while the chorus continued with another a capella carol.

Suddenly, from behind the hill, a spotlight beamed upon a teenage girl. In the darkness, she looked as if she were floating in the air, but Holly knew that she simply stood on a small platform on top. Still, the effect transported her back in time and filled her with wonderment, peace and hope.

"Do not be afraid. Behold, I bring tidings of great joy." Pastor Matt's voice floated out over the loudspeakers.

The words held double meaning for Holly.

A few heartbeats later, Mary revealed this year's baby Jesus. A wail ensued and the audience sighed.

"That part always gets to me." Holly gripped Ethan's hand tighter and leaned into him, absorbing his warmth and the feeling of protection. Moisture coated her eyes.

Maybe because it represented God's love for them that he gave His only son. Or maybe that it represented a new beginning.

Chapter Ten

"Where are we going?" Cameron's voice filled the interior of Ethan's SUV.

The boy apparently didn't like to get up early on the weekends, especially after his performance last night and the ice cream that followed. Ethan smiled to himself. The day had dawned bright and sunny, but that was expected to change later in the afternoon when another storm moved through right on the heels of the four inches they received last night. Now that the church service was over, it was the perfect day to chop down a Christmas tree. Or two. Or four.

"You'll see." He smiled at Holly, who returned it readily. Something had changed between them yesterday, and he liked it. She seemed a bit more relaxed, more settled, even though he'd admitted he'd found a new tenant for the shop. Guilt consumed him. He had no choice, though. He needed the rent money to help him pay his own bills while the sanctuary got off the ground.

"Cam's not a morning person."

"I've already figured that out. He'll grow out of it. Eventually." Just like the boy would grow out of his troubles. He was at a tough age. For now, Ethan was glad he was there to help guide him in the right direction.

"Are we going to the sanctuary?" Cameron's excited voice popped up from the backseat. "Are you almost done, Mr. P.? When are you going to move the dogs?"

"Yes, we are. We made a lot of headway this past week. If all goes well, we'll be in by Christmas."

"But how will I be able to get out here after school?"

Ethan didn't have an answer. "We'll worry about that when the time comes."

The snow hit Holly on the back of her head. She turned just in time to see another snowball flying through the air. "Hey!"

Both her son and Ethan had reloaded behind the quick barrier they'd built in the dog run. She ducked behind a pine tree and scooped up a handful of fresh snow. Heavy and moist, the snow was perfect for packing. Forming it into a perfect ball, she waited for one of the two to expose themselves. She didn't have to wait long. She hurled the ball and it hit Ethan square in the chest.

"Good shot."

"My mom was captain of the softball team. She was an all-star pitcher. I'm switching sides." Cam lunged from behind the snowbank and headed toward her. But not before Holly lobbed another perfect pitch and hit her son in the chest.

"Mom."

"Hey, all's fair in love and war." Yet she gave him the opportunity to hide behind the pine tree with her and lob a few more snowballs at Ethan until he cried uncle.

"Wow, I can't believe you really got beaten by a girl." His laughter filled the air as Cam ran from behind the tree, plopped onto his back into the fresh snow and began to move his arms and legs. A smile creased her lips. Holly hadn't seen her son this happy in a long time, and she owed it all to Ethan.

"Yeah, well, until you switched sides, you were, too." Holly helped Ethan dust the snow from his sleeve, but his amused expression told her he didn't mind. It hadn't really been a fair fight, but Ethan didn't seem to care.

"You are a good shot." The corners of his eyes crinkled as he squinted from the glare of the sun. "Is there anything else I should know about you?"

"I can't sing, I love sushi and I placed fifth in the state spelling bee in eighth grade." Feeling a bit childish herself, Holly let her reserve down and jumped in the snow next to her son. Cold bit her neck as she moved her arms and legs in a wide sweeping motion.

"A brainy athlete. That's an oxymoron if I ever heard one."

"Hey, I resent that." She grabbed a handful of snow and threw it up at him.

"What word did you place with?"

"*Metamorphosis. M-e-t-a-m-o-r-p-h-o-s-i-s. Meta-*

morphosis." She grinned. "Okay, smarty-pants, do you know what that even means?"

Ethan sank down beside her. "Of course. It's a transformation of one thing into another. Like a caterpillar into a butterfly."

A strange feeling passed through her. It was as if after two years, she was starting to break free of her shell and stretch her wings. In the Bible, it was the symbol for the Resurrection. Was she going through her own sort of change? She shook off the feeling. "But can *you* spell it?"

"I'm not even going to try. What word did you miss?"

"*Parliament.* I forgot the second *a.* But enough about that. Let's build a snowman. You make the base. I'll make the middle, and you make the head, Cam." Holly jumped to her feet. With the wet, heavy snow, they should be able to build a monstrous one that would take days or weeks to melt if the cold snap held up.

"You're on." Ethan pushed himself from the snow and formed another snowball. He gazed at her playfully and tossed it in the air.

"Don't even think about it," Holly warned as she molded her own ball. "I went easy on you last time."

Ethan laughed and started rolling the snowball around to form a bigger one.

Once assembled, the three balls of snow needed to be adorned. Holly took her hat from her head and placed it on top. Cam trudged to the edge where the woods met the snowdrift and broke off a few dead branches from a tree.

"Too bad we don't have a carrot." Ethan pulled out a few pennies from his pocket and placed them in as eyes and a nose. Then he removed his scarf and wrapped it around the snowman's neck.

"Now all we need is a mouth. If I had my purse, I probably could have found something in there to use." Holly shrugged. "But it seemed ridiculous to bring it out here."

"Why would you? We're going to have our hands full with the next activity. Cameron, there should be some rocks around here somewhere. Check the areas where the snowballs lifted the snow. If you can't find anything, then there should be some pinecones by the pine tree near where you got the arms."

"I'm on it." Cameron dashed away, a jumble of arms and legs. The corners of her mouth turned up. When he grew into his adult body, he'd tower over her, thanks to the Stanwyck side of his DNA.

After scooping up some snow, Ethan filled in an uneven spot on the snowman's trunk. "He's a good kid. He'll be okay."

"I know he will. Thanks for all your help." Holly readjusted the scarf around the snowman's neck. "Aren't you cold?"

"Aren't you? Heat escapes from your head."

"It does, but I'm used to this weather. You're not." Her fingers played with the scarf's dark fringe. Even though she couldn't feel the fabric through her gloves, she could imagine the rough wool texture against her skin. And if she dared think hard enough, she could almost feel Ethan's five-o'clock shadow against her palms, his lips caressing hers again. This time she wasn't sure if she would break it off so quickly.

Disloyalty stabbed at her heart.

"I'll be fine, but if it makes you feel better, we can come retrieve our stuff on the way back to the house." Ethan must have sensed her discomfort. "Are you okay?"

"I'm fine. Thanks for bringing us out here. We haven't had this much fun since—" Holly stopped short. The memories of Jared and their last winter together as a family surfaced. They'd gone sledding, had their own snowball fights and built a snowman, just days before the accident.

And in the blink of an eye—or tires against black ice—everything had changed.

Ethan gathered her in his arms and rocked her gently. The light kiss on the top of her head brought back more thoughts about her late husband. Letting go was hard when everything around her reminded her of what she'd lost.

But Kristen was right. She had to. Today brought that to the forefront. Somehow, somewhere feelings had surfaced for Ethan regardless of her attempts to close off her heart. The realization stung. She had to let go and move on. Living in the past wasn't healthy, but as Pastor Matt pointed out, she wasn't the only one who needed to realize that.

Shrugging out of his arms, Holly stepped away into some sort of hole buried by the snow. Her arms flailed as she tried to regain her equilibrium and footing. Not happening. She fell backward onto her bottom, the snow quickly finding its way under her jacket and sweater. She shivered, but it was more from Ethan's unguarded expression than from the cold.

"Are you okay?" He held out his hand.

"Just fine." But she knew her heart would never be the same.

Ethan released Holly's hand when he heard Cameron approach. Her son might misconstrue the gesture, especially after their conversation on Thanksgiving. Cameron wanted another dad and someone to make his mom happy, make her laugh again.

Ethan wasn't the guy to do that. People had counted on him before, depended on him for their lives, and he'd let them and their families down. But holding Holly in comfort had been the most natural thing in the world. Ethan took another step to the side, stooped down and packed on more snow to another uneven spot on the base of the snowman.

She glanced at him from underneath her lashes as if she understood, before her attention turned to her son. "What did you find, Cam?"

He held out his hands. "Pinecones. They were bigger than the rocks."

"Pinecones it is, then." Ethan stood and dusted the snow from his gloves. "Since you retrieved them, you may have the honors."

Once the snowman was complete, Ethan grabbed the saw he'd dropped by the edge of the meadow before the snowball fight. "Come on, our ultimate destination is just a bit farther."

They walked in a companionable silence through the

woods. Ethan loved the stillness of the day, the crisp air filling his lungs, the muffled footsteps on the fresh snow. An occasional bird cawed, and a few rabbits scattered when they wandered too close. Not wanting to disturb the peace surrounding them, he put a finger to his lips. "If we're real quiet, we may see a deer or two."

"Really? That would be cool," Cameron whispered back.

Too bad the deer chose not to cooperate. A few minutes later, they stepped into what should have been another meadow, but this one was filled with pine trees of various sizes.

Holly gasped beside him. "Wow. It's beautiful."

"Cool." Cameron ran into the stand of trees.

"Cam—"

"Let him go. He'll be okay." Holly's wide-eyed wonder and look of pure enjoyment of his special retreat pleased him. He knew the feeling. He'd been nine when his dad first brought him out here—a family ritual that took place at that special age. Eyes wide, mouth open, he'd run through the trees, arms outstretched, touching the spiny needles, laughing. They'd played hide-and-seek before deciding the right ones to cut down. His smile turned upside down.

It was also their last Christmas together. His dad had been dead for almost twenty-five years now, and Ethan still missed him. Bringing company out here with him might have been a mistake. He identified with Holly's son and knew what Cameron faced in the future.

While there was nothing Ethan could do to bring Jared back, he could make things better for Cameron, just like his old neighbor did for him. He glanced up. *Thank you, Lord, for bringing me into Cameron's life right now and helping him through this.*

Other images superimposed themselves in his mind's eye. He clenched his fists, realizing there was nothing he could do to bring those people back, either.

But he wasn't responsible for his father's death.

"Are you okay?" Holly placed a hand on his arm and knitted her eyebrows. His muscles bunched underneath her touch. "You have that faraway look in your eyes."

"Fine." He blinked. "I was just thinking about my first time here."

"Really? Then it's not a pleasant one. You're tense. If it's that painful, we can leave, but I have a feeling this has nothing to do with here but someplace far away. Afghanistan is behind you now." She knew him well, but not well enough.

"You don't understand. It will never be behind me."

"Only if you want it to be that way." Her voice softened and her gloved fingers ran up and down his arm. "You weren't the one who planted the bomb." He knew she was trying to help, but her words had the opposite effect.

"No, but I should have seen the signs. I should have recognized that they knew my weakness for dogs." Anger boiled inside him, begging for release. He should have brought an ax, but he doubted that the four trees he needed to cut down would be enough to release him from the tension.

"You weren't the only one there. There were others

who could have recognized them, too. What about the driver?" Her words struck a blow.

"But it was my job."

"And given the circumstances, I'm sure you did your best. Things happen. Just like the night Jared died." Holly's face resembled the snow around them. "I know what you're going through."

His anger dissipated into the air as he gathered her in his arms and held her close, inhaling her floral fragrance. He needed to gain control over his emotions and deal with what happened. Everyone told him it would take time. That the nightmares would cease; that he would recover emotionally as he did physically. Maybe Holly could help him. Or maybe this was something he had to do on his own.

But until he did, there could be nothing between him and Holly, despite his growing love for her. It wouldn't be fair to her or her son. He broke away moments before Cameron rejoined them.

"Look what I found." Giving them a strange look, Cameron held out his hands. Five small pinecones dotted his gray gloves. "I want to exchange these for the ones I put on the snowman. These are better." He handed them to Holly. "Here. Please hold them. This place is so cool. Why are the trees all in rows?"

"A long time ago, my great-grandfather decided to plant some pines right after he built the house and barn so we'd always have a supply of fresh Christmas trees. Once spring hits, I'll be planting a few more to replace the ones we take today."

"Can I help? How many are we going to chop down?"

"Well, let's see. I need one, so does my cousin Meredith, and my mom needs one. Am I missing anyone?"

"We need a tree, right, Mom?" Cam rubbed his hands together and tilted his head forward. His eyes widened in expectation.

Holly thought about the fake tree in the garage. They were easier to handle, but nothing compared to the real thing, especially the smell. Candle companies only wished they could bottle the scent.

"I believe we do. Which one do you think would be the perfect one?"

"Let me look."

As they tramped through the trees, searching for the perfect ones, birds chirped, and the sound of snow underfoot met her ears. Holly inhaled the earthy scent, unique to the area after a snowfall, mingled with that of pine.

Her mood lightened a bit, but some of the thrill had disappeared. Their guilt was the white elephant in the room that no one wanted to talk about. They both wore it like jackets that couldn't be shed.

Mindless of the slight tension between the adults, Cameron led them to an eight-foot-tall pine. "This one right over here."

"Are you sure? It might be too tall." Ethan looked at her. "What height is your ceiling?"

"Ten feet."

"This one it is, then."

Holly's heart filled with misgivings and joy at the sight of the two heads bowed together as Ethan showed Cameron how to hold the saw and cut the tree at the base. Cameron had blossomed over the weeks that Ethan had been working with him. He was turning back into the boy she remembered. But it should have been his father out here with him, and Holly had taken that away from him.

She let out a slow breath and digested Pastor Matt's words.

She couldn't control the weather that night or the patch of ice, and she'd done everything possible to avoid the collision. There was nothing more she could have done. A few snowflakes drifted by her visions as she glanced up past the dark, gray, snow-laden clouds, searching for an answer. Searching for God.

"There. It's up." Ethan dusted his hands against his jeans and stepped back. "Good job, Cameron. You've just put up your first live Christmas tree."

"Sweet." Her son beamed with pride. "Look, Mom."

"Awesome job. This calls for some hot chocolate." Holly carried the tray with three cups into the living room, the scent of chocolate mingling with the pine. Her heart rate changed when her fingers touched Ethan's as he accepted his cup. She tried to shake off the sensation that reminded her of the kiss in the shed. She'd been in a vulnerable position then and still was, with her emotions so close to the surface in recent weeks, and they were all due to the man fluffing up the branches of the pine tree.

"Thanks." Cameron grabbed his cup and settled down on the area rug covering the hardwood floor. Sighing, he leaned back on the plush sofa and crossed his legs in front of him before he took a sip. "Okay, the hard part's done. Don't we have to check on the dogs, Mr. P.?"

"Oh, no you don't. Don't get too comfortable. Now the real fun begins." Holly snapped her fingers and pointed at her son. "You don't get off that easily. Decorating is part of the deal. It's my favorite part. It's yours, too, remember?" Good thing, too, because she was doing a lot of that lately. Not that she didn't appreciate the extra money coming in; she did. Her gaze rose to the ceiling, and she managed to send up a silent prayer of thanks. Things were starting to get better. She had another job tomorrow for Mrs. Baker, another member of the congregation, to put up her tabletop tree and a few other decorations.

"Mooom."

"Don't Mom me. You know Figaro's only good for swatting the ornaments off the bottom of the tree. The lights go first, then the garland, then the ornaments and finally the star. Got it?"

"Got it." Her son sulked but pushed himself off the floor.

Holly wanted to wipe the amused grin from Ethan's face. "You're not off the hook, either, mister. Everyone under this roof is expected to help."

Ethan held up his hands in mock surrender. "Looks like we're stuck, Cameron. The boss has spoken."

"And don't forget it." Holly laughed, took a sip of her hot chocolate and sat back on her heels. The laughter felt good. The foreign sound had appeared at the most unlikely times in the past few weeks, and she owed it to one man.

Ethan caught her son's attention. "Your job for the next few weeks, besides the sanctuary, is going to be making sure there's water in the base every day. A dry Christmas tree could cause a fire."

"Got it."

Holly dug into the box marked Lights and pulled out a strand of multicolored ones. Before she could stand, Cameron walked over and held out his hand. "Here, let me have those. Let's put up the lights, Mr. P."

Reluctantly, Holly handed them over. Despite her earlier words about Ethan helping, somehow when she envisioned putting up the decorations a few weeks ago, it was her and Cameron doing the work together. The idea that she'd been pushed aside hurt, yet Cam's smile and willingness to help couldn't be overlooked.

"Come on, Holly. You're not going to let the men do all the work, now, are you?" Ethan held out his hand and pulled her to her feet.

"Of course not." But maybe she should, since her reaction to him seemed to grow stronger with each passing heartbeat.

"You're the decorator. Where should the lights go?"

"On the tree, of course, although the rest of these are all tangled. I have an idea. Cam, we need some help here."

"What?" Her son joined them at the box.

"We need to get these organized so it's easier to get them on the tree. Here." She handed a ball of tangled lights to her son. "Now, Ethan, you just stay right there and hold this." She found the plug and handed it to him, a smile on her lips. "Okay, now, as we unravel the lights, Ethan is going to be our human holder. Ethan, all you have to do is turn slowly so we can wrap them around you."

Cameron's laughter joined hers. "Cool idea, Mom."

A few minutes later, the first strand had been untangled and wrapped around Ethan's middle.

"I have another idea." Excitement and humor filled Cam's voice as he plugged in the extension cord and ran back to Ethan. "I'm gonna light you up."

The lights cast a multicolored glow on Ethan. Holly ran back to another box labeled Decorations and pulled out a hat. She flipped on the switch and placed the singing Christmas tree on his head. The tree wiggled around as the music filled the air while she and Cameron lifted their arms up and began to dance around Ethan, singing along with the song. Holly's laughter filled the air again. When had she lost the ability to have fun? The thought sobered her when she realized that only one person was responsible for how she felt.

And she suddenly found herself alone with him when Cam left the room to run upstairs to get his camera.

Holly stopped dancing and stood in front of Ethan, close enough to take in the clean scent of the outdoors underneath the fragrance of the tree. His eyes clouded with an emotion she hadn't seen for a while and her breath stalled.

Ethan placed his hand under her chin, forcing her to stare into his compassionate eyes. The scent of peppermint collided with the freshness of pine and pulled her to him. Holly wrapped her arms around his neck, needing to feel his warmth, his protectiveness, his trust. She claimed his lips. It was meant to be a light kiss, the kind between friends, but deepened into something more. Ethan made her feel alive again, and if she had to admit it, she enjoyed the kiss way more than the first time. Holly couldn't deny it any longer. She'd fallen completely in love with him.

Hearing Cameron tread on the stairs, she blinked to end the connection. Before taking a step backward, she removed the hat and tossed it toward the coffee table.

"Walk over to the tree, and as soon as Cam takes your picture, we'll transfer the lights."

Once all the lights were on and the garland in place, Holly pulled out a pewter Noah's Ark scene and motioned for her son. "Cam, here's your first ornament. And here's the ornament you made in Mrs. Beasley's kindergarten class." Holly held up the round wreath made out of construction paper with uncooked macaroni pasta glued to the outside and Cam's picture inside the circle.

Cameron blushed. "Mom."

"What? It's cute. Maybe we should make more ornaments this year."

"No way!" Her son retreated behind the tree with a bunch of ornaments in his hand. "Hey, aren't you going to help, Mr. P.?"

Ethan settled back in the armchair and put his hands behind his head. "No. I helped with the hard stuff and need a break. This is between you and your mom. Besides, I've got my own tree to decorate, and you can help with that tomorrow after your homework and chores."

The tree filled up quickly with ornaments.

"And now for the finishing touch." Holly handed her son the tree topper.

Cameron scampered up the old, rickety wood ladder to place the star on the top.

The rung broke beneath his left foot. Cameron tried to regain his balance, his arms flailing out, grasping for something to latch on to. He swayed, tilted and fell backward.

Cries escaped both Holly's and Cameron's lips.

Bile hit the back of Ethan's throat and adrenaline burned in his veins. But just like before, he was powerless to stop the chain reaction of events. He stood and moved forward, but it wasn't quick enough. As if in slow motion, Ethan watched Cameron hit the floor with a thud and lie next to the ladder.

Please, Lord, don't let him be hurt.

"Cameron! Sweetie, are you okay?" Holly dropped to her knees, her eyes wide and all the blood drained from her face when she saw the unnatural bulge near his wrist. With a shaky hand, she pushed the hair from his face. "Everything's going to be okay."

Her gaze met his, looking for confirmation. Ethan knelt down, tasting the fear. "Don't move, Cameron. Let me see what we're dealing with."

The boy nodded, pain creasing the skin around his eyes. His gaze scanned the floor and Cameron's arm. No blood or exposed bone, just a bump where the bone had snapped from the pressure. At least he was dealing with a simple fracture. "You've broken your arm. Does anything else hurt?"

This time Cameron shook his head.

Ethan's fingers probed up and down Cameron's other arm and legs. "Can you wiggle your fingers and toes?"

The boy did as instructed. Good. Nothing else appeared to be broken, but he needed immediate medical attention.

"That's great, but don't move again." Ethan took control of the situation. "Holly, after you get a bag of ice, I'll go get my first-aid kit from the SUV. I have something to make a sling, which will hold his arm in place until we can get him to the E.R."

Snow accumulating on the roads, along with encroaching darkness, made driving treacherous. In the backseat, Holly gripped the strap of her seat belt with one hand and held on tightly to Cam as Ethan's headlights barely made a dent in the whiteness swirling around them. Holly kept talking to a minimum, wanting Ethan to give his full attention to driving. Still, she could tell Ethan fought to maintain control, given the whiteness of the knuckles on his left hand as he gripped the steering wheel.

Another incident rose to the forefront, except it was Holly driving and fighting the conditions because Jared had had a headache. Her hands clenched as the memories paralyzed her. She fought to push them back where they belonged. That time was over and done. This was here and now. Everything would be okay. It had to be.

"Stop it, Mom. You're hurting me even more," Cam whispered from the middle seat.

"Sorry." Holly quit squeezing so hard and worried her bottom lip as the snow consumed everything around them.

Ethan's wheels lost traction on the pavement when he attempted to stop at a stop sign. Nausea roiled in her stomach as the SUV fishtailed but managed to stop just shy of the intersection.

At this rate, it would take them at least fifteen minutes to get to the hospital, but going any faster would be unsafe. *Please, Lord, keep us safe. Let us get to the hospital in one piece.* Repeating the prayer over and over, she clutched the gold cross she'd pulled from her jewelry box.

It felt good to be right with the Lord.

"Hang on!"

Holly felt the wheels spin as Ethan tried to gain traction and move through the intersection. Her gaze froze on the red car speeding toward them from the driver's side. Ethan tried to move the SUV forward, but he wasn't fast enough and the other car blew the stop sign and clipped the back of his vehicle.

Holly wrapped her arms around Cam's shoulders, squeezed her eyes shut and held on tightly as the SUV spun on the ice and snow. Time suspended as she waited for the vehicle to stop, the thud of metal against metal still reverberating in her ears. She grew dizzy and her stomach dropped to the floor as she braced for impact. Another thud jolted them inside the vehicle, and then muffled silence. Beside her, Cam whimpered in pain.

Holly lifted her head, opened her eyes and found Cam staring back at her. She gave him a quick once-over. He was okay. She kissed the top of his head and then looked beyond him. Glass fragments littered the empty seat behind Ethan's and cold wind and snow blew in through the shattered windows. They'd jumped the curb and were wedged up against a brick building, the driver's side caved in from the impact. Her heart stalled when she spied Ethan slumped over the steering wheel.

"Ethan!" There was no movement in the front seat. No! Not again. *Please, Lord. Not again.*

"Stay where you are, Cam." It took two attempts for Holly to free herself from her seat belt so she could scramble out the undamaged door. The cold wind bit at her nose and exposed skin as she opened the door and forced her way into the front passenger seat.

"Is he okay, Mom?"

"I don't know, Cam. I don't know." *Please, Lord, let him be okay.* Holly managed to wedge her hands between Ethan and the steering wheel and maneuver him back so he leaned against the seat. She cradled Ethan's head between her hands. Blood poured from the open cut on his scalp, but he didn't regain consciousness. "Ethan. Please. Wake up."

Tears burned her eyes. She loved him. There was definitely no denying it now.

Her fingers shook violently as she reached back for her purse and dumped the contents onto the seat, searching for her phone to call for help.

Chapter Eleven

Sitting in the front seat of the ambulance, Holly dug her fingernails into her palms and chewed her bottom lip, the paramedic beside her concentrating on driving. She closed her eyes, unable to look at the bleak scenery. She shivered. The scene replaying in her head wasn't any better than staring at the blizzard outside. Over and over the images replayed in her mind and the jarring sensation of spinning out of control consumed her.

There was nothing she could have done. Nothing Ethan could have done.

"We're almost there, Mrs. Stanwyck."

Holly opened her eyes. Amid the swirl of white, Dynamite Creek Memorial stood out in red letters against the tan brick building as they turned into the parking lot. She swallowed and her breathing came in short, erratic bursts when they pulled up to the E.R. entrance. She hadn't been here since the first accident.

Moments later, she hurried across the pavement, her steps keeping tempo with her heartbeat as she followed behind the paramedics pushing the stretcher carrying Ethan and the man in dark green scrubs pushing Cameron in the wheelchair. The door snicked open and she stepped inside the foyer; the odor of antiseptic filled her nostrils. Another wave of nausea hit her.

A woman looked up from her clipboard. "Please take Cameron Stanwyck to Room 1 and Ethan Pellegrino to Room 7."

Hesitation racked her as Holly glanced between her son and a now-conscious Ethan. She needed to be there for both of them, but how could she be in two rooms at once? Ethan refused to meet her gaze, though, and her heart cried out as he was wheeled away in the opposite direction. He had shut her out.

Holly followed Cameron.

"Is he allergic to anything?" the nurse asked as she transferred Cam to the hospital bed.

"No. No allergies that I'm aware of." Still running on adrenaline and fear, Holly moved to Cam's side and pushed the hair off his forehead. She caught her lip between her teeth again. How small and fragile he looked, seemingly lost among the white sheets in the adult-size hospital bed. And scared.

"I'm going to give him some morphine for the pain. Is that okay?"

"Fine." Wanting to give the nurse some space, Holly sank down in the chair opposite the bed. Now that they were at the hospital, she acknowledged the pounding behind her eyelids and that her stomach had twisted into knots until she thought she was going to taste what remained of her lunch.

How was Ethan doing? Was his head wound serious? Did he suffer any other injuries? She clenched her hands and bit down hard enough to taste blood, staring at the heart-monitoring machine when the nurse inserted the IV for a morphine drip into Cameron's left arm.

"Hi." An older man in a white lab coat entered the room. "I'm Doctor Hill. Let's see what we have here." He went straight to the bed and examined Cam's arm. "Yep, I'd say it's broken. Now, how did you happen to do this?"

After listening to the story, he pulled a small flashlight from his pocket and looked into Cameron's eyes. "Good. No concussion. We're going to take a few X-rays, young man, and then I'm going to set it. Then you can get out of here when the snow lets up, but no roughhousing for a while."

A few moments later, another staff member came in. Holly held the hand on Cam's unbroken arm as they wheeled the bed into another room.

"Okay, Mom, you're going to need to stand behind that wall with the window while I'm taking the pictures." The woman in the dark blue scrubs motioned to her left.

"Cam, I need to go check on Ethan." Holly squeezed her son's hand. She didn't want to leave her son, yet she had to know how badly Ethan was hurt. "Will you be okay?"

Cam nodded.

"Are you sure?"

"Mom."

"I'll be right back, then." She kissed Cam on the forehead and then retreated from the room.

Holly's heart fluttered as she made short work of the distance between the rooms. There was nothing she could do for her son right now, and she needed to know that Ethan was going to be okay. He'd taken the brunt force of the crash and looked as if he'd lost a fair amount of blood. She glanced down at the dark red drops staining the sleeve of her jacket. Ethan's blood. Another sob wedged its way into her throat. He had to be okay. She couldn't lose him, too.

"Hi." Holly knocked as she peeked into Ethan's room. Aside from the large bandage covering the wound on his forehead and being slightly pale, he looked good. Better than good. He was alive. "How are you feeling?"

"Like I got hit by a brick building."

"Funny. Very funny. Glad to see you didn't lose your sense of humor." Holly wedged her hands onto her hips and strode to the bed. "You gave us quite a scare back there, mister."

"How's Cameron's arm?"

"They're taking X-rays right now and then the doctor is going to set it. What about you?"

He stared at a spot behind her shoulder. "So far just the cut, but they're going to keep me here for a few more hours to do more tests."

Holly's stomach flip-flopped again. Was there something going on that he wasn't telling her about? She searched his self-loathing expression. "Quit blaming yourself, Ethan. You kept us as safe as you could. The accident wasn't your fault. In fact, it could have been a lot worse. What if the other driver had T-boned us?"

"It doesn't matter. I failed in my duty." His gaze shifted back to hers, yet she knew he didn't see her but the horrific scene from all those months ago that replayed in his mind. Anguish and pain distorted the features that she'd come to love.

"No, you didn't." Holly refused to back down. "This isn't your fault." She reached out and touched him, ran her palms across his face. The day's growth on his jawline was rough yet welcoming as she pressed her lips against his, trying to push away their nightmares.

He turned his head. "Allow me some dignity, Holly. This was all my fault. I can't keep anyone safe. Tell Cameron I can't have him out at the sanctuary anymore. You, either."

"Here, take this. How're you feeling?" Holly handed Cam the painkiller and a glass of water later that night. She sat down on the side of the bed and pushed away his bangs again.

"My arm hurts."

"Well, that's only to be expected. The painkiller from the hospital is starting to wear off, but what I just gave you should kick in soon."

"I'm sorry, Mom." Cam sat up in bed and hugged her as best he could with his good arm. Emotion laced his voice. "I was only trying to be helpful. If I hadn't fallen, I wouldn't have broken my arm and then we wouldn't have had to go to the hospital and Mr. P. would be okay."

"Of course you were trying to be helpful, sweetie." The endearment slipped out, but Cameron didn't seem to mind, even though he'd been embarrassed lately when she showed him any affection. She held him close and rested her cheek on the top of his head. "Ethan is going to be okay. He simply had a cut on his forehead and they were keeping him for a bit to make sure there was nothing else wrong."

"But if I hadn't broken my arm—"

"Shh. It was an accident. It could have happened anytime, anywhere. Accidents happen."

Accidents happen.

There was nothing Ethan could have done to prevent what happened today, just as she realized there was nothing she could have done two years earlier. Too bad Ethan didn't believe that. He was still consumed by a past that refused to release its grip.

No longer would she allow her past to continue to rule her life. She'd had a taste of happiness again and so had Cam. She was also sure that Ethan had felt it, too. Ethan. His image rose in her mind's eye. The caring and compassionate man had become a part of both her and Cam's lives. Maybe she could help him. If he'd let her. Which wasn't going to happen in the immediate future.

Giving her son one last gentle squeeze, she held him away from her and steadied herself for her next words. "But just like you, Ethan is having a hard time with what happened tonight. He doesn't want you out at the sanctuary anymore."

"Just until my permanent cast is on, right?"

How could she explain this when she didn't really understand the reasons herself? "No. You won't be going back at all. It's what he wants and we have to respect his wishes." She leaned down and kissed him on the forehead, hating to have to be the one to break the bad news to her son. "Good night."

Cam shrugged out of her grasp and hugged the covers to his chest, his expression laced with pain, disappointment and denial.

She left Cameron's room and lifted her gaze heavenward, staring at the ceiling before closing her eyes and breathing deeply. *I get it now, Lord. I understand. You give and You take away. Let go.* She had a lot of letting go to do. God knew what He was doing. By shutting the window, He was opening a door for her. She had to be ready to accept the new phase in her life by shedding the past and allowing a future into her heart. Pastor Matt was right. She had enough room in her heart to love a lot of people, Ethan included.

Her memories spun back to earlier that day when they cut down the Christmas trees, and she smiled.

Metamorphosis.

That was what she needed. In her life with Jared she'd been a caterpillar. When he'd died, she'd formed a cocoon and hid from the world. Now she was ready to break free from the chrysalis and start over as a new person.

Peace settled across her shoulders. She knew what she had to do. She didn't know what the future held for her, but she had to be ready to grasp it when it came.

* * *

"Cam?" Holly knocked on her son's door at six o'clock. He should be up by now. "Wake up. How are you feeling? You should be going to school in just over an hour."

No sound came from behind the door. Her stomach muscles clenched, upsetting the cup of coffee and yogurt she'd taken at breakfast.

"Cam? Come on, honey, it's time to wake up." She turned the handle, stepped across the threshold and flipped on the light switch.

Her son's bed was empty.

And not just empty; it looked as if Cam hadn't even tossed and turned in it last night. Sagging against the door frame, disbelief then terror ignited her blood. "Not funny, Cam. Where are you?"

As if her feet moved independently of her body, she entered the room and pulled back the sheets. Nothing. Not that she expected to see him without the telltale lump, yet her fingers ran up and down the cold fabric. She searched his closet, pushing his clothing aside, his old karate equipment, and even rummaged through the plastic bin of old cars. Then she checked every room in the house. Staggering back to his bedroom, she grasped the back of the chair to his desk and toppled it, daring to hope he'd wedged himself underneath.

Nothing.

"Cam? Please don't do this to me." She crawled back to the bed, tears ravaging her cheeks as she lifted the bed skirt and stared into the inky void. Not even Figaro hid in his favorite spot. In a vain attempt to find her son, she stretched out her arm and swept the area, only coming up with a few stray socks and one of his old Cub Scout T-shirts. She buried her face in the cotton. Cameron had run away.

Hoping that they'd released Ethan from the hospital last night, Holly grabbed her phone, her fingers stumbling across the buttons three times before she managed to dial his number. Cam had to be with him. He had to be, although she had no idea how he'd walk all the way across town in the dark. Clutching the phone like a lifeline, Holly clenched her other fist and pounded her knuckles against her forehead. "Answer the phone, Ethan. Please, answer the phone."

Her stomach clenched with each ring and her teeth worried her bottom lip. Maybe Ethan was outside with the dogs? Maybe he didn't realize that Cameron was supposed to be getting ready for school? Maybe they never released him and something far more serious was wrong with him? More panic twisted her emotions.

By the time his voice mail picked up, she'd already circled her kitchen twice. Holly hung up and reached for her winter jacket thrown across the kitchen chair. She had to do something.

Darkness pressed against the kitchen window. From outside, the sound of the wind chimes on her back porch echoed in her brain as she shoved her arms through the sleeves. Adrenaline spurred her out the door. Cold enveloped her in its icy grasp and her foot stumbled on the bottom step, but she continued to her car. After she rubbed her chilled, damp hands against her jacket, her fingers shook as she jammed the keys into the ignition.

Fifteen minutes later, Ethan answered the door as soon as she knocked. He looked good—really good— despite the accident last night. A bandage covered the cut on his forehead, but other than that, he showed no other signs of trauma. "Holly? Is everything okay? I tried to call you back but there was no answer. You didn't answer your cell phone, either."

Instead of soothing her, it set off another chain re-action of emotions. Holly bit back another sob. She must have left her cell phone on her nightstand. What if Cam was trying to call her? More fear gripped her lungs, making it impossible to breathe. The first time she opened her mouth, nothing came out. The second time, she managed a squeak. "Is Cam here?"

Ethan ran his fingers through his hair, instant con-cern etching deeper lines around his mouth and eyes. "No. Why?" Realization dawned in his eyes. Ethan pulled her to him and cradled her as if it were the most natural thing in the world. "I'm sorry. This is my fault. You told him what I said, didn't you?" He kissed the top of her head. "We'll find him, Holly. I promise. We'll find him. And I know just where to look."

Stepping in behind Holly, Ethan wedged the door to the barn closed with his shoulder and shut out the bit-ing wind. He knew Cameron was here; the footprints in the snow didn't lie. He just had to find him. With a flick of his finger, the lone lightbulb in the center of the room illuminated all but the corners of the large space. He stomped his feet to remove the snow and rubbed his gloveless hands together. Despite being on the inside, he saw his breath. This place still wasn't ready for the dogs—or the twelve-year-old boy hiding somewhere inside.

Cameron. This time his words had put another life in danger. But he could fix that when he found the boy.

As he thought of decorating the Christmas tree at Holly's house yesterday, memories rushed through his mind—the laughter, the friendship, the love. All the times they'd spent together held special meaning for him. Ethan grasped the reality of the situation. He loved the boy like his own. He loved the boy's mother.

Determination filled him. God had granted him a new day and another chance. This time he would seize the opportunity and not fail.

In the corner past the row of assembled dog kennels, Ethan saw the pile of blankets and towels that the church had donated. Amid the greens, browns and tans, he spotted an unusual lump in the center.

"This way." He grabbed Holly's hand and pulled her with him. With his heart beating a tad bit more than normal, Ethan made short work of the space between them. Cameron's pale face was a sharp contrast to the black beanie hat and the dark brown blanket covering him.

"Cam." Holly gasped in relief, sank to her knees and then reached out to touch her son.

At the same time, Ethan squatted and gently shook the boy's shoulder. "Wake up, Cameron. Your mom is worried sick about you."

After a few moments, Cameron woke up and glanced between them with a worried, nervous look. "Mr. P.?

Mom? You're here?" He tried to dig himself deeper into the pile, his scared gaze never leaving Ethan's face. "My mom said you didn't want me out here anymore. Did you mean it?"

The saliva fled Ethan's mouth, making talking difficult. What could he say when the words were true? He stared at the stricken look etched into the boy's features. In Ethan's preoccupation with himself and his own feelings, he hadn't thought about Cameron's. Just like he'd only thought about himself and blaming himself for what happened in Afghanistan.

Let go, let God. It was about time he started not just listening to the words, but living them, too. "I've been saying and feeling a lot of things, and I thought it for the best after the accident yesterday. I'm sorry if I hurt you, but your mother spoke the truth."

"Then you don't want me out here? You don't need my help anymore?" Cameron's bottom lip shook as he clutched the blanket to his throat.

Ethan stilled. Help? He needed a lot of help. He couldn't do it alone. He never could. God was always with him and He always made sure that His children had what they needed. Sometimes it just took them time to figure that out. "That was yesterday. Today is a different story. You don't think I can handle this all by myself, do you?"

Cameron shook his head, hope blazing in his eyes.

Ethan stood and held out his hand to help Holly to her feet before he reached out for Cameron. "How did you get all the way out here?"

Wide eyes stared back at him. "I hitchhiked. I told

the man that I'd run away from home and wanted to get back. He dropped me off at the end of the driveway."

"Cam!" Beside him, Holly gasped and stiffened.

Ethan wrapped his arm around the boy's shoulders and squeezed, careful of his broken arm. Things happened, despite all the precautions. There was no way he could have prevented the accident any more than what happened in Afghanistan. Peace finally settled within him. "We'll talk about the dangers of hitchhiking later. Right now we need to get you to a warmer place before you catch pneumonia. And if it's all right with your mom, there are some dogs that need some attention this afternoon."

After Cameron went to bed later that night, Holly pulled the old banker's box from where she'd hidden it in her closet. Sadness and anticipation filled her. Without opening it, she carried it downstairs, placed it on the coffee table and then rubbed her hands against her jeans. She knelt, sank back onto her heels and then scratched Figaro under his chin. "Well, Figgy. Here we go. Are you ready?" Her cat rubbed the top of his head against her palm. She hadn't looked inside in a couple of years. After Jared died, she hadn't had the heart to set it out that Christmas.

All because of her inability to let go of her husband and let someone else get close to her and her son. Jared was dead and nothing would bring him back. She'd made peace with that. So what was keeping her from admitting her love for Ethan?

Fear.

Because letting someone else into her life opened up the possibilities of losing him as she'd lost Jared. Except there were no guarantees in life. This year, she'd found the courage, thanks to Ethan.

Taking a deep breath to calm her nerves, she lifted the lid and stared at the crinkled newsprint used to protect the contents. The article for the annual lighting of the Christmas tree in the town square caught her eye.

Life went on. As it should. For two years, she'd put everything on hold, grasping the memories of what she'd had and closing her eyes to her future.

Or what she hoped to be her future.

The paper rustled as she unwrapped the carved wooden animals first. Fingering the carvings, she marveled at the intricate whittling, even down to the texture of the lamb's wool. Jared had worked on these for hours while they'd sat and talked about their days, their hopes, their dreams. Back then, she'd wanted to be an interior designer, but life had a funny way of intruding. Maybe now that the shop was officially closing December 27, she could revisit that dream.

She set the animals on the glass surface and reached in again as her cat sniffed at the wood figures. "Leave them alone, Figgy." Holly shooed him away. Mary and Joseph came out next, followed soon by the shepherds, three kings and then baby Jesus and the manger. The last piece she took out was the stable that sheltered the nativity set.

She'd missed her mantel centerpiece.

A quiet knock sounded on the front door, breaking the stillness in the room. Figaro fled and scampered upstairs as she stood. Holly flipped the switch when she walked by the stereo but resisted lighting another candle. The five candles in the fireplace were enough and the Christmas tree already fragranced the air. She glanced up at the ceiling between the living room and front hall and smiled. Her last impromptu decoration was ready.

After opening the door, Holly admitted Ethan, took his jacket and hung it on the antique coat tree. He looked tired, but good. Now what? Should she just come right out and blurt what she wanted to say or work into it and wait for the right opportunity? She ran her fingers along the roughness of his jacket, gathering her composure. *Okay, Lord, I could really use some support here.* Turning around to face him, she fisted and unfisted her hands. "Thanks for coming over on such short notice."

Not exactly what she had in mind. Guess she'd have to work into it.

"Is everything okay? You sounded—"

"Everything is fine. I wanted to share something with you." Inhaling deeply, Holly wrapped her hand in his and pulled him into the living room, feeling more nervous than a schoolgirl at her first Sadie Hawkins dance. Then she motioned for him to sit before she handed him a cup of hot chocolate she'd brewed while waiting. Another Christmas carol hung in the air and the candlelight flickered, casting shadows against the brick wall of the fireplace.

Holly sat on the couch next to Ethan as he examined the figure of Joseph. This wasn't how she'd envisioned the moment, but then again, she hadn't had much practice in this area lately. Butterflies took flight and even a sip of hot chocolate didn't soothe them. Her fingers tightened around her mug. Maybe this wasn't such a good idea after all. Ethan seemed almost as uncomfortable as she felt.

"This looks like Jared's work."

"It is. They took forever to carve, but the five nativity sets he completed sold for a thousand dollars apiece. This is the last one."

"You're not going to sell it, are you?"

Holly stared at the set on the table, emotion hovering near the surface, begging to be released. "Of course not." She took a deep breath and flexed her fingers. It was now or never. It was what she wanted and knew that Cameron wanted as well even though they hadn't discussed it. Holly figured she'd better see where Ethan stood on the issue. "I thought you'd like to see it. And maybe help me set it up."

His eyebrows rose. "This is amazing. The detail is incredible, but it's small. I don't see why you need my help."

Holly was tempted to throw a pillow at him but didn't for fear of damaging the carving. Was he that obtuse? Or had she and Kristen misread him?

No. His eyes twinkled and his lips twisted into a grin that she'd come to associate with him. He wasn't going to make this easy on her. "Really? Then I guess it's time for you to leave. Thanks for coming by."

"Not until you tell me why you wanted me to come over after nine o'clock at night." He set the carving back down on the table and stood. Seconds later, he pulled her to her feet and held her close. "So are you going to tell me or do I have to coerce it out of you?"

He inched her backward.

Her fingers splayed across his shirt and she allowed him to lead, one baby step at a time. "Thanks for knowing where to find Cameron today."

"Holly, I—"

"Shh." She put a finger to his lips and stared into his eyes. "And for making me realize I need to move forward."

After he removed her finger, he gently kissed the tip of it. "You're not the only one who needed to put the past to rest. I had a lot of time to think about things in the hospital last night. With all my Bible studies, I should know that everyone has only a finite time on earth before they are called home. I did the best I could over there."

"And you continue to do His work by taking care of our service men and women's animals while they're gone and reuniting them with the strays they've adopted once they're back here. Plus, you've worked wonders with Cameron. I think that's why you're here."

Ethan took another step back and dragged her with him. "He had his reasons, and I'm not the one to question it."

"I'm not, either. I realize now that Jared's time was done, but mine and Cam's and even yours still continues." Despite all her hardships over the past few months, she knew everything would be okay as long as she allowed God to remain a part of her life. Would Ethan remain part of it, too?

"So where does that leave us?"

Holly glanced up and realized Ethan had maneuvered her into the hallway, specifically under her impromptu decoration. "Where do you want it to leave us?"

"That depends." His head dipped down and his lips captured hers, and Holly returned the kiss with all the emotion and love she felt inside. "I like the mistletoe. Nice touch."

"I thought it might help move things along." She inhaled sharply. Ethan had awakened her, opened her up to understanding and forgiveness and made her want to take another chance. "I love you, Ethan." Holly never thought she'd ever utter those words again and yet she had no problem now. She'd managed to forgive herself and move on, and Ethan had done the same.

"I love you, too, Holly." He captured her lips again, bringing back her Christmas spirit.

Reluctantly, Ethan pulled away. "You know there's only one thing to do about it, don't you? But I'm not really prepared."

Holly hugged him around his waist. "Who cares about material things? It's what's in our hearts that counts."

A hesitant look flitted across the features Holly had come to love. "About the store—"

"Don't worry about it. That was Jared's dream. I have others. I've also decided that instead of keeping the woodworking shop locked up, I'm going to give the keys to Cam for Christmas. Those are the final pieces to letting go."

"That's a great idea. You are amazing. But still…" His gaze wandered past her shoulder. Seconds later, he pulled an ornament from her Christmas tree, strode back and got down on one knee. Maneuvering the ornament to the thumb on his right hand, he grabbed her left hand and pulled it toward him. He hung the small knitted wreath on her ring finger. "The physical therapist was right. It does get easier with time."

"Of course it will."

A smile lit his lips, yet she heard the seriousness and hesitation in his voice. "Holly, will you marry me?

"Yes." Tears filled her eyes again and a smile danced on her lips.

"So when do we tell Cameron?"

"How about Christmas? I think that would be the best family present we could give him."

"And that will give me some time to find just the right symbol to show my love. This just doesn't seem to be working." He picked up the wreath that had slipped from her finger and slipped it on again. "Maybe I can incorporate your birthstone somewhere in the equation. When's your birthday?"

"December 25."

"A Christmas baby?"

"That's why my parents named me Holly. It was the last thing my mom saw as they were leaving for the hospital. Apparently I wanted some Christmas ham, because I interrupted their dinner."

"At least it wasn't mistletoe she saw." He sneaked

another kiss. "So do I still need to help you with the nativity set?"

"Of course. I'm not going to let you out of my sight that easily." She dragged him back to the coffee table. "We set it up on the mantel. Of course, we didn't do it until Christmas Eve, but somehow I felt the need to do this now. I think it's the final piece of saying goodbye to Jared but still keeping a part of him in our lives at Christmastime. You don't mind, do you?"

"Of course not. Jared was my friend and a very important part of your and Cameron's lives. What do you say we start a new tradition, though? We did this in Afghanistan. We put the pieces apart from each other and moved them toward the stable as we got closer to Christmas." Picking up the stable and manger, he set them on the mantel, positioning them in between the two small silk poinsettias.

Holly picked up the donkey and lamb. "So by Christmas morning, everyone will be together. Like us."

Ethan nodded, the love shining from his eyes enveloped her in their warmth, and she looked forward to many more years to come.

"The animals should be in the stable, shouldn't they?"

"Yes, and Mary and Joseph should be over here." Ethan placed them on the far side of the mantel.

"The shepherds would be on the other side?"

"You're getting the idea."

"But where should we put the three kings? They wouldn't even be in the picture yet."

"We can leave them on the coffee table unless Figaro would be a problem."

"Maybe we'd better set them on the side table." Remembering the cat's curiosity earlier, Holly picked up the carvings and set them on the small table in the corner, where her cat wouldn't bother them.

"I think I'm going to like this new tradition." Holly dusted her hands and stepped back into the room so she could survey the scene. What they'd created was more realistic, and moving the characters each day would bring the real meaning of Christmas closer to their hearts.

Ethan reached for Holly and held her close again. "And I think I'm going to like creating new ones with you and Cameron, as well."

"You know what, Mr. Pellegrino? The future Mrs. Pellegrino is going to like that herself. She's also thinking another tradition might be to put mistletoe in each room, too." She wrapped her arms around Ethan's neck, pulled him closer and sealed her vow with another kiss.

Epilogue

Holly stepped out onto the back porch of the old farm-house and handed a glass of iced tea to Ethan. She sat on the rocker next to him and breathed in the last of the warm scent of the lingering summer. The diamond flanked by blue topaz in her wedding ring glistened in the September sun as she took in the green splendor of the trees and grass. Puffy white clouds dotted the light blue sky, and the sound of chirping birds surrounded her. More peace settled across her shoulders.

"Thanks, Holly. May I offer you a cookie?" Ethan held up the tray of chocolate-chip cookies he and Cameron had made earlier while Holly rested.

The scent of chocolate drifted by her nose and she put her hand on her middle. "I think we'd like that."

"Is everything okay?" In a flash, Ethan was on his feet, concern overriding the love etched into his features.

"Everything is fine. I've been through this before." She smiled and gazed at her husband before she looked up. *Thank you, Lord, for bringing us together. For showing us that there can be life after tragedy. And for giving me the strength and courage to move on.*

"But what took you so long? I was beginning to think I'd have to do a search and rescue."

More happiness filled Holly. Closing the shop and putting Jared's dream to rest had allowed Holly more time to do what she discovered she really loved—taking old things and recycling them into something usable. "I just got another call about a decorating project over in Flagstaff. Apparently, the man saw what I did with some of the old stuff from the Weaver estate and wants me to rehab some of his things."

"That's awesome. Just as long as you don't overextend yourself." He looked at her stomach before his gaze rose to her face again. "There's something you're not telling me. What is it?"

"I also took another phone call from a staff sergeant who leaves next month."

"And you told him we were full, right?" Ethan rubbed his neck, his gaze frozen on the barn to their right.

"Of course not." Holly laughed. "We also just received another check in the mail. I think it's time to start renovating the loft and build a real staircase and ramp. We can probably fit about eight kennels up there if we really squeeze them together." Holly bit down on her lip to keep her laughter in.

"What?"

"Hazel the ferret is about to get some company. Two cats are coming with the new dog."

Ethan groaned and sank back down into his rocking chair. "I hope they get along with Figaro."

"I'm sure they will." The topic of their conversation padded onto the porch and jumped into Holly's lap. She patted him, resulting in a satisfied purr. "So you never did tell me why you don't like cats."

"It's not that I don't like them. It's just that I don't understand them. They're just so aloof, and what's with all the things Figaro is constantly leaving on the doorstep?"

Holly couldn't help but laugh this time. "Those are presents. It's just his way of showing you how much he loves us."

"Funny way to show it. Why not lick your face like a dog? Never mind, don't answer that. Those cats will be your responsibility, except for the litter box."

"Why, thank you, Ethan. I'm glad you're going to let me do something to help after all this time."

Ethan grabbed her hand, held it to his lips and kissed each knuckle gently. "Despite your role as a board member and taking care of the books, you've been a bigger help to me than you'll ever know."

"Patrick, you're not doing it right. Let me show you again." An animated Cameron and Patrick emerged from the barn. Two other at-risk youths followed them with dogs in tow. Boys and dogs. Ethan's idea to do youth interventions had been accepted by the town, and there was currently a waiting list to get in. With the added dogs and work, he'd be able to take one more boy and hopefully turn his life around just as Ethan's had been all those years ago.

"And everything has turned out just fine, hasn't it?"

"Better than I could have ever imagined, Holly. Better than ever."

* * * * *

SOMEBODY'S SANTA

Annie Jones

To my family far and wide (yeah, the older we get, the wider we are!): for all the merry Christmases past and all the joyous new years to come, thank you and God bless!

She will give birth to a son,
and you are to give him the name Jesus,
because he will save his people from their sins.
—*Matthew* 1:21

Chapter One

Burke Burdett had lost himself.

The man he had always believed himself to be had vanished. Nobody needed him anymore. Nobody wanted him. Nobody even realized that he had gone.

It had happened so quickly he still didn't know where he fit into the grand scheme of his company, his family or even his own life. But he did know this—years ago he had made a promise and now he had to see that promise through, even if it meant he had to go someplace he swore he'd never go to ask help of someone he swore he'd never see again. Even if it meant that he had to trade in his image of Top Dawg, the eldest and leader of the pack of Burdett brothers, to become somebody that nobody in Mt. Knott, South Carolina, would ever have imagined. If Burke ever hoped to find himself again, he was going to have to become Santa Claus.

Fat, wet snowflakes powdered the gray-white Carolina sky. Dried stalks of grass and weeds poked through the threadbare blanket of white. Everything seemed swathed in peace and quiet solitude.

Winter weather was not unheard of in this part of South Carolina, but Burke Burdett had rarely seen it come this early in the year, nor had he ever considered it the answer to somebody's prayer. His prayer.

He looked to the heavens and muttered—mostly to himself but not caring if the God of all creation, maker of the sky, and mountains and gentle nudges in the form of frozen precipitation, overheard— "And on Thanksgiving Day of all times."

It had to be Thanksgiving, of course, one of the few days when Burke took the time to actually offer a prayer much beyond a mumbled appeal for help or guidance.

This time he had asked for a little of each and added to the mix a heartfelt plea, "Please, prepare my heart for what I am about to undertake. Give it meaning by giving me purpose."

If he were another kind of man, he could have waxed eloquent about love and honor and humbling himself in order to learn and grow from the experience. But he wasn't that kind of man. He was the kind of man who wanted to feel productive and useful. There were worse ambitions than asking to be useful to the Lord, he believed.

So he had left his prayer as it was and waited for something to stir in him. It had stirred outside instead. Snow. In November.

The whole family had ooohed and ahhhed over it, and for an instant, Burke recalled how it felt to be a kid. And just as quickly he excused himself and drove away from the family compound of homes.

Now in the vacant parking lot of the old building that housed his family's business, the Carolina Crumble Pattie factory, Burke did not feel the cold. Only a dull, deepening sense of loneliness that had dogged him after spending a day surrounded by his family. In years past that family had consisted of his mom and dad, Conner and Maggie Burdett, his three brothers, Adam, Jason and Cody, and maybe a random cousin or two in from Charleston. This year two sisters-in-law and a nephew had been added. But it was the losses that Burke simply could not shake.

Age and grief had ravaged the tough old bird who had once been the strong, proud Conner Burdett, left him thin and a little stooped, worn around the eyes and unexpectedly sentimental.

Sentiment was not the Burdett way and seeing it in his father made Burke think of weakness and vulnerability. Not his father's but his own.

Burke clenched and unclenched his jaw and squinted at the low yellow-and-tan building where he had worked since he'd been old enough to ride his bicycle there after school. It did not help that the realities of the changing market had their business by the throat and had all but choked the life out of what had once been the mainstay of employment for much of the town of Mt. Knott, South Carolina.

They had made a plan to deal with that, or rather, his brother Adam had. He had gone out into the global marketplace, learned new techniques and made powerful allies. He was the one, the family had concluded by an almost unanimous vote, who needed to take the reins now. That plan had come at a cost. Burke, who had always carried the title Top Dawg in the pack of Burdett boys, had been asked to step aside.

Step aside or be forced out. By his own family.

In doing so Burke had lost his place not just in the family but, he thought, in the whole wide world. Not that they had fired him outright. They had asked him to stay on in a different capacity, but they must have known he'd never do it. After all, who had ever heard of Upper Middle Management Dawg?

So he had tendered his resignation and never returned, not even to collect his belongings. Until now.

Adam was to take on the job that Burke had held, for all intents and purposes, for a decade now. Adam, with his expertise in international corporate business dealings. Adam, with his new ideas for marketing and distribution. Adam, with the one thing that made him the most honored in the eyes of Conner Burdett, the thing that would assure them all that their name and reputation and even their business would go on—a son.

Burke didn't even have a girlfriend. How was he supposed to compete with that?

He wasn't, of course. To know that, Burke only had to think about Adam and Josie and their son, Nathan, how happy they had looked today seated at the massive Burdett dinner table together. Love and joy and wanting the best for those you care about, *doing* your best for them, that was what mattered. Winning?

Winning, Burke decided as he let out a long, labored sigh, was for losers.

And for the first time in his life, Burke felt like a loser. Not because of the loss of his position with the company or the unlikelihood that he would become a husband and father anytime soon, but because he had failed at that one thing that really mattered in life.

Burke shuddered. The wind whipped at the collar of his brown suede coat. He pushed his gray Stetson down low, as much to hide the dark blond hair that everyone in town would recognize as to protect his head and ears from the cold. Today, Thanksgiving Day, he felt the cutting ache of the loss of his mother down to his very bones. She had died two years ago, come Christmas Eve. *Two years*.

Yet it felt so fresh that he could still feel the heft of her coffin as he led the procession of pallbearers that day. He flexed his hand as if to chase away the memory of the icy brass handle he had clutched to take his mother to her final resting place. But it had been too long.

He had let too much time go past and now he had to face the truth.

Until this year the running of "the Crumble," as everyone in Mt. Knott affectionately called the business, had kept him busy. It had occupied his time, his thoughts, his energy. He hadn't even had time for dating, much less a real relationship, for seeing friends or making a real home for himself or any of the niceties most people his age took for granted. He certainly didn't have time to take on some silly pet cause of his mother's. One he didn't understand, didn't approve of and had only learned about when she was on her deathbed. Even if it was the one thing she had asked that Burke and Burke alone, of all the brothers, undertake. Her dying wish.

He swiped a knuckle across his forehead to nudge back his hat, ignoring the sudden sting of a flake that swirled beneath his Stetson to land on his cheek.

His finger brushed over the faint old scar that jagged across his eyebrow.

Conner had given it to him—the scar, not the business. The Crumble he had had to fight for in every sense of the word. He'd used the law, his family's consensus and finally even his fists to win his birthright as oldest of the four Burdett sons. His birthright—his place as head of the Burdett household and CEO of the family's already foundering enterprise.

Burke had gotten that scar the night he'd taken over as head of the family business. He'd been running it behind the scenes while his mother was sick, without much input at all from the rest of the family, but Conner's name had always remained painted in gold on the glass of the door to the big office. Until that night. That night everything had shifted, like a great jutting up of land along a fault line. They had all known it would come one day but had done little to prepare for it.

That night Adam had cashed out his share of the Crumble factory, taken the inheritance his mother had left and run away. And Conner and Burke had pushed their always contentious relationship to the edge.

He hung his head. Even after all these years, even

though he and his father had made their peace, Burke felt a pang of regret that it had gone so far. But his father's grief over losing Maggie had driven them to the brink of bankruptcy. Adam's actions had sealed the deal.

It was either challenge his father and take over or lose everything that they had worked to achieve.

Burke stroked the memento of that fateful night. Two things had happened then that would forever shape the rest of his life. First, he'd become a man, the leader of his family, the one they would all depend on. And second, he had decided, as he saw his father sobbing in misery over the remnants of what had once been a proud life, that Burke would never let himself need another person the way his father had needed his mother. It was a man's choice, as he saw it. You cannot love one person that much and still have enough left to serve the many who depend on you.

He'd been true to his word on both counts. He'd applied the ruthless business tactics that his father had taught him, slashed jobs, cut the budget to the bone, stripped away bonus plans and reduced salaries, starting with his own. It wasn't enough.

And as for needing anyone?

Need was some other person's weakness. Not his. Ever. Except...

There was his mother's dying wish.

A wish too long ignored.

A job that no one in Mt. Knott could know about, much less help him with.

He *needed* to take care of that.

Christmas was only five weeks away. Time was running out.

He'd looked at his predicament from every possible angle. In order to preserve everything his mother had worked so hard to keep secret for so many years, he would require a certain type of person. Someone from out of town. Someone who would work hard, collect her sizable paycheck and then go away before December twenty-fourth to leave his family and his town to celebrate the sacred holiday, without so much as a backward glance. Someone who shared his beliefs that business is not a personal thing, that sentiment breeds weakness, and that needing someone is not the cornerstone of a good life but a roadblock on the way to the top.

He forced his hat back down low on his head and made his way toward the building at last. He would duck inside and grab the box that had been waiting there for him ever since he had cleared out of his office to make way for Adam. In it he'd find a phone number on a business card. Tomorrow morning, he'd have to make the trek to Atlanta.

Chapter Two

"Working on the day after Thanksgiving, Ms. Hoag? I thought you'd be out shopping with the rest of the country."

"Shopping?" It took Dora Hoag a moment to grasp the concept. "Oh, *shopping! Christmas* shopping. As in gifts and glad tidings and ho-ho-ho and 'Hark! the Herald Angels…'"

Dora let out a low sigh.

She glanced up from the paperwork on her enormous desk at the salt-and-pepper–haired man, Zach Bridges, owner of the company who cleaned their office building. She knew him, just as she knew everyone on his cleaning crew, the night security guards, the lunch cart girls, everyone at the nearest all-night coffee shop and the company maintenance staff. Dora knew pretty much anyone who, like her, was still working long after others had gone off to…well, do whatever it was people who did not work *all* the time did when they were *not* working. She knew them, but they didn't know her, not really.

Granted, each year she took off most of the month of December, using up some of the vacation days she hadn't taken during the year. After seven years she thought ol' Zach might have figured out that she did not need more time to go caroling, wrap packages or bake cookies. She was hiding.

Hiding from the hurt the most joyous time of year always had meant to her. After all, what happiness is there in the season of giving when you have no one to give to?

Dora supported all the charities, of course. She'd worked at missions serving food and dropped a mountain of coins in little red buckets. She went to the candlelight service at her church, and her heart filled with love as they sang the hymns about the baby born in the manger. But when the last parishioners had called out their goodbyes, Dora had always been alone. Like the last gift under the tree that nobody claimed.

"Let me guess. You're the type who has all her shopping done before the stores even put up the first display. Oh, say, long about the end of September." Zach's smile stretched beyond the clipped edges of his mustache. "That way you don't have to face the rush this time of year."

Dora would have loved a reason to brave the throng and chaos this time of year to find just the right thing to express how she felt, to make someone smile, to give them…well, just to give from her heart. Instead she had work to do, and if she hoped to take her yearly sabbatical starting next week, she had to get back to it.

She flipped over a piece of paper in the file and narrowed her eyes at the long column of numbers. "I'm shopping all right. I just have a different idea of what constitutes a bargain."

"Looking for a couple of small businesses to snatch up and use as stocking stuffers, eh?"

"Snatch up? You make me sound like a bird of prey swooping down for the kill."

"Eat like a bird," he said, emptying the day's trash— an apple core, a picked-over salad in a plastic container, half a sandwich with just the crusts nibbled away. "And you're always flitting around, never perching anyplace for long."

"I've been based in this office for seven years, now, Zach."

"Seven years, and I'm still dusting the same office chair. Ain't ever in it long enough to wear it out and requisition a new one."

"Point taken." She laughed. For a moment she considered quizzing the man on what else he had concluded about her over the years, but a flashing light and a buzz from her phone system stopped her.

"Ms.…." The barely audible voice cut out, followed by another buzz then, "This is…" Silence, another buzz. "…says that…" A longer silence, a buzz, then nothing, not even static.

She frowned.

Zach chuckled and gave a shrug. "Security. Brought

in extra help for the holidays and made the new ones work this weekend."

"Not like you, huh, Zach? You let your staff have the time off and came in yourself." She admired that. It showed the character to put others before your own desires and the integrity to make sure you still meet your promised goals.

"Just the way I roll, I reckon," Zach said matter-of-factly. Then he nodded his head toward the bin beneath her paper shredder, his way of asking if she wanted him to take the zillion cross-cut strips of paper away with the rest of the trash.

She shook her head. Nobody got a glimpse of her business, not even in bits and pieces. She glanced down at the pad on her desk and the silly little doodle of a very Zach-like elf pushing a candy-cane broom and suppressed a smile. It was only business, she admitted to herself as she tore off the page and slid it into the middle of the pile of papers waiting for the shredder. The man might come to some conclusions about her on his own, but she wouldn't supply any confirmation. That was the way *she* rolled.

Never show your soft side. Never reveal all your talents, even the more whimsical ones. Never let anyone get a peek at what you think of them. Never share your dreams. Never act on anything in blind trust, not even your own feelings.

And most importantly, never let your hopes or your heart do the work that is the rightful domain of your history and your head.

She'd learned that lesson the hard way and not all that long ago.

She looked at the nest of shredded paper and blinked. Tears blurred her vision. The tip of her nose stung.

For an instant she was in South Carolina on a lovely summer day at a family barbecue. Not *her* family, but one in which she had thought she might one day find a place.

Dora Burdett. How many times had she doodled that name like some young girl in middle school with her first crush? *Crush.* What an apt word for what had happened to that dream.

She cleared her throat, spread her hands wide over the open file before her and anchored herself firmly in the present. "If you'll excuse me, I have to get back to my work."

"Always wheelin' and dealin', huh, Ms. Hoag?"

"I head Acquisitions and Mergers, Zach." She raised her head and stared at the massive logo for GrimEx-Cynergetic Global Com Limited on the green marble wall beyond her open door, where professional decorators had already begun hanging greenery with Global gold-and-silver ornaments. "It's my job to find the best deals before anyone else does."

"One step ahead of all those poor saps who took the long weekend off to get a jump on the holidays, right?"

"Yeah," she said, her voice barely above a whisper. "Those poor saps."

How she so wanted to be one of them.

All her life that was what she had wanted most of all—to have somebody recognize what she had to give, and to accept it and her. Not as an obligation or duty or in hopes of currying favor but because…she mattered.

Dora had never truly felt that she mattered. She, the things she did, the things she thought, her hopes, her dreams, *her.* Not in that way when someone loves you despite your shortcomings. When someone not only wants the best for you but feels you are the best for them, that you bring out the best in each other. She did not grow up in a home like that.

Her mother died when she was born. Her overwhelmed father left his newborn in the care of a childless and already middle-aged aunt and uncle while he went away to "find himself" and "get his head on straight," as people said in the seventies.

Apparently he never did either thing, because he never returned for Dora. Sometimes when Dora thought about him she imagined a man wandering about with his head facing backward, asking total strangers if they had seen his lost self.

Aunt Enid and Uncle Taylor did their best to care for her as their own. They started this by naming her Dora, which already put her at a disadvantage among peers with names like Summer, Montana and Jessica. So she kept to herself and worked hard, trying to make her foster parents proud. And for her effort she drew the attention of teachers and administrators. They called her "the little adult" and made jokes about her being "ten going on forty" and tried to get her to lighten up a little. But whenever they needed something done— from choosing a child to represent the school at a leadership conference to helping out in the office or being

in charge of the cash box at the pep club bake sale—
they tapped Dora.

She learned quickly that hard work and efficiency
opened doors. It wasn't the same as fitting in or mat-
tering to someone but it came a close second. About
as good as Dora thought she'd ever see.

Still, she couldn't help wondering how different her
life might be if just once someone had reached out
and asked her to come through the doors her drive
had created.

A small thing.

A shouted invitation to join a crowded lunch table.

A remembered birthday.

An explanation of why a certain blond-haired, South
Carolina gentleman had slammed the door in her face
when she had only wanted to…

"I'm dreaming of a…"

"Please, no Christmas songs, Zach."

"Too early in the season for you?" the man asked,
as he tossed his dust rag on top of his cart and began
to back the cart out of the room.

"Something like that." Especially when her mind
had just flashed back to last summer and that family barbecue when she had thought that finally she
had done something so caring and constructive that it
would change her entire life. That the man she had offered to help, she dared hope, would change her life.

Dora Burdett.

She pressed her eyes closed.

Zach cleared his throat.

A twinge of guilt tightened her shoulders and made

her sit upright, look the man in the eyes and produce a conciliatory smile. "Oh, don't get me wrong. I'm not one of those who wants to do away with Merry Christmas or any of the wonderful trappings of the season. I just..."

She put her hand over her forehead, as if that would warm up the old thought process and help her find the right words to explain her feelings. Except, it wasn't her brain that was frozen against all the joyous possibilities Christmas represented to so many. She loved the Lord, and observed His birth in her own way. "I love going to church for the candlelight service on Christmas Eve. I love singing the hymns and all, but...."

"But after that you don't have no one to go home to and share it all with," Zach said softly.

"How did you know that?" The observation left her feeling so exposed she could hardly breathe.

"You don't dust around folks' knicknacks and gewgaws or throw out their calendars' pages or run into them working on the day after Thanksgiving year upon year without learning a thing or two about those folks."

The answer humbled her even if it didn't bring her much relief. "I'll bet."

"Anyway, don't think it's my place to say—or sing—anything more, but I hate to leave without at least..." He scratched his head, worked his mouth side to side a couple of times then finally sighed. "I'll just offer this thought."

Dora braced herself, pressing her lips together to keep from blurting out that she didn't need his thoughts or sympathy or songs. Because, deep down, she sort of hoped that whatever he had to say might help.

He lifted his spray bottle of disinfectant cleaner the way someone else might have raised a glass to make a toast. "Here's to hoping this year is different."

It didn't help.

But Dora smiled. At least she thought she smiled. She felt her face move, but really it could have been anything from a fleeting grin to that wince she tended to make when forcing her feet into narrow-toed high heels. Just as quickly she fixed her attention on the papers in front of her and busied herself with shuffling them about. "Thanks. Now I need to get back to work. Can't make a deal on merely hoping things will improve, can I?"

"On the contrary." The challenge came from the tall blond man who placed himself squarely in her office doorway. "I'd say that hope is at the very core of every deal."

Burke Burdett! Questions blew through Dora's mind more quickly than those fictional eight tiny reindeer pulling a flying sleigh. But the words came out of her mouth fast and furious and from the very rock bottom of her own reality. "How dare you show your face to me."

"Show my face? The view don't get any better from the other side, Dora," he drawled in his low, lazy Carolina accent.

Zach, who had worked the cleaning cart into the hallway by now, laughed.

Dora opened her mouth to remind him it wasn't part

of his job description to make assumptions about her or eavesdrop on her and her guests. The squeak, rattle, squeak of the cart told her Zach had already moved on, though. She was alone in her office with Burke Burdett.

But not for long.

She reached out for a button on her phone, hesitated, then raised her eyes to meet those of her visitor.

He had good eyes. Clear and set in a tanned face with just enough lines to make him look thoughtful but still rugged. But if one looked beyond those eyes, those so-called character lines, there was a hard set to his lips and a wariness in his stance.

"Give me one reason not to call security to come up here and escort you out," she said.

"Well, for starters, I don't think the poor kid you've got posted at the front desk knows how to find the intercom button to hear you, much less where your office is." He dropped into the leather wingback directly across from her.

Years ago an old hand had taught Dora that standing was the best way to keep command of an exchange. *Stand. Move. Hold their attention and you hold the reins of the situation.*

Burke had just broken that cardinal rule. And made things worse when he stretched his legs out in front of him, crossed his boots at the ankle to create a picture of ease. He scanned the room, saying, "Besides, he was the one who let me in."

Dora wasn't the only one who noticed and befriended the people everyone else looked right past. "And what did you use to convince that so-green-he's-in-danger-of-being-mistaken-for-a-sprig-of-holly security guard to get him to do that?"

"Use? Me? Why, nothing but the power of my dazzling personality and charm."

"I've been on the receiving end of your charm, Mr. Burdett. It's more drizzle than dazzle." She'd meant it as a joke. A tease, really. Under other circumstances, with another man, maybe even a flirtation.

Burke clearly knew that. All of it. He responded in kind with the softest and deepest of chuckles.

And Dora found herself charmed indeed.

"So the security kid is already sort of on my side in this deal," he summed up.

"Deal?" She stood so quickly that her chair went reeling back into the wall behind her desk. She did not acknowledge the clatter it made. "There is no deal. You made that very clear to me when you cut me out of your family's plans to save the Crumble and get things there back on track."

Last summer, after working his way quickly up the corporate ladder at Global, Adam Burdett had returned to Mt. Knott with a scheme to buy out Carolina Crumble Pattie and get some satisfaction for all the perceived wrongs done against him by his adoptive father. It had all seemed a bit soap operaish to Dora, but as a good businesswoman she knew those were exactly the elements that put other people at a disadvantage in forging a business contract. Emotions. Family. Old hurts. They could push things either way.

In this case, they had eventually gone against Global's proposed buyout. And in favor of Adam Burdett, and by extension, Dora. Together they had the where-withal to save the company and the desire to do so. It wasn't what either of them had planned, but then love had a way of changing even the most determined minds. Adam's love for Josie—now his wife—his son, his family. And Dora's for the town of Mt. Knott, its way of life, the thrill of a new venture based on the same kind of Biblical principles that had once moti-vated Global a few dozen mergers ago. And her love for Burke.

She hadn't loved him right away but by the end of the summer, she thought she did love him. And she thought he loved her back.

Only she hadn't been thinking. She had been feeling and acting on those feelings. Which had brought her full circle, only then she had become the one at a dis-advantage in the contract negotiations. Dora was out. Adam was in. Burke had been nowhere to be found.

Burke glanced her way, then went right on survey-ing their surroundings. "This is a *new* deal that I've come to talk to you about today."

"New deal? Why would I talk to you about a new deal? Or that old deal? You didn't talk to me about that then and I don't want to talk to you about…"

"Look, I'm here now, dazzling or not, with a new deal to discuss. The past is past. I can't change it. Isn't there anything more important for us to talk about than that?"

Only about a million things. Yet given the chance to bring up any of them all Dora could come up with was, "I can't imagine what we'd have to say to one another."

"I can. At least, I have some things I want to say to you."

Her whole insides melted. Not defrosted like an icicle, dripping in rivulets until it had dwindled to nothing but a nub, but more like a piece of milk chocolate where the thumb and finger grasp it—just enough to make a mess of everything.

"You have something to say to me?" She bent her knees to sit, realized her chair was a few feet away and moved around the desk instead to lean back against it. "Like what, for instance?"

"Like…" He tilted his head back. He narrowed his eyes at her. He rested his elbows on the arms of the chair.

The leather crunched softly, putting her in mind of a cowboy shifting into readiness in the saddle. Readiness for what, though?

She held her breath.

He leaned forward as if every decision thereafter depended on her answer, asking softly and with the hint of his smile infusing his words, "Like, what do you want for Christmas?"

She almost slid off the edge of the desk. "I…uh…"

What did she want for Christmas? "After six months of not so much as a phone message, you drove all the way from South Carolina to Atlanta to ask me what I want for Christmas?" She stood up to retake control of what was clearly a conversation with no real purpose or direction. "Are you kidding me? Who does that?"

He could not answer her. Or maybe he could answer but didn't want to. He just sat there.

And sat there.

She could hear him breathing. Slow and steady. See his eyes flicker with some deep emotion but nothing she could define without looking long and hard into them. And she was not likely to do that.

She cleared her throat. She could wait him out. She had waited him out, in fact. He had been the one who had come to her, not the other way around. Even though early on there had been plenty of long, lonely nights when she had wanted nothing more than to hop in her car, or in the company jet or hitch a ride on a passing Carolina Crumble delivery truck to get herself back to South Carolina to confront him. Or kiss him.

Or both.

She wanted to do both. Even now. Which made it imperative that she do something else all together. So she plunked down on the edge of the desk again and said the only thing that made any sense at all to her, given the circumstances. "What I want is for you to go back to Mt. Knott and just leave me in peace."

"Peace. Yes." His slow, steady nod gave the impression of a man who longed for the very same gift—but doubted he'd ever find it. "That I can't promise you. That's better a request for the One who sent His Son."

"Nice save," she whispered, thinking of how deftly he'd avoided her demand for him to leave.

"Best save ever made, if you think about it."

She looked out into the hallway at the Christmas decorations going up. Global would not have a nativity scene, or any reference to the birth of Christ, and yet they covered the place in greenery, the symbol of life everlasting. All around her this time of year, the world came alive with symbols of hope. They rang in the ears, they delighted the eye, they touched the heart. It was such a special time, a time when one could believe not just in the wonder of God's Son but also in the possibilities for all people of goodwill.

Maybe even for a person like Burke.

Maybe he *had* really come here because he wanted to know what she wanted. Maybe he needed to know that she could still want him, to tell her that he had made a mistake, to tell her that she...

He shifted forward again, clasping his hands. "As for me..."

As for me. He had asked what she wanted, ignored her reply and went straight for his real purpose in coming. *Me.*

Himself.

He didn't want to know about her, he wanted to ask her to do something for him.

The moment passed and Dora stood again. She had to get him out of here. She had to keep him from saying another word that might endear him to her, that might give her reason to hope....

"As for you, Mr. Burdett." She moved to the door and made a curt jerk of her thumb to show him the way he should exit. "I don't really care what you want for Christmas."

"Not even if what I want, only you can give me?"

Chapter Three

Burke had broken the first rule of negotiation. He had let his counterpart know the strength of her position. He had been upfront and told her that he wanted to make a deal and she was the only one he wanted to deal with. He might as well have handed her a blank check.

And he would have done just that if he had thought it would work.

It wouldn't. Not with a woman like Dora. So he had done the next best thing, given her all the power in the situation. Now that, that was something she had to find compelling. Right?

Burke swallowed to push down the lump in his throat. He was not accustomed to anyone questioning his judgment and actions. Even when they included his limited charm, fumbling coyness and… Christmas cutesiness.

Who does that? Dora's earlier question echoed in his thoughts. Who drives all the way from South Carolina to Atlanta to ask a grown woman—one who clearly hates his guts—what she wants for Christmas?

Certainly not Top Dawg, the alpha male of the Burdett wolf pack. Certainly not him. And yet, that's exactly what he'd done.

And he had no idea whom to blame for it.

"What do you want, Burke?" She folded her arms over her compact body, narrowed her dark eyes and pursed her lips, a look only Dora could pull off. A look that probably set countless underlings and more than a few superiors shaking in their boots. A look that made Burke want to take her by the shoulders and find the nearest mistletoe. "What could I possibly do for you?"

He forced the obvious and inappropriate answers aside and started at the beginning.

"It's a long story. Goes back to my mom." He squirmed in the fancy wingback. He tried to make himself comfortable but the back was too stiff, the seat too short, the leather too slick. Not to mention that his trying to pin his actions on his late mother, too flimsy.

He wasn't a man who needed to assign blame, it was just that something had brought him to this point and he sure wished he knew what it was.

"Your, um, your *mother?*" Dora did not flinch but her no-nonsense squint did soften as she prodded him to say more.

He jerked his head up and their eyes met. He hadn't planned on that happening. Hadn't prepared for it— hadn't steeled himself against the accusations he saw aimed like a hundred arrows right at him.

How could he have prepared a defense for those?

He'd earned each and every one of those unforgiving, poisonous points. She had every right to hate him, or at least not to want to see him and to turn down his proposal outright. "Uh, yeah. My mother. Thing is she started this…it all started a long time ago, really. Long time before she was my mom or met my dad or had any idea that her life would turn out, well, the way it did."

Dora looked away from him at last. Her shoulders sagged, but she kept her chin angled up, in that way she had that she thought made her seem brave and sophisticated.

Seeing her like that made Burke want to push himself up to his feet and take her in his arms and hold her close. To lay his cheek against her soft, black hair and tell her that when she acted that way he could see right through to the scared, lonely little girl he had seen in her since the first time she powered her way into the Crumble to try to buy it out.

She sounded the part, too, quiet with a tiny quiver that she forced to be still more and more with each word. "None of us knows the way our lives will turn out."

"My mom did." He matched her tone, without the tremor. "Or she thought she did."

"That's the kicker, isn't it? When things don't turn out the way you thought they would?" Try as she might to come off all cool and in control, his showing up like this had obviously thrown her off balance. "When you start down a path. You make plans. You pray about it and feel you've finally…"

She glanced out the door.

He uncrossed his ankles and set his feet flat, just in case he decided to up and bolt from the room. It wasn't his style to do that kind of thing, but then again, neither was the way he had treated Dora earlier this year. Something about her made him do things he'd never thought himself capable of.

"Things just don't…" She shuffled the files on her desk.

He looked down. He should have worn his new boots. Dora deserved for him to put his best foot forward, literally and figuratively.

Dora cleared her throat.

He crossed his ankles again, his way of making it harder to give up on his quest and hightail it back to Mt. Knott.

"Like you said," she murmured at last, "…the way you thought."

"Yeah," he said. "That's the kicker. When things don't turn out the way you wished they would."

She'd said *thought*.

He'd said *wished*.

He wondered if she would correct him and in doing so bluntly and unashamedly confirm that they were talking about their own failed plans. If only she would and they could get it out into the open.

Burke was an out-in-the-open kind of man. Always had been—except when the good faith of a woman who didn't have sense enough to give up on him was at stake. That's how he'd gotten into this predicament in the first place.

He'd wanted to be upfront with Dora from the get-go, but the underhanded way in which his brothers had cut him from his spot as top dog of the family business left him hurt, humiliated and wanting to tuck his tail between his legs and hide. He knew that about himself. Knew that what he'd done, dumping her by pretending the only thing between them had been a business deal, was wrong. If she would only call him on it maybe they could sort it out and then…then *what?*

He shook his head. "You see, my mom, she had this plan for her life."

Dora held her tongue.

He felt he had to forge ahead.

Fill the silence.

State his case for coming here after all this time.

And if he got what was coming to him in the bargain? He'd take it like he took every blow and disappointment he'd suffered in life, without flinching and letting anyone see his pain.

"College, travel, adventure. Mom had the brains, the courage and the means to do it all. Something I know you can relate…" Too soon. One look into her eyes and he could see he had tried to get her to invest in this on a personal level much too soon.

"Yes?"

No, not too soon. He'd read her all wrong.

He'd spent hour upon hour with her. They'd discussed everything from business to barbecue sauce. He'd even sat by her side and mapped out a future that would forever intertwine them, if only on their corporate income tax papers.

The things unsaid had promised more, and he knew

it. Their laughter, their shared beliefs, their dedication to their work. Those things made it easy to be around Dora, something he'd never felt with another woman. They also made it easy to let go of her when their business deal fell through.

Fell through. Pretty words for having been kicked out by your own family and finding yourself left with nothing more to offer anyone, least of all a woman like Dora.

No position. No power. No purpose.

Burke knew that Dora needed those things for herself and from anyone involved with her. After the family had put those—position, power, purpose—out of reach for him, a personal relationship with Dora had become impossible for him.

He pressed on with his pitch. "My mother changed her life plans completely so that she could give her all to her family and the new dreams we would create together."

Dora would never have done the same.

"So your mother made her choice," she said. "Most women do. We tell ourselves we can have it all, and maybe we can but most of us know we can't have it all and give our all, all the time. So we all make choices. That *is* something I can relate to."

There was an eagerness in Dora's eyes, an intensity. Did he dare call it hope? Or merely an openness to hope? It was so slim, so faint. He doubted she even knew she was revealing it. It embarrassed him a little and humbled him that he should have this advantage, no, this blessing. That he should get this tiny glimpse into something so personal, the best part of this woman he admired so much.

Not until this moment did he realize that while Dora Hoag might be living the life his mother had never realized, it was not by her own choosing.

That changed everything—save for the fact that he still couldn't pull off any of this without someone's help. Dora's help. But now instead of wheeling and dealing to get it, he knew he had to win her over, make her want to do it as much as he wanted her to do it.

Without giving her any warning, he stood and held his open hand toward her. "Let's get out of here."

She looked at his outstretched palm then at the door. "You go first."

"Stop playing games, Dora."

"At the risk of sounding repetitive—you first."

"I don't play games." He dropped his hand.

"I know." She folded her arms again. "And you don't make a trip to tell someone something face-to-face that could easily be said on the phone or by e-mail."

He acknowledged that with a dip of his head.

"So just say what you came here to say and then kindly get out," she said quite unkindly.

"You're right. I did come to tell you something. And ask you something. But first I have to show you." He reached into his inside coat pocket.

Her arms loosened slightly. Her shoulders lifted. "If you were any other man, I'd expect you to pull out a small velvet box after a statement like that."

"Small? Velvet?" His fingers curled shut inside his coat. "Oh!"

She tilted her head and gave him a smile that was light but a bit sad. "I don't play games, either."

"I'll say you don't." He shook his head. She'd gotten him. He'd come here thinking he knew what he was walking into and how to maintain control of it and she'd gotten him. To his surprise, he didn't mind. In fact, he kind of liked it. He liked this feisty side of her. "But you sure do a have an overactive imagination, lady."

"Overactive? Because I once thought of you as a man of his word?"

Suddenly he liked that feistiness a little less. "Hey, let's not go there, Dora."

"Where else would you like to go, Burke? You seem to be up for a lot of travel all of a sudden. Coming here. Wanting me to go someplace with you. Maybe we should add a little trip down memory lane to your itinerary."

"Memory lane?" He smirked.

"What?" Lines formed in her usually smooth forehead. She pursed her lips and waited for him to say more.

"Just a pretty old-fashioned term, don't you think? I'd have gone for a play on time travel." He was trying to lighten the mood.

She wasn't having any part of it. "I was raised in a pretty old-fashioned home by my great-aunt and uncle. It's the way they talked, I guess. It's not so unusual. You knew the meaning."

The meaning he knew. The tidbit about her upbringing he hadn't known. Did it make any difference? Probably not to his plan, but it did explain a few things about her outlook on the world and the world's outlook on her. Nobody got her, not really. Nobody knew her.

Try as he could to stop it, Burke found that she was bringing out the protective nature of his Top Dawg personality again. To keep from caving into that or allowing her to rehash how badly he had handled things between them last summer, he stepped forward. He pulled the business card he had gone to retrieve from the Crumble out of his pocket. He gazed at the off-white rectangle with raised black lettering atop brightly colored shapes for only a moment before he handed it to her.

"What's that?"

"That's where I want to take you."

"To a doctor's office?"

"A pediatrician's office."

"Why?"

He moved to the doorway. "Come with me and I'll explain everything."

She did not budge. "So far, you haven't explained anything. You haven't answered a single one of my questions. Why should I let you show me this place?"

"Showing is simple." He held out his hand again. "Answers are complicated."

She ignored his gesture and raised one arched, dark eyebrow. "Then uncomplicate them."

Uncomplicate a lifetime of mischief, hope, happiness, tough choices and intricate clandestine arrangements? Couldn't be done.

Rattle. Squeak. Rattle.

Zach and his cleaning cart went wobbling by the open door.

Burke grinned. Maybe he couldn't just hand her the whys and wherefores of his situation, but if Dora wanted answers he could at least give her one. "You asked me who comes all the way from South Carolina to Atlanta to ask someone what they want for Christmas. It's not so hard to figure out, really, if you think about it."

Zach's raspy voice rang out in a Christmas carol about Santa Claus.

Dora frowned.

Burke jerked his head toward the open door. "Go ahead. Say it. You know you want to. Who makes a trip to ask someone what they want for Christmas?"

"S-Santa Claus?" she whispered, as Zach rounded the corner and his song faded.

Burke gave a small nod of his head, then looked up to catch her eye and winked. "That's me. And if there is going to be Christmas in Mt. Knott this year, I am going to need your help."

Chapter Four

"Okay, we've been driving for fifteen minutes." Dora glanced out the window of his shiny silver truck. Her, tooling around Atlanta in a pickup with a South Carolina snack cake cowboy Santa-wannabe at the wheel—listening to country music's finest, crooning Christmas carols on the radio. What happened to her policy of not trusting anyone, especially anyone named Burdett, again? What happened to her plan of ditching Christmas again this year by making herself scarce before sundown? What happened to this place that Burke had promised to show her, the one that would give her a reason to forgo the not trusting and the ditching and make her want to...

The lyrics to a song she'd heard moments before—"I Saw Mommy Kissing Santa Claus"—popped into her head. Burke Burdett? *Santa?* Difficult to imagine. Kissing him? Hardly the kind of thing a serious businesswoman, an angry almost-girlfriend or a woman of good Christian character ought to be dwelling on! She stole a peek at his rugged profile and noted the way he seemed to fill up the cab of the truck and yet still leave a place for her to sit comfortably beside him.

"Burke?"

"Hmm?" He didn't look at her and yet the casualness of his reply gave her a sense of familiarity no quick cast-off glance in a truck cab ever could.

She flexed her fingers on the padded car door handle and forced herself to study their surroundings as she counted off their recent itinerary. "I've seen the art gallery where some lady from Mt. Knott had her first show. The jeweler's where your mother used to have special ornaments engraved. And the building of the accounting firm that employs the valedictorian of your graduating class."

She hoped she hadn't missed anything. He'd told her it would all make sense in time so, ever the bright, obedient girl, she had tried to make mental notes as they drove along.

"Yeah?" He seemed engrossed in reading the street signs.

If he didn't know where they were going then why had he brought her along? And why had she come? She squeezed her eyes shut to put her thoughts back on track.

She crossed her arms and tipped up her chin. "So far you haven't really shown me anything that supports your claim of needing me to help you play the jolly fat guy."

"Hey." He tapped the brake lightly and stole a sly,

amused glimpse her way at last. "Is that any way to talk to Santa?"

"*You* are not Santa."

"Maybe not," he conceded, with an expression that was neither jeering nor jovial but somewhere in between. Then he made a sharp turn, and used the momentum of their shifting center of gravity to lean over and whisper, just beside her ear, "But I'm on his team."

"Oh, right." She shivered at his nearness. "Team Santa. I suppose you have the T-shirt and matching ball cap?"

"No can do. Team Santa is strictly a hush-hush kind of deal." He sat upright behind the wheel again and fixed his eyes straight ahead. "Not that I wouldn't look devastatingly cute in said hat and shirt."

He would. He'd be downright adorable, with his suntanned skin and deep set eyes that twinkled when he knew he had the best of a person in a given situation—and Burke always had the best of everyone in any situation. He knew it and so did she.

She couldn't take her eyes off him now. So strong, so confident, so manly but with just a hint of boyish excitement over this odd adventure he insisted on dragging her into. This was the Burke she had known last summer. The one she had wanted so much to give her heart to, right up until his last quick, cutting phone call when he'd ended their professional and, by extension, personal relationship based on the results of the family meeting. Correction: the Carolina Crumble Pattie board of directors meeting, a board made up of the members of the Burdett family. This Burke and the man who had torn her dreams to shreds with a soft-spoken and deceptively simple, "nothing personal, just business," seemed to be two entirely different people.

A man like that…he was not to be trusted.

That reminder made it easier for her to sit back and create a little verbal distance. "I suppose next you will try to tell me that you're an elf?"

"Why do you think I let my hair get this shaggy?" He tapped the side of his head. "To hide my pointed little ears."

"Really?" She did not look his way. "I thought you let your hair grow out for the same reason I keep mine short."

"Because it makes you look like a little girl all dressed up in grown-up clothes?"

"No." She crinkled up her nose at his way-off-base guess. "Because…um, does it?"

She put her hand to the back of her head. If anyone else on earth had said that she'd have given them what for, but coming from Burke, it had a sweetness that took her by surprise. She had always suspected that he could see the young Dora, the frightened, lonely and longing-to-belong child who lurked just beneath her polished surface. The notion warmed her heart. And chilled her to the core.

"That's not…that is…the point is, we both keep our hair the length we do for the same reason."

"I hope not. My hair is long but I hope not long enough to make me look like a little girl!"

"I like your hair." It wasn't all that long, really, just grown out enough to add to the overall appeal of this man who was rough-hewn, unfettered by convention and free from any kind of vanity or fussiness.

"Do you?" he asked softly.

"Yeah," she said, more softly. Almost childlike, almost flirty. The CD had stopped playing a few minutes earlier and she didn't have to compete with sleigh bells and steel guitars to be heard.

He looked into her eyes for only a moment before he squared his broad shoulders and stuck out his chest. "Then I guess I'll cancel my regular appointment with the barber."

"You don't keep any regular appointments with a barber, Burke. Just like I never *miss* mine." She sat in the truck with posture so perfect that only the small of her back made contact with the upholstery. "I wear my hair short for the same reason you don't bother to keep yours trimmed. I'm too busy with my work to bother with upkeep and style."

He did not dispute that, just turned the wheel and took them down a quiet residential street in a part of town Dora had never seen before.

They fell silent.

The air went still around them.

Dora should have let it go. Let him make the next move, the next comment. He had brought her here to prove something, after all. She didn't need to ramble on, cajoling and teasing and then retreating, hoping he would follow. That phase between them had passed. Now it really was just business.

Nothing personal. Just business.

No, not even business.

Once he had shown her the last of these places—he seemed to think they would add up to something that would somehow affect her—and shared this story of his, she'd probably never see him again. If she were smart she'd just keep her mouth zipped and wait it out until he dropped her off back at her office building.

"So if your hair hides your ears then I guess you wear that cowboy hat of yours all the time to hide your pointed little head?" So much for keeping her mouth shut.

"Elves don't have pointed heads." He frowned. Actually *frowned* as if he had to think that over and make the point quite clear.

She gulped in a breath so she could launch into an explanation that she had meant it as a joke.

He beat her to it by adding, with a wink, "It's just our pointy little hats make it look that way."

She laughed at the very idea of Burke in a pointed hat. "Someone sure is aiming to get on the naughty list."

"Aww, you haven't been that bad. Lots of people make cracks about elves and helpers and Santa's weight issues."

"I wasn't talking about me. I was talking about you, for fibbing about wearing a pointed hat."

"I'm not fibbing." He looked quite serious, but couldn't hold it and broke into a big grin. "And I have the photo to prove it."

"Then prove it."

"Uh, I, uh, I don't have the photo with me."

She shook her head. "For a second there, you almost had me believing you."

He went quiet then. Not silent, not still, but quiet with all the power, control and even reverence that implied. She could hear the tires on the road, the squeak of the seat cushions, the beating of their two battered hearts.

Her skin tingled. Her throat went dry.

For only a moment it was like that, then Burke turned to her, his intense, serious eyes framed by playful laugh lines as he whispered, "Believe me, Dora."

Oh, how she wanted to—to believe him about the hat, his being Santa and, most of all, that he needed her in a way that he needed no one else in the world.

But life had taught her that those kinds of beliefs only led to disappointment. So she kept it light, played along. "You in an elf hat?"

His eyes twinkled. "With red and green stripes, a plump pom-pom and a brass jingle bell on the end."

"What are you going to tell me next?"

"That this is what I wanted you to see." He pulled into a parking lot, slid the truck into a space and cut the engine. "This is why I need you."

"To go to a pediatrician? What? You need me to hold your hand while the doctor holds your tongue down with a Popsicle stick and makes you say 'ahh'?" What was he trying to pull?

"No. Not to go to the doctor, to see what she's doing."

"What? Seeing patients?"

"On the Friday after Thanksgiving." He nodded, his gaze scanning the lot.

Dora took a moment to follow his line of vision. It did not take long for her to come to a conclusion. "This is some kind of clinic?"

"Every Friday, even holidays—except Christmas and when the Fourth of July falls on Friday." He watched as a little boy scurried ahead of a young woman carrying a baby and then held the door to the office open. "A clinic for people who have jobs but no insurance. Just the doc's way of giving back because once upon a time somebody did something nice for her."

"And what does that have to do with Santa Claus coming to Mt. Knott, South Carolina?"

He hesitated a moment, gripping then repositioning his large, lean hands on the steering wheel. He started to speak, held back, then took a deep breath. Finally, he worked his broad shoulders around so that they pressed against the window and his upper body faced her. His brow furrowed. His eyes fixed on her then shifted toward the children. He kept his voice low as if he thought one of them might hear. "Do you know the story of the first Santa, the real Saint Nicholas?"

She kept her backbone pressed to the seat and her cool gaze on the man. "I think the real question here is, do you know how to answer a question directly when it's put to you?"

"Humor me," he said with grim sobriety just before he broke into a crooked grin.

It was the grin that got her. She sighed. "The real

Saint Nicholas? Hmm. Turkish? Skinny fellow, too, not the bowlful of jelly Clement Moore described. Or the ho-ho-hokey, soda pop–swilling, round-cheeked invention of American advertising."

"Right. The Bishop of Turkey. He surreptitiously gave bags of gold to girls who otherwise would not have had a dowry so they wouldn't be pressed into servitude or prostitution."

Now she moved around in the seat, impressed. Suspicious but definitely impressed. "You said that like a kid reading off a plaque in a museum."

"Close. Only the museum is my mom's office in the attic of our family home, and the plaque is a caption under an old print from a book she has framed there."

"Really?"

"Really."

"I'd like…"...*to see it someday.* The rest of the sentence went unfinished. She had no business inviting herself, not only into the home where Burke had grown up, but into his late mother's office. "I'd like to know how that relates to this pediatrician's office in Atlanta?"

"Easy. The original saint gave money to girls in order to give them the power to make better lives for themselves, and by extension better lives for their families and their communities."

"And this doctor is doing the same?"

"Because?"

"Because she…" Dora looked at the office once again. On the sign with the doctor's name was the symbol of a gold coin with a wreath encircling a Christmas stocking. "Because once upon a time that doctor got a visit from Saint Nick?"

"Who is?"

"You."

"My mom." His gaze dropped for a moment and the grief seemed so real and still so fresh in him that Dora did not know how to respond. She didn't have the chance, as he quickly recovered and met her gaze with his sad and solemn eyes. "From the time she decided to stay in Mt. Knott and raise a family instead of traveling the world, my mother gave out grants and scholarships to deserving girls and young women who otherwise would not have had the opportunity to make better lives for themselves."

"Wow. She paid for their college?"

"She helped. And not just college. Private high schools. Vocational training. Trips. Conferences. Art supplies."

"Art…oh, art supplies. So the artist, the jeweler, the accountant were all…"

"Just the artist and accountant. The jeweler is where she has the gold medallions engraved that she gave the recipients to let them know they were chosen."

"She didn't present them in some kind of ceremony?"

"She kept it quiet. The jeweler sent them from here so no one would ever know who they came from."

"People suspected the Burdetts, though. They'd have to."

"If they did, no one ever said."

Dora studied the coin with new eyes and understanding. "There's writing around the edge."

"'We give to others because God first gave Christ to us,'" he said, without even looking at the sign or the coin he had just quoted.

"And no one knows about your mother's good works? Really?"

"Only the accountant who manages the financial side of things, me and now you."

"Not even your brothers? Or your dad?"

"It's a secret Mom entrusted with me alone on her deathbed."

"Oh, Burke." She reached out to touch his face, to lend support and comfort.

"But me alone? I don't think I'm up for the job."

Job. Only business. She curled her fingers closed and put her fist to her chest.

"That's why I need your help. I need someone who isn't from Mt. Knott to help me pull this off. Because as a Burdett I can't do anything in Mt. Knott in secret."

"Including taking me out there to manage this for you," she reminded him, switching swiftly into organizational problem-solving mode. "How would you ever explain that?"

"Oh. Yeah." He scowled. "Unless…"

"Yes?" She needed him to come up with this solution, not because she didn't have one to offer, but because it was his project. She had no intention of investing in it emotionally or even mentally unless he could find a way to win her over to it. Which meant she wasn't getting involved.

"Well, you were out there all last summer and no one questioned that."

"I was in negotiations to buy into your business then." She folded her arms and clamped them down tight. "I don't suppose you want to revisit that?"

"There's a lot about last summer I'd like to revisit."

And a lot of memories she wanted to send packing. She shut her eyes. "Burke, I…"

"Just come out and stay at the family compound, Dora."

"What?"

"We won't have to say why you're there. People probably wouldn't believe anything we told them anyway."

"I can't just leave work." It was the first thing that came to her mind. Not a lie or a means of deceiving him but just a gut reaction, telling the man the kind of thing he'd expect her to say.

The crooked grin returned. He shook his head slowly. "You save up all your vacation time all year and take it in December."

"How did you know that? Did Zach tell you?"

"Who?"

"Zach, the…" The closet thing she had to an old friend. She sighed. "Never mind. Just tell me how you knew that."

"Because you told me."

"I did?"

"One night when we talked about the future. You said if you ever got married you'd want it to be in December."

Her cheeks grew hot. She found it hard to swallow. Marriage? The future? She remembered that night, but not the things they had said—just the way it felt to be near Burke, to sit out on the porch beneath a blanket of stars. Had she really let her guard down so completely? "Was I under the influence of Carolina Crumble Patties?"

"Maybe."

"Sugary foods get to me, you know. Make me say things I don't necessarily mean." As did certain men.

"You meant this."

"You said a lot of things I thought you meant, Burke."

He did not say a word in his own defense.

He couldn't, she realized. And just that quickly she also understood that she could not help him, even with this worthy cause. She could not allow herself to be that vulnerable again, especially not at Christmas.

She looked out at the doctor's office building again. "Just because I don't go into my office most of December doesn't mean I don't have things to do."

"Yeah. Right." He nodded, his eyes downcast. "Everybody has things to do. We live in a busy, busy world. So busy doing the things we have to do we often let go of the things we should do."

That stung. It was true of course, which was probably *why* it stung. "Burke, I—"

"Oh, I don't mean you specifically, Dora." He looked at her, then at the pediatrician's sign, his face stormy with emotion. "Over the years my mom has given out a lot of time and money, and none of those people have ever tried to find out who their benefactor was so they could offer support."

"But this is good." She held her hand out to indicate the clinic taking place right before their eyes.

"Yeah, this is good, but I can't help thinking."

"What?"

"We have kids in Mt. Knott, too."

"What?"

"Everyone always says, why doesn't the Crumble factory do more? Why don't the Burdetts help out the town more? But how many of them ask, what more can I do?"

"I'm not from Mt. Knott," she felt compelled to remind him. She did not owe the town or its inhabitants anything. But then, who was she indebted to? Beyond her aunt and uncle and the unseen powers-that-be at Global? No one. No one needed her on a personal level.

"People don't seem to see that every doctor who goes someplace else to practice, every young person who goes off to college and never comes home, every citizen who gets his gas, does the grocery shopping or sets up business outside of Mt. Knott takes something vital away from the community. The Crumble and the Burdetts can't counteract all that."

"I know."

"We shouldn't have to try."

"I know."

"I just keep thinking that at some point somebody is going to step up."

"That's why you keep the Santa gifts a secret, isn't it?"

"Huh?"

"You're a big softie, admit it."

"Well, thank you for that much."

"But you could put some stipulations on the gifts. Say the recipients have to give something back to Mt. Knott, serve the town a certain amount of time."

"I couldn't do that. Mom never did and I want to carry on her tradition."

"Tradition shmadition. You do it because you have faith."

"I'm a man of faith, yes, but—"

"Faith in your fellow man. And woman, for that matter."

"I don't know what you mean."

"'We give to others because God first gave Christ to us.'" She read the words from the coin on the sign. "You want to keep this all a big secret because you are hoping that one day one of these girls who are gifted will turn around and do the right thing and give back to the town because they want to, not because they have to."

He didn't deny it but he didn't jump on her claim and praise her for seeing right into his thought process, either.

"Or, at the very least, that the town's people, knowing somebody among them has done these good things, will want to do something for the town, too."

"Is that a crazy thing to hope for?"

"That you hope to inspire people and make it easier for them to give to others?" It was all she had ever wanted. And the very thing she had worked so hard to keep herself from doing. Until now. "No, I think it's wonderful, especially at Christmastime."

"I can't do it alone."

"You don't have to, Burke."

"You mean?"

"I hope you saved that hat you said you had." She could not believe she was saying this but…well, she had known he would have to sell her on the idea to get her to join in. She also knew that the best sales were made by a person who truly believed in what he was selling. Burke, in his own raggedy, begrudging way, believed in Christmas and in his mother's dream. It was within Dora's power to help him realize that dream— a gift only she could give him. How could she refuse? "I may have to borrow it if I plan on becoming this year's Santa's helper."

Chapter Five

Monday was soon enough to get started. Too soon, really, for Burke's tastes. Yet, by his mother's standards, they were already eleven months behind schedule. For her, the undertaking she called the Forgotten Stocking Project was not a special holiday event but a year-round commitment.

If he had let Dora have her way they would have gone to work the day she accepted the position as his assistant. Why not? It's not like she had a bunch of family hovering around for the weekend wondering why she wasn't there diving into the leftovers with the rest of them. Or asking a lot of questions that they considered to show concern but really hinted that she needed to be doing something different with her life.

So, when will you be bringing someone special home for the holidays?

Don't you get lonely in that big house all by yourself?

Now that you aren't working at the Crumble practically twenty-four/seven why don't you start something new? Like, say a family of your own?

He didn't know whether to pity Dora or envy her for not having to endure that. He looked around at the people gathered in Josie's Home Cookin' Kitchen, at the people he had known most of his life chatting with friends and loved ones, then at his sister-in-law, *the* Josie of the Home Cookin' in the restaurant's name, and decided, in his grudging curmudgeonly way, that he did not envy Dora. Pity might have gone too far, but he did wish that Dora didn't seem so very alone in this world.

She'd mentioned her father. Gone off to find himself when she was still quite young. He wondered why with all her resources she hadn't tried to locate him.

She had probably weighed the risks against the potential gains and had come to the most practical conclusion. Dora was first and foremost a businesswoman, after all. Right?

Of all the people who knew Dora Hoag, Burke suspected he above all knew better than that. Dora was so much more than a businesswoman. She was the child she had been and the friend she could be, a good listener, smart, funny, a thoughtful Christian and a…a woman.

Dora was a woman, with all the faults and every fine quality that came with being one. But she had no person to share her joy with and no trusted friend to lean on when things did not go well.

Except she did. She had both, in him. Only maybe she didn't see it that way.

Burke settled onto a stool at the counter. He pulled out a menu, even though he'd had breakfast a few hours earlier and it wasn't quite time for lunch. He'd arrived only a few minutes before the hour he and Dora had agreed to meet. He'd planned that so he wouldn't have time for a lot of chitchat with the patrons, but it also meant he wouldn't have time for a piece of pie. If Dora would be anything—and to his way of thinking, Dora Hoag could be many, many things—she would be prompt.

"Coffee?" Josie lifted up a sturdy white cup turned upside down on a matching saucer.

Burke watched her, thinking how blessed his brother Adam was to have found someone like Josie.

"Sure." He nodded then slid the menu back in place, glad not to have to order something as a cover for hanging around the place. "Surprised to see you here today."

"Why?" Josie paused, his coffee cup still in her hand, to take money from a customer.

Ching. The cash register rang out. Its drawer popped open.

Josie tucked the exact change away then thanked the customer with a radiant smile and a soft word.

Burke squinted as he tried to figure her out. "Thought you'd given up all this to be a full-time mom."

"A *what?*"

"A, uh, a full-time mom?" Burke usually didn't have that much trouble making himself heard or understood.

"That's what I thought you said." *Whomp.* She sent the cash drawer slamming shut with a swing of her hip.

"Uh-oh." Warren, one of two older fellows who oc-cupied the stools at the diner almost every morning of the week, ducked his head.

Burke sat perfectly still, unsure what was headed his way.

"Burke Burdett!" Josie set the cup down firmly enough to make it clatter against the saucer. "Every mother is a full-time mother!"

With a flare of authority that made it clear she thought she had given the final answer on that, Josie spun around and nabbed the coffeepot.

He frowned. He should have let it go. He'd said what he'd said, she'd said what she said and…and she'd got-ten the last word. Being Top Dawg, he just couldn't drop that bone. "I thought some of them were work-ing mothers."

"What?" Josie held the coffeepot back as if she had half a mind not to serve him at all after that remark.

"Oooh. Should have just said 'yes ma'am' and quit while you was ahead," muttered Jed, Warren's cohort in café commentary. "You ain't getting no pie, after a remark like that, no sir."

"Yup. That boy's definitely going on the no-pie list," Warren confirmed, his head shaking forlornly.

"I mean, uh, *every* mother is a working mother?" Burke tried to slip back into his sister-in-law's favor by saying what he thought she wanted to hear. What did he know about this motherhood business, anyway? He'd always sort of thought that he'd raised himself, looked after himself. He hadn't really needed his mom for much. What was the big deal?

"That's better." Josie exhaled and took a second to regain her composure.

"Whew." Burke pretended to wipe his brow for the benefit of Jed and Warren, his counter-mates.

They chuckled.

"And I'm down here today because the place still has my name on it and I intend to keep a hand in running it. Also, I had to come to oversee the end-of-the-month paperwork." Josie approached the counter again. "Your turn."

"Huh?" Burke dragged the saucer and cup closer in front of him on the counter and flipped the cup over.

"I could say the same about being surprised to see you here." Josie held the pot up. The dark brew sloshed, sending its warm, rich aroma wafting his way. "The way you took off the day after Thanksgiving we all half-expected not to see or hear from you again until we got a postcard from you halfway around the world."

"Saying I'd joined some far-off army rather than spend the coming holidays with y'all?" He chuckled, though now that he thought of it maybe that wasn't a bad alternative, once this whole Santa mess got worked out.

"That's what the guys thought. The girls…" She dipped her head and the curls of her ponytail fell over her shoulder as if every part of her had to move in close to get in on this tidbit. "The girls thought maybe it would say you'd run off and eloped and were on an extended honeymoon."

He jerked his head up to meet her gaze. "Married? I don't even have a girlfriend."

"You don't have to have a girlfriend to get married, Burke." Josie laughed. "No one ever thought of me as Adam's girlfriend. I was his baby's adoptive mother, then I was a thorn in his paw, the next thing anyone knew, I was his wife."

Wife? Burke winced. Had he given anyone reason to think that he and…the one woman on the planet he had allowed to become the thorn in his paw…had ever considered…

"Who is getting married?" Warren wanted to know.

"Why do you care, you old coot? Ain't like they plan to invite you along on that fancy honeymoon." Jed gave his companion a nudge in the shoulder. "Way I hear it your wife wasn't too keen on you tagging along on your own honeymoon."

Jed laughed.

Warren joined in, grumbling something that sounded partly like a complaint about his friend's sense of humor and just a little bit like agreement with his assessment.

Burke tensed. He'd spent so much time with his head buried in the business of late that he had forgotten how easily gossip got started in this town.

Gossip? About his super-secret project involving his mother's dying wish and his…his… Dora?

Josie had already gone all demure and amused, looking down as if the task of pouring coffee, something she did a hundred times a day, required her utmost attention. She lifted the pot.

"On second thought…" Burke stuck his hand over the cup.

Too late.

Josie pulled up but not before a stream of steaming hot liquid splashed over his knuckles.

"I'm so sorry." Josie winced.

He yanked his hand away and, knowing every eye and, more importantly, ear in the place had suddenly fixed on him, gritted his teeth and merely said, "My fault."

He slid from the stool and wiped his hand on a paper napkin from the dispenser on the counter.

"Come back into the kitchen and run that under some cool water." She motioned toward the open door a few steps behind her.

"No, I'm not staying." He wadded the napkin up and, realizing the large trash bin was across the room, stuffed it into his pocket rather than prolong his time there. "I can't stay."

What a bad idea to meet Dora here. He had to get out before she came strolling through that door and fueled who knew how many rumors, spreading from this point like wheel spokes in every direction, to every home and family and inquiring mind in Mt. Knott. Ex-business partner, thorn in his paw, soon to be wife. The town would have them married before they finished their Christmas shopping!

He checked his watch. She was already a few minutes late. Not like Dora. He didn't have any time to…

"Sorry, I'm late." Dora stood in the open front door with a space-aged-looking gizmo attached to one ear, her hair an uncharacteristic mess. Fresh but still formidable. Without her power pumps to give her height or her tailored business suit to give her substance, she looked like a cross between a waif arriving at the gates of an infamous orphanage and one of those bright-eyed girls with big dreams getting off the bus in the big city. She wore a black fuzzy sweater, a single strand of pearls, some black-and-white checked pants and black shoes. With bows.

It was the bows that got to Burke. He didn't think he'd ever before seen her wear anything so out of character and yet so perfect.

She clutched her expensive leather briefcase to her chest, blinked those big, brown eyes and blew away a piece of straw that had tangled in the soft curl of black hair alongside her cheek. "I'd blame traffic but, well, is getting behind a slow-moving tractor hauling hay considered traffic around here?"

"Dora?" Josie, still standing close to the kitchen door, cocked her head. "*Dora Hoag?* Talk about being surprised to see somebody in here!"

A murmur moved through the room.

It had the effect of a bucket of cold water on Burke's head—a most unpleasant wake-up call but one that got the job done and quick.

Think fast, Burke warned himself. No. Act fast. That's what this situation called for. To act fast, talk fast and think about what he had done later.

"Yeah! What a surprise to see you come walking through that door today at, uh…" Another glance at his watch. "…Ten minutes after ten in the morning."

"What? Did we get our wires crossed? Is this the wrong day? Wrong place? Wrong…what's wrong,

Burke?" Dora spoke softly as though he were the only person in the room.

He liked that feeling.

Liked it a lot.

Too much.

He cleared his throat and took her by the upper arm, turning to, in essence, present her to the room and to emphasize to her that they were not alone. Then he leaned down and whispered for her ears only, "Play along, please."

"Play? Burke, what's going on?" she managed to ask, barely moving her lips.

Cool trick but not one a bulldog of a man like him, accustomed to barking out orders meant to be heard and carried out, could pull off. So he faked a cough and used his fist to hide his mouth as he said, "For the sake of secrecy. We can't be seen planning in a public place like this."

"No lies," she commanded, under the cover of slapping him on the back in a show of helping him with his sudden coughing fit.

Slapped him a bit harder than the pretense called for, he thought, but then maybe she felt she deserved the indulgence for the way his family had treated her. The way he had treated her. The way he was treating her right now.

"Okay, no lies." Even though lying would have been the easiest way to go. But it was Christmas and he was supposed to be a better man this time of year, right? "Not that I make lying a way of life, you know."

She shot him a look that suggested she did not know that.

It hurt but he understood her position.

"So, what are you doing in town?" Josie had made her way around the counter now and had her hand out to Dora, the woman who had been her husband's boss at Global not so long ago.

"Me? I, um, I have some time off," Dora blurted out.

"So you invited her here for the holidays?" Josie took Dora's hand but her eyes focused on Burke.

"No!" That was the truth. He fully expected Dora to be gone before the holidays rolled around. Once she'd finished her part in the vetting and selection process, he expected her to hightail it out of town to leave him, the town and his nosy, matchmaking family to tolerate, um, *celebrate* Christmas as usual.

He glanced down at Dora.

Usual? How could he carry on as usual knowing she was alone in the world during the season when so many, like it or not, came together with their loved ones?

"That is, I didn't invite her to spend the holidays with us but—"

"He told me about Mt. Knott this time of year and I wanted to come and see it for myself." Dora released Josie's hand then looked up into Burke's eyes, her expression reassuring him that she would not insinuate herself on him or his family. "I came of my own volition. I'll only stay as long as I feel welcome."

Burke felt like a jerk. Probably because he was one, from the way he had roped her into helping him, to the way he was treating her this moment. Then and there he vowed he would do something to make it up to her. Somehow. Someday.

"Well, as far as I'm concerned you are welcome to stay the whole season." Josie beamed. "Ring in the new year with us, if you like."

"The new year?" Burke scowled. Jerk or not he had no intention of having Dora Hoag all but move into this town—this very small, very up-in-everybody's-business town.

"Oh, I plan to be back at work the day after Christmas. I always am," she said, before Burke had the chance to say something awful that would hurt or embarrass her. "Like I said, I just came for, well, because Burke had said…it just seemed right to, well, you know. You all know your little town better than I do, surely you understand why I came."

Get the other guy to tell you his strengths and in doing so, you will discover where you need to be stronger. Burke recognized that Dora had the finely honed people-assessing skills of a seasoned CEO or sales executive. If the folks around them asserted that she had surely come here for the fresh air, she'd need to make sure they saw her soaking up plenty of it. If they discerned she must be trying to buy out the Burdetts again, then by simply spending time around the Crumble every day she would fuel that rumor and throw everyone off the scent of her real objective. And if anyone guessed the real reason? Ha! Who in this town would guess she had come to Mt. Knott to play Santa's helper?

It was an old negotiating technique that Dora had,

after a few false starts, fallen back on. She was clever, he'd give her that. And sharp witted. And—

He gazed down at her, smiling right at the two men sitting at the counter even as her knuckles went white on the handle of her briefcase.

And adorable. Dora was adorable.

"So?" she prodded. "Y'all know why I'm here, right?"

Another murmur went through the room.

Josie frowned.

A woman in a booth started to say something then thought better of it and shook her head.

Finally Warren sputtered in disgust, "Oh, c'mon, y'all," and slapped his leg. "Ain't it obvious? She come to participate in our fabulous downtown hoedown, all around, by the pound, glory bound.... Stop me, Jed, I can't seem to get to the end of this thing!"

"You got the name wrong, you old goat." Jed nudged his friend to show he'd have none of his tomfoolery. "It's Homemade Holidays Down on the Homefront."

"Down Home Holidays Downtown," Josie jumped in to correct them both. Then she turned to Dora. "We thought, to generate some interest in people coming into town to eat and shop, we'd have a big kick-off celebration with a parade, street vendors and that evening a lighting ceremony and sing-along and maybe carriage rides through the street."

"That's what she's talking about," Jed proclaimed. "That's what she came for. Couldn't be nothing else, could it, Top Dawg?"

Burke cleared his throat. No lies. This did give

them a position of strength. A reason for Dora to hang around. And he wanted her to hang around. For the work. Again he cleared his throat then nodded in her direction. "You really should stay. Give you a feel for the place like nothing else could."

Everyone looked at Dora as if her approval could make or break the whole event.

"I'd love to," Dora said, her eyes bright and her whole demeanor so light that Burke wanted to glance down to see if her feet had lifted off the ground.

"Great!" Josie approached as though she suddenly felt Dora were her personal guest. "Do you have a room at the motel or would you like to come out to the compound?"

The compound? Burke had asked her here to get a feel for the town, not to move in on his home turf. He frowned at her and maybe even shook his head, she wasn't sure.

Dora's shoulders slumped slightly, he thought, then rebounded and her standard straight arrow all-business poise returned.

"You didn't let me finish," she said. "I'd love to attend your Down Home Holidays Downtown."

She got it exactly right after hearing it only once. She would, of course, but it still impressed Burke and reminded him why she was the perfect person for the job.

"But I can't really stay around Mt. Knott indefinitely."

"Well, there's nothing indefinite about this, young lady," Jed noted.

"It's tomorrow night." Josie took her by the arm and began to lead her farther into the restaurant.

"A Tuesday?" Dora followed, her feet dragging slightly.

"No other time for it." Warren swung around to face the counter again.

"The Chamber of Commerce thought having it before Thanksgiving was rushing things a bit." Josie pointed to a seat at the counter for Dora.

Dora looked at Burke.

He smiled, though he suspected it wasn't a warm smile. If she wanted more, like some kind of affirmation that this was all a great idea, she wouldn't find it from him. Burke knew very little about any of this, seeing as he no longer played a role in the Chamber of Commerce, or in much of anything these days. He clenched his fingers and his jaw tightened at the reminder of all he had lost—all he no longer had to offer.

"And this past weekend, with people traveling to be with family and all, no sense in holding it then." Josie pulled a piece of green paper from beside the cash register and handed it to Dora.

"Not to mention that most any given Saturday half the town empties out, people heading elsewhere for shopping and entertainment and such." Jed stretched his neck out to peer over Dora's shoulder at the flyer with all the information about the event printed on it.

"Sunday is the Lord's day. Monday is get-back-to-work-and-already-realize-you're-a-day-behind day." Josie hurried to fetch another saucer and coffee cup.

"Wednesday it's back to church for the goodly lot of us."

"Shouldn't that be the Godly lot of us?" Warren pondered aloud.

"Thursday's middle school football—we're in the play-offs." Josie set the saucer down and flipped the cup deftly. She nabbed the coffeepot and held it up to ask silently if Dora wanted any.

Dora nodded.

Josie poured. "Friday—high school football. That's an all-day and way into the night deal, what with pep rallies before and bonfires after."

"Then there we are back at Saturday and the great exodus." Jed nudged his own cup forward as if it were a reluctant volunteer that needed coaxing to step up and claim its refill.

"So Tuesday really was the only practical time to have it." Josie filled the cups, one right after another, with all the precision of a machine at the Crumble factory and a lot more grace and goodwill. She also saw to it that Jed and Warren each got another slice of pie, something no machine, or expense-conscious business-woman, would ever have done.

"I see. Yes. I am interested in this." Dora waved the paper around in a way that made Burke think that if it had been on white paper instead of green it would have looked like she intended to signal her complete surrender to the persistent and wonderful citizens of his hometown.

That thought made his hand freeze with his steam-ing cup of java halfway to his lips. Dora giving in to

Mt. Knott? He never considered a thing like that could happen, but seeing her like this, all sweet expressions and hay in her hair, laughing at Jed and Warren's corn-pone jokes?

"You know, if Ms. Hoag says she can't stay until the big event tomorrow night, we should probably just—"

"Do you suppose they have a vacancy at the hotel where I stayed last summer?" Dora pressed her lips tight and those big eyes of her went flinty and fixed on Burke's face. She crossed her arms and tipped her sweet, slightly pointed chin up.

He supposed that look had scared many a brave man, but it just made Burke want to grin. The woman had fire in her, he had to admit that.

"Then you'll stay for it." Josie clapped her hands.

But Burke had been burned too often and much too recently to dare to play with fire. "I'm sure Ms. Hoag is much too busy to...."

"I wasn't asking, Burke, I was insisting." And just that quickly Josie had Dora by the arm again, this time guiding her to the best booth in the place.

A booth. Not a seat at the counter. A seat at the counter said you were in a hurry, either that or you were Jed or Warren. But a booth? A booth said you were settling in for a spell.

Burke watched the women, then realized that everyone else was watching him watch them. Some curious, the rest sort of smug about seeing him overruled by his own sister-in-law.

Jed and Warren grinned.

"You are in big trouble now, boy," Jed muttered, swiveling around to go back to eating his pie.

"Half the town already got you married to that gal in their minds." Warren shook his head.

Burke knew they were right. Dora had walked in here a woman alone in the world and less than an hour later she was practically his fiancée. Only he didn't have a fiancée and wasn't looking for one.

This, he thought, mostly to himself but also a little bit as a plea for help to the Lord of all creation, this could be a problem.

Chapter Six

Dora's head was spinning. She couldn't figure this guy out. First, he hadn't wanted her to stay for Mt. Knott's Christmas kickoff. He'd asked her to come here but now he did not want her to stay. Why?

Dora glanced over her shoulder at the man standing with one hand on the lunch counter and the other raised to his forehead. A strand of blond hair fell across his knuckles, and he shook it off.

Jed or Warren—even though she'd spent many hours in this place last summer, Dora never had gotten straight which one was which—said something. Both men laughed. Burke's expression turned icy.

Dora plunked down in the seat and cradled her coffee in both hands, though that did nothing to warm the chill she felt coming from Burke's blue eyes.

The man, Jed or Warren, had probably said something personal. Burke did not do personal.

But Mt. Knott and its residents? Nothing but personal. Too personal.

And personable.

They had taken Dora in today as if she had never left after last summer. They treated her like one of their very own. An old friend. No different from anyone, not even the town's Top Dawg.

To be treated like one of the crowd had to drive a man like Burke, a man who defined himself by his position, his accomplishments, crazy.

Dora smiled to herself. Mt. Knott might drive Burke crazy but she was just crazy about the place, and the people. She couldn't think of a nicer, warmer, sweeter place to be during the Christmas season, and she looked forward to the townwide event tomorrow night.

No, Burke did not want her here at all but here she was. She sighed.

She put her shoulders back against the seat and drew in a deep breath, savoring the familiar smell of Josie's hearty fare.

Dora had eaten lunch at Josie's Home Cookin' Kitchen almost every day last summer. Sometimes dinner. Now and again breakfast. And coffee. Lots and lots of coffee at all hours of the day and night while she and Adam Burdett and Burke had pored over the details of the business, discussing what they should do, what they could do and what they would never want to do with it.

The thing they had never wanted to do was to let it slip out of family hands. Dora probably read too much into that, right up until the moment Burke had let her know she was never going to be a member of their family or their future business plans.

If it were possible, she felt even more unwanted by

Burke now than she had sitting alone in her office on the day after Thanksgiving. What had she gotten herself into? And how did she get out?

She twisted around in the seat to look at the front door and the chalkboard wall caught her eye. Josie had painted almost an entire wall of the one-room restaurant with chalkboard paint to give the little ones something to occupy them while their parents visited with friends and ordered dessert.

Dora had to admire the younger woman's initiative and creativity. And, looking at how a portion of the wall had come to be used, she also had to admire Josie's heart. She'd allowed the townspeople to use the board to send messages, not just to each other, but in a special place sectioned off by vines and scrolled lettering, for prayer requests.

That section had been full last summer when many people had concerns about job security, the need for rain, the future of the Crumble. Dora fixed her gaze on the list now and shook her head.

The seasons had changed and, of course, the circumstances, but the things that people laid before the Lord varied little. Most people wanted the same things, after all, didn't they?

The sound of Burke's boots moving across the floor made her breath catch, but she kept on reading.

Prayers for health, well-being, peace of mind.

Prayers for prosperity.

Prayers for the people whom they loved.

People wanted to have a purpose, to have enough to sustain them in that purpose and to love and be loved.

That's all Dora wanted, when you boiled it all down. Same as the folks in Mt. Knott. Same as everyone, even those who thought they were above all that mushy stuff.

The footsteps stopped.

Dora swung her head around at last and looked up at the king of the mushy-stuff haters. She smiled, even as the promise of tears bathed her eyes. "I can see why you chose here to start on the proj—"

"Pie." Burke interrupted with a stiffly cheerful insistence. He shifted his eyes, reminding her that they did not have the privacy here they would have had in a café in Atlanta. "Yeah, Josie makes great pie. Mind if I join you and we order ourselves some?"

"Yes, I..."

"You mind?" He actually looked disappointed.

"I mean, yes, I'd like some pie, and no, I don't mind if you join me." She motioned to the bench across from her in the booth. "But aren't you worried you're keeping me, since you seem to think I'm so busy I can't stick around until tomorrow night?"

"Yeah, about that, Dora." He dropped into the seat. "No hard feelings."

"Of course not. Nothing personal. Just business."

"Exactly." He nodded slowly then slumped back in the seat as though a great weight had been lifted from his shoulders. His broad shoulders strained at the denim of his work shirt, shoulders that looked like they could carry the weight of the world as easily as lift a small child to see tomorrow's Christmas parade. "Just business. I'm glad you said it and not me."

But you did say it! Had he forgotten already? Dora

would never forget last summer, his hushed, hoarse voice, the clipped formality of his words, even the way he paused between one phrase and the next. *Nothing personal...just business.*

As if—well, she had never quite figured out why he had done that. Probably weighing his words so that he wouldn't give her anything to throw back at him.

Just like now. He'd let her use it as a justification for his actions, and how could she ever deride him for it? But it still hurt.

She tried to convey the message with her eyes and with the tension in her body. With the silence she left hanging uncomfortably between them and finally by jabbing the toe of her shoe into his shin.

Which he did not even feel through his jeans and cowboy boots.

"As long as we're clear on that...." He jerked his chin up and looked toward the counter, searching.

"You thought I wasn't clear on that?" She batted her eyes, doling out a measure of unspoken sarcasm to go with her, well, big ol' dose of spoken sarcasm. Another message the big galoot did not pick up on.

"No, not you. I know you, Dora. You are all business."

Now there was a kick she couldn't ignore. She opened her mouth to protest that claim.

"Not...not all business." He made a face like a kid trying to fit together a complex model kit or do long division in his head. He brushed his hair back from where it touched the scar cutting across his darker blond eyebrow. "I know that. But as far as this business between us is concerned, you are. All business."

"Tell me once again about how you dazzle people with your charm?" She pursed her lips but couldn't hold it and broke into a subtle smile to let him know she was teasing.

He chuckled and caught Josie's attention and called out for two slices of her freshest pie.

"Going to take one out of the oven in a sec. Give it fifteen minutes to cool, and I'll have it right to you."

"Thanks." He checked his watch.

"Waiting for pie? Sounds like a good enough excuse for you to sit here, and I won't have to rush off back to my busy, busy life."

He had the good form to wince a little at his own behavior. But not much. "I said all that just now because I didn't want to appear too eager to have you here."

Dora's turn to wince. "Wow, thanks."

"You're welcome."

"How do you do that?"

"What?"

"Only hear what you want to hear."

"I wish. If I could do that I'd…" He looked into her eyes. He shook his head and looked away and said no more.

Unlike Burke, Dora had a knack for hearing both things said and those unsaid. It had come in handy in her line of work, but now it made her feel a bit too vulnerable. She did not know how she could keep things between her and Burke merely professional if he kept telling her so much about himself by not telling her anything.

She reached her hand out across the table. "You actually care what people here think of you?"

He looked down at the place where her hand rested near his. "No. Not so much. As the head of the town's biggest business, I couldn't let that kind of thing get to me."

She touched his wrist lightly with her fingertips.

"I don't care what anyone thinks." He withdrew and dropped his hand into his lap, shifting back in his seat. "But I do care about what people *say*."

"Spoken more like a VP of marketing, not a CEO," she teased. "But I thought there was no such thing as bad publicity."

He squinted, looked left then right, then focused in on her. "Dora, you don't know how people get ahold of an idea in a small town and run with it."

Now Dora took a look around them, her eyes wide open. She observed the friendships all around them, the sense of community, the way that people wanted not only the best for themselves but for one another, too. She shook her head just a little and fixed her gaze on Burke again. "Actually, I suspect you are the one who doesn't know that, Burke."

"What do you mean?"

"Let's just say I don't think you are giving the people of Mt. Knott the credit they deserve."

"Yeah? Well, thanks to me and my lousy handling of the Crumble no one will give them the credit they deserve." He sat back, hearing what he wanted to hear all over again. "Going to be a bleak Christmas for a lot of folks around here, Dora."

"Money isn't the only thing that makes a merry Christmas, Burke," she said quite softly, since she doubted he'd listen.

He cast his eyes downward and nodded. "Yeah, but money is what I've got to give, thanks to my mom's life mission. Now you and I have to decide who to give it to."

"I can't help do that if you don't want me to stay here in Mt. Knott."

"I didn't mean for you to not actually stay, Dora. I only felt I had to put up some resistance to your hanging around town."

She nodded. "To protect yourself."

"To protect you."

From what? *Humiliation*, he would have said and she knew it. Knew it because she had already lived through it once.

"Fair enough," she conceded. "You don't want people to know about, um, about our *business* or thinking they know too much about our personal lives."

"Yeah."

"Then why meet me here? Your sister-in-law's place is the social hub of the whole town."

"Nowhere else much to go on weekdays if you're retired or work second shift or are a farmer who doesn't have much to do this time of year."

Or are out of work because the Crumble laid you off, or a business dependent on people laid off by the Crumble closed. He didn't say it, but Dora only had to read the prayer requests on the chalkboard wall to know the thought had occurred to him.

"That and there's pie."

He smiled the most genuine smile she'd seen on him all day. "And there's pie."

"Good choice then." She pulled out a pad and pen and began to write. "Not to mention that the wall alone gives me enough information to keep me busy for days."

Burke's hand closed over hers. "What are you doing?"

"Making notes."

"You can't be seen doing that."

"Then how do I collect the information?"

He scowled and glanced around them. "You have a camera phone?"

She tapped the earpiece attached to the side of her head.

He studied her Bluetooth a moment. "Can you read them off, like into voice mail or something?"

"Or *you* could."

"What?"

"Pie!" Josie set down two plates in front of them with practiced stealth. "Won't bother you. If you need anything else, holler."

And she backed away. Didn't turn and walk away. Oh, no, backed away with her eyes on them the whole distance back to the counter.

Dora tried to hide a chuckle. Maybe Burke could control the things he said, but he had no sway over his friends and family. They would think what they liked and say what they thought.

Good for them.

Even if it would make her job—and maybe her holiday—a bit tougher.

"Where were we?" Burke asked, steadfastly ignoring the cherry pie filling that dripped from his raised fork.

"You were going to call and read the names to me so I wouldn't be caught writing them down."

He set the bite of pie down on the plate, his silverware clattering.

"Well, it makes sense, doesn't it? To me they are just names and a brief request," she said. "You should be able to give me more background."

From the look on his face, she realized he didn't think he could do that.

"Well, if you can give me anything more to go on, that would help." A sentence she had longed to say to this man time and time again over their brief courtship and at least a time or two since they had parted ways. *Give me something more to go on, help me to understand this.* Dora sighed. "If we want to keep up the appearance of my having come to town just to look around—"

"Which you did."

"Which I did." She took a bite of pie. It was as good as she remembered it. No, better. Maybe that was because she was enjoying the company. Or maybe because she was enjoying getting the best of that company. If Burke had wanted to call all the shots on this project he shouldn't have called in a corporate hotshot. "Then I should go and look. Poke around a bit. Maybe start with some churches, the library, the newspaper."

"And do what?"

She outlined the list, touching her fingers to count down the tasks she had in mind as she did. "Ask at the churches if there is anyone in need I could consider for a donation. Read up on the town as a whole and its history. Then, at the newspaper, maybe look up stories on past recipients."

He clasped his hand over her raised fingers to cut her off. "Those I have in my mom's files."

She cocked her head and smiled. She did not slip her hand away from his. "Are you inviting me out to the Burdett compound to look them over?"

He let go of her hand. "No."

"Of course not." *Business. All business.* "Just as well, because I need you to stay here."

"Here?" He went for another bite of pie.

She gave him a look meant to scream, *you really do just hear what you want to hear,* and said, in a crisp, hushed voice, "To call me up and leave the names from the wall on my voice mail."

He wolfed down the bite. "Won't that look odd?"

"I thought you didn't care how you looked to other people?" Which was a shame because he looked terrific. Except for that… "You've got a…" She waved her hand over the side of her mouth. "Just a little…"

He frowned at her, confused.

"A…" Another wave of her hand. "Oh, here."

She stretched up from her seat, reached over the

table and dabbed away a blob of bright red cherry filling from the corner of his mouth.

"Thanks." He laughed and swiped the pad of his thumb over the same spot. "Of course, now everyone in this diner is going to talk about this."

"About what a sloppy eater you are?" She sat back down.

"About how you and I shared some pie and how you found a reason to touch my face, to make it your business to look after me."

To make it your business to look after me. The thought made Dora sad and wistful all at once. "All the more reason for you to stay here and make the call. It will look better than the two of us heading out of here together."

"Good point. You certainly don't let anything slip by, Dora."

"Hey, what's a good little helper for?"

He looked at her a moment but said nothing.

A good helper. A helpmate. The thing she had always wanted so much to be for one man. For this man, she had once thought. Now she had her chance, even though it could not last.

"Hey, Josie, can I get a refill on coffee?" he called out, as if to remind Dora that in his world he had plenty of helpers. They were his employees, servers and beneficiaries. Though she had taken on this job strictly as a volunteer, he did not see her any differently.

"Anyway—" She started to slide out of the booth.

"Stay." He did not reach for her with anything but the most sincere look deep in his eyes.

Her heart stopped. She did not move.

"Wait until Josie gets over here, then we'll make our goodbyes. If we do it in the open like that it gives people less reason to try to guess what we said or why we said it."

She sat and felt her whole body sag a bit. "Funny, sometimes you can be right here hearing every word and still be left wondering those things."

"Hmm?"

"Eat your pie," she said. "We have a lot of work yet to do."

Chapter Seven

Burke could not read a single name on the list without stopping to wonder about the story behind the request. He knew some of them, but far too many held no larger meaning than they would for a stranger passing through town.

Conner Burdett had had a rule about knowing too much about the people who worked for him. He was against it. In much the same way kids learned in 4-H never to name the animals they later might have to sell for slaughter, the old man thought it best not to have any personal connection to a worker, because you might have to fire him later.

Adam, Josie's husband, the second Burdett son, had followed that edict to the letter. Made him a better manager, some said. Most must have said it, Burke decided, since he was the man in change of the whole shebang now.

But Burke wasn't made that way. Despite being the adopted son, Adam was Conner all over. And Burke was his mother, in conscience, in commitment to a calling and, by her design, now in Christmas spirit.

So where he had initially intended to pick and chose only the people most in need of some kind of grant, he ended up reading the entire list into the phone, each with a notation, a personal observation or bit of encouragement.

"The Sykes family asks for prayer for their daughter, Jenny, who is serving in the army overseas. Would be nice to do something for someone in the military."

And.

"The cheerleaders need to raise money to go to a competition this spring. It's not exactly what Mom had in mind, but I think it would give the whole town something to get behind. They need that. They deserve it."

And later:

"The Pennbreits simply say they are praying for everyone because it's all they can do right now. There's a story that would break your heart, Dora. I don't know if they have sons or daughters, though. Does it matter?"

He didn't think so but he trusted that Dora had the wherewithal and the detachment to make the right call on that. Still, he felt compelled to remind her, "They're good folks. They're all good folks, Dora. I wish I had the means to help them all."

I know, but maybe you aren't meant to help them all, Burke, he could hear her soft words in her head. He could imagine her soft reply clearly in his mind. *Did you ever stop to think—*

"I am thinking, Dora. Can't help but think." He said out loud he'd meant that just as he had meant the last thing he said before flipping the phone shut and leaving the Home Cookin' Kitchen. "Guess sometimes you don't realize how blessed you are until you stop dwelling on all the wrongs you think have been done to you and look around at what other people are dealing with, and ask yourself, what can I do to make things better?"

What he had decided to do was head home. Yes, *home,* not the house, as he had taken to calling it since his mother had died.

Home. The place where he had grown up and where he had returned to live after his mother's death, for Conner's sake. As the oldest son and the one who had unseated the old man from his position as CEO of the company he had founded, it was Burke's duty to move back in. His place both as a son and as a brother. The only place he still retained now that Adam had taken over at the Crumble.

He sat in his truck and gazed at the house at the center of the Burdett compound. Five structures, each indicative of their owner.

Stray Dawg, the second son, the loner tamed by love who now had a wife, son and the reins of the business, had an upscale log cabin on a wooded two-acre lot. Jason, dubbed Lucky Dawg because he was born after Conner and Maggie had given up ever having another child and for never having broken a bone, despite a love of extreme sports, had designed an Irish cottage, complete with a meandering stone path and hunter-green shutters. While Cody, the youngest of the bunch, still called Hound Dawg despite having answered a call to the ministry, lived with his wife, Carol, in an old-fashioned-style farmhouse complete with wrap-around front porch, like something right out of *The Andy Griffith Show.*

Burke's house, a small, simple ranch style, looked more like a guesthouse than a place where a man would want to spend his free time or one day raise his family. Dora had stayed there last year when she had been in negotiations to buy into the family business.

Burke had not even crossed its threshold since she had left. Not that they had happy memories there. She had always come over to the main house to avoid even the appearance of impropriety. But still, just knowing she had eaten breakfast at their table caught his imagination. She had rested her head on the pillows and dreamed who knows what dreams, about being his partner in life as well as business, he supposed. They had never discussed that eventuality outright but it had been an unspoken possibility that had woven itself through their every moment last summer. She had lived in his family's home, learned the ropes of his work, spent her days with his family. She had even attended Cody's church with him.

Home, work, family, church. She'd seen all the sides of the man that mattered and hadn't run off—until he had chased her off. It had humbled him then to think of a woman like Dora even considering caring for a man like him. Now? Well, now he wasn't that man anymore.

She must be counting her blessings today that she had escaped ending up with him. Here in South Carolina without a job or any real plans for the future.

Burke had invested his all in the company, in his

place there and among his brothers, and his own family had sized him up and found him unworthy. Still, he had tried to fight for her. He had championed her cause of allowing her to buy into the Carolina Crumble Pattie Company and he had failed. He had been determined to get for Dora whatever she wanted one way or another, but in the end he had failed to get her a place in the business. The whole house of cards—home, work, family and all their unspoken possibilities—had caved in.

He gripped the steering wheel and gritted his teeth. By now she surely understood that she was better off without him.

He got out of the truck and stood, trying to decide whether to go to the main house where he had taken up residence—if by residence one meant that he had been sleeping on the pull-out sofa in his father's old office—or to finally return to his old house. The house he had once moved away from with a sure conviction of his station in life. The house that Dora had probably imagined the two of them would one day share.

He looked skyward for a moment, not seeking guidance from above, but just to find some respite from the choices laid out so plainly before him.

Following the brief flurries of Thanksgiving Day the temperature had warmed considerably. The clouds had cleared away. In fact, the sun shone so brightly that by nine in the morning people could shed their lightweight jackets. Everyone needed a baseball cap or dark glasses to shade their eyes, and here and there the summery sound of flip-flops could be heard along the sidewalks of Mt. Knott. In other words, the weather matched Burke's mood—totally inappropriate for the approaching holiday and the task that lay ahead for him.

There was only one way to change his mood. Something that he had to do, that he had promised Dora he would do. Something he had put off doing for two years now. He had to go to Santaland.

That made the choice of houses for him. In a matter of moments he was outside the locked doors of the attic office that no one had entered since his mother's death. Before that, only she had been allowed through those doors. Her office. Her sanctuary. Her domain. Right up until the night she had given him the key, told him what she had been doing all these years and to go and see it for himself.

He put his hand on the doorknob. He took a deep breath. Dust assaulted his nostrils. He sneezed. Once. Twice. Three times. Silly him, he half-expected to hear his mother's voice from the other side of the door call out, "God bless you, baby."

In the deafening silence that greeted him instead he thought better of the plan to come here. He turned, started to tuck the key away then paused. He sniffed, lightly this time, cautiously. What was that smell?

Pine. Probably from some scented candle that his mom had had on her desk to keep her in the holiday mood all year round. He imagined it, deep green in a large glass jar sitting right where she had placed it before she got too sick to climb the stairs.

It seemed to draw him back.

He had to do this.

For his mom.

For all the good folks of Mt. Knott.

For Dora.

"Dora," he said softly. He pulled his phone from his pocket, flipped it open and pressed the button to show his last placed call. If he were the kind to go in for a lot of heavy self-analysis, he'd say wanting to leave a message on Dora's voice mail at this precise moment was his way of not facing his memories and concerns all alone.

Instead he said out loud as he pushed Call, "I'll map the place out as I go so if she needs to get to files or anything I won't have to come back with her."

A soft electronic purring ring filled his ear.

He cranked the doorknob to the right and gave a nudge with the toe of his boot just above the threshold where age and weather had swollen the wood and made it stick.

Another ring.

The door swung open.

R-r-r-ring.

He flipped on the light.

Correction: Lights. Hundreds of them. Maybe thousands. Not just the two large overhead low-watt bulbs that glowed dimly from their frosted fixture-coverings, but string upon string of tiny twinklers strung from every rafter, framing every window and running along every surface. They even outlined the huge old desk painted gleaming black with bright gold scrollwork accents, in the same style as an old sleigh Burke's mother had purchased years ago and restored to perfection.

Guilt tugged at Burke over that. They had always stored the sleigh in the barn where they housed a couple of horses and countless cats. Each year when his mother had announced it was time to get the sleigh out and go caroling, Burke had been the one to go get it, hitch up the horse and bring it around.

That last year, the year his mother died, she had asked him to bring the sleigh out for her. "I want to give you boys one last happy memory."

"We don't want a memory, Mom. We want you to get better. You can't get better if you go out in the cold night air."

"Burke, I'm not going to get better. I certainly won't be well enough to go Christmas shopping this year. Memories are all I can give you this year."

Burke had refused.

Refused to fetch the sleigh. Refused to accept the memory-making experience. So a few days later when his mother had asked for another favor?

He glanced around him. From every nook and cranny statues, dolls and likenesses of Saint Nicholas peered out from under a robed hood, a red and white fur cap or even, in a couple instances, a cowboy hat.

"Take over my legacy, son. Continue the good work. Don't be afraid to change someone's life for the better."

When his mother had asked him to do this, he could not refuse.

Rr-r-r-r-ing.

The tone drew him into the present again. In a moment Dora's voice mail would pick up.

His gaze fell on the credenza behind the desk and all the framed photographs of the girls his mother's charity had helped over all these years.

All those stories. All those fresh starts and new opportunities. All those changed lives. How had she chosen? How had she known who was deserving and how had she dealt with the disappointment that so few had given back to the cause?

That hadn't bothered her, he knew. She'd told him even at the end of her life that her responsibility was to be a cheerful giver and to act in the name of the Lord. She couldn't control what the receiver did after that. If they squandered their gifts or used them for ill, that would be between those receivers and God.

The lack of appreciation and failure to give back to the town was his issue. And one of the reasons he felt so inadequate to take this all on.

Maggie Burdett.

Saint Nicholas?

Top Dawg?

"Uh-uh." He pulled the phone away from his ear. There was one name he knew did not belong on that list and it was...

"Burke? Burke Burdett? Is that you?"

"Dora?"

"Don't sound so surprised. You called me."

"I thought I'd get your voice mail."

"You want me to hang up? You can call back and let my voice mail pick up."

Yes. That was exactly what he wanted. Oddly enough, it was also the one thing that he did not want—to lose contact with Dora. "That's kind of silly, isn't it?"

She didn't confirm or deny it.

"Yeah." He cleared his throat. "Okay. Well, I've got you now. That is, we have each other...on the line."

"Good. I actually found out a lot today and have some good leads. One thing I need your input on, though, is when to call the jeweler."

"The jeweler? Why?"

"It's the Christmas season, Burke, maybe not where you are but for the rest of us—"

"Oh, it's Christmas where I am." He shifted to take in the full panoramic view and chuckled. "Definitely Christmas."

"That's a busy time for a jeweler. We need to get our order in so he can have the charms ready and engraved with everything but the names of the recipients. I bet your mom had records about when she ordered them and all the specs on them."

"I'm sure she did." From the looks of it, his mom had never thrown anything away.

"Great. If you can just read them off to me?"

"Hold on. I'll just look over...here." He tried to maneuver without tipping over tiny trees or stomping on delicate glass baubles. He yanked open a drawer only to find a small snow scene made from a mirror and cotton batting where file folders should have hung. "I'll tell you what. Why don't I handle everything with the jeweler?"

"Are you sure? I'll be headed back to Atlanta soon anyway."

"You will?" He shut the drawer with the snow scene in it and a puff of glitter sprayed up onto his hand. "Why?"

"Because that's where I live," she said, and left it at that.

Burke didn't need the lecture that could have followed. He thought she showed great restraint and good manners by not pointing out that he had left her little choice by not providing her a place to stay. "You can stay as long as you need to and bill your room at the motel to me, of course."

"What? I would never ask you to pay for that."

"You expect Global to pick up the tab when you travel. This is no different from that." He opened another drawer and then another searching for the information about the jeweler, or about his mother's selection system, or at least a tissue or hankie to clean the glitter from his hand. A dozen boxes of old-fashioned icicles tossed in with a ledger for the project, from a decade ago. Some tin noisemakers. The template for the letter she must have once meant to send with the coins but never finished. A sheet of self-adhesive gift tags. "Just a business expense. You may not take a salary for your time, but I can't let you pay out of your own pocket to help me do my job."

"Don't you mean your mission?"

"Do I?" He paused to give that a moment's thought. "Or maybe a calling?"

Mission? Calling? The terms exuded a higher purpose than trying to assuage his guilt over his many failings. Burke couldn't own up to that. If he were to chose a word he'd pick *obligation. Responsibility.* An expectation that came with being born a Burdett. "No, *job* is the right word."

"Well, then I guess you're one of the lucky ones in Mt. Knott. Asking around all day I've heard that unless you work for the Crumble, there aren't any jobs to be had around here."

"How do you think I'd do at crumb cake inspecting?" The next drawer he tried stuck after opening only an inch. Were those files inside?

"I suspect you've known a few crumbs in your life," she shot back.

She didn't name names but he got the idea she meant him and felt it an unfair categorization. Instead of telling her so, though, he channeled his annoyance into freeing the stuck drawer with one mighty tug.

"Christmas cards?" And not new ones that someone could use, either. But old ones, from people they hadn't known for years if they had known them at all, probably saved for the pretty pictures. "And speaking of pictures…"

"Were we speaking of pictures?"

Burke stared at the faded color photograph of him dressed as an elf for a kindergarten play. He chuckled under his breath. "Yeah. Yeah, we did speak about pictures. The one in my hand in particular."

"The…not the…the elf?"

He laughed at the unabashed delight in her voice.

It was a sound he had heard almost daily during their summer together. He'd missed it. He'd missed her.

"Oh, this I have to see," she said. "Of course, I suspect to do that, I'd have to slide down the chimney by night and rifle through the house until I found it for myself."

"Actually—" He looked around, then at his hand, then at the boxes of junk and cabinets, also filled with junk. "You may be right."

"What? I, uh, Burke, I may be thin but I don't think I can actually fit down a chimney."

He chuckled.

"And as for rifling through a house? Not my bailiwick, buddy. Legal history, financial documents, tax records, ask me to find my way around those and I won't quit rummaging until I found out who owned the land the house sits on before Carolina was a state."

"That would be a Burdett," he informed her, half-wondering if he might turn up an ancestor or two in the dust and mayhem of his mother's office. "And that would be exactly the kind of dedication this situation calls for."

"Burdett dedication?"

"Dora dedication." He picked up a receipt for hundreds of dollars' worth of school supplies paperclipped to a pamphlet of illustrated Christmas carols. "The only way to get the information we need fast is to get someone to come to the house and organize my mother's things."

"I would be proud to help with that, Burke. All you have to do is—"

Ask. His mind went instantly to all those things left unsaid between them and he knew that if he did this, he had to be clear about what he wanted from her from the very start.

"You couldn't just come in and work up here in the office. No one else knows about this place. It's just a small space across the hall from where they think my mother used to spend her days." He wondered how anyone could have known his mother and believed that she could ever get anything done in the tidy yellow decoy room with the white furniture across the hall from her actual "office." "Whoever came in would have to pitch in and get the downstairs in order by day then work up here after hours when everyone thinks they have gone to bed."

Dora cleared her throat. "Is that a job offer, Mr. Burdett?"

"Well, it's not as glamorous a job as crumb inspector."

"Why would anyone believe I'd do that kind of thing—putting your mother's things in order—for you?"

"You wouldn't be doing it for *me,* really."

"No one would believe I was doing it for my health, now would they?"

"We'll tell them the truth. We needed an objective person to go through Mom's things but we also wanted someone familiar with the family. All we have to do is throw those two ideas out—a person who knows the Burdetts and can still be objective about us, and the list suddenly gets very narrow."

She hesitated.

He knew if he said anything more, asked her from his heart, gave just the tiniest insight into how much this meant to him, into what she meant to him, she would do it in an instant. And be hurt all the more when their work ended and she realized that he had nothing more to offer a woman like her. He remained silent.

She said nothing.

As negotiating tactics went, this was one of the oldest of the bunch. It went back to children in the school yard. First one to blink loses.

Finally, after what seemed forever, Dora sighed. "When do I start work?"

Burke tried not to sound too pleased with himself. "I'll move from the main house back into my old place in the morning. You can move in here anytime after noon tomorrow."

"Move in? I didn't really bring enough stuff to move in, Burke."

"You know what I mean."

"No, I don't. How long do you anticipate me staying?"

"Until the job's done."

"The job. Yes. Of course. Just business, huh?"

"Just business," he echoed. "Is there anything else?"

Tell me. Tell me, Dora, that there is something else.

She held her tongue for so long that he almost wondered if they had lost their connection. When she finally spoke he realized that their connection had been lost long before today, as she said in a quiet voice just before ending the call, "No, Burke. I guess there is nothing else. I guess maybe there never was."

Chapter Eight

Dora's heartbeat kicked up a notch. She'd come for the day, thinking she'd spend a few hours discussing things with Burke, gather what information she could then head back to Atlanta to sort through things. But here she was, already more than a day later, standing before the main house of the Burdett compound—moving in!

"Just visiting," she murmured firmly to keep that particular little flight of fancy in check. "No different than whatever five-star hotel I'd pick to spend the holidays in these last few years."

She gripped her purse and briefcase—she never went anywhere without it—in both hands, took a deep breath and marched up the front steps. She paused in front of the large door with its glass inset, looked down and saw four sets of footprints stenciled onto the painted floor. Hound Dawg's, the smallest, showed the treads of tennis shoes. Lucky Dawg, the name under the next set of prints preserved by a tough protective finish, had the feet positioned in such a way that Dora could almost see that brother's cocky stance. Adam, Stray Dawg's, prints faced toward the steps and the last set.

She moved to the full-sized boot prints, pointed directly at the door, of a man who knew where he belonged and had no intention of budging.

Dora looked around a moment. She wet her lips. She held her breath. This was it. Crossing the threshold back into the world she had once hoped would be hers meant…she didn't know what it meant, really, only that once she did this she couldn't undo it. Just like this past summer when she worked so closely with them—with Burke—she could only move through what happened next. No turning back.

If she were smart or, rather, wise, she'd run. She exhaled at last, looked straight ahead then stepped inside Burke's footprints.

They made her shoes look almost childlike. And though the footprints were only made of paint and many years old, she felt as though, through them, she had made a small connection to the man.

She put her hand on the doorknob and a shiver shot through her body.

Who was she kidding? No different than a five-star hotel? This was the Burdett family home.

The place where the man she had once hoped to have a future with was raised. Where he had lived these past two years. Where the people who had first invited her into their midst and into the middle of their business, then later tossed her out without so much as an explanation, met over deals and meals alike.

Dora reached out to touch two fingers to the ornate *B* etched in the glass of the oval inset on the dark green door.

"Five stars?" She looked at the grime on her fingertips then at the chipped paint around the broken brass and plastic doorbell, then at the footprints strangely preserved against the faded blue-gray of the weathered porch. "I don't think this place would even rate a lone star." She peered through the glass to the darkened rooms beyond. "A falling star, maybe."

At least at a hotel she got the hustle and bustle of holiday activity and a beautiful tree to gaze upon. Not to mention she usually enjoyed a roaring fire without having to go outside in the elements to gather wood. That and the lights and excitement of the city cheered her up.

Where were the Burdetts' decorations? The tree? The lights? What was there here to offer her a sense of warmth, of hope, of excitement?

The door swung open.

"Welcome to my home. It's good to have you here." Burke stepped up to the threshold, his hand extended.

Dora's arm trembled as her palm met his. Trembled! She had shaken hands with some of the most powerful people in her industry and never let her nerves get the better of her. Why couldn't she get control of herself now?

Burke's expression was an odd mix that Dora couldn't quite call delight but wouldn't deny held a certain amount of pleased relief. He was nervous, too.

"I was beginning to think you'd changed your mind about coming."

She had changed her mind. Multiple times. Yet somehow it always got changed back and so here she was. Standing in Burke's shadow and in his footsteps. Giving up her usual holiday activities to give other people a Christmas while in return she would have—

She lost her train of thought as the smell of turkey and gravy, pumpkin pie and coffee filled the air.

"Dora's here!" Burke called over his shoulder.

"Don't make her stand outside, bring her in, we're waiting for her!" Josie pecked at her from the wide arching doorway that led to the dining room.

A cheer went up from the entire Burdett family.

She would give up her usual holiday and in return she would have the best shot at a real Christmas she'd ever known.

Dora came inside and before she could even thank them for welcoming her, Burke had taken her briefcase and someone else had scooped up the plastic bag of personal items she'd picked up at the one store in town, a chain discount, general mercantile type of place.

"Can we eat now?" Jason, the third of the dog pack, howled.

"Ain't fitting. T' have company like this fine lady come here and not provide her with a proper spread." Conner Burdett, who had probably once stood almost as tall as Burke, pushed his way past his sons and daughters-in-law. Rail thin and aged by grief, he still had a hard edge to him that said he wouldn't be taken advantage of.

Or fooled.

Or even charmed by anyone.

The grip of his handshake told Dora he recognized her as not just anyone. He knew who she was, what she did for a living and that in another place and time she would have been a powerful ally—or opponent— in business.

"Though I admit I find myself perplexed as to why you are here, Ms. Hoag. Why you would *want* to be here," he amended, his tone and demeanor changed from when he had barked at his wolf pack of a family.

Message received. Conner didn't want her here.

The old man turned and walked toward the arched doorway.

Dora shifted her gaze from one face to the next, ending with Burke. He prodded her to move with a nod of his head. Dora understood this as her cue to follow Conner and she did so.

"It's just leftovers, buffet style with these mangy mutts, nothing fancy," Burke warned her. "I hope that's okay."

"Okay?" Here was her out. She could simply say she thought she should find other accommodations, that an old house and Mt. Knott, South Carolina, simply did not meet her standards. Except…

She took a second to study those accommodations. The smiles, the smells, the light in the family's eyes and Burke, trying to smooth her way, and once again her mind changed.

"There a problem?" Conner demanded, turning

slowly. "What's good enough for my kin not good enough for you, young woman?"

Dora eased out a long breath, brushed a glance Burke's way then met Conner's unyielding stance. "It's better than good enough, Mr. Burdett. Your home is grander and more agreeable than any five-star hotel in any exotic city in any corner of the world."

"What?" Conner turned and fixed a hard, squinty-eyed gaze on her. "What did you say?"

A lot of people would have been intimidated by the strange look on the old man's face and the energy with which he asked his question. Both seemed determined to push her back a step, knock her off balance, challenge her.

Obviously the man had not considered his target. If she did not know how to stand her ground, keep her equilibrium and rise to a challenge, she certainly would never have spent a day in the company of Burke Burdett. And she sure wouldn't be standing in his home now.

She raised her chin, trying to make herself an imposing figure, and smiled, because, well, the old man looked like he needed a kind smile. "I have traveled all over the world. Paris, Rome, Tokyo, I've stayed in fancy hotels and even a palace or two and I have to say, Mr. Burdett, your home has them all beat."

"You, little girl…" He stabbed a bony finger directly at her face.

She braced herself for a tirade, not sure if he would go into detail about everything he found lacking in her or merely call her a liar, which she wasn't.

Burke stepped up and put his arm around her shoulders. "Mind your manners, old man."

"No, you mind yours. I'll remind you not to go grabbing on our honored guests like a crate of Crumble Patties ready for loading on a bakery truck." Conner plucked Burke's hand from Dora and batted it away.

"What?" Burke stepped back, his hands up, clearly more from surprise than from sheer obedience.

"Honored guest?" Dora asked.

"Why, yes." Conner beamed down at her and put his arm where Burke's had been moments before. "Such a perceptive, wise and well-spoken young lady, you are welcome in my home anytime."

"B-but don't you want to know why I'm here?"

"Yeah, you've come to put my house in order." Conner came off gruff but his pale eyes shone with gratitude and more than a little grief. That quickly shifted to something more like accusation as his attention went to Burke, then to impish sweetness as he turned to her and added, "And I couldn't think of another person on earth I would want to do it."

That shut Dora up.

At least long enough to try to take it all in.

"Seems a waste of a powerful executive." Adam, who had once worked under Dora's tutelage at Global and now ran the whole operation at the Crumble, eyed her cautiously.

Her cheeks burned. She had been so focused on her feelings about Burke that she hadn't thought about having to play the humble servant to people who had treated her so shabbily.

"But Burke said you volunteered," Adam went on. "He said you were the cheerful little helper type."

"Volun—? Cheerful little helper?" She shouldn't have been peeved by that and if it were just the two of them, she'd probably laugh off the whole elf connotation, but to let everyone think she'd pushed her way into this with such a flimsy excuse as being a helper type? This whole deal was Burke's doing and he needed to own up to some part in it. "I'd have never presumed to offer, of course, if Burke hadn't—"

"You know, I never even asked if you wanted to put your things away and clean up before we eat, Dora." Burke grabbed her by the elbow and pulled her gently against his chest.

At his touch, her anger faded more quickly than she would have liked. Anger, after all, had often proved a reliable ally in protecting her from people getting too close, and from any weakness on her part for trusting too much, too soon, too… "I'd like that."

As soon as they were out of earshot, she dug deep and tried to rekindle her initial feelings of embarrassment. "I volunteered?"

"What's wrong with that? Volunteering is nice."

"It makes me seem like I couldn't wait to worm my way back into…" *Your heart.* She struggled to take her eyes off him and tear her mind away from thoughts of what might have been between them. Maybe she shouldn't have come away alone with him, even just a flight of stairs or two. Even if it was all only a business proposition. That thought snapped her back to the reality of the situation. "It made me seem far too anxious to worm my way back into your family's good graces."

"Trust me, they would never even consider that was what you were doing."

"Because they see me as a serious professional?"

"Because…" He turned and winked at her over his shoulder. "My family is worm proof."

She opened her mouth to make a cutting remark about this not being the time for joking, then it dawned on her that he probably was not making a joke so much as a painful private observation and covering the truth of it with a joke. The Burdetts had shut him out as well as her, and it had to have left its mark on him. That concession was the most personal glimpse he'd given her into what was really going on with him these days. She accepted it, and his offering of closeness by opening up, with a gracious nod of her head.

He led her on upstairs, took her luggage and set it outside the door then beckoned her to a narrow doorway. It opened to a secluded stairway.

"Besides, I had to let them think it was your idea to see to my mother's things and that meant helping my father deal with her estate, because I couldn't very well tell them that this is why you had to come." He flipped on the light.

Dora gasped. No wonder they didn't have any exterior decorations. They were all here.

"Oh, Burke. You really are…"

"Don't call me that name."

"Name?"

"Jolly old you know who." He pressed one finger

to her lips. "Please don't call me that. I'm just me. A flawed man without a clue how to accomplish the task before him."

His first concession about his family had been more than she expected from him. This uncustomary humility, this way of telling her how much he needed her without really telling her how much he needed her, this was a precious gift, indeed.

She closed her eyes and whispered, "No, you're not, you're the Top Dawg," placing her fingertips on his hand as he swept it along her cheek.

"Not any more." He shook his head. His hand fell away. "You saw it yourself. We're in my father's house. My brother speaks for the family and runs the Crumble. This is all I have."

"This seems quite enough, Burke. If you do the right things with it all." After a moment measured by no less than a heartbeat, it dawned on her she had said that while looking into his eyes.

He held her gaze for just one fleeting second, then looked through the door, his jaw clenched. "It is what it is."

Just business. He did not say it, but he did say it, in his posture, in his grim expression even as he fixed his attention on the wonderful landscape of the office before them.

She flushed, cleared her throat then hastily flung her arm out toward the glittering space. "It's a great, um, jumping-off point."

"It's just a mishmash of an inheritance, not by my

own doing. Plus I have to hide it away, which is not my style."

"Oh, I don't know. You seem a very private person to me." From *me,* she might have said instead but decided not to push it here and now. With her trust issues and all the things she had yet to say to him or his family about the way they had ended things, she was hardly one to throw stones.

"Yeah. I guess. But guarding your privacy and actually hiding things from people that matter to you? Very different. Doesn't feel right and yet...." He held his arms out to indicate the cluttered, covert office.

"Not your style."

He met her gaze and with an expression that admitted he was only half-kidding asked, "You think it's too late to change my nickname to Lost Dawg?"

"You're not lost. You can't be. You've always got someone to guide you." She reached down and picked up a multipointed silver star meant for the top of a Christmas tree.

He nodded then looked around at all the clutter of Christmas items overwhelming the small space. He rubbed his eyes and groaned. "I'm sorry I got you into this."

She set the star down and came to stand beside him. "I'm not."

His hands dropped from his face and he bent his head to look down into her eyes. "You're not?"

"I really do like it here," she whispered. She started to step back, literally moved by her own surprise at her confession, but Burke stopped her, taking her by the shoulders. She stilled and murmured, "I really, really like it."

"I like having you here."

"I'll try to be here every evening."

"What?" He cocked his head.

"In this office." She peered beyond him into the room. "I said I liked it here. You said you liked having me here. You did mean in the office, right?"

"No, Dora." He inched in closer.

"No?"

"I mean in my arms." He placed his crooked knuckles beneath her chin and nudged it up into just the right position to place a kiss on her waiting lips.

She wanted to tell him she couldn't allow that kind of overture. They were business associates, after all, nothing more. But in Burke's arms, kissing him, all that fell away. For the briefest measure of time, and despite the sparkle of Christmas ornaments and lights all around them, it was summer again. Anything was possible and—

"Dora? Burke? We went ahead and blessed the food. Served ourselves and now Jason wants to know if he can start on seconds or if he has to wait for you?" Adam's voice carried up the stairs and sliced between them as effectively as if he had pushed them apart and sent them to neutral corners.

Only Dora could not imagine a place in this house, in this town, in her heart or mind, where she would feel neutral about this man. That scared her.

A lot.

But fear alone could not account for the rabbit-quick beating of her heart.

"Sorry about that." He tipped his head to one side to make clear that he meant the interruption. "Hope having all these people around while you try to get things done doesn't drive you crazy."

"Are you kidding?" Dora embraced the chance to talk about anything that took the spotlight of awkwardness off what had just happened. "Spending time around your family is one of the reasons I came here. This will be the first Christmas in a very long time that I won't feel utterly alone in the world."

Quick thinking! Take the spotlight off how readily you gave into his kiss and put it right on the humiliating reminder that you have not a soul in the world who cares enough about you to share the most wonderful time of the year with you.

"Dora…"

He pitied her. She could tell. And she hated it.

Her whole life she had just wanted to give from her heart and find someone who would take what she had to offer gladly. People didn't take anything from those they pitied. They became objects of sympathy and charity, not wellsprings from which to draw love and support.

Suddenly Dora realized that this might be the loneliest Christmas she'd ever known.

"We should go." Dora stepped backward and fussed with her hair.

"Yeah." Burke cleared his throat and jerked his thumb toward the open door. "By the way, I'll do whatever I can to help go through my mom's belongings downstairs for you."

"With me," she clarified, her head held high. "Expecting others to do the work I have committed to as mine is not my style."

Her clipped, driven business persona rose to the surface again.

"I know. That's why Global values you so much."

"Global? Values?" She tried to piece those words together so that they made sense to her but she just couldn't do it. Global was a huge corporation that thought of her as a cog in the machine. As long as she kept on churning and the wheels kept going round and round she had a job. The second she stopped? She harrumphed. "Where did you get the idea that Global cares anything about me?"

"You said they had been founded on Biblical principles." He repeated something she had told them when they had still been in discussions about the Carolina Crumble Pattie operation selling out to the megacorporation.

"Yes, a long, long time ago. They've grown. They've changed. They're no longer a family business, like yours."

"Hey, from where I'm standing mine's not strictly a family business anymore, either." He grumbled then he opened the door and held his hand out to allow her to go first.

The sounds of laughter, of plates clattering, of conversation wafted up from the lower story.

They washed over her, each one pricking at her raw emotions.

"That—" she pointed out the door "—is not something I would ever hear at Global. Global is just a big, faceless and heartless corporation."

"That may be, but at least your heartless corporation hasn't kicked you to the curb. You don't see the faces at Global every time you get up in the morning and find you have nowhere to go. You still have a job."

Dora found it hard to feel sorry for Burke, who had so much, in contrast to her. She had, well, a job to do. "Speaking of jobs, when can I get back into this office?"

"My dad usually is asleep by nine."

"I can pitch in going through your mom's estate by day then, and come up here by night."

"I'd appreciate it. If you can make some sense out of her system that would help me next year and the year after and the year, when—"

"I get it." She cut him off because she did not want to hear the rest of that sentence.

"When you won't be around to help me anymore." He said it anyway.

"You just won't take a hint on a silver platter, will you?" She hurried past him and out into the hallway.

"Hmm? Hint? You mean—" He shut the door, turned the key in the lock then spun around and in one fluid movement snagged her arm and pulled her close. "This?"

"This is not a hint, Burke," she whispered, finding

it hard to breathe. "This is either the real thing or nothing at all. It's not a game."

"Do I look like a man who plays games, Dora?"

"No." *Then kiss me again and make it mean something,* she wanted to demand. Of course, she didn't. She wouldn't. A kiss like that from Burke was something he would have to give, his gift to her. And something he had to be willing to receive in return from her with the commitment that their kiss would mean more than a fleeting physical connection.

They had once had a future together, or more accurately, the promise of a future. That had changed and Dora did not completely understand why. But she was willing to try again. If he was.

He gazed deeply into her eyes.

She held her breath. Her heart pounded. She had no idea what he would do next.

"You're right." He let her arm go and moved away. "We can't let ourselves get distracted from the work ahead."

"Work," she said softly as she followed him down the stairs. "That *is* all there is between us, I guess."

"Did you say something?" he asked over his shoulder.

"I, um, I—" *If you can make some sense out of her system that would help me next year and the year after and the year, when you won't be around to help me anymore.* Burke had made his choice. She had to accept it.

They went down the stairs and headed for the dining room.

She should never have expected more. "I knew what I was getting into, Burke. I don't think you have to worry about me getting distracted again."

Chapter Nine

...This will be the first Christmas in a very long time that I won't feel utterly alone in the world.

Dora's words had kept coming back to him as they ate their meal, cleaned up afterwards, then all hurried off to the heart of Mt. Knott to join with the community to welcome in the coming season of goodwill.

"You know if it hadn't warmed up the way it has, I'd say drag out the old sleigh and ride into town," Jason announced, as they all headed for their cars outside their family home.

"Oh, I wish we could have." Carol turned to Cody, clapping her hands. "I only got to ride in it that one time. Of course, I'll never forget what happened that night."

"What happened that night?" Dora leaned in to whisper to Burke. "Did they get in an accident?"

Jason, who was passing by them at that very moment, barked out a laugh and promptly broke into the chorus of "Jingle Bells."

"Worse." Burke tried to maintain a proper scowl as he swung open the passenger door of his truck for his guest.

Dora put one hand on the door but did not climb up and into the cab right away, instead stopping to challenge him. He found that awfully charming, her fearlessness to stand up to him about the smallest things, even as a joke. "Worse?"

She clucked her tongue, shook her head and acted shocked to even imagine what could be worse.

"They got engaged," Burke answered, adding a jerk of his head to prod her to get into the car so they could get going and put this conversation behind them. He was not looking forward to having to spend his evening with the entire town of Mt. Knott, including a whole lot of people he had personally had to lay off from the Crumble. All of them acting as cheerful as possible. Trying to make it through the best they could. With him feeling guilty, both that he would be snooping around to decide which of them had the most pitiful circumstances, and that he could not simply help them all.

"Getting engaged is worse than getting into an accident?" she asked as he hurried her along.

"Doing anything that showy, like proposing in a sleigh, is worse because if you don't get it right or she turns you down, you will never hear the end of it."

"I can see that, especially in a small town like this where people are liable to talk," she agreed, joining in his jest.

"What do you two plan to get up to, to get people talking?" Cody asked, using his very most serious look of keeping an eye out for trouble, as any good preacher should.

"Nothing. Honest." Burke held his hands up like a kid who had been caught rattling the lid to the cookie jar. Then, for good measure, he gave Dora a quick wink. "We're on our best behavior."

"That's too bad," Conner grumbled, as he made his way slowly down the steps of the house, too proud to allow anyone to help him. "Don't know how this family is ever going to have any more grandkids with that kind of attitude."

Dora looked at Burke, a bit shocked.

"I'm not sure he actually heard what I said," Burke explained.

"Then again I'm not sure he didn't hear every syllable," Cody warned. Carol and Cody laughed, apparently having heard the old fellow's views about abandoning good sense and reason now and then in order to add a few new branches to the Burdett tree.

"Don't mind them. Sometimes they forget how to talk to people who aren't beholden to the Burdetts for their bread and butter." Burke stuck his hand out this time, trying to hurry her into the truck at last.

"I don't mind." She slipped her hand in his then paused for a moment. "I enjoyed sharing bread and butter with the Burdetts, so I guess I can stand it. In fact, I find it all endearing, the stories, the teasing and the bickering."

"I like her," Cody said, flashing the dimple that so many young women had sighed over that it had earned him the nickname Hound Dawg.

How could you argue with a woman who found your family's senseless babbling endearing? Went back to having spent so many holidays alone, he figured. Only explanation for finding charm in the Burdett clan. If only she had her own clan, her own relatives to laugh and bicker with.

"Anyway, it's not so bad getting talked about, you know." Cody gave Burke a playful punch in the arm.

Burke considered striking back, not hard but firmly enough to tell his baby brother he did not want a lecture on what he should do regarding Dora.

"After all," Cody went on, even before he dropped his fisted hand to his side. "Jesus was the talk of the town a time or two if you recall."

"Still is," Dora noted.

"So right." Cody nodded to her then gave Burke a no-nonsense look that suggested he thought his big brother should not let this woman go. "I'm telling ya, man, I like her."

"Maybe they should stay behind and rig up the sleigh," Carol whispered in her husband's ear loud enough for all to hear. She then wriggled the fingers of her left hand so that her diamond ring flashed in the light from the open truck cab. "Cody proposed to me in that sleigh on a winter's night three years ago."

"How romantic!" Dora folded her hands high on her chest and spoke directly to Cody. "Your idea?"

Cody pressed his lips tight and rolled his eyes in just the right way to silently rat out his older brother.

"You?" Dora looked at Burke with undisguised awe and surprise.

"Yeah. Well. I just—"

"Had to come from him." Conner passed his oldest son, clapping him hard on the shoulder as he did. "It's his sleigh. His mama bought it for him when he was a little tyke, before any of these other mangy mutts even came along."

Suddenly it dawned on him that his mother had been planning his taking over for her for a very long time. He'd certainly let her down these past two years.

Well, why not? Hadn't he let down everyone he cared about, as well as plenty of people he didn't even really know, these last two years?

"Your sleigh?" Dora cocked an eyebrow at Burke. "You own an actual sleigh? Is it red with gold trim and silver bells?"

He had cut her off before she could ask him where he kept his reindeer or make some other joke about the irony of the man who would rather not be Santa owning that particular kind of conveyance. "No. It's black and gold, just like—" Then he realized he had to cut himself off before he gave away where she would have seen the desk with the same high-gloss black paint and gold filigree. "Just like in an old Currier and Ives print."

"Oh, I'd love to see it sometime."

"Out in the barn." Cody helpfully pointed the way. "Though I can't for the life of me think of a reason he'd want to find an excuse to get you off alone in a dark, secluded place like that."

"I did ask if he'd put the wheels on it so we could take it into town tonight, maybe give some rides up and down Main Street and around the courthouse like the other people with wagons are doing," Josie chided, as she tucked her son into his car seat in the minivan parked next to Burke's truck.

"Guess he was too busy for that." Conner climbed into the seat beside his beloved grandson.

"I don't know doing what. Ain't like he had to get up and go to a job like the rest of us." Adam tossed his car keys up and caught them again in the same hand.

"Maybe *busy* isn't the right word. *Distracted.* That's more like it." Cody, ever the peacemaker, rushed in to verbally separate the two older brothers, who seemed to have forever been warring with each other since Maggie and Conner had adopted Adam. Burke had seen him as not just a rival but a replacement.

"Right." Adam did not relent. He never did. He was like the old man that way, except he knew when to pick his battles. Adam didn't push the things that didn't need pushing. It was what made him the ideal candidate to run the newly reorganized business and made Burke want to grab him by the scruff of the neck and tell him to back off when Adam concluded, "Guess the man was too distracted by *something* to do the few things we depended on him to do."

In the past, Burke would have put his brothers in their places, or at least stood his ground to defend the scraps of his place in the family. Not today. Today, he had to try to digest the fact that his mother had been quietly asking him to take on this job his whole life and he had failed her. He had failed Josie with her simple request. Just as he had already failed Dora by not securing her investment in the Crumble—just as he'd surely fail her again if he let down his guard around her.

He caught a glimpse of Dora's face and the joy the exchange brought to her. He had failed her, but he would not do it again, starting here and now. These fleeting moments were all he could give her, after all.

"Yeah, yeah. You guys are just jealous because Mom bought you a car or a motorcycle, which none of you still owns, by the way, and she gave me a truly classic and classy mode of transportation."

"Because she knew you'd need it," Dora whispered.

He could not give her a home—his had been empty the last two years. Or a real job, the kind equal to her achievements. He had no idea what he would be doing once he'd fulfilled his obligation to follow through on his mother's pet project.

"At least once a year," she went on.

Beyond that...

There was no beyond that for them. Only the work before them. "Only this one Christmas," he reminded her.

"Then we should make it a memorable one," she murmured.

...the first Christmas in a very long time that I won't feel utterly alone in the world.

Burke understood how Dora felt. It was a cliché, Burke knew, that old saying about feeling alone in a crowd, but that didn't keep it from resonating deep within him.

A few minutes later, he looked out, mostly over the heads of the people milling around on the sidewalks of downtown Mt. Knott. People he had known his entire life, his family, his former employees, even his fifth-grade teacher, and yet Burke felt completely alone.

His gaze fell on Dora's sweet face.

Well, not completely.

What could he do to make this time memorable for her? To keep her from feeling the way he did now, deserted and misplaced, when her work here ended and she had to return to Atlanta alone for Christmas? Now that she'd heard about the sleigh-ride proposal—two things not on his agenda, marriage and sleigh rides—every small effort he might make would fall short.

"I don't think I've ever been to anything like this." She stood on tiptoe and made a sweeping search of the scene as if she feared missing something.

"Sure you have." He squinted at the clusters of people representing churches, schools, clubs and causes in town. The booths left over from the Fourth of July, done up in greenery and plastic red ribbon and candy canes, did seem a bit shabby and worn. "Well, maybe not *just* like this."

His mind went to the great decorations stored in the barn with the sleigh. He had worked a lot of hours organizing the outdoor lights with a system so that he could put them up single-handedly, because his brothers never seemed to be around when that kind of chore popped up. Of course, the best thing was the huge nativity scene, the kind usually seen in front of a church.

The figures were plaster casting that stood about three-quarters of a person's size. His mom had repainted their robes in vibrant colors to reflect the joy she felt for the occasion. It had always seemed gaudy to his tastes but people seemed to like to visit it set up on the courthouse lawn, until the year the town council got "nervous" about it and asked her to move it to the Crumble.

Instead she put it in crates in the barn and left it there. They hadn't been opened in ten years or more and now sat beneath tacky pink-and-blue-and-white sparkly fake fiber-optic trees, and three-foot-tall figures of Victorian carolers that rang bells when the right switch was flipped. He should have volunteered some of those things, not the nativity but other things to make this downtown festival a little brighter.

"So you did stick around, Miss Dora. Glad to have ya." Jed raised his whole arm and swung it back and forth in a greeting from across the way. "Too bad you couldn't get a handsomer date!"

"Someone's trying to get our attention." Dora gave a small wave back.

"That what he's doing?" Burke didn't mind that Jed found him unattractive, but the man did not have to go shouting things that made the whole town think he was Dora's date. "I thought maybe he was signaling to bring a small aircraft in for a landing."

"Small aircraft? Oh, you mean like a flying sleigh full of—*oof!*"

The gathering crowd pushed them closer together.

She put out her hand to brace herself from going face-first into his chest.

"Yeah, a sleigh full of *oof* and Saint Nicholas, too," he teased her softly, then bent his head and met her gaze. Just for a moment he knew they shared the same thought, the same memory—of the kiss that they shared.

Just this one Christmas. They should make it memorable.

She looked deeply into his eyes then broke contact and used her hand to steady herself. She smiled briefly then stepped away again.

They were wise not to follow through on another kiss. Still looking down at her now, he couldn't say the urge to pull her close had subsided so much as it had been subdued. It would be wrong, of course, to pursue a relationship with Dora at this point in his life. And he could not delude himself. If he kissed Dora again, with their already fragile history, he was as good as making a promise. A foundation from which the rest of their lives would be built.

It would imply trust and hope, things Dora clearly did not take lightly. Things that Burke would not offer lightly.

He fought the temptation to move still closer to her, to smell her hair, touch her face and see the light glow of a blush work across her cheeks. Then to lower his head and...

"Dunk the elf and win a prize!"

Burke blinked then looked around them again. The whole while he had been lost in Dora's eyes they had moved along with the cluster of people around them to the small midway of games and food booths.

All around them people laughed and greeted one another.

Overly loud Christmas music poured out of poorly placed speakers, crackling, crooning, then crackling again.

Adam and Josie had gone on into the Home Cookin' Kitchen leaving Conner to parade baby Nathan around, making sure nobody had any doubt as to the kid's lineage.

Carol and Cody met up with their youth group to check on proceedings at their Dunk the Elf booth. Some of the larger boys tried to convince Cody he should take a turn on the board above the murky tank of water.

"No one would dare dunk you, Preacher," someone called out.

"Ought to be *one* Burdett who'd step up and do it," came another observation.

"No," Burke said, before Dora could even open her mouth to volunteer him.

"I was going to suggest Adam," she shot back.

"Adam?" It should not have hurt his pride to hear that. But it did.

"He's the CEO. He's the guy they will take the most delight in soaking to raise money for the needy folks in town."

"Yeah, only he isn't the one who made them needy." He scanned the crowd knowing full well that this threadbare, makeshift gathering was going to be the highlight of more than one family's holiday, especially now that the Burdett party at the Crumble was a thing of the past. "I did that."

"No, your father did that. You tried to keep as many people employed as possible."

He looked at her, not sure whether to be impressed or wary.

"You have to know," she continued, "that I did plenty of research before I ever even considered investing in your company."

"Sure." He did know and just then it dawned on him that Adam probably had known, too. And Conner and the others. Could that have been behind the huge risk of not allowing Dora to buy in? She knew them too well, and she might have too readily stood with him against them.

Not that he saw his family as wicked or scheming. They had just come to one conclusion while Burke, and maybe Dora, had come to another. The other Burdetts were doing what they thought best, protecting the business they all loved just as much as he did.

It was one of those no-win situations, Burke thought. Only not winning had cost Dora and the townspeople more than it had any one of the Burdetts. Burke felt worse than ever now.

"Combing over the data, I believe your plan for the Crumble was working." Dora did not look at him as she spoke but strained her neck to get a good look at the goings-on in the church youth group booth. "Slowly. However, with a fresh infusion of cash things would have turned around soon."

"*Your* cash?"

She shrugged, still avoiding eye contact.

"I wish it had worked out that way," he said,

"So do I."

"Yeah?" He couldn't help smiling to think of her on his side.

At last she turned to him, her smile coy and a bit crooked. Her eyes glittered in the mix of streetlights and bright Christmas decorations. "If you had stayed in the top spot, it would be you on the board about to take the plunge right now."

For a split second Burke considered doing it, if just to show her he could take his lumps.

But before he could volunteer, Adam climbed into the seat and donned the baseball cap with the pointy ears that the kids had provided for him.

"Sure it wasn't your brother in that elf picture I've heard so much about? He looks awfully cute."

"I'm sure," Burke growled.

Carol took the first pitch and missed by a mile.

Cute? She thought Adam was cute? And for what? Doing the job Burke had done long before he got a shot at it? Taking the place in the business and in the dunking both that was rightfully Burke's? Dressing like an elf? Burke had done *that* long before Adam as well. "No. It's not Adam. It was my job long before he even came into the picture."

The crowd shouted for Carol to try again.

Adam laughed, put his thumbs in his ears, wiggled his hands and stuck out his tongue.

"What was your job?" Dora asked.

Carol cocked her arm back, placing the softball in perfect position—for Burke to take it.

"To be Top Dawg," Burke came back. He threw the ball with all his might at the small target.

Wham! The ball hit the mark.

Adam went down into the tank with a *yeowl,* his hat flying up in the air.

Some people whooped and started a chant, "Top Dawg! Top Dawg!"

Everybody laughed, even Adam.

Well, almost everybody. Burke couldn't shake Dora's assessment. It should have been him in that tank.

Not that he would have ever gotten in it.

He stared at his younger brother who rose from the water, dripping wet. He bent to pick up the cap he'd tossed to safety earlier and waved it to egg on the crowd.

Josie, standing ready with a towel, leaned in to kiss Adam and found herself in a big, damp hug. She laughed, too.

The townspeople cheered some more.

Dora clapped.

For a fleeting moment everybody seemed content with their lives, happy even, and Burke had the odd sensation that maybe things were exactly as they should be.

Adam as the head of the business. The new leader of the Dawg pack.

"Isn't this a hoot?" Dora applauded Adam as he walked by, waving and enjoying the appreciation of the crowd.

"Oh yeah," Burke droned even as he found it in

himself to give her a lopsided grin. "It's a regular hoot and a half."

"Be nice," she whispered.

"I am nice," he protested.

She narrowed her eyes, more flirting than challenging, and opened her mouth as if she had every intention of refuting his claim.

"Okay. You win a prize, Burke." Carol strolled up to them with a plastic mug with the church's name on it in one hand and a trio of glow-in-the-dark necklaces in other. "What do you want?"

He looked at Dora.

She mouthed the word *necklace* and, while he stored that preference away for future reference, he shook his head. "I want…"

Maybe it was the way he drawled it out. Or the fact that he spoke a bit too loud. That he stood a good five inches above the tallest person there. Or maybe, just maybe, it was because even after everything that had happened he really was still the Top Dawg—but everybody seemed to pause and listen.

"I want…" Burke nearly closed one eye and drew a bead on his younger brother. He pointed his finger. "I want his hat."

People whooped.

Dora beamed her approval.

"The hat isn't one of the prizes," Carol whispered.

Burke reached around to his back jeans pocket, tugged out his wallet, withdrew every last bit of cash he had on hand, tucked it all into the plastic mug in Carol's hand and said, "It is now."

"Give the man that hat, tank boy!" Cody demanded.

Adam obliged. Or rather, Josie obliged for him, giving it to Burke with a curtsy and a giggle.

Burke accepted it with a nod of his head then turned and presented it to Dora.

"This should come in handy," she said, giving it the once-over.

"I hope you don't already have one," he said, enjoying the look of excitement on her face. He helped her tuck her hair behind her ears and settle the hat on her head.

"How's it look?" She posed and batted her eyes for him.

"I don't know," he said softly.

She stopped still. "You don't know how my hat looks? Why not?"

"Because he's not looking at the hat," Jed called out.

And he wasn't.

He wanted now more than ever to kiss her. To make that promise.

"Okay, enough of this! Who's brave enough to go next?" Cody barked out.

Dora gave Burke a weak smile.

The younger brother pressed his hand to Burke's back to thank him for the donation and dunking Adam, and to prod him to take his obvious flirtation with Dora out of the church parking lot.

Burke moved on before Jed could make a bad marriage pun about him and Dora taking the plunge.

"So, do you like that hat or not?" she asked again, clearly making nervous small talk.

"I like it." He wished now that he'd put that childhood picture of himself in his pocket and brought it to show her. "Reminds me of somebody I've seen a photo of lately."

"Don't see how it could." She walked ahead a few steps then turned to look at him over her shoulder. "I don't *have* anybody."

...the first Christmas in a very long time that I won't feel utterly alone in the world.

He couldn't give her much. Not a home or a position in the business or a future. But this? With a little help, maybe he could give her the one thing that would end her lonely Christmases from this year on.

Chapter Ten

The next week flew by faster for Dora than the final countdown of "The Twelve Days of Christmas" sung by a bunch of third-graders who knew that as soon as they finished the last *e-ee-e-eeee* of the partridge in a pear tree they'd be excused for cookies and punch.

During the daylight hours, Dora kept to the downstairs part of the family home, sifting through the remnants of Maggie Burdett's life. After a quiet dinner with Conner and sometimes Burke she would excuse herself and head upstairs, where she tried to sort out the remarkable woman's more private and encompassing legacy.

There was so much to learn about the town and its people. So many angles Dora could imagine taking to bring order to the eclectic mangle of a system Maggie had developed over the years. Should she consider granting the coins on merit or need or both? What about potential? Or doing the maximum good for the most people?

Would eight smaller gifts accomplish the goal? Or did it have to be one spectacular award to do Maggie Burdett justice? The only thing even resembling a mission statement Dora had found was what Burke had told her early on: *We give to others because God first gave Christ to us.*

All the while the days went whirling by. Those geese were a-layin', those swans a-swimmin' and those lords, Dora could practically feel those fancy-footed dudes doing a number on her poor aching head.

For the most part, Burke gave her no input. He always seemed to have mysterious work to do elsewhere or he just kept to himself in his ranch-style house sitting a half-acre away on the compound grounds. And yet everywhere that Dora looked she saw him, or something of him. And more often than not it gave her a glimpse into the man that his real and guarded presence never had.

She dragged her thoughts away from the man who had involved her in the project and then conveniently disappeared as she fixed on the task at hand.

"This single place setting doesn't seem to go with anything, Mr. Burdett." On her knees on the dining room floor, Dora held up a piece of china in a regal black-and-red pattern with gilded edging. With it she brandished a gold-plated knife, fork and spoon with clean, modern lines and a bold letter *B* engraved on the handles.

She carefully cataloged them on a yellow legal pad to leave a record so the often-squabbling siblings would know everything they came across and what had become of it. Often, while Conner Burdett told her the story of this thing or that, she doodled a quick sketch of an object or how she imagined it was used.

She flipped back to the first page of the pad to peek at the doodle there, a big shaggy dog wearing a Santa hat and elf ears. She considered drawing a Bad Dog sign beside the pooch and held back her smile as she turned again to the list and that troublesome lone place setting. "Should I box these up or put them with the things to give away?"

"Oh, no. No, no, no." Conner had dragged everything out of the linen closet and into the room, which was large enough to accommodate a long, dark table, eight straight-backed chairs, a buffet, a china cabinet and still leave room for a person to move all the way around with a serving cart. He held his hand up. "Don't go and do either of those things."

Dora took a deep breath and braced herself to hear what Conner had said about every scrap of paper, piece of clothing or useless knicknack she had held up— "There's a story behind that." Which he would then proceed to tell her.

At length.

In detail.

Twice.

"No, no, no." He shook his head, squinting. "Put those back in the china cabinet where you found them."

Dora waited for more.

Conner went back to shuffling through a stack of tablecloths.

Maybe he hadn't understood her question. Or perhaps in the dim light from the dingy, aging crystal chandelier, he hadn't actually seen what she had held up. "Mr. Burdett?"

"Now how many times have I asked you to call me Conner?" He gave her a sly smile and then a wink. "Mr. Burdett is my firstborn."

Dora had to chuckle at that, even though she completely understood and agreed with the comment. "Conner, then. I..."

"Look here." He yanked up a crisp pink, white and olive-green cloth with a motif of funky Santas and Christmas greetings in odd-size text. "Maggie got this the very first Christmas after we began keeping company." Conner, sitting in the chair at the head of the table, unfolded one corner then practically caressed the cloth with the palm of his weathered hand. "Before we were married, or even engaged yet."

"For her hope chest?" Dora wondered aloud. Her great-aunt had had one of those and tried to start one for Dora, who had told her that none of the other girls Dora's age had one. The truth was that Dora would have loved one but the last thing she needed was yet another thing to single her out, make her seem out of touch.

"Hope chest?" Conner scratched his head. "No. Not for my Maggie. Her hopes ran in an entirely different direction than tablecloths and putting away things for home and hearth. That's why when she showed me this, I knew."

Dora leaned in to get a closer look. "Knew what?"

"That she was going to be my wife."

Upon closer inspection the tablecloth made her almost laugh out loud. She couldn't imagine old sour Burke growing up eating Christmas dinner off this.

"I had just about given up the whole idea that Maggie would want to settle down and stay here in Mt. Knott with me. But this tablecloth changed all that. Perfect fit for this table, which had belonged to my parents."

"Let's keep it out, then." She accepted the cloth from his hands as though it were made of spun gold. "I'll launder and press it and we can put it on the table for Christmas in honor of your marriage and your Maggie."

"Thank you, Dora, for doing this with me." His eyes got misty, for only a second, then he cleared his throat. "You're the only person in these past two years I would have trusted with the task."

"Me? But Mr., um, Conner, you really hardly know me and what you do know, well, I got the impression, no, actually, the legal notice of failure to complete a contract that made it pretty clear your family didn't really have much use for me."

That was the sore spot. All her life Dora had found her niche in being useful. To be told she wasn't?

"That were the case you wouldn't be here now, would you?" He scoffed and went back to sorting through the other tablecloths, hardly able to hide the tears welling in his eyes with each memory they brought.

"I see" she murmured, humbled at the freshness of the man's grief even now.

There was so much sadness in this house, so much gone unsaid between family members that might have healed it, or lessened it. It made Dora's heart ache for them. Was it really so hard, she wondered, this relationship between parent and child?

She shook her head and went back to the work at hand. "But this? Why would you want to keep a single place setting?"

"It's Burke's."

"Burke's?" She held it up. It was hardly big enough to serve a slice of Josie's pie and had no companion pieces. "Burke has a china pattern?"

"It was his when he was a baby."

"Baby? But it's fine china."

"Nothing but the best for my son."

"So they each have one?" She looked up and tried to find three more plates with utensils.

"No. Just Burke. Just our little prince."

"Your Top Dawg," she said softly.

"From the day he was born," Conner confirmed. "By the time we adopted Adam we had figured out how impractical it was, feeding boys off fancy plates."

"Guess Burke taught you a thing or two." She smiled.

"In his own way, yes."

"And what way was that?" she asked.

"The hard way, my dear," he said with a gleam in his eye and unabashed pride in his voice. "Always the hard way."

Dora laughed, but not from the heart. Her thoughts went back to trying to teach herself how to run the Forgotten Stocking Project and her head throbbed anew. "I'm surprised this plate survived intact."

"I ain't rightly sure he ever used it." The older man reached out and took the plate for his own inspection. "But, oh, the plans we had for that boy when we bought it and then…."

"Then you realized he had plans of his own," she said softly. Suddenly the parent/child conflict became clearer in her mind. What, she wondered, had Conner expected of Burke that he could not give?

Giving, she realized in that instant, was not Burke's strong suit. And giving was the only thing a parent would want, that a child not act grudgingly or out of teeth-gritting obedience but to submit freely and from the heart. Yes. She could imagine the conflict between father and son now, and had a new insight into the reasons the Bible often taught about the relationship with God in terms of a loving Father wanting the best for His children.

"For I know the plans I have laid for you," declares the Lord, *"plans to prosper you and not harm you, plans to give you hope and a future."* Being a lifelong planner who always feared for her own future, Jeremiah 29, verse 11 had always held a special appeal for Dora.

"That's nice." Conner folded his hands and gazed at the plate again. "That's all I ever wanted for my sons. For them to prosper. For them to have hope and a good future."

"You provided for that, Conner, when you built up the family business."

"Exactly why I did it." He nodded, still not making

eye contact with her. "And exactly why I didn't think—don't think—all of my boys should carry on in it."

Wow. What an odd and yet profound statement. The kind of thing Dora suspected the old man might never have said to anyone else. The kind of thing she wanted to hear more about. "Are you saying—"

"I'm saying this work won't do itself." He clapped his hands. "We still got a week's worth of work ahead, and that's not taking into account the barn or the upstairs."

"Week? Barn? Upstairs?" She didn't know which to worry about first. She had planned to head back to Atlanta in a couple of days. She hoped that distance and her own surroundings would help her gain perspective on the best approach for the project. "I don't think I can stay out here doing this for that long. I have things that need my attention."

He trained a beady eye on her. "You were a jiggler, weren't you?"

"A—" Dora didn't know whether to be insulted or charmed. "What?"

"When you were little. I bet you were the one who crept in under the cover of darkness, lay on your belly under the Christmas tree and gave each and every one of your presents a little—" He raised both hands as if holding a package then demonstrated as he said, "—a jiggle."

Dora laughed and hoped it didn't come off too awkward and iffy. "No, Mr. Bur—"

"Eh, eh, eh."

"Conner. I was not then nor have I ever been a jiggler."

"Of course not." Burke leaned in, plucked up the yellow legal pad and began glancing over it as he said, "Way too unreliable a means of checking inventory for our Dora."

"How long have you been standing there—" She turned away from Burke, leaning against the doorframe with a heart-melting smile on his lips, to his father as she shared an inside joke with the older of the two men, *"Mr. Burdett?"*

Another of the brothers would have naturally protested that Mr. Burdett was their father. Given the old man his props, as it were.

Not Burke. Not Mr. Business. Not the real *Mr. Burdett*.

He wasn't going to give anybody anything. Not even a direct answer.

"Where you been?" Conner wanted to know.

"I had things to do," he said cryptically.

"Apparently you didn't get them all done." Conner dove back into the work before him.

"What makes you say that?" Burke asked.

"You forgot to pick up dinner."

Every evening since she had gotten here Burke had shown up about this time with "to go" boxes from Josie's restaurant. The food was good and plentiful and Dora hadn't minded one bit not having to add cooking to her list of duties. But she had felt a bit strange that it probably looked to Conner as if she were too snobby to pitch in and pull together a simple meal.

"I'll go back to town in a minute," Burke said. "How are things going here?"

"We found your baby plate."

"Can't say you ever ate off it." Conner gazed at it and whispered, "But, oh, what plans we had...."

"I don't see any use in keeping it." Burke handed her the legal pad, pointing to the plate listing, as if to order her to move it off the list of keepers.

Dora took a breath but did not take the pad, not just yet. Taking it implied agreeing with him and she couldn't do that as long as Burke would not even give his father a moment of sentimentality. She wanted to—well, never mind what she wanted, she decided, reining in the temptation to lose her temper or to cross the line between personal and professional behavior. Burke wouldn't give anything, including a hoot, about what his father was really saying to him.

"Bad dog," she muttered under her breath.

"What?" Burke pushed the pad toward her again and when he did the pages flipped to reveal the drawing on the front.

He paused, studied the blatant representation of himself with elf ears and finally chuckled softly before handing it to her again. "I'll go back to town to pick up dinner now. Is the special okay with everyone?"

This time she did take the pad. Maybe the man wasn't so bad.

Dora had already given plenty, but then she had come here looking for a way to give as much of herself as possible. Maybe that meant she needed to set an example and give a little more. "How about I do the cooking tonight?"

She worked her way over toward Conner on her knees, intent on using the arm of his chair to climb to her feet.

As she wriggled by, Burke nabbed her by the arm and helped her up, peering down into her eyes with a hint of doubt as he asked, "You cook?"

"I sure do." She freed her arm from his grasp and tipped up her nose. "When there's a fridge full of Josie's wonderful leftovers to throw together into a casserole or hash."

"Oh. Yeah? Well, in that case, I cook, too," he shot back with a grin, showing a glimpse of the man who had assured her that he was actually this nice at the downtown holiday event.

"Then maybe you should give us all a break and do the honors tonight," she teased. Only she wasn't completely teasing. She honestly thought it would serve this man well—this high-born prince of snack-cake bakers, this sometimes very bad dog—to do some good for others instead of deciding for them or directing them or even dogging them.

Of course, that was the part he picked up on. The kernel of truth beneath the jest. Dora should have seen that coming. It's exactly what she would have done, only she liked to think she'd arrive at a more accurate reason to have taken offense at the remark.

"I should cook because I'm the only one who hasn't been working?" Burke still had her hand in his, and his hurt and anger held her attention as though they were alone in the room. "Is that what you're saying?"

"No." *Well, sort of.* She had, if she confessed, been aiming to change him, because she thought he could do more, be more. She had no business prodding him that way, of course.

Because the only thing between them *was* business.

"Just laying out the terms of the contract, Mr. Burdett. You know, always ask for more than you think the other guy will ever give when you begin negotiations." A smart tactic usually but since Burke wasn't about to give anything, just opening her mouth had blown the whole deal at the onset. "We have leftovers and both of us are equally capable of—"

"I submit that capability in cooking is a pretty subjective thing, Ms. Hoag." He shifted quite easily into CEO mode.

Something that did not put her off one bit. "I gladly accept your submission, Mr. Burdett, and I—"

"Knock it off, the pair of you!" Conner moved the table linens from his lap to the floor, signaling the end of his task and his patience. "You both know how to cook. The kitchen is thataway. I'm hungry."

Burke and Dora exchanged a brief look. In a boardroom, they probably would have shaken hands as a sign that they had reached an agreement. Instead they started off in the direction Conner had just pointed.

"Good. Go. About time you two turned up the heat." Conner waved them away, calling after them. "And while you're at it, make some dinner, too!"

"I'm sorry about him," Burke said as he ushered her into the kitchen.

"Don't be. I like him." She went to the fridge and started pulling out the remnants of earlier meals.

"Well, he likes you, too."

"You say that like you think we both have bad taste in the company we keep."

"Did I?" He frowned but she wasn't sure that it was a comment on how she had read him, or because the food in the container he had just opened had gone bad.

So she went on, getting out a big ceramic casserole dish and pulling salt and pepper from the overhead cabinet. She knew where it all was, having gone through this room cataloging every gadget and gewgaw.

As she worked she made the kind of small talk she usually heard other people making in the break room. A question couched as a thought. A tidbit of information thrown out for comment without the formality of requesting a comment or opinion. "Um, your dad thinks we have a week's worth of work left but I think I should go back to Atlanta for a few days."

"I agree." He threw the box he'd just sniffed into the trash can.

"With what?" This was why she never engaged in that break room chitchat. She wasn't any good at it. And, of course, everyone at work was so afraid of her they usually emptied the room before she could attempt to join the conversation. "Staying for another week or going back to Atlanta?"

"Atlanta." He scanned the boxes and picked up another one. A quick peek inside then he handed it to her. "Start with this."

She took the box and peered inside, too, feeling more like part of a production line than a participant in a conversation or creative endeavor. "Okay. Then what?"

"Then you tell me where I can meet you there."

She'd meant *then what do I add to the mix of leftovers?* not *then what happens with you and me?* "You and me? In Atlanta? At the same time?"

"Sure."

She clutched a wooden spoon in her hand until her knuckles went white. Maybe she had read him all wrong. Maybe he was more giving than she thought and right now he was giving her a chance to make something more of their relationship. "In Atlanta?"

"If that's where you'll be, then that's where I need to be."

She stopped filling a casserole dish with macaroni and cheese from the box Burke had passed to her. How long had she waited to hear him say just that? She took a step toward him.

"Yeah. Makes sense doesn't it?" Another box, this time set aside. "Down there we don't have to have any secrets."

"Secrets? About the project?"

"About the... Oh! Yes, the project. Yes. That's right. How could I forget the project? It's the reason I'm here. I do have a lot to talk to you about." She flipped the last of the boxes open and studied the contents. "We need something to hold all this together."

"The project?"

"The food, you know, some canned cream-of-any-thing soup?" Dora jerked her head up. Actually, yes, that was exactly what they needed for the project, something to hold it, and them, together long enough to see it through. "Now that you mention it, though, we do need something to make this project cohesive. It's all over the place now. I can't seem to find any formula for how your mom made her choices. If we—"

"Save it." He plunked down a can with a pull-top lid then made a stirring motion with one hand to ask her to hand him the spoon. "In Atlanta we can meet someplace, you can give me your report and answer any questions I have then."

"Okay," she murmured, as the glop from the can fell on top of the noodles with a slurpy plop. She had come here because she thought she had something to give, but in reality what she had given had always been his to begin with, his to take and his to reject if he so desired.

She slapped the spoon into his palm, not angrily but more like a nurse handing a surgeon a scalpel. They would be in Atlanta just what they were here and now, a couple of professionals with a deadline on a job they had both committed to see through. "Then after that I can go over things with the accountant and get an order in with the jeweler."

"I'll do that." He stepped in and took over the construction of the casserole as well.

"I don't mind." She held her hands up, feeling absolutely useless. Her least favorite feeling in the world.

She watched him a moment and realized that he

had already begun to pull away from her, the way one does when a collaboration nears conclusion. *Correction,* she thought, *feeling useless is my* second *least favorite feeling in the world.*

He churned the food in the dish and added salt and pepper, never once turning to acknowledge her. "Dealing with the other team members, that's my place, Dora."

And she had just been put in hers.

"Besides, if you and I are both gone at the same time then we both return at the same time, people will talk." He yanked open a cabinet, pulled out a half-empty bag of potato chips and sprinkled some on top of the mix. "I won't have that."

She leaned back against the counter, trying to get some satisfaction from the fact that he had taken over the meal-prep duties after all. "Protecting your reputation, eh?"

"Protecting yours."

"Gallant but unnecessary." Just how she felt about him taking charge of the kitchen instead of offering to do it out of kindness and generosity. "I don't care what people think of me if I know my actions are honorable and right."

"Yes, but you're working in my home. And though people don't know it, on my mother's project. I can't have that compromised."

Right. Business. It always came back to that with him. Everything did. She suspected that after the Christmas festival he had made his brother write out a charitable donation receipt with a notation at the bottom: For elf employment.

"So, Atlanta?" he asked.

"Atlanta." She nodded then suggested a place for them to meet.

"I'll put it on my calendar." He slid the casserole into the oven and set the timer.

"Me, too," she said, watching him walk away, leaving her with the less glam job of cleaning up the small mess they had made.

She looked around her. She was spending her yearly vacation in an old house in Mt. Knott, South Carolina, playing helper to the world's surliest Santa.

This was her gift, not to Burke, but to the town, and now to dear, still-grieving Conner Burdett and to Maggie. They deserved her best.

Come to think of it, *she* deserved her best.

She was going to do this the way she would if it were her project from the get-go. Then she would find a way to bring it all together and when they met in Atlanta she would give her all to Burke with no strings, no expectations and, like that fellow who sent the rings, the hens, the drummers, dancers and maids a-milking, a strict no-givebacks policy.

Chapter Eleven

"Job hunting? That was your story?" Dora slid into the back booth in the small coffee shop at the address she had given him to meet her. "You told your family you were off job hunting?"

"Sure? Why not?" And by that Burke meant, *why not do a little job hunting* as much as, *why not tell the family that's what I'm doing?* He took the other side of the booth, making the table wobble with every inch he scooted along the shiny-red vinyl and gray duct tape–patched bench. "Nice place you picked to meet, by the way."

"I like it." Dora pulled her laptop from its case, flipped it open. "It's quiet, out of the way."

He checked out the clientele, more of a "can't never tell" lot, it seemed to him. A couple of bleary-eyed types with one hand affixed to a computer and a coffee cup in the other. And in the corner a fellow who clearly felt invisible to the world, and liked it that way. "Yeah, the place is practically abandoned."

"Hey, it has ambiance." She connected her Wi-Fi service with the push of a button.

"Good. I think people who eat here sometimes *need* an ambulance."

"Ambiance. Atmosphere. It's cozy. Quaint. A piece of Americana. One of those, what's the word?"

"A dive?"

"A mom-and-pop operation," she corrected with a hint of a smile and a steely-eyed glower.

Mom-and-pop. Suddenly he understood the appeal it had for a woman who had neither. So he tried to find something positive to say about the place where Dora had practically set up an office away from, well, her office. "I see they have a bottomless cup of coffee."

He pointed to a sign, smiling, trying to make nice.

She barely took her eyes off the computer screen.

Forget nice, he wanted to see the fire in her eyes. "Of course they don't say if that means they keep refilling your drink, or if the coffee is so strong it eats the bottom right out of the cup."

That did it. She gave him the look, all flash and polish and a touch of little girl ready to defend her corner of the playground.

"I like their coffee," she said.

I like you, Burke wanted to say. Instead he just sighed and shook his head, grinning like a fool.

That softened her up a bit and she conceded, "So the place is a bit of a greasy spoon."

"I don't think the grease is limited to the spoons, Dora." He picked up his water glass and held it up so that the fluorescent light shone through, highlighting the smudges.

"Enough of that. So, it's no Josie's Home Cookin' Kitchen—"

"Or Dora's home cooking for that matter." He meant that as a jab at his having come all the way to Atlanta to meet with her and her not inviting him to her home, but she didn't seem to pick up on that.

"But it's got big tables where they won't chase you off if you sit for a while, a Wi-Fi hotspot and the coffee keeps coming."

Or maybe she had brought him to the place where she spent more time than home. "Spoken like a woman who comes here often."

"Not *that* often."

"Hey, Dora. The usual?" A chubby-cheeked waitress in a bib apron with the strings wrapped around her thick middle and tied in front—which gave her a soft, lumpy look that seemed to say "hey, the food's great here"—offered up a half-empty coffeepot.

"No, thanks." Dora put her hand over the top of her coffee cup and glanced nervously at the waitress. "I, uh, think I'll have hot chocolate."

"Hot chocolate? Really? This early in the—"

"No time of day too early for hot chocolate." Dora beamed.

"—Season," the waitress finished. "I mean you don't normally switch to the sweet stuff until the week before Christmas."

"What can I say? I'm in a holiday mood," Dora droned, her beam decidedly bummed.

"Last year you held off right up until Christmas Eve. Or was it two years ago?"

Dora blanched.

Burke loved it.

And hated it.

Loved seeing her squirm like this, getting this tiny glimpse into her secret indulgence of hot chocolate around the holidays, but hated, hated, hated the thought of this bright-eyed, brilliant woman spending Christmas Eve in this greasy spoon. Granted, he could see what drew her to the mom-and-pop operation but he couldn't help thinking that even Mom and Pop found something better to do on December twenty-fourth than hang around here.

"And for you, sir? Hot chocolate as well? It's good. I can highly recommend it."

Burke scowled. "I don't usually go for the—"

"He's already so sweet as it is," Dora needled.

"I was going to say I don't usually go for the rich stuff."

"He rich enough as it is?" The waitress didn't so much as smirk to apologize for the directness of her question.

"As a matter of fact…" Dora gave him a look.

"I'll take the hot chocolate," he said.

"With a shot of Dairy Dream on top?" she asked, pointing to a laminated picture clipped to the menu of a frothy whipped-creamlike substance floating on a cup.

Dora opened her mouth but Burke cut her off. Much as he'd love to hear her say out loud that he was, indeed, *dreamy* enough already, he actually wanted the stuff in his drink. "That would be fine. Thank you."

The waitress snapped a very professional "Yes, sir" and scooted off, calling out after herself, "I'll bring your whipped cream in a dish on the side, Dora, just like always."

"Don't come here that often, eh?"

Dora bit her lower lip and raised her shoulders sheepishly as she gave Burke a guilty glance.

He would have gloated at being proven right so eloquently, so unarguably, so...deliciously, except that seeing her like this he didn't feel like gloating.

"Shall we get down to work? Or do you have to rush off and put in your application someplace?" She whipped her head around toward the front door. "Hey, you know, I think I might have seen a Now Hiring sign in the window here. If you want I can put in a good word for you."

He shifted awkwardly and the cushion beneath him sighed and groaned. "Yeah, I want to talk to you about that."

"About the work we need to do or about your claim that you are job hunting?"

"Can't I do both?"

"Oh, Burke, really. You have such a noble cause to tend to." She sat up all prim and proper in her navy-blue business suit and gleaming but simple gold jewelry.

Suddenly he wished he had chosen the glow-in-the-dark necklaces as his prize at the church dunking booth. He'd have loved to see her in those, and the elf hat, and.... "Excuse me, did you say noble cause?"

"Your mother's legacy." She rolled her eyes, something he figured she'd never do in a bona fide business meeting, and pressed on, "I don't believe for one second you want to do anything, especially anything as demanding as job hunting, to distract you from that right now. Or ever."

"Ever? A man has to work, Dora."

"And there is plenty of work to be done with this, Burke." She slapped down a stack of file folders onto the table even as her eyes fixed on the computer screen. "I can see why your mother worked on it year-round. It's a full-time job in its own right. Or could be. If you did it right."

If you did it right. The reminder that he had not done it, or much of anything, right stung. Suddenly the thought of asking her to put in a good word for him at Global seemed pointless. Silly, even. Besides, Adam had worked at Global. Burke was looking to blaze his own trail once again, as he always had, not to follow in his younger brother's footsteps. But the job interview he'd had there this afternoon had gone so well, and the position they had open sounded like a perfect fit for him.

His teeth were on edge. He wanted to defend his work ethic and record to her on one hand, but, on the other, she had offered him the single best hope for doing something meaningful with his life since his family had so lightly dismissed him. Between a rock and a hard place. Only there was nothing hard about Dora, though many people thought of her as tough as nails. He saw right through that to the little girl all alone in the world, and to that scared and lonely child all he could say was, "I'm listening."

"I've been thinking a lot about this." She scooted forward, her eyes lit with enthusiasm. "You could create a foundation to build on your mother's dream."

"I think my mother has already laid a pretty good foundation, Dora."

"Not that kind of foundation, Burke. This kind." She pressed a button on her keyboard and spun her laptop around.

There, on the screen was a logo, a hand-sketched image of the coin that his mother had made at the jewelers in Atlanta with a glimmer of light bouncing off the rim. Below it, in simple but elegant script, the words *The Forgotten Stocking Foundation*.

He pointed to it. "What's this?"

"Just a rough example. I toyed with the idea of a stocking or a something more, oh, you know, Santa-ish, but then I thought it was a better idea to honor the One who moved the original Saint Nicholas and us to action." She stroked her fingertip over the upper right curve of the coin on the screen.

Burke blinked and when his eyes focused in he realized what he had taken to be a flash to show the shine of the gold was really the image of the cross at the center of a star of Bethlehem.

He nodded slowly. He liked it. "But I don't really understand it."

"Your mom accomplished so much, Burke, but in a way that only a person who lived and worked and listened and learned about the goings-on and needs of a small community could."

The waitress brought their hot chocolates and clunked them down, the cups clattering against the saucers, the saucers thumping against the table. She opened her mouth to say something but Burke spoke first.

"Go on." He'd meant to encourage Dora to keep talking but the waitress must have taken it as a direct command, and she hurried off.

"Maggie did so much."

"You said that."

"But—" She wet her lips.

"I thought so." He sat back. "She did so much but what? She didn't do enough?"

"I'm not criticizing her, Burke. I'm not trying to downplay any of the work she did."

"But?"

"Just looking over the records I have been able to pull together, I am in awe of her." She placed her hand on a thick file folder. "She helped so many people, created the recipe and the logo for the Carolina Crumble Pattie and raised four very competent and compassionate sons."

"But?" He was a Dawg with a bone.

"But I think we could do more. Much more."

We? She had no right to include herself in his family business. No more place in it than he did. And he guessed, in a funny way, that did make them a *we*. "What makes you think *we* need to do more?"

"See for yourself." She worked a second file from

beneath the first one and slid it across the table toward him.

"More rough examples?"

"No. More harsh realities."

He frowned then flipped open the file folder to see a name along with a page full of neatly typed notes on the person's situation. He picked that up and beneath it found another name, another summation. And under that another and another. He raised his gaze to meet Dora's.

She sighed and tugged a piece of paper from the pile. "Look here. A budding scientist who can't go away to college because her mother died last year and there are two younger siblings to care for."

"I know them."

"A talented painter who just needs a little space for a studio."

He nodded at the name on the page. "She's good."

"A family who—"

He put his hand down over the page she was peering at. "Dora. I know all this. I know there are a lot of worthy folks in need, that's why I hired you to sort them out."

"Sort them how, Burke? By depth of desperation? By the most potential good to be seen, and if that, whose good and over how long? Does someone who can be a doctor take precedence over someone who wants to go to a technical school and be at work in six months? Does the scientist get a coin while the artist gets an empty stocking?"

He looked again at the papers lying side by side and shook his head. "Maybe we could do both."

"Maybe so but we can't do all of them."

Now he got it. Now he saw her quandary. "Let me guess, you want to help all of them, don't you, Dora?"

She didn't say yes, but she didn't have to because it shone in her kind eyes and the way she pressed her lips tightly together to keep from blurting out something totally unprofessional.

"Dora, I don't see how—"

"I thought you'd never ask."

With that she launched into what Burke could only call a high-powered, take-no-prisoners, this-was-why-Global-paid-her-the-big-bucks-and-gave-her-a-company-car, smokin' sales pitch for the establishment of the Maggie Burdett Forgotten Stocking Foundation.

It sounded great.

Correction. Her voice sounded great.

"This year we make the announcement and give small grants with multiple recipients. What we can't do we ask locals to pitch in and help with. Someone probably has empty space for that studio, and surely someone can help with day care for those kids if we pay for reliable transportation so the college-bound girl can come back and forth on weekends."

Her *enthusiasm* sounded great.

"Then the real work begins. First we set up the means to raise money to serve just the immediate region. In a year or so the whole state. Eventually we should be able to reach anywhere they know the name Carolina Crumble Pattie."

Even the way she paused and took the tiniest sip of hot chocolate then smacked her lips ever so slightly sounded great. The pitch? Burke really wasn't listening.

He didn't have to listen.

"It sounds good, Dora."

"I'm so glad you think so. When can we—"

"Never."

"Never?"

His brothers and father had displaced him, and he did not owe them anything. The town had all but forgotten his years of dedication and sacrifice in favor of the promise of a new start with Adam, while they themselves made no effort to invest in Mt. Knott or one another. He owed them even less. He had made promises to Dora and to his mother—those he would honor but even they had their limits. Or, rather, he had his limits. He did not have it in him to do what Dora was asking. "Just this one Christmas, Dora. That's all I committed to. That's all I have in me."

"But why? You sat right here a few minutes ago and told me you were ready to take on a new job."

"I am." He flipped the file folder in front of him closed. "I plan to take a job, too. I feel that I have a lot to give if someone would have me."

I'll have you.

She'd never say it. She didn't want him any more than anyone did, he supposed, but he would give her ample opportunity to prove him wrong. When she sat there, her eyes narrowed and her lips pressed tight, he went on. "As soon as this one Christmas is past, I will be back hard at work again, but not as Santa Claus to the entire South."

"So you're rejecting this out of hand?"

"No, I'm rejecting it out of common sense."

Her face went pale. Her lower lip quivered so slightly he doubted anyone else would have noticed it. Then she rallied and raised her chin. The disappointment in her eyes cleared. She nodded. "I see."

"Look, Dora, it's not personal. It's just—"

She held her hand up. "As an early Christmas present to me, I'm going to ask that you not finish that sentence."

He shut his mouth. Nodded once.

She nodded, too. Then forced a mild, tense smile and nodded again.

For a few minutes he felt that they might sit there like that for the rest of the night, like two silent bobble-head dolls. Nodding and smiling. Nodding and smiling.

In his capacity as CEO, this was the point where he would have stood up, shaken her hand and thanked her for her time before walking away. Nice and tidy. But today he was acting as a person, talking with another person, dealing with feelings and history and... and nothing about it was nice or tidy.

Well, last summer had been nice right up until the part when his whole world fell apart. He flexed his hands around the mug of hot chocolate and tried to think what more he could say. "So, how do you plan to spend the rest of the day?"

"Foundation or not, the job isn't done."

He reached for the files. "I can take it from here."

"I mean the job I'm doing for your father. I owe it to him to see that through until the end."

"You're going to Mt. Knott?" He hadn't expected that.

"Don't worry. I'll try to finish up before you get back." She clicked her laptop shut, tucked it in the case and slid out of the booth. "That will be my Christmas present to you."

Chapter Twelve

Dora stood in the dining room of the main Burdett house, trying to look inconspicuous while three brothers and two wives finally faced the mountain of memories left by their mother. Burke had not returned from Atlanta nor had they seen one another after their tiff in the coffee shop.

She'd given it her best shot and been turned down. Only business, she reminded herself, nothing personal.

Her part was over. In reality she probably should have excused herself and gone upstairs to finish up there. But she really didn't think she could manage that without drawing attention to Maggie's secret office and the project that she had kept hidden from the family her whole marriage.

Families. Dora didn't know what to think of them. Of this one, at least. Her own, she had always believed was the exception to all the rules.

"What was Christmas like when the boys were

young, Conner?" She asked a unifying question to try to make herself useful.

"A lot of grabbing and arguing and pushing and pulling, and a lot of laughter and love. Basically just like every other day around here."

"Hey! That's mine." The next to the youngest brother, Jason, lunged for an old tin box, the kind Boy Scouts used to sell filled with peanut brittle or log candy at fundraiser time. Dora had found a whole stash of the things in the back of a closet, most of them empty but a few holding the kinds of treasures young boys might have stowed inside—marbles, rocks, four-leaf clovers.

"No, yours was red." Cody held the box up high, just out of reach from the brother a scant year older, but a full four inches shorter. "This one, the blue one, is mine."

"You're both wrong." Adam, the eldest, and shortest, of the three, leapt up and whisked the box away from the grasping fingers of his younger siblings. "That's mine. I know because I left a dent in the underside of it when I banged Burke over the head with it when he said it was his."

"Ha! That proves it can't be yours. If this metal had ever met with Burke's hard head it would be dented beyond repair," Jason observed.

To which the other brothers paused, shared a look, then broke into laughter.

Adam turned the box over in his hands. "Bet Burke still has his tin squirreled away someplace. Man, you can't get that dog to turn loose of anything."

He'd turned loose of her pretty easily, Dora thought before it dawned on her. Maybe he never really had ahold of her—maybe the connection she felt last summer had come from her alone?

"Hey, like we don't know that." Jason eyed the tin as if he weren't quite sure he was ready to let Adam keep it. "Hasn't forgiven us yet for ousting him from the Crumble."

"I still feel pretty lousy about that," Cody confessed.

Dora tensed. She wondered if she should excuse herself, or start humming Christmas carols really loudly to remind them they had an interloper in the midst. Except she really wanted to hear this.

"Don't none of you try to carry the burden for that decision." Conner pulled himself up to his full height for the first time since Dora had been here. He set his jaw in grim determination, but kindness and care flickered in his eyes. "That was strictly my doing."

"Yours?" It slipped out before Dora's decorum could lock it inside her.

"Yes, young lady. Me and that firstborn of mine been at odds since long before I decided he ought to eat off fine china."

She looked once again to the plate.

"He's the one you thought shouldn't follow you into the family business?"

Conner's mouth twitched. He gave his other sons a once-over then he turned to her. "Too much of his mother in him. Too much of the little prince we expected him to be. Both those things always at war inside him."

That's why the old man kept that place setting. It wasn't just a reminder of the plans he had for Burke but of how he had tried to shape his son into something he wasn't meant to be and the price they had both paid. The conflict between them, the things he felt he had robbed his son of doing.

"So you corrected that by kicking him out of the business?" she asked.

"We had words. We had legal battles. We even came to blows at one point. But in the end I bested him with the one thing I knew he'd have to accept—good business."

Dora tried to take all that in. "Is that why you turned my investment down?"

"Didn't seem right to invite you into the family just when we kicked Burke out." Cody gave a sympathetic shrug.

"Personally, I was all for that." Adam threw his hands up to show he had no part in her rejection. "You would be way more nice to sit across from in board meetings."

"Prettier, too," Jason agreed.

Dora had to smile at that even while she had no idea what to do with the rest of the information. "Have you ever told Burke any of this?"

"Did she suggest trying to reason with Top Dawg?" Adam asked, laughing.

"Reason he'd go for, like telling him we were doing it for his own good? He'd pull an Adam just to prove us wrong." Cody gave his older brother, the one who had run off with his inheritance and taken a job with

Global to try to run the family out of business, a jab in the ribs with his elbow.

"Neither the business nor the family could have withstood that," Conner told her.

"Hate to contradict you, sir." She folded her arms and looked at the lot of them. "But I've gone over your business with a fine-tooth comb and seen the inner workings of your family and I have to say both are far stronger than you are giving them credit for."

"Flattery ain't going to change our minds." Adam tossed the tin in his hand up a few inches and caught it again.

"Yeah, if you want to be a part of the business or the family, you're going to have to do it the old-fashioned way," Cody warned.

"Hostile takeover?" she asked, one eyebrow cocked.

"Some might call it that." Conner chuckled. "But we were thinking if you want to be one of this pack, you're going to have to marry into it."

With that they all dove back into the once neatly stacked piles of things that Dora had spent days going through and organizing to see what they wanted to keep, store away for future generations or give away.

Marry? It wasn't even within the realm of possibility. Dora knew that, but why ruin this shot at making a lasting memory with something so impermanent as reality?

Boxes got shuffled from hand to hand. Papers avalanched onto the floor. Grown men whooped like children at coming across some long forgotten memento.

"Some things never change." Conner chuckled softly.

"Some things have changed, though. A lot." Dora moved her gaze away from the undoing of all her hard work to the closet where she had relegated box upon box of Christmas decorations, filling the small storage closet from floor to ceiling. "I take it you once went all out with the decorations."

Conner followed her line of vision. "We haven't had any of that stuff up since we lost our sweet Maggie. She passed at Christmastime, you know."

"I know." Dora put her hand on the old man's arm. "It must be hard for you to see all those things. If you'd like I'll just shut the door and leave them for you to deal with another time."

"But?" He stopped her in her tracks.

She inhaled and held it, then let it out with a soft chuckle. "Did anyone ever tell you that you sound a lot like Burke?"

The man's forehead wrinkled in confusion.

Dora laughed.

"I guess maybe the real issue is that the men of this family have no difficulty reading me like a book. They don't just hear what I say, they listen to what I am *not* saying." Dora looked from Conner to Adam then to the single place setting she had carefully, some might say lovingly, placed front and center in the china cabinet, the one that had been for Burke. "And unlike the people who work for me, they have the gumption to call me on it."

Conner had seen through her lame attempt to suggest that it was time to return to their old family traditions. Adam had stayed ahead of her in business negotiations and sent her packing before she had known what hit her. And Burke?

Being a master of not having to say much to speak volumes, Burke had seen through the razzle-dazzle of her Forgotten Stocking Foundation to the heart of the matter. She had tried to horn in on his territory. To make herself a part of his work, his family and his life.

Dora wet her lips. "Okay, you got me. I could close that closet door and leave it all for you to deal with at some later date. To let another Christmas go by without a tree or any lights or even a manger scene that I suspect your wife would have set up in a prominent place year after year."

"You know about that? We haven't set that thing up in more than a decade."

"You haven't had a crèche in your home for that long?"

"A crèche? Oh, no. I thought you meant the near life-size one we used to set up for the whole town."

"You have a nearly life-size nativity scene?" She whipped around to look at the boxes, sure she wouldn't have missed *that*.

"We did. Not too sure what became of it after Maggie had a meltdown over the town council kicking the holy family off the courthouse lawn, though. Burke might know. His mama always went to him to deal with things like that."

Dora chose not to respond to that, out of respect for

Maggie and the objective of keeping secret what Maggie had asked Burke to deal with.

"There is a smaller crèche in there someplace though. She picked it up on some island. Can't recall which—" His face contorted with the strain of trying to remember.

"Fiji? Hawaii? Crete?"

"Long!" He snapped his fingers.

"Long Island?"

"Got it at a dime store. Little plastic thing." He made a frame with his hands to indicate the size. "Got it before she even met me and said she always dreamt of starting a collection of nativities from everyplace she traveled. Wanted a whole roomful but then she met me and ended up with just the two—the big one and that plastic thing. Not enough to even fill a box."

"What she ended up with could not be contained by even this one house," Dora reminded him, and with a hand on his shoulder, drew his attention back to Adam and Josie with their son, Nathan, to Cody, Carol and Jason, all talking at once, holding up objects and sharing their fondest feelings about their mom.

Conner smiled at last. "I reckon you think it's time to let some of what she loved spill out again?"

"I do."

"What do you have in mind?"

She hadn't actually gotten Burke a Christmas gift besides her promise to leave before he returned. Which she still planned to do but somehow, after all they had shared, she felt she should do more. No, it was more than that.

She still saw so much good in Burke. So much, well, as much as she had tried to avoid the emotion her whole life, *hope*. He had so much to give if he would only let go of it. So much to share. Not with her, she understood that. He felt undone by the loss of his job, his lifelong work, his place at the top. He associated her with that loss, and she, of all people, understood that.

But he had brought her here to give something that only she could. She had yet to do that. The work on the project? He could have hired someone else, someone who had no contact at all with the town or the workers at the Crumble or his family, to compile all that and even make recommendations for him. What he could not appoint anyone else in the world to do was to tell him the truth.

She owed that to him. And he owed her...one memorable Christmas.

"Well, we have all these things and the house is so drab...."

And just like that Dora found herself in the middle of a family. Not an outsider. Not an observer. A member.

They heard her out then flew into a decorating frenzy. The sisters-in-law worked on the inside of the house, hanging swags of faux pine with red-and-gold ribbon over the fireplace and around the banister and filling every empty space with knicknacks and baubles. The brothers tackled the outside. That didn't take as long as Dora had expected since a whole system of hooks and latches that were hardly visible during the year had been installed and the lights, which had all been stored in neat rolls with tags showing where they went, fit right into them.

She and Conner took on setting up the large artificial, pre-lit tree and had just finished putting the star on the top when the doorbell rang.

Dora gasped. "I didn't think Burke would come back for another hour or more."

"Burke? Since when does he ring the doorbell?" Josie asked, even as she hurried to answer it.

"We three kings…" the three Burdett brothers belted out their own version of the old song, this one extolling their hard work and success at outdoor holiday lighting.

The women laughed.

Conner joined them. They stepped out onto the porch and, as the final note of the song warbled through the rafters, Adam flipped a switch.

"Oh!"

"Wow!"

"You did all this?"

A thousand white lights twinkled around them, warming the dusky late-afternoon sky like candles lighting the way on an overcast day. Framed by a semicircle of glittering pastel trees set of Victorian-style carolers stood, some moving mechanically from left to right, others lowering and raising songbooks and all of them opening and closing their mouths silently.

Cody pointed to them and laughed sheepishly. "We couldn't find the music but Burke just drove up so we can ask—"

"Who did this?"

"Burke?" Dora stepped from behind Conner, her

heart pounding. She had wanted to do this for him and be gone, to leave him with this wonderful sight and never see him again. But here he was.

Here *she* was.

And here was her heart, laid out and exposed in this small token she had wanted Burke to have—his family Christmas restored to him. "I planned to leave before now but it all took a little longer than I expected."

"So this was your doing?" he responded in quick, barely controlled anger.

Indifference. Mild amusement. Even gratitude, those she might have anticipated. But anger? Why anger?

The old Dora, the woman she had been before spending these last two weeks going over other people's troubles, thinking of ways to be of service, acting in a small way as a part of a family and a community, would have seen this coming. That Dora knew to never let your heart or your hopes do the work of your history or your head. "It was my idea, yes, but I only wanted to help."

He shook his head and anger faded to something else. Pain? Embarrassment? "If I need help, I hire it."

"You hired me to help," she reminded him.

"Not anymore." He moved past her, then looked back. Framed in the glow and flicker of thousands of lights, he fixed his eyes on her alone, angled his chin up and set his jaw as he said quietly, "You're fired."

Chapter Thirteen

"Fired? Fired? I'll tell you who is fired, mister. You. You are the one who is fired here. I should have known you wouldn't be up to the job."

"Burke was working for Dora?"

Dora and Burke both startled at hearing Adam's voice. They looked his way then at the rest of the family staring unashamedly at them.

"I am not working for anyone, least of all you, Adam. Or any Burdett. That means I don't owe a one of you an explanation." Burke nabbed Dora by the arm and pulled her, gently but firmly, into the house.

She cooperated and went with him but the second they crossed the threshold, she yanked her arm free.

The door fell shut.

Dora turned on Burke, her eyes flashing. "Unlike your family, I may not have the power to actually fire you from the work we're doing, Burke, but somebody should. Someone as stubborn and prideful as you has no business setting himself up as some kind of icon of giving during the most joyous season of the year."

He stepped back. He'd come home thinking he'd find things much as he had left them, without decorations and without Dora. Instead he had returned to find all the people who had shirked the duty of decorating the house for their mother standing around congratulating themselves on a job well done—using his system. And now Dora was standing here telling him he didn't belong in the only role he had left?

Actually, that he sort of agreed with, in principle, if not in the personal emotional toll it would take. "Hey, I never wanted that job in the first place."

"Good, it doesn't suit you," she snapped. This time when her lower lip quivered she did not control it well. Tears glittered in her eyes. The little girl who he had always known lurked just beneath the surface of her unflappable, businesslike exterior came out of hiding and in full temper-tantrum mode to boot. "In fact, you'd look pretty silly in the suit that comes with the job, anyway."

That hurt. It shouldn't have. After all, what she'd told him was he couldn't pull off the jolly old elf look in red, fur and jingle bells. No rosy cheeks. No snowy white beard. No belly like a bowlful of jelly for him, no sir. In a way it was a compliment.

Only Dora didn't mean it as a compliment.

And that bugged him.

The fact that it bugged him, well, that scared him. Because it meant that deep down he wanted Dora to—no, not see him as Santa Claus—but to think that maybe he had some of the same stuff as the Saint who had worked so hard and risked so much to give others a better life. He wanted Dora to believe in him.

But he knew she was right not to. Nobody else had, why should she? "I'm not Santa Claus. I never was."

She folded her arms, pure defiance. "That's not what you told me in my office the day you recruited me to come here and help you."

He opened his mouth to deny her claim, then realized she was right. Not that he'd ever tell her so. She was right. He was wrong. All wrong.

He shut his eyes for a moment and bowed his head. Not to pray, as he really should have, but to hide. To stall. To give himself a moment to gather his thoughts so that he could say something tender, profound, healing.

"I, uh, you know you're not really fired, right?" he stammered at last. Was that the best he could do? Maybe his family had a point when they ousted him from the office of CEO. "Of course. You know you're not fired because you were volunteering your services but...."

"You don't have to tell me that." She waved away his response then turned and faced the front room. "But I'd appreciate it if you'd share that with your family."

"My family?" For the first time he realized the decorating hadn't been limited to the outdoors. His gaze brushed over pine boughs and ribbons and the little plastic nativity scene his mother had treasured for so long, and the Christmas tree, with a tinfoil star on the top.

"Yes. Please tell your family you did not really just fire me." She frowned, cast her eyes down, then exhaled as if to say *moving on now*. Only she didn't move on. "It may seem like a small thing to you but I care what they think of me. And, well, I've never been fired from anything in my life."

"I have." His gaze moved slowly again to that star. A knot tightened in the pit of his stomach. "Let me tell you, it's not fun."

She softened a little then, her shoulders shifted. She ran her delicate fingers through the fringes of her dark hair, which now touched her earlobes and fell over her eyebrows. "A lot of really powerful and successful people have been."

"Fun?"

She smiled, though not a cheerful or genuinely amused smile. "Fired."

"Oh, yeah. Yeah. You hear that all the time but when it's happening to you it's not as inspiring as people think it will be." He tore his gaze from the tree, whisked it back over the room, then shut his eyes and rubbed his temple in defeat. "Maybe it's because for every person who rebuilds and goes on to bigger and better things after a failure there are a lot who don't ever rebound wholly."

"Being fired is not necessarily a sign of failure."

Eyes still tightly shut, he rubbed the bridge of his nose, his forehead, as if somehow he could erase the whole scene from his mind. "Says the woman who does not want anyone in my family to think it had happened to her."

"Just tell them at some point, okay? I won't stick around for it. I should have left already so you could get back to—"

"No, Dora." He looked up at last. "There is no going back."

"What?"

He wished he could just leave it at that but he knew she'd find out sooner or later. "I got a job offer when I was in Atlanta, and I think I am going to take it."

"You'll be working in Atlanta?"

"The company is headquartered in Atlanta but they have jobs all over the country. All over the globe, actually."

"You're going to work for Global?" Her expression brightened. Her gestures became lively as she shot off questions without giving him a chance to answer. "In what department? What's your job title? Do you need me to show you around? Where will you be based?"

He didn't meet her gaze as he answered only her last question. "London."

"London?" She took a moment to process that. "London, England?"

"I don't think they have an office in London, Kentucky." He cocked his head and studied her. She looked different than she had in the coffee shop yesterday. Softer around the edges. Less angles to her. Less business. "You haven't kept your hair appointment since you've been here."

"I, uh…" She tucked a c-shaped curl behind her ear.

"I like it," he said. "It will go nicely with the ball cap with the, um…" He made a motion with a couple of fingers toward the side of his head. Suddenly he wished he had shown her the picture of him as a kid, pointed hat and all. Too late for that now. Too late for so many things.

"With the elf ears," he finished.

This time her smile came freely. "So, London?"

"Yep."

"They're taking a second-generation Southern snack-cake business king and sending him to London?"

They weren't sending him. He had made it a stipulation of taking the job that they send him as far away Mt. Knott as possible. "Yeah, their only concern was whether I could learn the language."

She did not laugh at his lame joke. "Isn't that a waste of a resource? You know the market *here*. The tastes of the South. This is where you have street cred."

"Street cred? As a guy who runs a snack-cake bakery? All I have from that is crumb cred." He chuckled with a tinge of bitterness.

"What about your family?" Dora pressed on. "How can you just leave them behind? What about…"

Me.

If she said that one word everything might change and Burke knew it. And so he prayed that she would not say it.

"What about the Christmas project?"

He had entered all of this with a prayer that God prepare him for what lay ahead. He had spent hours in Atlanta going over every step that had led him to this moment. He exhaled trying to shore up the unexpected ache in his heart that came with the reminder,

Careful what you pray for, you might get it. "That's my concern now, Dora, not yours."

"Then, I *am* fired?"

"No. You've done your part. Your job is finished."

"But I was going to…" She shut her mouth and pressed her lips until they went white. Her eyes grew still and sad. Clearly she knew that what he'd said was true. Her part in all of this was done. "So the foundation—"

"There is no foundation." Again the double meaning of that stung. His own foundation had been kicked out from under him. He and Dora had no foundation for a relationship. He had no intention of turning this yearly whim into an obligation that he would commit to only to find himself unseated by a better man, or woman. "Dora. Give it up. It's over. I am letting you go."

"Letting me…go." She nodded. For a second her eyes shimmered with unshed tears. Then she rallied, raised her chin, squared her shoulders and smiled. "Well, I may not have any experience being fired but being let go? That's old hat to me by now. Everyone I ever cared about has let me go or let go of me. I've survived that, and I suppose I'll survive your doing it, too."

Burke opened his mouth to say something but couldn't find the right words.

Dora did not share this problem. "In fact, I may be the one getting the better end of this deal."

"What?"

"Because I didn't just get something for my trouble, I *gave* something. I'll leave a part of myself here in Mt.

Knott, but I'll take a part of it with me, as well. Can you honestly say you will do the same?"

"What are you talking about? I have given practically my whole life to the people here, to the business and well-being of this community."

"But what have you let them give to you?"

"Huh?"

"You ever ask your family why they voted you out and Adam in, Burke?"

"I didn't have to ask. They liked his ideas. The direction he wanted to take things. I made my pitch. He made his. They voted. I was out. That simple."

"I have known your family for a few months and though I learned the most about them these last couple of weeks, you have known them all your life and you don't seem to know them at all."

"Huh?"

"When is anything simple with the Burdetts?"

She had a point.

"They voted you out because your dad never thought you should be there in the first place."

"Yeah. Yeah, that's the story of our lives. Me and Dad always locking horns. I should have figured he was the one who—"

"The one who wanted the best for you," she finished on his behalf.

"What? No. Dora, this, this gentle old frail figure of a man you've seen around here, that is not Conner Burdett. Not the one who raised me and founded the Carolina Crumble Pattie bakery. He was ruthless. He was hard and driven. He was a man of good business."

"A man of good business? Isn't that the way Dickens described Scrooge?"

He opened his mouth to refute it but said instead, "Close enough."

"And you were on your way to being just like him. When all along, your family could see that you should have been more like your mom."

He stared up at the star then at the plastic nativity. He thought of that picture of him helping his mom one Christmas long ago. Of the light system he had worked to perfect to make his mom happy and of the Forgotten Stocking Project she had entrusted to him alone. "Funny, I always thought I should have been more like myself."

"Well, there's something to be said for that." She tipped her head to acknowledge his thinking. "I've spent a lot of my time here trying to figure you out, Burke."

"Surely there were more interesting things to focus on." He shifted his weight, uncomfortable with the idea of Dora's fascination yet curious about what conclusions she had come to—and if she thought him completely beyond all hope.

She moved farther into the room. "I've seen your baby plate, gotten to know your family, gone through your mother's most prized and even private things and yet I don't think I know you any better now than I did when you showed up in my office the day after Thanksgiving."

"I never planned to—"

"I know. You never planned for me to know you. But

that day, I did. I saw the real man beneath the CEO, beneath the Top Dawg. I saw someone who wanted to make a difference in the world."

He did want to do that, he couldn't deny it. But how could he when he couldn't even make a difference at the Crumble or even in his family home? He focused on the star again.

"But you can't make a difference in a world that you won't fully participate in, that you set yourself above, even if you do it for what you consider all the right reasons."

"Is this lecture for my benefit or yours, Ms. Checks out of the world for the whole month of December and when she is in it, she's in her office, on the road for work or in a coffee shop at all hours doing business on her laptop?"

"Fair enough." She held her hand up. "But there is a difference between the two of us, Burke."

"There are several, actually, but my mama raised me too polite to point them all out." He smiled, hoping to break some of the tension.

She relented and chuckled quietly. "The difference I was talking about is that we both started this out as people too busy to—"

"Be bothered by hair care?"

She looked up at him in a quick, startled motion then laughed. "You've been to the barber!"

He nodded and ran his fingers through the closely clipped hair along the side of his head. "I've had a little free time lately."

She nodded. "Me too. And I've put it to good use."

"You don't like my haircut?"

"I like it just fine."

"But?"

The single word made her look away, almost as though he had caught her staring at him too long.

"The difference I'm talking about is that during this season, this one Christmas that I will always remember, I have changed."

"How?"

"I guess I did what you said you should do."

He shook his head. "I don't know…"

"I took the time to become more like myself."

"Yeah, but when you do that, you become more like, well, somebody pretty terrific. If I would do that, who would I be like?"

"I suppose you should try to be like someone who is at the very center of Christmas."

"Saint Nicholas?"

"Christ."

"Oh." He hung his head. He should have thought of that. "Is that what has happened for you, Dora? Has your time here strengthened your faith?"

"In ways I hadn't expected, yes. While I was here I gave my time and attention and in return I was given kindness and a glimpse into another way of life." She moved to the tree, touching the tips of the branches so that the lights bounced and set the ornaments sparkling. "And stories. Wonderful stories. Some that touched my heart and others that will have me laughing every time I think of them."

He looked around him. "I know a lot of stories."

"And people. And pie. And memories. I've only been around this town a couple of weeks this time and I've gotten all that." She stood at the far side of the tree so that he could not see her whole face and she looked at him. "And you?"

Yes. You've got me. If you want me. The problem was, of course, the thing that kept him from blurting that out—nobody wanted him. At least not as he was. And he was too old to change, wasn't he?

"Burke, you complained about people not doing their part for the town. About them not shopping here, not setting up businesses and medical practices here, but this town already had its primary business, yours. Maybe no one ever felt the town was big enough for anything else."

"Hey, it's a Top Dawg's instinct to bark and snarl and chase off any threats to his, um…"

"Top doggishness?"

He grinned.

"Only you are not a dog, Burke. No one here was ever any real threat to your position in the community and in the end, what did all your snarling and snapping get you?"

"Nothing, I guess. But then, I never wanted—"

"Anything from anyone. That's it." She stepped out from behind the tree. Her dark eyes had grown wide and somber but shone with a warmth and kindness that Burke did not know how to take. "I thought for a time you didn't know how to give. Then I thought you didn't know how to share."

"You really thought those things about me?" That

hurt even more than saying he'd look bad in a Santa suit. "People think those things about me?"

"No." She shook her head. "People know you are capable of those things and so much more."

"People?" He wanted a definition. He wanted names.

She did not offer them. Instead she turned and moved to the mantel where the plastic manger scene sat. "Everyone talks about this being the season of giving. There's more to it than that, Burke. Giving is nothing if no one is there to receive what is offered. The baby Jesus came for all of us, but for those who turn away and do not accept the gift of salvation, it's just a story. It's a package wrapped in pretty paper that is never opened."

He wasn't sure what she was trying to tell him.

"You have the power to open you life, Burke. To not just give but to welcome what's given to you."

"*What* has been *given* to me, Dora? Nothing. I worked for everything I have and even so have seen it all taken away from me, from my position at the Crumble to having a chance to decorate the Christmas tree with my own family."

"Burke, that's just not…" She launched into a denial but cut herself short. She stood there, blinking for a moment. She looked down. She shook her head. "Oh, Burke. I never thought of you wanting to help decorate."

"I used to always put the star on top of the tree for my mom. You know, just because I was the oldest, and the tallest, so I had to do it."

"Sure," she said, as if she really bought his premise that he had acted solely from a sense of duty.

"Not that I won't take you words to heart but…."

"Do. Please. Because…"

Because I love you.

That's what he wanted to hear her say. *Careful what you pray for,* he warned himself.

She had already turned to walk away and as she reached for the doorknob she added, "Merry Christmas, Burke. And happy new year—in London. Maybe you will finally find what you're looking for there."

Chapter Fourteen

"You better not cry, you better not... Ms. Hoag? Are you...are you crying?"

Dora sniffled and began hastily reshuffling files on her desk. "It's the day before Christmas Eve, Zach. I didn't think you'd show for work today." With Christmas falling on a Wednesday this year, the building would be pretty deserted all week long. "Nobody else is."

"That's why I am here, ma'am." He came into her office, leaving his pushcart of cleaning supplies in the hallway. "So nobody else on my crew has to be."

"You're a good employer, Zach."

"Rest assured I'll be out of the building like a reindeer with its tail on fire the minute I finish up my rounds. Won't see my sorry old face again around here until the second of January, either."

"I think it's a nice face." She slid the files marked Personal into her briefcase then met his eyes and smiled.

"You all right, Ms. Hoag?"

"I'm…" She paused to think about that question for a moment, to really think about it. "I'm better than all right, Zach. And please, we've known each other for so long, please call me Dora."

"Won't that raise some corporate eyebrows? The head of a janitorial service and a big boss lady on a first-name basis?"

"Corporations don't have eyebrows, Zach. They are not human. They don't have faces, which they like because if they did they'd have eyes and have to actually see what they do to people. No facial expressions, either, because they have no emotions. Nothing is personal with them, it's all business." She stood at last. "And I am going out of business."

"No! You? Say it ain't so. Global would never turn loose of a big-time team player like you."

"Global did not turn loose of me, I turned loose of them." For once she had been the one to let go, to stop trying so hard to win approval, and it felt *wonderful*.

Wonderful and just a little bit scary. Burke had called it though, no turning back. Her time in Mt. Knott with the Burdetts had changed her.

"I recently came to understand I was wasting my gifts and decided I need to do something more meaningful. I don't want to be part of Global's team anymore, Zach. I'm getting in a whole new league."

His neatly clipped silver mustache twitched, hinting that he wanted to break into a broad grin or let out a celebratory whoop. His eyes twinkled. "I know how you feel."

"You do?"

"Yep. Was on the fast track myself for a lot of years. Corner office, stock options, racked up enough frequent flyer miles to jet to the moon and back. Then one day, fffttt."

"Fffttt?'

"Company downsized and I was gone."

"So you became a…" She pointed to the dust rag thrown over his shoulder and the cart waiting in the hall.

"Independent contractor?" He chuckled. "Well, made sense. I knew offices. I knew what the sixty-hour-a-week crowd expected. Started my own business. Became my own boss. Twenty-three years later, I have a nice home, a thriving business and time to play with my grandkids."

"Sounds great." She sniffled again. "I wish I'd known your story earlier. I know someone who might have benefited from hearing it."

He shrugged. "It's nothing special."

"I disagree, Zach. You're special. So is everyone who puts in a full day of work, does their best and still finds time to make the world around them a little better."

"I do that?"

"You always make me feel better when our paths cross. Oh, that reminds me!" She yanked open a drawer and pulled out a red envelope and handed it to him. "It's a Christmas card. I don't think in all these years I ever gave you one before."

"Why, thank you, Dora, dear." He poked his thumb under the flap.

"Oh, don't open it here—"

Too late.

His eyes went practically buggy at the check inside the card with the Star of Bethlehem on the front. "Oh, Ms. Hoag, I couldn't…"

"Dora, please."

"Dora, I can't accept—"

"But you have to accept, pal," came a deep masculine voice from the doorway. "It's a gift. Like life. You have to welcome what's given, then it's up to you to make the most of it."

"Burke!" Dora plunked down into her chair with a thud. She hadn't realized she was doing that until the wheels rattled and she suddenly found herself looking up at the two astounded faces of the men standing just inside her office.

"Hello, Dora." He stood there in his suede coat buttoned up to the neck, new jeans and a gray cowboy hat. "Did I come at a bad time?"

"No," she said softly, when what she wanted to say was: It depends on *why* you came.

"I better get back to work." Zach touched the corner of the envelope to his eyebrow in salute. "Thank you, Dora. If I don't see you again, Merry Christmas and my hopes for the very best in the coming new year."

Burke moved into the office to let Zach out. He tipped his hat.

Zach shot him a warning look then took up his pushcart again. "He knows if you've been bad or good so be good for goodness' sake! Oh…"

Burke chuckled as he turned around. "You sure it's not a bad time?"

She shut the drawer she had taken Zach's card from and gave her desktop a final scan. "If you'd shown up a few minutes from now, I'd have already left."

"Starting your holiday early?"

"I'm leaving Global." She stood again, this time taking up her briefcase.

"When? Why?"

"When? Now. Why? Because it's long overdue." She came around the desk, trying to look brave and serene when she felt scared and shaky. And more than a little heartbroken. She wanted to demand of him: What are you doing here? Haven't you hurt me enough? Instead she said, "If you like, you can walk with me to the door."

"Maybe we could head over to your favorite coffee shop, then?" He stepped quickly to the coatrack and lifted her long black wool coat from the hook, holding it open as she approached. "You'll want to bundle up. It's turned cold finally."

"I know." She reached out to take the wrap away from him but with one elegant move he slid the sleeve over her outstretched arm.

This brought him so close that she found her face shaded by the brim of his hat, creating a private world where it was just the two of them gazing into each other's eyes.

"They were predicting snow in Mt. Knott when I left this morning. A white Christmas for sure."

"A white Christmas in Mt. Knott? Sounds…" Romantic and lovely and a wrenching reminder of how, despite giving her all, she was going to spend another Christmas all alone.

"I got the sleigh all prepped." He held up the other shoulder of the coat for her.

"Oh." She fidgeted with transferring her briefcase so that she could put her arm through the sleeve.

"Hoping to take it out tomorrow." He helped her with her coat then left his hand on her shoulder.

She couldn't help smiling, just a tiny smile, then she met his eyes again. "Why are you here, Burke? Surely you didn't drive all the way from South Carolina to tell me that you are planning a sleigh ride on Christmas Eve. Who does that?"

"Gonna find out who's naughty and nice," bellowed Zach from a couple of offices away.

Burke laughed and gave a jerk of his head in Zach's direction. "You know who does that."

"So, now you're back to claiming you are Santa Claus?" She fussed with the collar of the coat.

"No." Burke lifted her hair from where it pressed against her neck and arranged it over the back of her collar. "But I am on his team, remember?"

She pursed her lips, not sure of what she would say to that but feeling she had to say something.

Then he produced a small, square photo of himself, in full elf regalia.

"You found it!" Dora took the picture and studied it

with sheer delight, her anger and hurt over the man's actions forgotten momentarily.

"You were adorable."

"What do you mean *were?*"

"And your mom was so proud." She ran her fingertip over the image of Maggie Burdett standing off to one side.

"No. My mom was tickled at seeing me like that. I didn't give her cause to be proud for a long, long time." He took the photo back from Dora's hand. "I plan to change all that now."

Her pulse raced. What was he trying to tell her? "You…what do you…have you selected a…"

"Let's go to the coffee shop. I have a lot to tell you."

"Tell me here." She stepped over and shut the door. "I'm in a hurry."

"You leaving town?"

"No, I have some last-minute Christmas shopping to do."

"Oh?"

"You say that like you don't believe me. What? You don't think I have anyone in the world to give to?"

"I think you give to everyone you know, Dora." He took her hand. "Only some of us were too stubborn to see what amazing gifts you were offering."

"What do you mean *were?*" She threw his own earlier question back at him with a more cautious tone. Okay hopeful. She did not say it cautiously, she said it with hope. Lots and lots of hope.

"I've changed, Dora." He took a deep breath, then

cocked his head and amended, "I'm trying to change. I want to."

"That's something."

He laughed. "I can't do it, though, Dora, without help. I can't do any of the things I want to do, that I feel called to do, without accepting the guidance, the hard work, the...love of some very good people."

"You're truly blessed, then." She cleared her throat trying to banish the quiver and hoarseness from her voice. "Because you have a lot of good people in your life."

"Yeah." He took her hand. "More than I deserve."

"Burke—"

"Dora, I have a confession. I didn't come all the way to Atlanta to tell you about the sleigh and the snow."

"I thought as much." There was that sliver of hope in her voice again.

"I had to come, you know, to go to the jeweler's and to stop by the accountant's to set a few things up before—" He cut himself off, his expression concerned.

That *hope*. It did her in every time. She clenched her hand around the handle of her briefcase. "Before you take that job in—"

"I'm not taking that job."

"What?"

"London? Are you kidding me? You know what they call Santa Claus in London?"

"Father Christmas."

"Father Christmas!" he said a half beat behind her. Then he laughed. "No thank you. I am definitely not ready to be a father."

She laughed because it was the polite thing to do, and because if she thought about that statement too long, it would haunt her the whole Christmas holiday and beyond.

"'Course that doesn't mean I'm not ready." He reached into his coat pocket and went down on one knee.

"Burke? What are you—"

"Oh." He reached up and whisked the hat off his head. Only to reveal another hat there, a striped one with elf ears.

Dora burst out laughing, at the hat and in the sheer joy of what was happening. Or what she *hoped* was happening.

"Dora, I don't have a ring. The jeweler told me I would be a fool to just go and buy one without accepting some input from you."

"I wouldn't have minded," she said, surprised she could speak at all.

"*Now* you tell me." He frowned and shook his head, sending the tip of his elf hat wobbling.

Dora laughed in earnest then drew in a deep breath. "Um, I think you were about to ask me something?"

"No, I wasn't."

"You weren't?"

"Nope." He pulled a flat velvet box from his pocket. "I was going to *tell* you something."

"Oh." Her joy subsided. She could hardly breathe.

"Dora, I decided who I am going to give the Forgotten Stocking coin to this year." He adjusted his body, shifting the knee he was balanced on. Then he lifted the lid of the box and held it out. "It's you."

"Me?" She stared at the marvelous golden coin which, unlike any she had seen before, was on a slender gold chain. Above the image the words, "We give to others because God first gave Christ to us," and below it, "The Forgotten Stocking Foundation." "Foundation? Burke, do you mean…"

"Yeah. This year I am giving this coin to someone who can set things up so that anyone who wants to can be on the Saint Nicholas team. I have some other coins, too, and I hope you will come back with me to Mt. Knott to distribute them."

"Oh, Burke!" She threw her arms around him and hugged him close, asking, "I won't have to wear these ears, will I?"

"Not if you don't feel like it." He wrapped her in a tight embrace and laughed. "Oh, and one other thing."

"What?" She pulled away just enough so that she could look into his eyes.

"Will you marry me?"

"Yes! Yes! Yes!" She kissed his cheek, his temple, his jaw, then paused, her lips just inches from his, "On one condition."

Chapter Fifteen

"I can't believe you made me go Christmas shopping before you'd pick out an engagement ring," Burke muttered to his bride-to-be as he hitched the horses up to his very own shiny black sleigh.

It had snowed yesterday and then again this morning. It had stopped an hour earlier but stayed cold enough that they could use the sleigh over the fluffy white covering on the ground.

"How else was I supposed to carry all those gifts?" She settled into the seat, arranging an old family quilt over her legs. "What is the use in marrying a gigantic elf if you cannot use him to haul your Christmas loot?"

"It wasn't *your* loot." He finished up then checked the time on his cell phone. "I think you bought something for everyone in town."

"Not everyone. Just the people I came across for the project. And the people on the prayer list. And your family. And a few extra things in case I left anyone out."

"Don't forget those gaudy ties for Warren and Jed." He went around to the back of the sleigh where they had stored the gifts they were about to take into town.

"Hey, with those blues and reds and purples and yellows, they can spill virtually any kind of pie Josie makes on those ties and no one will ever know!"

"I wish we'd come up with a way to buy replacement nativity figures." He looked back where his brothers were hard at work loading the best and the least busted-up figures from his mom's long stored-away nativity scene into his truck bed.

"I was so sorry to see what bad shape they were in. We'll work on getting the whole scene completed for next year."

"Don't we have enough to do with starting a charitable foundation, planning a wedding, getting married, going on a honeymoon, extending the honeymoon…"

She laughed shyly.

Her laughter sounded sweeter than bells, even Christmas bells.

"Oh, please, organize, delegate, take charge, we can do all that in a flash and standing on our heads." She snapped her fingers then paused, and rushed to say before he made a questionable joke, "Except the honeymoon, of course."

He cupped his hand beneath her chin and brought his lips to hers.

"Whooo-hooo!"

"I cry foul! They don't even have mistletoe!"

"He sees you when you're smooching…"

Adam, Jason and Cody began to holler and tease.

She kissed his lips lightly again. "You have given me hope again and restored my trust, Burke."

He glanced over his shoulder at the brothers carrying out the last of the statuary to the truck. He raised his hand and pointed. "Nope, not me. Not my job description. Not even within my means. But I do suspect who had a hand in that."

She looked at the Burdett dog pack, minus the Top Dawg, carefully lowering the figure of the baby Jesus into the truck and wrapping it to keep it safe. They had to add extra padding because so few of the pieces had survived the years intact.

Adam jumped down and shoved the tailgate into place with a wham. "Sure won't be much of a display this year."

"I had no idea that belonged to y'all. Always thought it was owned by the town and, when they stopped setting it up, that it was gone for good." Carol tugged her gloves on as she hurried toward the minivan to ride with Josie and Adam to the Crumble. "Remember how everyone in town used to look forward to visiting it?"

"Noticed none of them fought for it when the council wanted it removed." Jason made one last safety check then strode to the truck cab where he would be entrusted with driving the precious cargo to town behind the sleigh.

"Hey! Mom never gave anyone a chance to fight for it. Just stashed the whole set away and never even told folks we had it. I think that was the wrong way to go about things. This is a town full of good folks who want the best for one another. Mom never let them prove that.

None of us Burdetts have had enough faith in our community that they would pitch in and help us do what is good for us all." Burke couldn't believe those words had come out of his mouth. But he believed them and he was going to stick to them. "And I think maybe it's high time we corrected that."

"How we going to do that?" one of the brothers called.

Burke only had to think a moment before he reached down to the floorboard at Dora's feet and raised the elegant burgundy shopping bag from the Atlanta jeweler. It contained six boxed coins with the recognizable logo on them, but no names, as he'd never been able to narrow it down to the most deserving. His plan had been to give them out this evening as he was moved to do so.

And at this moment, he was so moved.

"All of us Burdetts have been so very blessed." He kept the bag aloft as he spoke. "Not just with money and opportunities but also with health and common sense—"

"Don't forget good looks," Jason called out.

Everyone shared a laugh.

"Yeah, with *devastating* good looks," Burke embellished. "And with faith and with, though we often take it for granted, the blessing of each other."

"Hear, hear!" Conner bellowed, and each brother and wife and wife-to-be echoed softly in agreement.

"And with the wonderful gift of having known or benefited from the love of an amazing woman—Maggie Burdett."

Conner again raised his hand but he could not speak

to lead a cheer. His sons did that for him, with joy and gusto. "Hear, hear!"

"With these blessings comes the responsibility to give to others. We have always given to our community as we were able. It is my proposal, my wish, my *gift* to you that you share our blessings in a way only the Burdetts can in Mt. Knott, this year."

The men shifted in their boots.

The women leaned in, listening.

Adam, Mr. Get-Down-to-Business, was the one who asked, "What is this about?"

Burke told them about their mother's secret and about his decision to start a foundation, then he laid out his own plan, the one inspired by Dora's assessment of him. "Give this coin to someone you trust and ask that they pass it along to the people they think need their Christmas wish answered the most." With that he handed out the coins.

Everyone murmured and oohed and aahed over them as the boxes came open.

Burke took Dora by the hand, gazed out on the newest members of Team Santa and said, "I say, let's give our friends and neighbors the gift of being able to give of themselves."

Chapter Sixteen

After taking a moment to run inside and make some phone calls, Adam and Burke and Jason had led the caravan through town. The truck and minivan had stopped every few houses to pick something up or to explain what they had in mind while Burke and Dora had gone along ahead in the sleigh distributing presents.

The kids loved their toys, even though they were small. And the families in need appreciated the gift baskets of necessities paid for from the Forgotten Stocking Project funds.

"I hope you don't mind I've been showing off my necklace and going on about the plans for the foundation more than I've been talking about our engagement," Dora whispered, snuggling close to Burke as they pulled up in front of Josie's Home Cookin' Kitchen.

"I'm just amazed at how many people always knew the coins were my mom's doing." He made a shushing noise and the horses stilled. He got out first then helped Dora down.

She ran around and picked out the packages for the regulars. Travel mugs for the commuters. Some soft fuzzy slippers for "Bingo Barnes," the mailman with the aching feet. And those ties for Jed and Warren.

Inside they found the counter piled high with cakes, cookies and candy.

"Folks 'round here may not have much, but long as somebody's got the fixin' nobody will go hungry," Jed observed.

Dora had never seen anything like it. "Let's check the prayer list and see if we missed anyone."

But there were no names there this happy day. In their place someone had written simply and in beautiful lettering: Peace.

And everyone who had come in seemed to have added his or her name.

"That's so awesome," Dora had said, then turning to the man she loved, added quietly, "I wish they hadn't erased the whole board, though, because—"

"Don't worry. I got it." He pulled out his phone and showed her the picture he had taken of the chalk drawing of a shaggy dog wearing a Santa hat. "When I saw it on the prayer list I knew you still had hope for me. I didn't give you hope, Dora, you always had it in you. You always had all this love and trust in you just waiting to give."

Tears welled in her eyes.

He gave her a hug and a kiss on the nose then hustled her off.

By dusk all the gifts had been handed out, the cakes and cookies and candies shared, anyone who wanted to had taken a ride in a genuine open sleigh and the townsfolk began to gather in the parking lot of the Crumble for the big display.

No matter how many new, handcrafted, specially-made, carved or even gilded figures they brought to Mt. Knott for future nativity displays, none of them would ever come near the sheer wonder and joy and beauty the haphazard, disorganized, motley, messed-up jumble of mayhem that was this year's pageant.

Four-H-ers brought live animals. Plastic blow-mold wise men knelt in awe around the original plaster holy family. Plywood palm trees from the high school theater department swayed in snowy gusts alongside a cluster of children from Cody and Carol's church meant to represent an angel choir.

"This has got to be the most ragtag group ever brought together," someone observed.

"Which is as it should be." Cody stepped forward, his hands out. "Because Jesus was born in a come-as-you-are kind of gathering not unlike this one. He was put in an impromptu bed and Mary and Joseph had to make do with what they had, but you and I know, friends, that they were giventhe most precious gift of all."

"Amen," someone shouted.

"The gift of that long-ago night is the gift we share

to this day—the hope of eternal life through God's Son, the light of the world." Cody made a signal and Jason pushed a plug into an extension cord and the whole scene lit up.

Everyone oohed and ahhed.

Then someone called out, "What about the Santa coins?"

"Yeah, what happened to them all?" Dora asked, going up on tiptoe and holding up the one she wore around her neck as if anyone in that town didn't know what they were talking about.

"I got one," the young artist called out.

"Me too," called the girl who had lost her mother and her hopes of attending college.

Burke and Dora shared a smile, feeling their own instincts on those grants had been validated until—

"And then I gave mine to the Sykes!" the artist concluded.

"I passed mine along to Mrs. Beck, the lunch lady at the high school," the would-be college-bound girl announced.

"I got one!" someone called.

"Me too!" someone else chimed in.

"Gave it to…" The first voice shouted out what had happened to their coin.

One by one everyone in town who had been given a gold coin told the story of the gift and how they had shared it with someone they thought more in need than themselves.

As far as anyone could tell the tokens were, in fact,

still on the move throughout the county, spreading good cheer and hope and allowing everyone who touched them to share in the experience of giving.

"That's the way it is around here," Jed finally summed up. "Got to look out for one another. Always someone worse off than you if you think about it and count your blessings. Merry Christmas, everybody!"

The cheer went out, "Merry Christmas!"

Burke pulled Dora close, her back against his chest.

As they stood there enjoying the sight, she murmured, "You certainly made good on your promise. This is a Christmas I will never forget."

"Just the first of many," he assured her.

And she believed him.

Then someone began humming "Silent Night."

"God meets us where we are." Cody took center stage—well, left of center, for he knew he was not the real star of the evening. "Whether we are in a manger in Bethlehem or a bakery in South Carolina, He says, 'Behold! I bring you good tidings of great joy! For unto you is born this day in the city of David a Savior, which is Christ the Lord.'"

And the crowd began to sing.

The snow began to fall.

And Dora thanked the Lord that she had found a place in the world and that because of the baby in the manger, she had never really been alone at all.

* * * * *

Get 4 FREE REWARDS!

We'll send you 2 FREE Books plus 2 FREE Mystery Gifts.

Love Inspired books feature uplifting stories where faith helps guide you through life's challenges and discover the promise of a new beginning.

FREE
Value Over
$20

What happens when a beautiful foster mom claims an Oklahoma rancher as her fake fiancé?

Read on for a sneak preview of
The Rancher's Holiday Arrangement
by Brenda Minton.

"I am so sorry," Daisy told Joe as they walked down the sidewalk together.

The sun had come out and it was warm. The kind of day that made her long for spring.

"I don't know that I need an apology," Joe told her. "But an explanation would be a good start."

She shook her head. "I saw you sitting with your family, and I knew how I'd feel. Ambushed."

"I could have handled it. Now I'm engaged." He tossed her a dimpled grin. "What am I supposed to tell them when I don't have a wedding?"

"I got tired of your smug attitude and left you at the altar?" she asked, half teasing. "Where are we walking to?"

"I'm not sure. I guess the park."

"The park it is," she told him.

Daisy smiled down at the stroller. Myra and Miriam belonged with their mother, Lindsey. Daisy got to love them for a short time and hoped that she'd made a difference.

"It'll be hard to let them go," Joe said.

"It will be," Daisy admitted. "I think they'll go home after New Year's."

"That's pretty soon."

"It is. We have a court date next week."

"I'm sorry," Joe said, reaching for her hand and giving it a light squeeze.

"None of that has anything to do with what I've done to your life. I've complicated things. I'm sorry. You can tell your parents I lost my mind for a few minutes. Tell them I have a horrible sense of humor and that we aren't even friends. Tell them I wanted to make your life difficult."

"Which one is true?" he asked.

"Maybe a combination," she answered. "I *do* have a horrible sense of humor. I *did* want to mess with you."

"And the part about us not being friends?"

"Honestly, I don't know what we are."

"I'll take friendship," he told her. "Don't worry, Daisy, I'm not holding you to this proposal."

She laughed and so did he.

"Good thing. The last thing I want is a real fiancé."

"I know I'm not the most handsome guy, but I'm a decent catch," he said.

She ignored the comment about his looks. The last thing she wanted to admit was that when he smiled, she forgot herself just a little.

Don't miss
The Rancher's Holiday Arrangement *by Brenda Minton,*
available November 2020 wherever
Love Inspired books and ebooks are sold.

LoveInspired.com